splintered hearts

THE NEW HOPE TRILOGY

A boxed set of the sexy and emotional New Hope series
that includes *Unbreak Me*, *Stolen Wishes*, and *Wish I May*.

splintered
hearts

THE NEW HOPE TRILOGY

A boxed set of the sexy and emotional New Hope series
that includes *Unbreak Me*, *Stolen Wishes*, and *Wish I May*.

NEW YORK TIMES BESTSELLING AUTHOR
LEXI RYAN

other titles by
Lexi Ryan

New Hope Series
Unbreak Me
Stolen Wishes: A Prequel Novella
Wish I May

The Here and Now Series (A New Hope Series)
Lost in Me
Fall to You
All for This (August 2014)

Hot Contemporary Romance
Text Appeal
Accidental Sex Goddess

Stiletto Girls Novels
Stilettos, Inc.
Flirting with Fate

Decadence Creek Stories and Novellas
Just One Night
Just the Way You Are

unbreak
me

unbreak me

by LEXI RYAN

Copyediting by Editing720
Cover © 2013 Sarah Hansen, Okay Creations
Interior formatting by E.M. Tippetts Book Designs

to Jack and Mary

about this book

Unbreak Me is New Adult contemporary romance. Due to sexual content and heavy subject matter, it is intended for mature readers.

"If you're broken, I'll fix you…"

I'm only twenty-one and already damaged goods. A slut. A failure. A disappointment to my picture-perfect family as long as I can remember. I called off my wedding to William Bailey, the only man who thought I was worth fixing. A year later and he's marrying my sister.

Unless I ask him not to…

"If you shatter, I'll find you…"

But now there's Asher Logan, a broken man who sees the fractures in my façade and doesn't want to fix me at all. Asher wants me to stop hiding, to stop pretending. Asher wants to break down my walls. But that means letting him see my ugly secrets and forgiving him for his.

With my past weighing down on me, do I want the man who holds me together or the man who gives me permission to break?

chapter one

Maggie

"You're not going to flake out, are you?"

I blink before realizing what my sister means. It's time. Time for me to face this. Time for me to pretend *everything is just fine.*

Time for me to walk down the aisle.

The words swim in my head. *Walk. Down. Aisle.* As if it's no big deal. As if I'm okay with this.

Lizzy gives me a shove toward the doors.

I can hear it now. The organ. Processional music. The hum of the crowd's whispers.

"Put a smile on your face and *march*," Krystal hisses.

I show her my middle finger before pushing through the doors.

"It's going to be okay," I hear Lizzy say. "She's going to do it."

My sisters' murmurs fade as I focus on my task.

My stomach pitches and my hands shake behind my bouquet, but I plaster on a smile and time my steps to the organ's heavy chords.

That's when I see him.

William Bailey stands at the front of the church, hands clasped in front of him. His eyes are hot and desperate and all over me. Can the guests see it too? The longing that rolls off him in waves as I approach?

Is he thinking the same thing I am? That this is supposed to be us? That this is supposed to be *our* wedding?

Or is he thinking I was the biggest mistake of his life?

I can't go there. Not here. Not now. I pretend not to notice the questions in his eyes, pretend not to notice the hum of gossip swelling around me.

But underneath the taffeta and flowers, underneath the hoopskirt and pretense, I'm overwhelmed with the thought that *this* is what my life has come to. Just a bridesmaid. Just a bridesmaid in my sister's wedding.

Just a bridesmaid in my sister's wedding to my ex-fiancé.

A vocalist joins the organ and the hum of whispers quiets—a swarm of killer bees distracted from their target as they remember the reason for their presence.

I reach the end of the aisle, ankles and dignity still intact, and breathe a sigh of relief as the congregation turns their attention to the next bridesmaid.

My sisters march one by one, coordinating with the hydrangea-blue décor like giant chameleons.

The flower girl appears at the end of the aisle, and the crowd stands.

Something in my chest tugs long and hard at the sight of my youngest sister. Even at ten years old, she's a delicate little thing with a tiny voice and a big brain. Too young to be a bridesmaid but too old to be a flower girl, she looks like a child bride half-drowned in white tulle.

Finally, Krystal enters. Thick brown curls piled high on her head and a smile curving her lips, she embodies every little girl's wedding-day dream.

Cameras flash. Women sigh. Tissues abound.

My eyes slide to Will again, and I'm not surprised to see he's watching me. For the hundredth time since I returned home last month, I find myself remembering the comfort of his arms. Why couldn't I have stayed there?

As his bride reaches center aisle, Will takes a step toward her.

He's going through with this. He's really going to marry her.

The same moment he takes her hand, the air conditioning kicks on.

First there are murmurs, whispers that carry back through the congregation and have me and my sisters exchanging confused glances.

Will shuffles back, scrambling to cover his mouth.

My mom's eyes roll back in her head, and she falls to the floor.

A breath later, I smell it. The scent guarantees Krystal's wedding will be as unforgettable as she dreamed.

No one would forget the wedding that smelled of rotting carcass.

A gag settles at the back of my throat as the smell grows.

My sisters hide their noses in their bouquets.

Seconds later, the bride gasps. Her face crumbles and she *howls*.

The sounds of retching echo through the church as the guests run toward the exits, pushing and shoving their way to fresh air.

The priest looks lost, and I nail him with my gaze. *Do something, damn it!* And he does.

He gags right into his microphone.

Chaos breaks loose. More gagging. Scrambling. Pushing.

No one cares about the wedding anymore. No one cares about vows or five-thousand-dollar dresses—not in the middle of stench warfare.

My little sister's face is white with panic. Her jaw slack as the chaos grows.

I offer my hand. "Come on."

She stares at me, then opens her mouth and throws up all over her dress, her face crumbling in horror.

Poor thing.

Grabbing her hand, I urge her toward the exit. "Abby!" When

she doesn't move, I gather her lanky frame into my arms and sweep her out of the church.

We make it out the doors and to the sidewalk where Krystal is crying into Will's arms. He strokes her hair, helpless, and whispers something in her ear.

When he lifts his head, the evening sunlight frames his messy blond hair and our eyes lock. It feels like we have a lifetime between us. A lifetime since my lies fooled us both. A lifetime since I believed a girl like me could have a happily-ever-after.

THE RECEPTION tent glows with candlelight, and the soft May breeze floats up from the river, jingling the wind chimes. Krystal and Will's reception is set up on the vast green expanse of my mother's backyard, just like mine was supposed to be last year.

Just like *ours* was supposed to be.

They're words I can't dwell on, but avoiding them leaves my mind hopping from place to place like a panicked rabbit in a den of wolves.

Topiaries line the path down the hill and to the river, and I follow them, needing to see the rushing water and escape the music and laughter and joviality. I can feel Will's eyes on me as I slip from the tent, but I don't go to him.

Krystal begged me to come home for the wedding, to be her bridesmaid so everyone would know things were okay between us, so everyone would know I was okay with her marrying my ex. I had my own reasons for doing it, but I can't talk to Will.

Not yet. Not here.

I can't stop thinking about what happened at the chapel. My mother and the wedding planner awkwardly organized the guests and directed them to the reception, where dinner was served. Now dancing is in full swing. But what about the ceremony? Does this mean Krystal and Will aren't married? They never said vows. Did they find some dark corner to sign the papers?

Of course, I can't ask. Everyone will think it's because I want Will for myself. They'll think I'm asking because I'm not over him.

I'm halfway down the path when I spot a man a few yards beyond my mother's dock. His black dress pants and a dress shirt draw my attention to the wide expanse of his shoulders and the narrow taper of his hips. I don't know him, but I recognize a kindred spirit. He looks hurt and far away, hands tucked into his pockets, gaze locked on the water. A broken heart left behind when Krystal put Will's ring on her finger?

I hesitate for a minute. I was looking for some solitude down here, but I'm drawn to this man who looks as lost and lonely as I feel.

I hop off the paved path, and my heels sink into the soft earth as I approach him.

"You look a little lost," I say. When he turns to me, his eyes are weary. I recognize that too and stall mid-step. "I don't think we've met. I'm Maggie Thompson, sister of the bride."

"I'm Asher."

Asher. Asher. I scan my memory for the significance of the name but I can't find it. New Hope is a small town, and I don't recognize him, but that doesn't mean much since my mom invited half the state of Indiana and a good portion of Kentucky. "Asher what? Friend of the bride or groom?"

"Just Asher. And I'm not a wedding guest."

Oh. That explains it. "Just one name? Like Madonna?"

His lips quirk. "Something like that."

"Nice to meet you, Just Asher." I offer my hand, and when he takes it, I can't help but notice the size and heat of his. An image flashes through my mind—rough fingers skimming over my bare skin, those eyes sweeping over my exposed body.

Asher should be the poster child for the sexy bad boy. I bet he even has a few tats under that pressed dress shirt. He's a big guy, not just tall but large, solid, filling his black oxford in a way that makes it difficult to keep from staring.

Hell, staring is inevitable. Not *drooling* is difficult.

His dark, messy hair has a little curl to it, the kind of hair a woman can slide between her fingers while her lover explores her body.

His stubbled cheeks inspire some inappropriate fantasies, and that cocky grin says he knows just what I'm thinking.

"Maggie?"

The little voice stops my thoughts and my heart, and I turn to see my youngest sister.

Abby changed clothes after the would-be ceremony and now wears a little pink dress. Just looking at her makes my heart ache. She grew up so much while I was away, and knowing how much I missed gnaws at me. I wasn't around to protect her from our mother's unachievable standards. Abby may be the one person in this world who really needs me.

"Hey, sweetie," I say.

"Hey, Mags." She toys with the hem of her dress. "I'm sorry about what happened at the church. I freaked out."

Something unwelcome sticks at the back of my throat at that insecurity in her eyes, that need to be everything to everyone at only ten years old. "It's okay. We all panicked a little."

"I missed you," she whispers.

Even though I've been home nearly four weeks, I've been making myself scarce, and this is the first she's mentioned my absence. The words claw at my heart and I pull her into a hug. She wraps her arms around my neck and I inhale deeply.

"Are you mad I got upchuck on your pretty dress?"

I flash a grin back to the sexy stranger and shake my head. "I don't know what pretty dress you're talking about. I've been wearing this ugly thing all day."

Abby stifles a giggle behind her hand.

"Abby," someone calls.

William.

He's headed down the hill toward us. "Your sister needs you for a few more pictures," he tells her.

"But I don't want to take more pictures," Abby whispers, a rare complaint from a people-pleasing child.

"Go on now. It's important to Krystal."

Abby nods. "Bye, Maggie," she says as she scurries away.

Will watches her go. When he turns to me, his expression shifts from stoic to pained.

"Are you married? Is it official?" How ironic that he's the only one here I trust enough to ask.

"No." The word is so soft I almost miss it.

"So...now what?"

His eyes devour me. It's been a year since I was his, and it's like he's trying to catalogue every new freckle, trying to account for every missed smile. "We haven't decided yet."

I open my mouth to speak then close it. My throat is so tight there's no room for words. I can't identify the emotion strangling me. Hope that he'll give me another chance? Fear that he might?

"Maggie." He breathes my name like a prayer, but then says, "It doesn't change anything. We're getting married. I love her. She wants to make a life with me."

I force a smile to hide that he's just smacked me with his words. Krystal wants to make a life with him, and I hadn't.

Not true, my mind objects. But I know that's what he must think. It's what I'd made him think.

Will notices the stranger for the first time. I'd forgotten about him, but he's still there, watching us carefully. "What's he doing here?"

"He's with me," I blurt. "Krystal said I could bring a date." The impulse to make Will think I'm attached is kneejerk, but I regret my words as soon as I see the man's eyebrows lift. I didn't mean for him to hear me, and horror sweeps over my face in hot waves.

But instead of calling me on my lie, Asher comes to my side and wraps his arm loosely around my shoulders. "I didn't want my girl to have to dance alone."

Will blinks then jerks back, and, as if we're tied together by invisible threads, I have to fight the instinct to follow.

"The bar opens in ten," he says. "Enjoy yourselves." With that, he turns and heads back to the reception.

When he's gone, I step out of the stranger's embrace. "You didn't want your girl to dance alone?"

"You started it." He grins full-out now, and my heart damn near stops in my chest. Sexy Stranger goes from hot to *panty-melting* when he grins.

"Are you prepared to continue this charade all night?" I ask. "To dance and pretend you like a total stranger just to help her out of an awkward conversation?"

He shrugs. "I can think of worse ways to spend my time." He slides his gaze over me. When he returns to my face, I notice his eyes for the first time. Wolf eyes. A blue so icy it's nearly colorless, rimmed by a dark ring.

This might not be the worst day of my life after all.

"Want to check out that open bar?" I ask, nodding toward the reception. "My family is loaded, so I'm sure it's stocked with the good stuff." I'm already heading in that direction, hoping he'll follow, hoping the company of a stranger will keep people and all their polite inquiries far away.

"Do you dance?" Asher stops me before I can make it to the bar.

"Not even a little."

He has Bad Boy written all over him, and my mom is going to flip when she sees me on his arm. Of course, this only enhances the appeal.

"Okay. I give up," Asher says. "I can't figure it out." His eyes connect with mine and send a little buzz through me.

I thought I'd lost that—the ability to get a buzz from the way a boy looks at me.

This is no boy, my mind tells me. *This is a man.* I'm no stranger to older men, but when I came back to New Hope, it was with a promise to myself that things would be different. That *I'd* be different. And yet here I am, preparing to spend my evening with a sexy stranger who breaks all the New Me rules.

"What's making you crazy?"

"I know you from somewhere…"

I have to laugh at that. "That line? Really? If you're trying to pick me up, can't you at least amuse me by coming up with something unique?"

He flashes that wicked, devil-may-care grin again and my goddamn stomach does a little flip. "Is that what you think I'm trying to do?"

I shrug. "I don't really know. It's been a long time since I bothered with games."

He steps closer, looking down at me. "Because you get right to the point?"

He guides me to the dance floor, and I let him.

Etta James croons from the speakers as this beautiful bad boy pulls me into his arms, his eyes roaming over my face like this is foreplay. He's a man who makes dancing easy, guiding me around so smoothly I could be walking on clouds.

When he dips his head, his mouth brushes my ear. "You know, don't you, that by dancing with me, you're going to make people whisper about you all night?"

I squeeze my eyes shut for a moment. They are whispering about me, it's true, but the whispers have nothing to do with some mystery man.

It was a year ago, but my wedding to William Bailey is still the hottest kind of gossip. A wedding called off two days before the bride and groom were scheduled to say their vows? Young bride ran away to God-knows-where for an entire year? Hell, the people of New Hope usually have to steal the mayor's cable to get stories that juicy.

"It doesn't matter," I murmur. Over Asher's shoulder, my three older sisters watch me with unhinged jaws. What's with them?

The song ends and the crowd on the dance floor shifts. Some couples return to their seats and others slide into each other's arms.

Asher grins. "I thought you didn't dance?"

"I don't. Couldn't you tell?" I shiver under his hot gaze. One dance and I'm contemplating bridesmaid clichés and one-night stands.

The DJ transitions to another song, and I find myself moving into his arms again. We fall into the rhythm of the music, and I'm rethinking my aversion to dancing when I feel a vibration from his hip. He's busy tracing my shoulder with the rough pad of his thumb and doesn't notice.

"Is that a cell phone in your pocket," I whisper up at him, "or did I misplace my vibrator?"

He pulls away and reaches for his phone. "You're something else." He glances at the number on the display. "I have to take this. It was nice to meet you, Maggie. Thank you for the dance." He winks at me as he backs away, leaving me grinning on the edge of the dance floor, dumb with lust.

My good mood vanishes when I turn and see Will and Krystal dancing.

My Will, I catch myself thinking. Which isn't fair, and I know that, but I keep remembering his arms wrapped around me and his breath in my hair as he whispered, *"If you're broken, I'll fix you."*

His thumb brushes her cheek, and he's looking at her with such tenderness, I stumble over my own feet in my rush to get off the dance floor. Loneliness claws at me, digging into my flesh just deeply enough that my eyes wet with tears.

chapter two

William

I AM an addict.

I am the cocky asshole who thinks he's bigger than his addiction. I am the ignorant son of a bitch who thinks he can look temptation in the face and walk away.

I have never been so wrong about anything.

Like most addicts, I can't tell you when my addiction began. I can't tell you the moment when my fondness for her became something more compelling. More dangerous. Was it when she was fifteen and showed up in my dorm room at Notre Dame? The girl next door suddenly a curvy vixen with sad eyes and hungry hands? Was it when I came back home for graduate school and she became a constant in my life? Or did it only begin when I tasted her lips for the first time, the sun reflecting off the water, the breeze ruffling our hair?

Maybe addictions don't have a beginning. They certainly don't have an end.

The bathroom door jars open and I remember myself. Who I am. Where I am.

She's staring at me, arms wrapped around herself as if her long, hot shower left her cold. "You could feign a little disappointment, you know."

Krystal is pissed. Hell, she should be. Today was everything to her. She'd planned every detail, as if the perfect wedding might make the guests forget I was supposed to marry her sister first. But it was ruined. And no one forgets.

"I am disappointed," I protest. Even to my own ears I sound apathetic, but I'm not, dammit, I'm just...weak.

"You need to tell me the truth." She settles on the bed, the hotel's fluffy white robe enveloping her petite frame. "Are you relieved? Do you feel like you dodged a bullet?" Her voice wavers, as if she's struggling to hold back tears, and I feel like the world's biggest asshole.

"No." I take her hands in mine. Squeeze her fingertips against my palms. "I want to marry you."

Her big brown eyes search my face, reading it for signs of a relapse. "You haven't been the same since she's been home."

There's no correct way I can respond to this and we both know it. Agreement will only prime her insecurities. Disagreement would be the lie that will drive this growing wedge between us. "I want to marry you," I repeat. "Let's do it again. A new ceremony. A new reception. Whatever you want."

She blinks at me and forces a smile. "Okay."

"I love you." I sound a little desperate. Maybe I am.

She leans her head against my shoulder, and her wet hair seeps through my shirt and chills my skin. One month ago, this bond between us was enough. One month ago, when I told Krystal I loved her, I didn't have a devil on my shoulder weighing that love against my love for someone else. One month ago, Maggie was out of my system.

I close my eyes with every intention to focus on Krystal, on my love for her, hers for me. Our future. Instead, I see Maggie lying by the river after a heavy rain, her hair splayed in a red sunburst against the lush green grass as she listens to the rushing water. I see Maggie's sprinkle of freckles and Maggie's bright green eyes laughing at me.

Krystal sniffs into my chest and I draw her tightly against me, focusing on the feel of her in my arms, trying to stay in *this* moment, with *this* woman. But my memory has taken hold and I feel Maggie's soft exhale against my lips, Maggie rolling under me in the dewy grass, Maggie's mouth connecting with mine.

"I love you too," Krystal says, and I can only faintly make out the words over the sound of the river rushing in my ears.

I am an addict and Maggie Thompson is my drug.

Maggie

TECHNICALLY, I am trespassing. *Technically*, trespassing is not part of the New Me plan. But it hardly feels like trespassing to use the neighbor's gorgeous, well-maintained pool when a) I've been doing it since I was sixteen, and b) the rich dude who owns the place is never around. I like to think I'm doing him a favor. He must spend a crap ton of money to maintain this place, but he doesn't get any use out of it because he's always away at his house in Vail or wherever. It would be wasteful for me *not* to use it just because of some technicality.

I hoist myself over the gate and feel greedy anticipation. Surrounded by lush landscaping and featuring a cascade of water that circulates from hot tub to pool, the space is more water feature than swimming hole. I don't know Rich Dude, but he has excellent taste, and this little oasis is one of my favorite places on Earth.

I could have headed home after the reception, but I knew I wouldn't sleep tonight. I told my mom I wanted to stay over, and I waited until everyone was in bed before grabbing a robe and trekking across a couple acres of lush grass for a moonlight swim.

I'm no stranger to insomnia, but it's been worse since I returned home. In the silence of the night, there's too much room for my thoughts and they expand until they fill every corner of my mind. While I was away, I could be anyone I wanted to be, but in New Hope, everywhere I turn, someone's labeling me. When I was young, I was just *one of the Thompson girls,* but now the labels aren't so innocuous. *Black sheep. College dropout.*

Slut.

I drop the terry cloth robe from my shoulders and dive into the water completely nude. Most pools would be intolerably cold in Indiana before June, but the water circulating from the hot tub keeps the temperature comfortable from spring to fall. Even if it was cold, I'd still be here. Exercise is the only thing that calms my mind. Tonight, I'll swim laps to escape the demons.

Until last year, small-town life was the only life I'd ever known, so I should be used to it, but you can be cut open a hundred times, and the slice of the blade still hurts.

I just never expected Will to be the one holding the knife.

Does he love her? Would he marry my sister out of spite?

Did he tell Krystal the truth about our canceled vows?

I turn and pull my limbs through the water, asking myself the question I've been avoiding for weeks. *Can I live here and watch Will and Krystal build a life together?*

I count out twenty-five laps. The rhythm of my breathing calms me. The water rushing over my skin salves my wounds. Finally, I rest forearms on the edge of the pool and gulp in air, focusing only on my breath and the water dripping from my face.

"Training for the Olympics?"

I snap my head up in surprise. In the soft glow of the moon, I can make out the bad boy from the reception. He stands in swim trunks three yards from me, a towel draped behind his neck. I was right about the tats. He has some sort of starburst on his left pec, another circling his thick biceps.

"Sneak up on many girls?"

"Only the special ones." He drops the towel on a chair and dives into the water.

When he surfaces, my heart kicks up a beat. He's close. I could almost touch him if I reached out.

But even as my eyes tour his broad chest and sculpted shoulders, I back away. "What are you doing here?"

His eyebrow quirks. "I live here."

I snort. "No you don't." Then, when his expression remains stoic, "Shit. Really? You're Rich Dude?"

"Rich who?" He looks puzzled. And annoyed.

Giggles bubble up and slip past my lips. I've always pictured the owner of this property to be some white-haired old man with a cane and a monocle. Asher is so far off the mark, I can't help my laughter. "Shit. I'm sorry. I just…" I laugh more, and it feels damn good. My muscles are spent from my swim, my mind is calm, and laughing feels like a long-denied decadent treat.

"You haven't come to swim in a long time," he says softly.

That cuts my laughter short. "You watch me?" I want to feel violated by the idea. But the thought of *this* man watching me swim nude in his pool zips potent arousal through my veins.

Asher shakes his head, studying me. "My groundskeeper told me a young girl used to sneak in about once a week. I assume that was you?"

"Yeah," I say softly.

"Why'd you stop?"

"I left town for a while."

"Looking for something?"

I shake my head. "Running away."

He nods, as if my answer is perfectly reasonable, and I get the sense that he doesn't just accept it, he *understands* it. His gaze settles on my mouth. When his eyes drop to the water and my bare breasts, his breath catches, and I feel that rush that comes from being desired, that false sense of worth I'm willing to be fooled by tonight. Suddenly, I want him to kiss me. Touch me. More.

I want to bury my loneliness under the weight of a man's body on mine, to erase unwelcome memories with his mouth.

This man's body. This man's mouth.

"Sorry I had to disappear earlier." His voice is low, husky as he watches me.

"I'd let you make it up to me," I murmur, closing the distance between us. I hesitate, but his gaze—hot, hungry, all over me—is all the invitation I need.

"You've had a long day," he says. "You want to talk?"

I drape my arms behind his neck. "Why would you think I want to talk to you at all?"

He grunts. "Because you're looking at me like a starved woman at a prime rib buffet."

"Yes," I murmur. "What does that have to do with talking?"

His eyes are so damn sexy. The kind of eyes you see in magazines, where the man staring at you from the pages seems to invite you to strip bare while promising you'd enjoy it.

"Don't you want us to get to know each other before you indulge?"

I pretend to consider it. "I'm more about the meal than the conversation."

"You're a kid." If it's supposed to be an objection it rings weak against the pressure of his hand on my hip.

I trace a rivulet of water down his neck. "I'm twenty-one." I bring up my knees and wrap my legs around his waist, satisfied when he draws in his breath with a sharp hiss.

"Is this about him?" he asks.

I frown. "Who?"

"The groom at your sister's wedding? He has some kind of hold on you. I saw it in your eyes. In his."

"This has nothing to do with William Bailey."

He looks unconvinced but doesn't call my bluff. Instead, he brushes his lips over mine. Gentle. Careful. Sweet.

The only thing that can break me tonight is sweet, and I won't be broken. I bite his full bottom lip and dig my nails into his shoulder blades.

A quick study, he gets my message. His hand tangles into my hair while the other digs into my ass and pulls me against him. The hard length of his cock rests between my legs and lights a hot coil of pulsing energy.

He rubs his tongue against mine and moans. Or maybe that's me, because I'm pulling him closer. I wrap my arm tighter behind his neck, and I'm practically crawling up him in my efforts to get closer and *closer* still.

I break the kiss and make myself back off. I'm not the kind of girl who loses control. I don't lose my mind over men and expect to be saved. I don't want Asher to save me.

His fingertips are at my hip, tracing an invisible path down and under, moving ever closer to that coiled ache between my thighs. His lips part and our breath mingles as I savor the heat of his body against mine, the sweet anticipation of his fingers inching closer to where I want them.

I slide a hand down his bare chest and between our bodies and cup him through his swim trunks. I'm rewarded with another hiss and then his lips, his tongue, his teeth, hot and desperate against my neck, nipping, toying, playing. Electrifying the sensitive skin.

He cups my breast, and this time I know the moan I hear is my own.

"So goddamn sexy." His thumb flicks across my nipple, a strangled sound escaping his throat.

I graze my fingertips under the waistband of his swim trunks. I want to feel him in my palm. I want that power to whip through me as I wrap my hands around his hot flesh and it pulses thicker, harder.

For a moment, that's where this is headed. His hands are greedy, all over me, his mouth doing delicious things to my neck.

"You have protection, right?" I ask.

He laughs and stops toying with me, his head leaning against my shoulder. Slowly, he slides his hands to my back. "That's not exactly something I keep tucked in my swim trunks."

I'm so aroused it hurts. Asher is stunning. Solid. Delicious. I want to bite into that corded muscle of his neck. Want to explore that smattering of chest hair with my fingers while I drag my mouth down his flat stomach.

But he doesn't have protection, and that's a deal breaker.

"In your house?" My breathing's unsteady, my heart pounding.

He cups my face in one big hand. "Why don't you run home and get dressed? I'll take you to breakfast."

My jaw goes slack. Who the hell is this guy? Who has brakes that good? "Are you serious? I mean, you don't want to..." Rarely am I at a loss for words.

"Sure, I want to do a lot of things. But sweetheart, you don't know a damn thing about me."

"You're really hung up on that." I unwrap my legs from around him and run a hand over my eyes.

Just my luck that I'd pick a bad boy who's all Mr. Sensitivity and wants to *get to know me.*

So be it. That's a better fit for the New Me plan anyway, right?

"Good. Because, you know, I'm not that kind of girl anyway." I wait a beat, but God doesn't strike me dead. "I'll be back in fifteen minutes?"

His lip twitches.

"What?"

"I've just never met a woman who can really get ready in fifteen minutes."

I hoist myself out of the water. "I'll bet breakfast on it. If I take longer than fifteen minutes, I'll cook for you."

Asher runs his eyes over my body, lingering at all my best parts. "Deal."

I grab my towel, making no effort to minimize the swish of my hips as I exit through his gate for the first time.

I pad through the dewy grass back to my mother's house and slip in the back door. I take a quick shower to wash off the chlorine. After a towel-down and some lotion, I slip into jeans and a tank, and pull my wet hair into a ponytail.

When I head toward the door again, my mom is blocking it. Her arms are crossed and worry creases her features. "Is there something you want to tell me?"

That old shame slithers up my spine and I immediately imagine she knows what I've been up to tonight. The trespassing. The strange man. The lust.

So many deadly sins, so little time.

"I don't live here anymore. I don't need your permission to go to breakfast with a friend."

She looks at her watch skeptically. "It's 3 a.m."

"I'm hungry."

She shakes her head. "I want you to think about how important that wedding was to your sister. And then I want you to think about how you can make it right."

My jaw drops. "What?"

She tucks a piece of chestnut hair behind her ear and cocks her head. "We're a family, Maggie, and we'll forgive you for your mistakes. But we can't do that until you own up to them."

My fists clench until I feel the bite of my nails against my palm. It's a lecture I've heard so many times I could recite it in my sleep. It's a lecture I deserved more times than I can count. "I didn't have anything to do with the stink bomb." The words are hard and gritty, pushed through clenched teeth.

"Maggie—"

I push past her, through the door and into the moonlight, anger and hurt a burning fist in my chest.

When I finally steady myself and make it to Asher's, he's waiting for me on his patio, sipping out of a steaming mug.

"You *lose*."

I tense, still wound up from my confrontation with my mom. "What?"

He smiles and points to his watch. "Twenty-five minutes. You lost the bet." His smile fades. "Are you okay?"

"Oh, right. Yeah." I wave a hand. "I'm fine." I let out a long, slow breath and settle into a chair. The moon shines bright and stars sprinkle across that infinite span of darkness. "I've missed this."

"What? Breakfast? First dates?"

"The stars. The light is constant in the city. Inescapable. I missed seeing the stars," I say, more to myself than him.

Suddenly his words register and I shift my eyes to him. "And this isn't a date."

Asher raises an eyebrow but doesn't question me. "So you left for a while but now you're back...for good?"

I wrinkle my nose. "You still insist on playing the get-to-know-you game?"

"Absolutely." He grins at me and leans forward. "I like hiking, seafood, and long walks on the beach at sunset."

I can't help but smile. "You'd think we had a country full of avid hikers," I say. "Every trail at every national park would be packed if everyone who says they like to hike actually did it."

"Your turn," he says. "Tell me something about yourself."

Is this guy for real?

I steal his mug from his hands and take a long sip of hot, rich coffee.

"I'm waiting."

I let the heat sink to my belly and relax my shoulders. "Well, I *should* tell you one thing."

"What's that?"

"I am *that kind of girl.*"

His laugh is rich and deep and sexy. "Sure you are."

"You don't believe me? Ask...oh, anyone in this town."

Something changes in his eyes. If sadness had a color I'd say I could see it circling his pupils. "I don't put much stock in the things people say. Anyway, I'd rather hear about you from your lips."

He can't possibly know what that single statement means to me. The silence stretches between us as I consider how to abbreviate my life into a series of simple sentences. He doesn't rush me. Doesn't seem intimidated by silence like so many people are. That alone makes me want to share myself with him.

"I'm just Maggie." I fight the urge to say too much. Months trapped in a self-constructed prison of silence have left me hungry for a confidant, but sexy Asher isn't it. "Black sheep. College dropout. Famished. Painfully turned on."

He groans, a low, guttural sound that speaks to his own arousal. "Well, I can fix the famished part, but the last will have to wait."

But I don't want to wait. I need to…escape. Forget. "I pay my bets." I wrap my fingers around his biceps. "Let me cook for you."

"You really cook?"

My eyes flick to the large French doors at the back of his house, but I dismiss the idea, ready to be on my own turf. "Follow me to my place and I'll show you."

I think we both know I'm not the slightest bit interested in food.

Asher

Maggie takes her coffee black. Straight from the pot, no sweetener, no fancy cream. Just coffee. She puts herself out there in the same way—no frills, no pretense, no bullshit. Just Maggie.

I like that. I like it more than I want to. I like *her* more than I want to. More than I've liked any woman since Juliana fucked me over.

We're at her shitty little rental house in New Hope, and our breakfast dishes litter the kitchen table.

"I've decided I'm not going to sleep with you," she informs me between bites of feta omelet.

"Really?"

"Yeah, my food is so damn good, I don't need you to get off." She takes a sip of coffee. Her tongue darts out to taste her bottom lip after every sip, an innocent gesture that makes me think of mouth and tongue and tasting in a very different context.

"Hmm," I say, as if considering. "You make a damn good omelet, but I promise you I'm better."

"Are you sure?" She slips another bite in her mouth. "Because

I'm bordering on foodgasmic about now." Her eyes float closed, and she makes a little sound at the back of her throat, tilting her head back a fraction of an inch.

I put down my fork. In the battle between my throbbing dick and empty stomach, my dick has won. It's not just that she's gorgeous. There are plenty of gorgeous women in this world. Maggie is more than that. She's a study in contradictions and I am an eager student.

My time in New Hope is coming to an end, and I don't know what I was thinking when I joined her in the pool tonight.

That's a lie. I know exactly what I was thinking. I was thinking of big smiles and bright green eyes that are so damn familiar I'm sure I've seen them before. I was thinking of soft skin and bare, sun-kissed shoulders.

I was thinking of the way her face looked by the river when the asshole in the tux told her he was marrying someone else. I didn't understand the conversation. Didn't need to understand it to know she needed me. To feel it.

"Do you make a habit of cooking breakfast for strange men?"

She runs her eyes over me, lingering on my chest and the tat snaking around my biceps. "Only the good-looking ones."

Or only when she's trying to get another man out of her mind. "Are you in school?"

"Not at the moment." She pushes her plate across the table. "Do you want any more? I can make you another."

I'm used to women trying to tell me their life story, trying to play on my sympathies. I'm used to women who want me to rescue them, but not this one. "Is there a reason that you change the subject every time I ask you a personal question?"

She leans back in her chair. "I'm a private person."

My mind is flooded with images—her hair slicked back from her face, her breasts rounded under the surface of the water. When her tongue darted out to taste my lips and she wrapped those long legs behind my back, I lost sight of all sense.

Maggie chews on the corner of her lip and my brain paints a

picture of those lips working their way down my stomach, opening over my cock.

"*Don't you want to...*" she'd asked.

"You didn't seem so private in the pool."

"That was just about sex, Asher."

Another contradiction. That openness. That in-your-face sexuality matched with complete avoidance of any kind of intimacy.

And hell, I could use some just-about-sex right now. It's been too long since I've tasted a woman, since I've felt a woman's mouth on my dick and buried myself inside her.

But I'm not about to end my celibate streak with someone as vulnerable as Maggie. Because no matter what she says, what happened in the pool wasn't just about sex. It was about *him*. The groom. The man her eyes kept returning to as we danced.

"You want to meet my little girl?" Her words rip me from my reverie.

"You have a kid?" Where are all the toys? There are dog toys all over the place, but no signs of a baby doll or Barbie.

Maggie would probably hang by that thick red hair before she'd let a child of hers play with Barbie dolls. But what about Little People or picture books? I hope she's not one of those moms who always pawns her kid off on the sitter. That makes me uncomfortable as hell.

Then, like a fucking genius, I put it all together. "Your little girl is a dog, isn't she?"

Maggie hops up from her chair and tugs the back door open. "Come on, baby girl. It's okay. Lucy! Come say hi to Mama!"

I love the idea of this rough woman owning a spoiled little dog.

The image in my mind is turned on its head when one hundred and fifty pounds of Rottweiler runs toward Maggie with the frenzied glee of a ten-pound pup.

When Lucy reaches Maggie's feet, she immediately drops to the ground and rolls onto her back.

"I should have known," I mutter.

"What?"

"I should have known you'd have a big-ass guard dog to match your big-ass guard dog personality."

Maggie scoffs. "Lotta good she does me. Lucy's the biggest coward I've ever met. Aren't you, sweetie?" she coos to the dog, rubbing on her belly. Lucy writhes in pleasure.

"So you *don't* have any kids?"

Maggie stands and the dog cowers behind her legs. "It's just me and Lucy here."

I drop to my knees and extend a hand. "Come here, sweetie."

Lucy howls in half excited whine, half terrified cry.

"We're still getting used to each other," Maggie explains. "I adopted her from the shelter when I moved back to town last month."

I'm still waiting with my hand out, but I flick my eyes up to Maggie. "Most people would have gotten a puppy."

"That's why Lucy needed me." Her eyes go soft as she studies her dog and she adds, quietly, "I needed her too."

Finally, Lucy edges toward me.

Maggie gapes. "You've got to be freaking kidding me!"

I shrug. Lucy drops to the floor at my feet, rolling to her back so I can rub her belly. "Dogs like me."

"Lucy's afraid of everyone. Even my *mom*."

"Maybe your mom's scary."

She snorts. "You have no idea." Then she grabs my hand and pulls me up. "I can't have her liking you more than me."

Her face is inches from mine and something's nagging at the back of my mind again. Do I know this woman? Maybe I saw her around town during my rare visits to my river house before this year, but the recognition, the *déjà vu* I feel when I look at her is something more.

Her skin is fresh and clear. Freckles scatter across the bridge of her nose. And I swear she smells like clean laundry hanging to dry in the summer sun.

Fuck. I'm in trouble.

"Let me take you out sometime, Maggie."

"I don't play games." She says it in a husky whisper that makes me think of lazy Sunday mornings in a warm bed, the sun slanting in on us as we explore each other's bodies.

"Who said I'm playing a game?"

"Isn't that what dating is?" Her eyes drop to my lips. "If I want something, I take it."

"And you think you want me?"

A smile spreads across her face. "Why don't you come find out?" She cocks her head and walks toward the hallway.

I follow like a smitten fool.

She leans against a doorframe and pulls her tank over her head, revealing creamy skin, heavy breasts in a simple black bra. No lace. No frills. And so damn sexy. I can still feel the weight of them, slick with pool water, her pebbled nipple against my palm, her breath quickening against my neck.

"Maggie, what are you doing?"

"I haven't figured out all the details yet, but I figure we can play it by ear. We have"—she glances over her shoulder to the clock—"approximately five hours before I need to play the good daughter for a family brunch at my mom's house."

The shirt drops from her fingers to the floor, and I groan involuntarily as she moves to the button on her jeans. I stop her hands with one of mine.

"Oh, sorry." She looks up, laughter in her eyes. "Did you want to do it?"

She has no idea. I could do it. I could fuck her today and forget her tomorrow. No one would be surprised. Half the world thinks I'm a selfish asshole, so why not prove them right?

"I'm not going to sleep with you, Maggie. Not yet."

Her eyes narrow. "I told you I don't play games. I'm not about that."

"And I don't make a habit of screwing women who are hung up on other men."

"I don't see any other men here, do you?" Her lips curve in amusement.

She shimmies out of her jeans, watching me as she steps out of them. She's in nothing but her bra and a black scrap of thong. I fist my hands against the temptation to trace the curve of her hip, tighten my jaw against the need to press my open mouth against the flat of her belly.

Grabbing the doorframe, I take a deep breath.

"I'm going to jump in the shower." Maggie pulls the tie from her hair and a thick curtain of red falls around her shoulders. "I'd love some company, but you do what you must."

She disappears around the corner and I count backwards from ten.

Ten. Nine…

Ancient plumbing squeals and the shower kicks on. I imagine her under the spray, all that soft, pale skin slick with water.

Eight. Seven. Six…

It would be so easy to follow her, so easy to pretend I didn't see that pain in her eyes.

Five. Four…

But I'm so damn drawn to her already. She has this magnetic pull on me.

Three. Two…

This lust is so powerful it nearly has me snarling with need.

One. I won't slide inside of her while her mind is full of another man.

Been there. Done that.

Turning around and walking out the door is on my top ten list of hardest things I've ever had to do.

chapter three

Maggie

MY EYES are heavy. Even amidst the constant chitchat of the Thompson family luncheon, I can't stop yawning.

Before I left my house for brunch, I found Asher's number on my kitchen table, a note scribbled under it.

Call me when you're ready for that date.

"Isn't this fun?" my mom asks me now. People are milling around with low-calorie mimosas and chattering about Krystal's wedding, but the guest of honor is fashionably late, as always.

Fun? It is the final day of a torturous three days. Rehearsal dinner Friday, Krystal's wedding yesterday, and today a lunch at the Thompson house with people so distantly related it would be legal for us to marry in most states. Fun would have been Asher joining me in the shower. I stayed under the spray of the water for a solid twenty minutes before accepting that he wasn't going to join me. *Sadist.*

Mom folds her arms. "I wanted to talk to you about your date last night. Some scruffy bum with piercings is the most respectable man you could find for your sister's wedding?" She shakes her head. "Where'd you even find him?"

I shrug. "Just wandering down by the river."

"You're not funny," she hisses.

I bite my tongue. I came home to begin Operation New Me, which includes a better relationship with my mother. She doesn't appreciate my "sass," as she calls it.

Gran waddles toward me. The scent of her makes me smile. Lavender soap and whiskey. "I had a vision during my meditation yesterday."

Mom nudges Gran. "Your devil games aren't welcome here." She produces a tube of lipstick from her pocket. "Just one coat, Margaret. People will think you have no self-respect."

Granny slaps at her hand. "Leave the girl alone!"

I roll my eyes.

"Maggie," Granny continues, "your past is going to visit you and bring your future as a gift."

I try to look interested. I love Gran, even if I think her brand of spirituality is a little kooky. "That's...profound."

"Are you seeing anyone, Maggie?" My mother's voice is low, the whisper reserved for talk of scandal—like premarital cohabitation and non-procreative sex. "Are you even *trying* to find love? Or do you intend to continue fornicating with random men outside the sanctity of marriage?"

"So if I were married I'd have your blessing to *fornicate* with random men? Maybe I should reconsider my stance on marriage." The words are out of my mouth before I can stop them. I'm batting zero on the New Me plan.

"Margaret Marie!" Mom's scowl is so fierce, it threatens to bust through the Botox. "Watch your mouth this instant! I do hope you still go to confession."

"Maggie's on a spiritual journey, Gretchen," Granny defends.

I frown. That's what Gran says about her crazy clients, and I don't want to be categorized with them.

"You need to let her find her own way," Granny continues. "But Maggie, your aura does seem terribly dark. You should come to my office sometime this week and we can do a cleansing."

"My aura can't help it, Gran. It feels fat in anything but black."

Granny grins. "Clever girl."

I'm quickly reaching my fill of family togetherness.

"So, Maggie," Aunt—Sally? Sophie?—asks, "you're getting married, right? When is your wedding, again?"

The other aunt shoots the first a hard glare. "Don't you remember?" Then to me, "Did it bother you to see him marry someone else, dear?"

I grit my teeth.

"It must be hard to see someone you once planned to marry fall in love with your sister."

As if mentioning her summoned the devil, Krystal bursts into the room, bringing the hot breath of Indiana summer with her.

"I'm so sorry I'm late!" she says, waving a hand in front of her red-tinged cheeks.

A bright-eyed blonde claps her hands. "Of course you're late after your *wedding night.*"

Krystal smiles at her friend and shakes her head. "Will and I never made it official yesterday. It just didn't feel right to let someone else control our day. We appreciate everything you all did this weekend, and we hope you'll join us when we try again later in the summer."

The chatter screeches to a halt. Damn it. Now they're all staring at me.

My sister Lizzy comes over to stand by my side.

"I'm so happy for you both," I manage, but I can't bring myself to exhale until they stop looking at me.

When everyone finally returns to their conversations, Granny leans over the table. "Are you okay?"

"I'm fine, Gran. It really doesn't bother me. My relationship with Will is over, and I'm okay with that."

Granny nods, but it's clear by her expression that she's unconvinced.

"You're really okay?" Lizzy whispers this time.

Across the room, Hanna gives me a pitying half-smile.

"Okay, no," I admit. "I'm not fine. But only because I don't want people looking at me like Hanna is right now."

One of Krystal's friends is asking about her wedding night in a stage whisper as clear as her wriggling eyebrows. "We're going to wait until it's official," Krystal says with a hand pressed to her chest.

"That's my girl," my mom says with an approving nod.

I stifle the urge to snort. Maybe Krystal hasn't had sex with Will, but she's no virgin.

"You NEED to settle a bet for us," Lizzy tells me as our server settles three chocolate martinis on our table. "Was that *Asher Logan* you were dancing with at the wedding last night?"

"It wasn't," Hanna says. "Though he's a dead ringer for him." She hums and—

"Did you just lick your lips?" I narrow my eyes at my sisters. I can't remember if he ever told me his last name. "How do you know Asher?"

Hanna's jaw drops. "No way!"

Lizzy hides her smile behind her martini. "Apparently they're on a first-name basis."

With a French-tipped nail, Lizzy tucks a long lock of blond hair behind her ear. Tonight, she's dressed to kill in a pale pink strapless, show-off-the-legs-that-go-for-miles dress. Next to her, Hanna is dressed a bit more modestly in a black capris and a lavender sweater set. She's as drop-dead gorgeous as her twin, if in a different way. Since good daughters spend time with their family, martini night with the twins is part of Operation New Me. So far it's been my favorite part of my ill-conceived plan.

"I just met him last night," I explain. "How do *you* know him?"

The girls giggle.

"How do we *know* Asher Logan?" Lizzy asks.

"Asher 'Sexy Beast' Logan?" Hanna adds.

I fold my arms. "That's what I asked."

The girls exchange a look.

"She's clueless," Lizzy mutters.

"He was only the hottest lead singer in the history of rock bands," Hanna says.

"But Maggie was always more into that angry chick music."

I wave a hand in front of them. "Hello. Quit talking about me like I'm not here."

Lizzy narrows her eyes. "You really didn't know?"

"All I know is that he is the Rich Dude who owns the house next door to Mom."

"Shut up!" Hanna's eyes go wide. "Asher Logan lives next door to Mom?"

Lizzy's eyes light up. "I take back every bad thing I ever said about New Hope."

"If the Asher I was dancing with last night is the Asher you're talking about, then yes, he owns the house next to mom's. But I don't think he *lives* there, or if he does I don't think he has for long."

Lizzy downs her martini. "This is so huge." She waves to the waitress. "I'm gonna need another."

"We need details," Hanna says, leaning forward.

"I met him at Krystal's wedding. He was down by the river and I thought he was a lost wedding guest." I snort, realizing for the first time why he was really there. "But I guess he was just in his own backyard."

Hanna grins. "Yeah, because Mom's backyard is right next to *Asher Logan's* backyard. God, this is epic."

Lizzy waves her hands excitedly, urging me to share more. "So you met at the wedding. And then?"

"We talked, danced. We ran into each other after the reception was over."

"Where? Did Maggie go out carousing?" Lizzy presses her palms into the table. "It's finally happened. Hell froze over."

I roll my eyes. "I hardly went out carousing. He caught me

swimming in his pool and…things happened."

Hanna wilts. "If you tell me you got to have hot pool sex with Asher 'Sexier Than God' Logan, I may never forgive you."

"Right, but that's just it. We didn't have sex. We messed around, and then I took him back to my place for breakfast and took off my clothes."

"And this is a problem because…?" Lizzy quirks a brow. "You're not thinking of changing your naughty girl ways on us are you? Has Mom's constant harassment finally broken you? Because, seriously, Maggie—if Asher Logan is in the picture, now is *not* the time."

"No. He rejected me. Told me he wanted to *get to know me*."

"*Oh*," the girls chorus. Judging by the disappointment on their faces, you'd think they were the ones left high and dry.

"Yeah. What the hell?"

Lizzy throws back her head and laughs, a full-stomach laugh that has everyone in the bar looking at us.

I scowl. "It's not funny."

She's doesn't even attempt to stifle her damn giggles of delight. "Yes, yes it is."

Hanna nods. "It kind of is, Mags."

"It's not like I go after one-night stands often, but the few times I have I've never been *denied*. Now I know how guys must feel."

"Maybe he's gay," Lizzy says.

"That would be a tragedy," Hanna whimpers.

Lizzy nudges her. "Don't be so narrow-minded. Gay boys deserve hot men too."

I roll my eyes. "He's not gay. Trust me. His attraction was physically evident."

"Oh, yeah?" Lizzy props her chin on her hands. "How's he measure up?"

I groan. "Why the hell do you think I took him back to my place and stripped down to my skivvies while he was trying to get out the door?" If I wanted Asher to distract me, I was successful because I can't stop thinking about him.

I smile into my chocolate martini, wondering if the girls would be offended if I tainted "Martini Night" with a beer.

I am nothing like my sisters. They do things like have makeover parties and martini nights. They ooze femininity from every pore, from their hair to their designer jeans and Gucci heels. Me? I'm all about comfort and practicality. My favorite outfit consists of worn Levi's and a ribbed tank top, and I'm convinced that heels are medieval torture devices. The girls primp and fuss, and make semi-annual shopping trips to the Big Apple, whereas I have discovered I can make a twenty-dollar dress from Target look damn good.

"You still got more action than I did," Lizzy says. "I was trying to hook up with that groomsman. You know, Will's friend from college?"

Hanna snorts. "He's not into girls."

Lizzy frowns. "A tragedy."

"Gay boys deserve hot men too," Hanna says, parroting Lizzy's words right back at her.

"I guess," Lizzy pouts. "Did you see Krystal's eyes today? I think she cried a lot last night."

"Poor thing," Hanna says. "Who do you think did it?"

Probably by some bored kid with nothing better to do with his Saturday. "I don't know. I figure it'll remain a mystery."

"Hmm," Lizzy says, "like the mystery of who stole those fraternity boys' clothes the night they went skinny dipping in Lake Lemon?"

I can't help but smile at the memory from my first semester at Sinclair. All those beautiful men searching for their clothes in the moonlight.

"Or the mystery of how the Sigmas all came down with stomach cramps after outing your friend Ed?"

Her implication clicks into place in my mind and I lift my hands, palms up. "You think *I* did this?"

The girls shake their heads, saying "Oh, no! Not us" in unison.

"Why would I want to ruin Krystal's wedding with a stink bomb?"

"*We* don't think you would," Lizzy says. "It's just…"

"There's been some talk," Hanna finishes.

"And your name's been mentioned," Lizzy says.

Hanna pats my arm. "It's no mystery how much you hate weddings."

Translation: Everyone knows how much I must hate seeing Will marry Krystal.

"We'd hate weddings too if—" Lizzy cuts herself off.

Hanna finishes for her. "You know."

"I do"—I soften the truth—"*dislike* weddings, but not because—"

"Of course not," the girls chorus.

"I would never—"

Lizzy holds up her hand. "You don't have to say anything else. I guess it just occurred to Hanna and me…"

Hanna nods. "…With the talk and all…"

"…How insensitive it was for Krystal to ask you to be in her wedding after…"

"You know," they say together.

"It's fine. I'm the one who canceled the wedding. I don't have any hold on Will."

"Was it weird?" Lizzy asks in a whisper. "Being a bridesmaid in Will's wedding?"

Hanna bites her lip and watches me.

"So, Asher's some sort of rock star?" I ask to change the subject.

Lizzy huffs, unimpressed by my non-sequitur, but Hanna's drawn in by more talk of the sexy rocker and gapes at me in dismay. "The *lead singer* of Infinite Gray?"

"Infinite Gray?" I frown. "Isn't that the band that put out the song 'Unbroken?'" I listened to that song on repeat during my sophomore year of high school, but then…I don't remember anything else. One-hit wonders? "A rock star," I mutter, trying to fit it all into place. There was something familiar about Asher—those *eyes*. This must be why.

"Former rock star," Lizzy corrects. "The band dissolved after their first tour. Same old story—hit the big time too young and got caught up in booze and drugs."

"I heard," Hanna says, "that he beat the shit out of some dude in a bar last year and got tried for aggravated battery."

My jaw goes slack. Now I really do want that beer. *Aggravated battery*. "Really?"

Hanna bites her lip. "No one but Asher knows what really happened that night. I'm sure he's a nice guy."

Right. Because nice guys get charged with aggravated battery all the time.

"Doesn't matter anyway, right?" I shake my head and force a smile. "He's had that house for, what, five years? And this is the first time we've seen him around? It's not like I think I'm going to see him again."

chapter four

William

THE BEST part of living in a small town is that everyone knows everyone. This is also the shittiest part of living in a small town, a fact I'm reminded of every time I take my grandmother to her bi-weekly salon visits.

"I'm so glad you're okay," Cecilia says as Grandma gets situated in her chair. "It's just terrible what they did to your wedding, Willy."

I cringe but don't bother to correct her on my name. Cecilia has been calling me Willy since I was a toddler. If my red-cheeked embarrassment didn't stop her when I was a teenager, a polite objection isn't going to stop her now.

"I think it was that Maggie," Grandma says with a knowing nod. "She didn't want to see you marrying her sister."

"Grandma." My voice is hard, making Grandma's shoulders drop, her face go sad. "Maggie wouldn't do that," I say, softer now, because as much as I hate the way she talks about Maggie, I know it's all out of love for me.

Grandma shakes her head. "That's what you said when I told you about the rumors back in high school. Then the truth came out. It always does. Poor Ann Quimby's whole life was torn apart by the girl."

"Mom, she's the county *prosecutor* now and has a new husband and children. I think she survived."

Gran turns to Cecilia and whispers, "Boy's got no sense when it comes to that little girl."

Cecilia shakes her head and combs her fingers through Grandma's hair.

I let out a slow breath. "Grandma, I have my cell. Just give me a call when you're done." I head to the door before they have a chance to say anything else about the wedding or Maggie or gossip that should have died years ago.

When I hit the sidewalk, I'm swarmed by the greetings of the bookstore patrons next door. They're sitting out on the patio, sipping coffee and sharing "local news," more easily recognizable as gossip.

"So sorry to hear about your wedding, Willy," Mrs. White calls.

I close my eyes. God *damn* do I hate when people call me that. "It's okay," I assure her, forcing a smile. "What matters is that we have each other. No stink bomb can change that."

"Of course it can't, and Krystal's mother tells us you're opening an art gallery in the old Beatlemeyer building."

"He is?" the woman across from her croons. "Well, that's what we need around here. More young people investing in this town. Putting roots down. Good for you, young man. Not like all those snotty college kids running away as soon as they get their degree."

"Thank you," I say. "We're lucky to be in a position to do it."

I excuse myself, but I don't turn to my car. The Curl Up and Dye sits just three blocks off campus and I need the walk to clear my head.

New Hope is simultaneously a young and aging community. The largest population is our community of seniors who lived and worked in this little town their whole life. Our second largest population comes from Sinclair, a small liberal arts college that families all over the country spend a small fortune to send their spoiled, privileged children to. In between, there are a few of us staying for jobs at the college or family ties or, in my case, both.

I can't leave Grandma. The woman raised me and she doesn't have anyone else. So I'm here with Krystal, and we are going to make the most of it.

My steps slow as I approach the county library and my breath catches in my throat.

At a seat by the window, Maggie sits with her laptop open, headphones on, and a soft smile on her lips. My feet stall under me as she leans toward her screen and her smile grows.

Suddenly, she turns to the window, and our gazes lock through the glass. Her smile falls away.

My chest is heavy with regret and longing and...fuck, I'm *angry*. She's the one who left. She's the one who called it off.

So why does she look at me like I've broken her heart?

Maggie

I MIGHT as well be sixteen again, I'm so obsessed with Infinite Gray.

I made a little trip to my local library to use their internet access—because Operation New Me means I can't steal it from my neighbors anymore—and now my hard drive is loaded with the band's album and a couple dozen half-nude pictures of Asher. The more I listened to the album, the more the memories came back—my ceiling fan spinning above my bed, my heart frozen in my chest, that low, mellow voice crooning from my MP3 player as I did my damndest to sink into my numbness and disintegrate into nothing.

"Come back and break me, don't let this go unspoken. I'm numb when I'm whole and you left me unbroken."

And the pictures? Dear God. If I had been the kind of teenager who watched music videos instead of the kind who broke her father's heart, I never would have forgotten that face or body. Turns out half-naked pictures of a rock star dubbed "Sexy Beast" are plentiful. Thank you, Internets. But there still weren't enough. Not when you consider how when I close my eyes I can feel his muscles flexing under my fingers, still taste his salty skin on my tongue.

I pack up my laptop and head to the parking lot with a sigh. I just wasted half a day obsessing over a rock star who will never sleep with me. Maybe I am sixteen again.

Stepping out of the library, I squint into the setting sun and see Asher "Sexy Beast" Logan leaning against my car.

My steps stutter and his lips curl into a grin as he looks me over.

Play it cool.

"Your wife kick you out, Pretty Boy?"

He looks damn fine standing there, his dark shades blocking his eyes from the setting sun, a tiny silver hoop glinting in each ear. He is all hard muscle and tan in his fitted black t-shirt and faded jeans. I always said there's no man as hot as my car. Now I'm not so sure.

My first thought is that we could be naked and in my bed in twenty minutes. My second is of the story Lizzy just told me, a story that makes Asher the worst kind of bad boy—capital B, capital N, Bad News.

I pull my keys from my purse. "What are you doing here?"

His too-goddamn-perfect mouth quirks into that cocky half grin. "I wanted to see you."

"Aw! That's what all my stalkers say."

He chuckles. "You owe me a date."

"How'd you even know to find me here?"

"How'd you get the cash for such a sweet ride?"

I drive a deep blue Mustang GT, a gift from my granny. She's terrible with money and we love her for it.

"Marry an old man for his money?" he asks.

"Sure. But I was screwing his brains out when he died, so he didn't mind much."

His smile never wavers. "I want to take you out."

"We discussed this already," I say, my traitorous gaze dipping back to the bulge of his biceps. *Lord have mercy.* "I don't do dates."

"So we'll call it something else," he says. "Try not to get hung up on semantics."

"And what if I say no?"

Asher's smirk should piss me off. This is a man who gets what he wants, and it's written all over his face.

I sigh. "Fine, but only if you have a signed note from your wife that says it's okay if you play with others."

"It's one night. What? Are you afraid you can't resist me?"

Damn. That's a challenge. "Dinner," I say, punching my key fob to unlock my doors. "But none of this macho, He-Man, I-drive-the-lady crap. I have free will and I like to keep my vehicle at my disposal. You might be hot, and I might be joining you for a meal, but you don't own me."

"Are you done?"

I try to stop the smile that's coming, but I can't resist. I don't meet many men willing to call me on my bullshit. "Yeah."

"Do you like Cajun food, loud atmosphere, a good beer list?"

I look him up and down again—a visual journey that is worth it every time. "Goddamn, Asher. You keep going and I might just think you had my number. Cajun Jack's?"

"I'll see you there." He heads toward his Jeep. When he turns back to slide his eyes over my body, I have to tell myself that the heat rushing through me is only a product of the scorching May afternoon sun.

"You're staring at me," I protest between bites of crawfish etouffee.

Asher lifts a shoulder. "Just watching in case you get foodgasmic again."

I hum as I swallow a particularly decadent bite. "I'm close. You like to watch, huh?"

His pupils dilate and his jaw goes a little slack as his gaze drops to my mouth. Just like that, we're not talking about food anymore. Maybe we never were.

I take a sip of my beer to cool off the heat his eyes send through me. Asher isn't drinking. He didn't explain and I didn't ask, but I'm curious. He doesn't strike me as a straight-edger. Hell, he's a former rocker. Maybe he prefers something with a little more punch than beer.

Jack's is slow tonight, and it will be until classes start up at Sinclair in the fall. New Hope is a tiny little town of contrasts—a bizarre mix of yuppie affluence and rural simplicity. The businesses within a two-block radius of campus cater to the private school students—a gourmet coffee shop, an Aveda hair salon, a sushi bar. Outside of those two blocks, residents are served with gas stations that advertise "Live Bait" on their marquees and greasy spoon restaurants where the closest thing to fresh sushi is the fried catfish—locally caught, cleaned, battered, and fried.

"So did you grow up in New Hope?"

"You want to know why I hate dating?" I counter. He frowns and I hold up a hand before he can protest. "I hate dating because dating protocol requires I keep it positive, that I feed you some bullshit about how my childhood was wholesome and awesome blah-blah-bullshit-blah."

He folds his arms on the table and leans forward. "It's a date, Maggie. Not a job interview." When I just stare in response, he says, "My childhood was shitty. I was poor. My dad was a drunk. He put his hands on my mom, and then, when I was old enough by whatever fucked-up standards he had, he put them on me."

"I…" What do you say? "I'm sorry."

He shrugs. "I'm grown now. I have more money than I know what to do with, Mom's all right, and the son of a bitch is dead.

Life's not so bad after all."

I let out a breath. Something about Asher compels me to open up. Something about the way his blue eyes take me in. It's like he sees something good when he looks at me, and I want to throw my ugliness in his face to prove him wrong.

I take a long draw from my beer. "I grew up in New Hope," I say in answer to his question. "And I stayed here for college at Sinclair. I probably should have gone away but there's a good art program here." *And Will,* I thought, remembering how Will's decision to come home for graduate school had solidified mine to do undergrad at Sinclair.

"So you're a brain," he says.

I laugh. "In my family, you don't have a choice. Good grades, good behavior, good fashion sense. It's all expected." I realize I've said more than I want to, so I wave it away. "Not that I was ever any good at any of those. Not anything other than painting, actually."

"When do you graduate?"

"Well, I dropped out last year, so that all depends on whether or not they'll take me back."

He exhales sharply. "Fuck, what a relief."

"What?"

"Well"—he starts ticking off reasons on his fingers—"you're gorgeous and sexy and smart. It's intimidating until you throw in the college dropout stuff. I was ready to find a new date."

"*I'm* intimidating? You're the freaking rock star at the table."

Some of the humor drains from his face, but he keeps his smile in place. "You know about that, huh?"

"My sisters told me. You could have mentioned you're in a band."

"I *was* in a band." He wipes his hands on his napkin and shrugs. "Past tense."

With a dreamy sigh, I prop my chin on my fists. "Who knew that one day I'd be on a date with the lead singer from a famous boy band?"

He scowls. "Infinite Gray was not a *boy band*."

"Were there any girls in the band?"

"No."

"That makes you a boy band."

"It made us an all-male rock group."

I bite back my smile. He's so cute when he's irritated. "Right, like 'N Sync."

He winces. "*Not* like 'N Sync. Jesus, watch where you hurl those things. Words hurt, Maggie."

I giggle.

He glowers. "You need a musical intervention."

I perk up. "Ooh! Are you going to make me a playlist?"

"Maybe."

I laugh again, but this time a little snort pops out, making me laugh harder.

He narrows his eyes. "You're playing me, aren't you?"

"Sorry. I couldn't resist."

"So you don't need that playlist?"

"Says who? No boy has ever made a playlist especially for me before. *Please*?"

"Not even in high school?"

That takes some of the wind out of my sails. "I wasn't that kind of girl."

He studies me for a minute and just when I think he's going to dig, he drops it. "Okay. It's your turn. Ask me anything."

I study him for a moment. The ice-blue eyes that keep dropping to my mouth. The stubble I can still feel against my neck. When I finally speak, it's to ask, "What do you have against a perfectly good shower?"

He releases a burst of laughter. "If I'd let you have your way with me, you wouldn't be sitting here with me tonight."

"Oh, you think I would have moved on to another rock star in my long line of rock stars?"

He shrugs.

"You know how much you can hurt a girl's ego by turning her down when she's stripped in front of you?" I put my hand to my chest. "I'll probably be in counseling for months to repair the damage."

"Somehow I think you can handle it."

"Games," I mutter. "Emotionally speaking, I'm going to be the man in this relationship, aren't I?"

"You certainly aren't like any woman I've ever met before."

"Thank God," I say, but my cheeks warm because I know he means it as a compliment. I try damn hard not to care what people think about me, but with Asher, I care. And that worries me.

He pays the bill and we walk out into the dusky evening. When he takes my hand, I don't pull away.

"How do you feel about weddings?" I hear myself ask.

"Proposing already?" He cuts his eyes to me. "I don't know. Seems like we're moving a little fast."

I bite back my smile. "I need an escort."

"To a wedding?"

"To my sister Krystal's wedding. I mean, if you're still in town or whatever. I'm not asking that you make a special trip."

He quirks a brow. "I thought she already got married."

"She wants a do-over. But don't worry, she promises it's going to be *fah-bu-lous.*"

He's silent. Can you blame him? He didn't want to sleep with me, and I think *this* is a more appealing proposition?

"Sure," he finally says. "I'd be happy to accompany you."

"Really? Because there's a pretty good chance the twins might maul you at the reception."

He chuckles and cuts his eyes to me. "I can handle a couple of fan girls. Anyway, I know you wouldn't ask me if you didn't feel like you needed to have a date. I've never said no to a woman in need."

"Humph," I snort. "My experience says otherwise."

A block away, a pickup screeches forward at the traffic light, and a guy in a ball cap sticks his head and chest out the window and points at me. "Loooose!" he calls out into the night, drawing out the word. "Loooos-eeee!"

The word, once a sharp knife, is now the sawing of a dull blade against my calloused heart. The truck screeches down the road, and hatred clogs my throat and blocks any response.

"Lucy?" Asher asks. "Isn't that your dog's name?"

Suddenly, I'm overwhelmed by my own naiveté. I really thought I could come back to this godforsaken hole-in-the-earth town and live a normal life? New Hope will never offer me *normal*. If I live and die in New Hope, I imagine they'll carve my tombstone with the word *loose*.

I swallow down my anger and shake my head. "*Loose*," I explain. "As in *loose woman. Promiscuous. Slut.*"

Asher's breath draws in with a raspy hiss and his nostrils flare. Those blue eyes burn as he looks after the offender. He's long gone now, and I'm glad because the look in Asher's eyes says what he'd like to do to them. It should scare me, given his reputation, but instead it helps the insult roll off my back.

I can handle the nastiness now. But I wish I could send Asher back in time to be indignant on behalf of my fifteen-year-old self. She wasn't so hardened.

"Can you tell me a name?" he asks, his voice low and deadly steady.

"They're just stupid townies from my high school." I press my hand to his arm. "It doesn't matter."

He doesn't call me on my lie, but we both know it *does* matter. What had he said in there? *Words hurt.*

He takes my hand and walks me to my car, toying with my fingers.

"Assholes notwithstanding," I whisper, "I had a good time."

"Me too." He rubs the inside of my palm. Soft. Gentle. This man may look rough with his tattoos and piercings, but there is nothing rough about the way he treats me. And, where the violence that flashed in his eyes didn't scare me, this gentleness does.

"Listen," I say. "About the other morning, I just—"

He cuts me off with his mouth. He touches his lips to mine, and I feel frozen for a moment—I am the statue I once trained myself to be. But his mouth is soft and slow and patient. I melt into him, curl my fingers into his chest, slide my tongue against his.

It's the kind of kiss I dreamed about as a girl and never got.

When he pulls away, he traces his thumb over my bottom lip.

"Come home with me?" I ask, breathless from his kiss, his touch.

"You're so damn sweet."

That gets me right in the solar plexus. Men call me *hot*. Men call me *sexy*. Men don't call me *sweet*.

"For a woman who claims to be an open book, you hide so much." He runs his thumb down the side of my neck, over the hollow in my collarbone. "Next time you strip for me, you're taking off more than your clothes."

I step back. "Goodnight, Asher." I climb in my car and drive away—from him and from this aching inside my chest that feels a whole lot like falling.

chapter five

William

MAGGIE THOMPSON is wandering around my art gallery, lips parted, eyes wide. At first, I think I'm imagining it. After all, this place was her dream too. We were going to get married and open New Hope's first art gallery. We'd sell her paintings and my photography. We'd feature Sinclair faculty and students. We'd sell art that people wanted to put in their homes. We'd get a liquor license and serve wine and champagne for clients to sip as they studied the selections and made their choice. And tucked into a corner of the back office we'd keep a bassinet.

My stomach lurches and my breath leaves me in a rush. My gut aches where the memory sucker punched me.

I must have made a noise because Maggie lifts her head and stares at me, mouth in a perfect, surprised circle. And I want to kiss it. Fucking scum of the earth *addict*, I can hardly think of anything but tasting her.

My fingers curl around the loft railing, and I force them to relax, force myself to walk down the stairs and greet her.

"Hi," I say as I hit the last step.

She looks around again. The gallery doesn't officially open for a couple of weeks, and it hasn't been staged yet. Paintings are propped against the walls; sculptures sit in odd groupings.

When she returns her eyes to mine, awkwardness sits between us like a chaperone with too many elbows. I hate it, and I hate myself for thinking about how it felt to hold her together, how it felt to be the thing she needed most in this world, her rock.

"Maggie," I repeat. My voice is a little hard this time, as if it's her fault I can't just let it go. "What are you doing here?"

She swallows audibly. "Sorry, I…" She shakes her head. "There was a flyer in the art building about a summer internship at a new gallery, and I…" She takes a step back. "I should go."

"No. Don't." I don't even realize I've reached for her until my hand touches her arm. The moment that electric zip of contact zings through me, I recoil. "You don't have to go." But even as I say it, I'm backing up, trying to put distance between us.

The click of heels echoes through the cavernous space.

"Hi, Krystal," Maggie says softly, a sad smile on her face.

I clear my throat. "Maggie's here about the internship I advertised on campus."

Krystal's face brightens and she claps her hands together. "Perfect!" she says at the same time Maggie says, "I didn't realize… What?"

Krystal looks between us. "Maggie's good at this stuff—right, Will? And between moving into the new house and planning the second wedding, you need someone you don't have to babysit."

"Krystal," Maggie says, "I don't think…"

Krystal raises a brow, waiting for Maggie to finish. When she doesn't, Krystal turns to me. "I don't see any problem with it, do you?"

"Maggie would do a good job," I acknowledge.

"It's settled, then." She smiles, but I can see the strain around her once soft eyes.

"I'll think about it," Maggie says, edging toward the exit. "I'll let you know. Thank you."

When the door closes behind her, Krystal's smile falters.

"Is this supposed to be some sort of test?" I ask.

She wraps her arms around herself. "Why would you say that?"

I stare at her. The tension between us isn't something we're used to, and neither of us knows how to deal with it, how to fit it into the previously comfortable territory of our relationship.

"Anyway, I'm not worried about her. That guy she was with at the wedding is some sort of rock star. Rumor has it he's cozying up to Lucy."

I set my jaw. "Don't. Call. Her. That."

She takes a step toward me and runs her eyes over my body. "My sister isn't a fifteen-year-old who needs the big, bad college boy anymore, Will. This isn't high school, and you two aren't going to live happily ever after, so stop trying to relive the past."

"Who are you?" The Krystal I fell in love with was never this cold, never this hard, not even when it came to Maggie—*especially* when it came to Maggie.

She's unbuttoning my pants with one hand and cupping me in the other.

I step back, evading her touch and escaping her ugliness. Only then do I see the tears glistening in her eyes.

"If you can't handle her taking some stupid part-time summer internship in this gallery," she says softly, hands hanging limply at her sides, "if that's too much of a fucking temptation for you, then we shouldn't be getting married."

She walks away and I'm left with the uncomfortable truth of her words.

"My sister isn't a fifteen-year-old who needs the big, bad college boy anymore."

I never realized how much I needed Maggie to need me. Until she didn't.

Maggie

I'M TORN from a fitful sleep and bolt upright at the sounds of a baby's cries.

I stumble out of bed, fighting free of my tangled sheets, tripping over my own feet. I'm halfway down the hallway before I realize my mistake, but the cries from my dream seem so real they echo in my ears.

Silent, tearless sobs rattle my chest and bring me to my knees.

I crawl toward my bedside table, to the anxiety medication I keep in my purse. Better to stay ahead of it, better to take the meds at the first signs of panic than to let the anxiety grab ahold of me with its sticky, suffocating hands.

I snatch the purse and dump the contents. A white slip of paper flutters out and down to the bed.

I frown at it. Who's leaving me notes?

But when I read it with sleep-gritty eyes, the words leave me cold, and an old, familiar sickness eats at my stomach.

Hands shaking, I look around my room as if a ghost might step out from a darkened corner.

The church hands these bookmarks out like candy, and it could have easily gotten pushed into my purse. And yet, as innocuous as it is, the words give me pause.

I don't know how long I stare at it. The cries from my dreams have faded in my ears, and my eyes have adjusted to the light pouring in the window. My stomach churns as I grab a book of matches.

I ignore my ringing phone as I drop the note in my bathroom sink.

The answering machine clicks on, then my mother's voice

says, "Maggie." She sighs audibly. "Krystal said you showed up at the gallery yesterday. I'm sorry we didn't tell you, sweetie. We just weren't sure how. I hope you understand that she never wanted to hurt you."

I squeeze my eyes shut in frustration, wishing for blackness and oblivion. I want to forget. Will. Krystal. The last year. The sound of my father's voice in my head, as if he rose from the dead to leave that reminder in my purse. I want to forget the words typed so neatly on the church bookmark. The words that make me want to crawl out of my own skin.

I light a match and throw it into the sink, watch the words that have been ground into my brain since birth flame and turn them to ash.

Confess your sins and be forgiven.

"I'll have a twenty-ounce Guinness," I tell the scruffy middle-aged man behind the bar. My day started off like shit and didn't get much better. I made myself go to campus to re-enroll and discovered I lost my scholarship by dropping out last year. But, hey, my consolation prize is that they have an art studio available. That almost makes up for the thirty grand a year I'll be paying in tuition to finish my degree.

Brady turns his best glare on me and props his hands on his hips. "You still hell bent on making me lose my liquor license, girl?"

I offer him my ID from between two fingers. "I am legal now, old man. You can't kick me out anymore."

Brady examines the card with a furrowed brow. I handed him enough fake ones over the years, I can hardly be insulted by his skepticism. Before coming back home a month ago, I'd never legally had a drink in New Hope—not that I hadn't had my share of alcohol, mind you, just not legally.

Brady grunts and hands back my ID. "I guess I woulda known

if I'd done the math." He shakes his head and draws me a beer.

I take a slow sip and scan the bar. My sisters were busy tonight—Lizzy with a date and Hanna with some sort of summer research gig for school—but I couldn't face my empty little rental tonight, couldn't handle the bare walls or the silence. After feeding Lucy, I decided to check out what it was like to be a patron at Brady's without having to dodge the proprietor.

Sadly, it's a little disappointing. It's a Thursday night, and apparently Brady's doesn't cater to a large, thirsty Thursday crowd in the summers. The place is nearly abandoned, save a couple guys in baseball caps playing a game of pool and a couple speaking in soft tones at the bar.

I'm bemoaning the silence when the screen at the front bangs shut and someone calls, "Lucy!"

I don't even flinch at that damn nickname anymore. I became numb to it when half my high school started using it—some behind my back, others to my face. In fact, I decided to reclaim it when I adopted my dog and bestowed the name upon her. Me and Lucy against the world.

Nevertheless, I turn around to see what asshole I have the pleasure of meeting tonight.

"I think you've got the wrong bar, sweet thang," Kenny Riles says, running his eyes over me and leaving a trail of slime behind. "The strip club is down the road."

"Fuck off, Kenny," I mutter.

I went to high school with this asshole and when shit hit the fan my freshman year, everyone was cruel, but Kenny and his buddies were the worst. And they never seemed to let it go.

He sidles up to me. Too close. I can smell his aftershave, a smell that might be pleasant if it weren't for its host. "When you were fifteen, I didn't get it. I didn't understand why a man would risk it all just to fuck you. But now..." His lips curl into a meaningful smirk as he trails off.

I feel sick.

The guys at the back table call to him, and he gives me a final once-over and winks before walking away.

My hands shake as I reach for my beer. I want to leave. I want to get as far away from here as possible, but I won't let him have that power over me. Instead, I settle into a stool at the bar and order something stronger.

chapter six

Asher

*KNOW ANY hot men who can meet me down at Brady's and take my
mind off a shitty day?*

She summoned me with a simple text message. I programmed
my number into her phone last week during our date—or, rather,
our not-a-date—and I'd been beginning to wonder whether she'd
ever use it.

The woman has driven me to distraction. Her laugh, her mind,
that shield of indifference she hides behind. I keep thinking of the
wicked look in her eyes as she stripped in front of me. My lust, the
hungry desire to take her, hasn't faded. If anything, it's grown more
intense.

Then there was the look on her face when that asshole called
her *loose*. The flash of hurt, a wounded girl resurfacing for a split
second before she pushed her away again. Physical attraction is
something I can ignore. But this need to protect her from the
pickup-driving assholes of the world? This need to uncover the
woman hiding behind those walls? I'm consumed by it.

I walk into the bar and instantly spot her. That fiery red hair.

Those wide green eyes. That smile that eats up her face.

Tonight she's wearing a little black number and knee-high heeled boots she had to have chosen for the express purpose of making me lose my mind.

There's an exposed strip of freckled skin between where the boots end and the skirt begins—two inches of soft flesh that make me want to drag her to the nearest closet and press her against the wall, slide into her hot, fast and hungry, her skirt bunched at her waist, her mouth hot against my neck.

Those two inches of skin are enough to make me forget that she's still hung up on some other guy.

Her lips tilt into a grin as she crosses to me, a little unsteady on her feet. "You came."

"You're drunk." The words come out with an unintended sigh.

She hooks her fingers into my belt loops and tugs me against her. "Not quite drunk. Not quite sober. Wanna take me home and take advantage of me?"

"Not if you're drunk," I say against her mouth. She smells so damn good, and I want to taste her, to touch her. I want to kiss my way down her body and find her sweet spots.

The tables in the front of the bar are empty and some guys sit at a booth at the back. "Who are you here with?" I ask.

"You now," she whispers.

"You're here drinking alone? You didn't bring a girlfriend to keep you company? To watch your back?"

She shakes her head and loops her arms around my neck. "I don't have girlfriends. Girls don't like me."

I'm sure this isn't something she'd share sober, so I let it drop. "How was your day?"

She leans her head against my chest. "Do you know what it feels like to have someone take away something you desperately wanted?"

Something jagged pushes down my throat at those words, but I don't reply. This isn't about me.

The jukebox thumps with a rock song and she rocks her hips

against me to the beat, trailing a finger down the side of my face. "It's like she stole it from me, but I'm not allowed to think that because I'm the one who left him."

I'm not sure what she's talking about but I'm not about to interrupt. Apparently, Drunk Maggie is less averse to sharing.

"It was supposed to be our gallery," she whispers. "It was our dream but she took my spot. She stole my happily-ever-after."

"Your sister," I say, but she doesn't seem to hear me. She's rubbing against me like a cat, lost in her own pity party and the rhythm of the music.

"Girls like me don't get happily ever after." Her lips curl into a wicked smile that looks maniacal under such sad eyes. "Instead, the prince marries the good girl, and girls like me get to fuck him behind his wife's back. Lucky us."

"Jesus." I pull her into my arms and she burrows her head against my chest.

We dance, rolling our hips to the music, her body pressing closer and closer to mine. She's slipped a hand up my shirt. It's pressed between our bodies and her fingers are splayed against the hot skin of my abdomen. I like her here. Against me, curled into me like she might let me protect her.

She looks up at me with those big green eyes and seems to remember herself. She stutters back a step, pulling her hand from my shirt. "I need another drink," she says softly.

I grab her hand before she can go too far. "Don't. Please?" I draw her back to me and she tilts her chin up to look into my eyes.

"Why are you here, Asher?"

"You sent me a text inviting me, remember?"

She cocks her head. "But you won't have sex with me."

"Not tonight."

She crooks her finger and I lean down until her lips brush my ear. "But I want you. You won't regret it."

I straighten and look past her shoulder. "I will if you're thinking about *him* the whole time."

She spins around and spots Will and her sister. She backs into me, consciously or not, I'm not sure, but I wrap my arms around her, just under her breasts, and she settles her hands over mine.

"Maggie!" her sister calls, looking me up and down. "We were just talking about you." Krystal slides her hand into Will's and Maggie's hands squeeze mine.

Will's jaw ticks with tension, and when he looks me over, there's no hiding that he's sizing me up. But if I'm the competition, why is he marrying Krystal?

"Maggie's going to take an internship at our art gallery," Krystal is telling me.

"I haven't accepted yet," Maggie says stonily. Gone is her softness from earlier. She's put up her walls, sobered by the sight of this man.

"Consider it, Maggie," Will says. "Krystal's right. You're a perfect fit. You should be a part of it."

"Asher and I were just leaving." She turns toward the door, pulling me behind her.

I nod my goodbye and follow without question.

The door clatters behind us as we cross the gravel lot to her Mustang.

"Are you going to tell me what's between you and him?" I ask when we're alone.

"Not yet," she says softly, her voice and eyes more sober than they've been all night.

"I'm going to keep asking."

"I know." We lean side by side against her Mustang, and her answer is enough—for now. We let the sticky Indiana humidity lick at us, and she slides her hand into mine as we stare up at the country stars.

"When I was a little girl," she says softly, "my sisters and I would sneak out in the middle of the night and walk down to the river. We weren't allowed to be down by the water without an adult, but we didn't care. We'd lie on a blanket, just counting stars until we fell asleep."

I could imagine her there now, sitting on the riverbank after dark and watching the moonlight play off the water.

Sorrow creeps into those normally sharp eyes. She's kneading the corner of her lip between her teeth, and I want to dig deeper, but I know she'd tense her shoulders, put up that wall that says *Do Not Get Personal!* I don't want her to shut me out tonight, so I turn to her and put my hands against the car, pinning her in.

Her eyes change in an instant. The sorrow fades, swallowed up into that part of her that holds the rest of her secrets. Just as quickly, awareness flashes in its place. Her eyes turn hot.

I want her. Want to hold her. Want to feel her. Want to get inside and see what she is so desperate to protect. And I know the last is what she'll resist the most, but I'll start here.

I drop my lips to hers, and she lets me taste her.

I start with small kisses at the corners of her mouth until she relaxes beneath me, and her arms settle around my neck.

She tastes like beer. Beer and heat and that wildly addictive, odorless, tasteless drug that is Maggie.

Her tongue strokes mine. She sucks it into her mouth until my cock strains painfully against my fly.

I pull back and let my lips hover over hers.

"You could take me home," she whispers. "And leave me all hot and bothered again."

"I could."

"Or you could finish what we started in the pool."

I groan, pressing against her, my hands finding her waist, her hips, her ass. Nipping at her neck, sucking. I don't just want her, I need her. I need this. For reasons bigger than months of abstinence.

Maggie arches into me then tilts her head to give me better access to her neck. I sweep my tongue over that sweet juncture of her neck and shoulder and she shudders in my arms. I want to make her shudder in my bed. Suddenly I'm struck by an image of her bound and blindfolded. Vulnerable. Trusting. Open. *Mine.*

"I need to get you naked," I growl.

"Naked?"

"Or in that scrap of lace you wore when you did your striptease for me."

"I thought you weren't going to have sex with me."

I suck her earlobe into my mouth and tug it with my teeth. "We can get naked without having sex."

"I think you're doing it wrong." She licks her lips, eyes hot. "But you might convince me to try. As long as you don't mind spectators."

I groan into her neck. "Get into your car before I take you up on that."

I open the passenger door, and her keys jingle as she hands them over with a satisfied smile.

It takes about two minutes to get from Brady's to her house, but it feels like an eternity. She doesn't touch me, but tucks her finger in my belt loop like she's afraid I might sneak away. The air between us pulses thick and hot with sexual tension and anticipation.

When I pull into her driveway, I cut the engine and pull her against me. I kiss her, taste her, my fingers tangling in her hair.

Her hands snake up my shirt and she nips at my mouth with her teeth.

When I break the kiss, we're both breathing heavily.

She shoves lightly at my shoulders. "Inside, Exhibitionist Boy."

I grin and climb out of the car. Her hips sway as she leads the way into her house. My hands itch with the need to get her bare, to squeeze her ass as I taste her, to scrape my teeth over the flesh at her hips.

When Maggie opens the door, Lucy races toward her in big, bounding leaps. Then she spots me and immediately turns, tucks her nub of a tail, and runs for cover.

"Batting zero with the kid today." Maggie laughs as she heads to the back door. "Luce!" she calls, opening the screen. "Let's go outside."

The dog skitters past me with a pathetic combination whimper/bark/howl and runs for the door.

When Maggie turns back to me, her eyes are hot as they trail over my body. "Strip."

"Have you ever even *tried* letting someone else take the lead?"

She saunters across the kitchen and plucks at the buttons of my shirt. "What fun would that be?" Halfway down she abandons her task and pushes it off my shoulders, pressing open-mouthed kisses to my abdomen.

I reach for her dress, and she pushes my hands away and presses them against the counter.

"Oh no you don't," she warns. "Keep those hands right there."

I know she needs this—to take, to be in control—so I obey.

Her fingers finish their work on my shirt as her mouth explores—sucking, nibbling, making me lose my fucking mind.

"Mag—"

"Hush." Her hands work the button of my jeans.

I want to protest. Want to touch her, to watch the pleasure on her face as I taste her, but suddenly I'm against the counter, my shirt hanging from my wrists, my jeans around my thighs as Maggie drops to her knees. Her skirt hikes up her hips and exposes the tops of her soft thighs.

She cups me through my boxer briefs.

"Jesus," I gasp. I reach for her but she backs away.

"My house, my rules."

I'm lost as she frees my dick from my boxers. I want to be tender with this woman the world has battered, but I'm helpless as she strokes me with those soft hands. My hands itch to dive into her hair. To touch her breasts. To dip into her and make her scream. But I clasp the edge of the counter.

"I want to put you in my mouth." She's breathing hard, chest rising and falling, my cock a breath from her lips, wrapped up in her hand. "Are you safe?"

"Safe?" I swallow hard as she strokes me again, try to blink away the haze and translate words into meanings.

"I can get a condom for this part."

I tighten my grip on the counter. Because I don't deserve the woman on her knees, offering to suck latex to get me off. "Safe," I manage. "I haven't been with anyone without protection for over-"

I'm cut off by my own moan as she takes me into her mouth, gently laving the underside of my cock with her tongue. Her mouth closes around me, and I'm swallowed up by the wet, by the heat.

I won't close my eyes. I wouldn't miss the sight of her swollen lips around my cock. She pulls me deep and moans softly as her mouth contracts around my shaft. She draws back and returns, draws back. I fight the instinct to rock my hips but she curls her fingers into my thighs as she opens for me, her lips nearly to the base of my shaft.

"Maggie." I can't let it end like this. God, not tonight. Not yet. "Maggie."

I draw her up to me and kiss her.

Her lips are red and swollen from taking me. I want to remember her like this, want to stop for a minute and memorize the lust in her eyes and the flush of her cheeks. I'm ravenous for her and need to back off a little, to slow down, but she pulls me closer and strokes me between our bodies, and I'm drowning in need.

"Let me touch you," I whisper.

"Fuck me."

"No." I slide my hand between her thighs where I can feel her slick and swollen even through the thin lace of her panties. I squat before her, kissing my way down her thin cotton dress as I lower myself and her panties in a single motion. I pull them off over her boots and slide them from one foot at a time.

She tugs at my hair, drawing me up. "*Please*, Asher."

I have to kiss her. I have to taste those lips again. I press her against the refrigerator, pictures and take-out menus flying. We're just limbs and heat and desire. She clings to me as I rock my hand between her thighs. She draws one leg up and wraps it around my waist as I slide a finger inside her, watching her face, reveling in her slick heat.

"You're so damn hot, so damn sweet."

Her hands tug lightly at my hair, and she makes little sounds at the back of her throat. I don't need to hear her cry of "*Please*" to know she wants more, but I resist the need to fuck, to claim, to bury myself in her.

She's a dream to watch. Masses of red hair, flashes of green eyes as she rolls her hips and loses herself in the pleasure I bring with my hand. I want her to break, to let go, but she's clinging to control.

I lower my mouth to her ear. "I don't fuck women who belong to someone else."

"I don't belong to anyone."

When I find her clit with my thumb, swollen and needy, she arches into me hard and her pussy squeezes me so damn beautifully as she pulses tight in orgasm.

Twenty thuds of my heart later, I come to my senses. Here's this woman in my arms I was so determined to treat gently. Her skirt's bunched around her waist, and bite marks swell at her neck.

Maybe it's seeing that red head pressed against my chest. Maybe it's the feel of her in my arms. Or maybe I hadn't wanted to remember before now.

But as I stand here, dizzy with arousal, I remember where I saw her before.

New Hope. The river. Jesus. How had I not put it together when I first looked into those big green eyes? I couldn't place them, and I've seen so many faces in my life, they all start to blend together.

Now the words slip out of my mouth before I can stop them. "God, Maggie. I'm so sorry."

Maggie

HE IS being ridiculous. One second I'm coming my brains out, his hot body pressed against my front, the cold refrigerator pressed against my back, the next he's apologizing to me? We were just about to have what I'm sure would have been off-the-charts hot kitchen sex, and then Mr. Nice Guy had to go and ruin my fun by apologizing. He's turning out to be one piss-poor excuse for a bad boy.

He sits at my kitchen table now, eyeing me. "Has anyone ever told you that you're moody?"

He's probably referring to the fact that I've been stomping around the house since that stupid S-word came out of his mouth and tarnished my after glow.

I grab two beers from the fridge and shove one in his hand. "You're *sorry*? How can you be sorry?"

He's pulled his pants back on, slid his arms back into his shirt—though it is still unbuttoned. We should be closing the deal. Maybe for a second time by now. In the bedroom, on the couch, in the shower. But instead I'm trying to figure out what the hell he thinks he needs to apologize for.

He narrows his eyes at me. "Because I had you up against the fridge with your dress hiked up around your waist. Because I didn't even take my goddamned shoes off, because whether you believe it or not, you deserve more than that."

I groan, running a hand through my hair and flopping into a kitchen chair. What am I thinking, getting involved with this man? He is too touchy-feely for me. "Asher, wake up and smell the third-wave feminism. Women have fantasies too. I happen to find a little frantic, half-clothed kitchen sex hot."

That makes him smile. "Me too." Then he ruins it by sighing and getting all serious again. "Listen. We need to talk."

I lean back in my chair. I'm not trying to get away from him exactly, but I'm never anxious to be closer to a man uttering those words. "You're not going to ruin this by declaring your eternal love for me, are you?" I take a pull from my beer, noticing he hasn't touched his. "Because, damn it, Asher, I thought better of you."

He averts his gaze, making me feel a little panicky until he says, "I do know you from somewhere."

"Wait. What?"

"I know you from somewhere."

"That wasn't just a line after all?" My laughter dies on my lips when I see the gravity in his eyes.

"We met twelve months ago."

I feel myself pale, the blood draining from my face and gathering low in my belly where it roils. I push away from the table.

Granny was right. My past really is returning. Because twelve months ago, my world changed.

chapter seven

Asher

"I WAS going to name her Grace."

When I first saw the girl sitting by the river twelve months ago, there was so much blood on her hands, I worried she had slit her wrists.

"Miss?" The redhead sat on the bank of the river, knees drawn to her chin. She ignored me and stared at her bloodstained hands like a tragic Shakespearean tableau.

"Are you okay?" I inched closer and saw a smudge of blood under her eye, streaked where the tears had run through it. I couldn't get a good look at her wrists, but assumed she had cut herself there, come to my little edge of river to let the life bleed out of her. "Where are you hurt?"

She blinked at me, seeming to register my presence for the first time. God. She was probably doped up on all sorts of drugs.

She shook her head frantically. "I'm not hurt. I'm fine. It's just a little blood. This happens to some women."

But then she squeezed her eyes shut, clung to her legs, and rocked herself back and forth.

"What's your name?" I kept my voice low, gentle, as I inched closer.

"I was going to name her Grace," she whispered, eyes focused on the river as if it could save her.

"Who?"

She bit her lip, shook her head. "I didn't want this. Not this."

She reached a hand down, cupped herself between her legs as if she were trying to hold something there.

I understood then. I lowered myself on the ground next to her, felt the dampness of the riverbank seep into my pants. "You're having a miscarriage?"

She shook her head again. "I was going to make it work. It wasn't ideal, maybe not right, but I was going to make it work. I didn't want this. This can't be happening."

"You need to go to the hospital."

Her eyes grew wide, and I was struck by how her irises were a solid jade green. "Would you go with me? I don't think I can be alone when they tell me I'm losing my baby. I"—she gasped for air, choked on a sob—"I'm so afraid."

And then I surprised us both by pulling her into my arms and holding her while she cried.

I never forgot the way all concern seemed to leech out of her as we approached the hospital. I never forgot the way her voice changed, became monotone, as if, so young, she'd already lost all faith in life. I hadn't been able to forget her haunted expression as I parked in the hospital's circle drive and she'd watched the sliding doors that lead to the ER. *Do you believe God punishes us for our sins?*

I thought about her after that day. I wondered what had happened after the nurses took her back. I waited two hours, smudges of a strange woman's blood on my shirt.

How could the Maggie who keeps a steel cage around her heart be the same woman who cupped herself between her legs to keep her baby inside?

Maggie

THERE'S SO much pity in Asher's eyes, I can't stand it.

"I didn't realize," he says. "I couldn't figure out how I knew you. You look so different now. Healthier than you did then. Your hair's different, maybe? I only knew what you looked like when you were crying. I found you by the river. Took you to the hospital."

Asher Logan was the stranger who took me in that day? Is the world really that small? Is fate really so cruel?

I was such a complete wreck that day at the river. I remember a man. Remember him trying to get me to go to the hospital.

I stare at my hands, almost surprised to see them clean. No blood, no horrible nightmare making me face my sins.

How can this all be coming back? But then, I never escaped it, did I?

"You held me."

"Yeah," he whispers, "I did."

I was praying by the river that day. Confused. Guilty. Mixed up as hell. I was pregnant, and I was getting married in two days, and I had no idea when my life had gotten so completely out of control.

Then, when I started bleeding, it was like some sick answer to my prayer. *Dear God, please make this right.* And then blood.

I don't hear Asher move, but when I look up, when I take my eyes off my unstained hands, he is standing next to me, extending a hand.

I could take it. No doubt, he'd hold me again. No doubt, it would feel damn good. He'd stroke my hair, murmur in my ear. He'd listen to me blubber like an idiot woman who can't deal with a traumatic situation—or even the memory of one—without the strong arms of a man to hold her together.

I'm tempted. I'm truly tempted, and I hate myself for that. Even twelve months later. Even after therapy and endless affirmations of self-forgiveness, I'm tempted. I want to tell someone. I want to start at the beginning. I want to start with my father. With being fifteen and seeing the word *CONFESS* appear like a phantom in the steam of the bathroom mirror. I want to spill my ugly soul out onto the cold, scarred linoleum of the kitchen floor.

At least then I wouldn't need to worry about any unwanted declarations of love—because then he would know just how damaged I am.

Asher reaches for me, but I ignore his hand. I wrap my arms across my chest because I won't let myself need his.

"I'm sorry you had to see me that way," I say. I need to get away from him. Away from the reminder. Coming back to New Hope is hard enough with all these pieces of my past returning, threatening to stir up questions I can't answer. This month—the anniversary of Asher pulling me from the riverbank and taking me to the hospital, the anniversary of the cancellation of my sham of a wedding, the anniversary of making the hardest decision I've ever made in my life—this month is the hardest yet. And my life has been no day at the fair.

"I hope you'll respect my privacy and keep that day between the two of us."

To Asher's credit, he doesn't come to me but neither does he retreat. He holds his ground, stands solid. "Of course."

I nod, and I'm so confident I can trust him that I want to weep. "Listen, it's been fun, but I think you should go. Do you need a ride back to your car?"

"No. I can walk." He doesn't move for a long moment, and I wonder if he'll argue. I wonder if he's having fantasies of holding the pieces of me together while I sleep. Will's words haunt me.

"Maggie, if you're broken, I'll fix you."

I won't be the woman who needs that from a man. I won't.

Asher is staring at me—waiting for something—but I can't meet his eyes.

I wait until I hear the clang of the front door.

I run the water hot at the kitchen sink. While squirting liquid soap on my hands, I think of the bookmark I found in my purse. *Confess your sins and be forgiven.*

My sins? I don't even know where to start.

I raise the mallet and hesitate a single heartbeat before bringing it down on the glossy purple serving tray. The sound of cracking ceramic lifts that ever-present weight from my shoulders, and I slam the hammer down a second time, and a third, until there's no platter, only purple shards that send my right brain spinning.

Next I have an aquamarine vase I found at a thrift shop. I can't wait to shatter it. And the mugs from the Salvation Army, and the ceramic tiles from my mom's bathroom renovation.

This is my new obsession. Mosaics. I came to Sinclair on a scholarship for painting, and I know how my professors are going to react to my new medium when I return in the fall. Ethan Bauer will call it a waste of my talent. Mosaics aren't *real* Art, he'll say, not the kind with the capital *A*. They're backyard tinkering. They're the layman's work. They're—Ethan's biggest insult to an artist—a *craft*.

But I think that's why I've fallen in love with them. I like finding beauty in these discarded treasures. I like making something where there was nothing before.

Being back on campus feels odd. A little like returning to a former life after being reincarnated. Being in this studio gives me a sense of *déjà vu*.

I take another sip of cranberry juice and smile at the rising sun peaking in the window of my art studio. Getting studio space means getting a key to the fine arts building, and after Asher left last night, I grabbed my keys and headed to campus. The only stop I made was for a bottle of cranberry juice and a bottle of vodka.

And if I'm a little drunk at seven in the morning, who am I hurting?

I'm unsteady on my feet—from the liquor and the exhaustion—and I have to balance myself with a hand against the table.

Glass pops, snapping under my palm. I see blood before I even register the pain. A little blood smeared across the bubbled glass, then a lot of blood. Then the pain—dull and throbbing as red liquid puddles on the floor.

I put my hand to my mouth. My fingers tighten around the wound. I'm okay. Maybe I need a few stitches, but I'll be all right.

But then I look at my hands. Really look. And the sight of them covered in blood sends me back to the river. Back to the day I thought I was losing my baby. Suddenly, breathing is too difficult. The air is too thick and the path to my lungs too narrow.

Then I'm crying. My tears are hitting the floor, mixing with the bright red blood.

I have to get to the bathroom. Wash this up. But I'm stuck in the past. My feet and my brain, frozen in time.

I don't know how long I stand there before Will shows up at my door.

"Maggie!" He rushes in and grabs my hands. And now the blood's on his hands too and that's not right. He's innocent in this. He doesn't deserve to be stained by my mistakes.

He's murmuring something and I realize he's wrapping up my hand in some sort of cotton. Where did he…

His shirt. He's torn off his shirt and is wrapping the gash in my hand in the soft cotton. Damn, that's sweet. And now he's standing in front of me in nothing but his jeans. I'm bleeding through his makeshift bandage, but I can't take my eyes off his chest.

"You're so gorgeous." Did I say that out loud? I didn't mean to. But he is. Will pushes his body hard—long runs and strict appointments with the weights. I always laughed at how regimented he was with his fitness, but now I'm thinking the world would be a better place if more men were so dedicated. There would be more happiness. Less war. Fewer children would go hungry.

I hear myself giggling and I'm looking into Will's face. He's taken my face into his hands and is saying…something.

Were his lips always so perfect?

"Maggie." He gives me a soft shake.

They were always that perfect. I remember. I remember wishing I were a different kind of girl so I could kiss those lips without feeling like I was tarnishing something so beautiful. "I'm sorry. What?"

"I'm taking you to the hospital."

I smile. "You're going to take care of me? Don't you just want me to bleed out? Wouldn't that be…easier?" Then I laugh because I sound so damn dramatic.

He frowns, says something about shock. Then he leans so close to my face I think he's going to kiss me. I tilt my lips up and wait. I miss the feel of his mouth on mine.

He draws in a deep breath through his nose. "You're drunk."

I lift a shoulder. "I'm legal now."

"Jesus," he mutters. He's saying something else, looking around my studio for something, but I can't take my eyes off his gorgeous bare skin, the expanse of his back. Did I kiss him there when I had the chance? Why can't I remember?

He grabs my purse and wraps his arm around my waist. The next thing I know, we're on the elevator, and I'm leaning into him. He's so warm.

"Yeah, and you're drunk," he says.

I frown. Did I say something?

Then we're walking again and he's settling me into the car, and I think I might have fallen asleep a little because now he's opening my door and pulling me to my feet. He has a shirt on again. When did that happen? Why did it happen?

"Why are you being so nice to me?" I ask.

"I'm not being nice. You're just too drunk to notice I'm pissed at you."

His arm is wrapped around my waist, and we're moving through sliding doors. He says something to the man sitting behind the counter, while I blink, my eyes objecting to the fluorescent lights.

"You're mad at me?"

He settles me into a chair and inspects my hand. The cotton is soaked through with bright red blood that doesn't look real at all. It looks like something out of a B-grade film.

"Do you often get trashed and play with sharp pieces of glass?"

Oh. I hear it now. He is pissed. I smile. I like when Will gets pissed. He's being all sweet and protective, and it makes me feel like I'm worth something more than the trash we all know I am. "I can't create art if I'm not relaxed," I object.

"It's stupid and it's dangerous." He settles into the seat next to me, and I lean my head on his shoulder. He's frowning at me, so I smile up at him. I've ruined his night. Then I laugh because it's not night anymore, and Will was probably starting his day. He probably had work to do. Department meetings. Curriculum development. I've ruined his day.

"You haven't ruined anything." His eyes meet mine and even twelve shades of tipsy, I can see the pain there, the confusion. His eyes stay locked on mine for so long, this should probably feel awkward. But this is Will and I've loved him forever. I could look at him forever. I could let him look at me forever. If I didn't believe he deserved better.

"That's you," he says.

I blink and realize they're calling my name.

Nodding, I only teeter a little as I push myself to standing.

I'm two steps toward the door before I realize he hasn't moved. I stop and turn to him. "Come with me?" I bite my lip, watching the battle play out across his face. I don't want to explain. The loneliness. This fear that it might swallow me whole and I'll just disappear. The bigger fear that everything might be easier if it did. "Please?"

He stands and wraps his arm around me, and as he leads me back to the examination room, I tell myself I'm only leaning into him because I'm drunk. I tell myself it's okay because I'm hurt. But the pleasure I feel at having his arm wrapped around me? The way his heat and low murmurs chase away the loneliness so much better than the vodka did?

I don't have an excuse for that.

William

SHE'S DRUNK. She's drunk and she's hurt and she's in shock.

But that doesn't change the fact that I love the feel of her in my arms. I love having her *need* me like she does right now.

The doctor stitched up her wound, a gash that extended from the palm of her hand down into her wrist and required twelve stitches.

She's stitched and bandaged and now they want her to sober up before they'll release her.

"How'd you find me?" she asks. The alcohol is leaving her system. I can tell by the way she's pulling away, remembering herself.

"You were making enough noise to wake the dead. I just heard all this glass breaking, and then I heard you crying."

She blinks. "I wasn't crying."

I tuck her hair behind her ear. She still has streaks of blood on her cheeks. The doctor wanted to do a psych eval, but I talked her out of it, convinced her Maggie wasn't a threat to herself, but I'm not even sure I believe that. When I saw all that blood…

Her eyes are on my mouth, and her lips are parted just so. "You saved me."

"You would have sobered up enough to get yourself to the hospital eventually," I offer, more for myself than her, because this thing that has me holding her so tightly is the soul-scorching fear that she wouldn't have, that by the time she came to her senses she would have lost too much blood, and then it would have been too late.

She leans her head back, taking her eyes from me to focus on the ceiling—thank God. "You're always there when I need someone. You're always ready to save me."

"Not always," I say softly, and her eyes connect with mine so quickly, I'm sorry I said anything at all.

"That wasn't your fault."

I shrug. "I wasn't there." My gut twists at the memory. How many times can one man fail Maggie Thompson?

She gives me a sloppy grin. "Look, Will. I broke and you fixed me."

"Maggie." I remember that promise. It's a promise I'd keep today if she'd take me up on it. There's nothing I want more than to see her whole after years of walking around broken.

"Why didn't you hate me? After? Everyone else hated me, but you…"

I focus on her bandaged hand as the memory takes me back to fifteen-year-old Maggie showing up unannounced in my dorm room in Notre Dame, her eyes sad, though she promised she was fine; her hands greedy, though I wouldn't let her touch me. "Just don't make me go back there. I can't do it anymore. Let me stay. Please." But I'd taken her to the bus station and sent her home. A month later, the town was overcome by the scandal. They blamed her, but I knew better because if she'd wanted any of it, she wouldn't have been in my dorm room begging me not to send her home.

I rest my hand over her bandaged palm. "I could never hate you, Maggie. Not when you were the pipsqueak neighbor girl and not when you were breaking my heart by leaving me."

She lifts her good hand to my face, her eyes on mine. "I was an idiot." Then she leans toward me and our lips brush.

Hot, electric arousal grips me. "Would you ask me to leave her?" I whisper against her lips. "Would you tell me if you still needed me?"

She flinches as if I've struck her. "I can't do that to her."

chapter eight

Maggie

LAST NIGHT, I dreamt of my father. His hurt, disappointed eyes stared back at me from behind my bathroom mirror, making me feel dirty in my own skin. Because of my own skin.

Then he was pushing me into church, but I wasn't the fifteen-year-old girl he'd shamed into confession. I was an adult. Blood stained my hands as I folded them in prayer and he whispered in my ear, *"Confess your sins and be forgiven."*

I woke to the sounds of a baby crying and jumped out of bed. I tripped over my feet as I scrambled toward the bassinet I don't own to comfort a baby I don't have.

Then I took a hot shower and scrubbed my skin until it was red and angry, and I dressed for church with my family. Operation New Me puts me in a church pew next to my mother at least once a month. Mom would prefer this happen weekly, but I've read that when you're committed to a change, you should set realistic goals.

I could have done without the sermon—a self-important speech about the decline in American family values as illustrated by teenage promiscuity, extra-marital affairs, abortion, and babies born out of wedlock. The priest nailed me with his condemning gaze again and again as he spoke. I don't have proof, but I'm pretty sure he planned this one for my return.

Asshole.

I sat through the whole sermon with Will's voice in my head. *"Would you ask me to leave her? Would you tell me if you still needed me?"*

I tried to tune out the priest by figuring out what Will had meant by that. Does that mean that he wants me or that he wants to protect me? Does he even know there's a difference? But I couldn't come to any conclusions with the priest warning the congregation against Jezebels and guilt surging up in my throat.

Mom always has Sunday brunch at her house after church, but the food isn't much to look forward to. As I study the buffet, my stomach growls in protest. Today's fare consists of fresh veggies and yogurt dip, fresh fruit, low-carb deli "sandwiches" wrapped in lettuce, and mimosas made with half-calorie orange juice. Mom is clearly on the warpath again, attempting to prove her worth as a human being by the size of her daughters' jeans.

Hanna is convinced this obsession is her fault and has apologized countless times for her "weight problem," resulting in bland family meals. Hanna's heavier than the rest of us, but she's gorgeous and wears it so well she's even been approached to be a plus-size model. Of course, that only embarrassed her, so she never pursued it.

"Hey," Hanna says with a slight bob of her head toward the door. "Don't look now, but I think Mrs. Bauer just came in."

"Claudia? Ethan's wife?" The words are out of my mouth before I realize the "Ethan's wife" part would have been better left unsaid.

"I personally think she's dense," Lizzy says. "What woman in her right mind would stay married to Professor Infidelity? You can't tell me she doesn't know."

I stiffen. "Know about what?"

"Oh, come on!" Lizzy turns her calculating gaze on me. "Everybody knows he sleeps with half his models. Be honest, haven't you fantasized a little about getting yourself a piece of delectable art professor ass?"

"Me?" I clutch my chest. "What the hell does that mean?"

"Come on, Maggie, every girl at Sinclair with a pulse and an inclination toward men is hot for Dr. Bauer. I saw the way you looked at him. Hell, it's the only time I've seen you go *all gushy* over a guy."

"I did not go all gushy. There's not a gushy bone in my body."

"There was with Dr. Bauer!" Lizzy sings.

"I'm an artist. I admire his work!" I'm quickly edging into *doth protest too much* territory, so I back down. "Anyway, I've grown up since then." And I have. Too bad I had to do it the hard way.

I fill my plate and take a seat between Hanna and Lizzy.

My youngest sister settles into a seat across from me, her plate heaping with fruit and low-carb sandwiches.

My mom clears her throat. "Portion control, Abby," she says softly.

"She's growing," I protest.

"I'm just trying to save her the heartache of being overweight."

Hanna winces beside me.

I push back from the table.

"Where are you going now, Maggie?"

"I need a cigarette." I say, though I find smoking repulsive.

I step onto the back deck and close my eyes. The sound of the river rushing beyond the backyard calms me as I sink onto the steps.

"Are you okay, Maggie?"

Claudia Bauer closes the door behind her as she joins me on the deck. Just the sight of her makes guilt settle over me. My mom seems to have taken Claudia under her wing, and since I've been home it seems like she's at the house as often as I am.

The woman has this classic, old-money kind of beauty. High cheekbones, delicately arched eyebrows, and a perfectly straight nose. Claudia keeps her hair bleached a platinum blond and cut just past her chin. Two-carat diamond stones sparkle at her ears.

Does Claudia know that her husband purchased those earrings for his mistress?

"I'm okay," I lie. I'm not okay. I don't want to be here, and I don't want to pretend to be the good daughter. I don't want to see my little sister grow up with the same unrealistic expectations I did, and I don't want to continue to dodge my past.

"No, you're not." Claudia lowers herself next to me. As an awkward teen, I always wished for the grace of women like Claudia. As a cocky college student, I finally accepted it wasn't in me.

Claudia sighs. "I always knew when you weren't okay, darling. You can fool everyone else, but I've got you figured out."

I turn to her. "Do you, now?" Though it's a possibility. Like her art professor husband Ethan, Claudia is an artist, and my mom sent me to her studio for lessons as a teen. She always looked out for me. Then, when I started at Sinclair and moved into a little rental house with Lizzy and Hanna, Claudia looked out for all of us.

I choose one hell of a way to return the favor.

My gut folds on itself under the weight of my self-loathing.

"Yes." Claudia's pink lined lips curve up in a smile. "You were always so tough. It never occurred to anyone that you might have some of those same college-girl insecurities as your sisters. I could always tell when you were upset. You'd storm into the studio worried about Hanna or on a mission to save Lizzy from flunking out when she'd been on another party binge."

"So, you're saying I was *always* upset?" I say, trying for humor.

"I'm saying"—Claudia twirls the cross at her neck—"that you don't fool people as well as you think you do." She smiles sweetly. "Now I'm going to go back inside. After you finish that cigarette of yours, I hope you join us."

"Thanks," I mutter, suddenly wishing I did smoke so I could delay my return.

When I join them, Claudia is chatting with my mother in the corner, and a small shiver runs from my toes all the way up my spine.

At fifteen, I fell from my father's grace. He would tell me I was a harlot sent by the devil to destroy men. He never said this to my sisters, never suspected they were anything but innocent. I was special in this way alone. Of course, I'd given him all the proof he needed.

Over the last year, I've wondered if he knew who I would become, what I would do. Or if I became what I am because his speeches were so damn convincing.

William

MY ALWAYS-BEAUTIFUL fiancée is forever exfoliating and moisturizing and wrinkle-removing. I watch her as she rubs lotion onto her utterly perfect legs.

"I kissed her. I kissed Maggie. At the hospital."

Krystal freezes for one heartbeat. Two. Then she swallows so hard I can hear it before she resumes her task. "Is that all?"

"Krys, it was stupid. I was caught up in the past, so worried about her. I wasn't even thinking." I force myself to stop. There's no explanation that can make this *okay*. "I'm worried about her."

"Thank you for telling me," she says softly.

"Don't do this. Don't pretend it's no big deal. This matters, Krystal. I fucked up and it's not okay."

When she lifts her gaze to mine, her big brown eyes are so sad they make my chest ache. I wish she'd say something, anything. I wish she'd scream at me. At least then I'd know she still cares.

"Let's just leave town." I'm pacing the length of the bedroom. "We can open a gallery somewhere else. We can start a new life somewhere."

"You know we can't do that."

"We'll take Grandma with us. Some of her friends moved to a

retirement community in Naples. We could take her there and find a place of our own." I squeeze her hands between both of mine. "You love the beach."

"What happened to wanting to raise your kids in New Hope?" she asks softly. "What happened to not wanting to uproot Grandma?"

I look at the floor. When Maggie wasn't around, I didn't doubt for a minute whether our love was strong enough. How do I explain that all changed the minute she came back to town? "I want this to work. You are so damn good for me."

Her hand touches my jaw, and the contact is so unexpected, so overdue, my nerves flair to life under her fingertips. "Do you love me, Will?"

"Yes." I want to lower my mouth to hers, to kiss her until we both forget everyone else, but I'm too afraid it wouldn't work.

"Do you still love her?"

The words wrap their fingers around my heart and squeeze painfully. "Don't ask me that."

She gives me a sad smile and pushes herself off the bed. "I'm going to bed," she says softly. "I'll see you in the morning."

"And then what? What happens next for us?"

She freezes, her back to me. "Do you think she was trying to commit suicide?" Krystal hugs herself and rubs her bare arms. The house is warm, but ever since I told her about finding Maggie this morning, she's been shivering.

"You can imagine why she might consider it, can't you? Even her own goddamned sister has taken to calling her *Lucy*. And you and me..." I trail off. Making Krystal feel guilty about Maggie's "accident" isn't productive, and with the tension between my fiancée and me right now, we need our conversations to be productive. Because this limbo is hell.

"When I called her that the other day, I was angry. Scared. It was the only time I've ever called her that." She bites down on her lower lip. "Do you really think the you and me part..."

I close my eyes. "Her accident wasn't your fault. She was

drunk…" The truth is, I have no idea if Maggie's injury was a drunken accident or a botched suicide attempt.

Krystal shakes her head and watches the river run by on the other side of the glass. "She drinks too much." Her voice is heavy with worry.

"You can't save her."

In the mirror, I see her close her eyes. "Says the pot to the kettle," she murmurs softly. "I'm just so worried."

"Me too." I watch her leave the room, but I don't know if we're talking about Maggie or us.

At the other end of the house, I hear Krystal locking up for the night and then the soft thump of her bedroom door as she goes to bed. We don't sleep together. She doesn't want us to have sex until our wedding night. Well, our *next* wedding night. She's become more conservative in the last few years, more concerned about pleasing her mother or her church or her God. Maybe all three, I'm not sure. I just know it's important to her so I don't push the issue.

In fact, since Maggie's been home, it's been a bit of a relief. Krystal's right. I've changed. But so has she, and I can't imagine fucking her right now. And *making love* is out of the question. There's too much tension between us, and we can't snuggle close when we're both wound up so tightly in thorny vines of doubt.

I lie on top of the covers and turn off the light. I stare up at the ceiling in the darkness.

I'm not sure I can go through with this wedding. When that stink bomb went off, it was so surreal, and then everyone started running out of the church and I was just…*relieved.*

Krystal has been a constant in my life since we were kids. We went through school together and went to college together. We both decided to move home after graduating from Notre Dame.

She was always there. Always a friend. And when Maggie canceled the wedding and skipped town, Krystal was there to hold my hand.

Our relationship was so *normal*, and I found comfort in that normalcy. When Maggie didn't take my calls or return my emails,

Krystal became a fixture in my life.

While Maggie always thought I was too good for her, Krystal had every confidence that she was good enough for *any* man.

I force myself to close my eyes, but my mind spins wildly with the implications of the decision I need to make. I love Krystal. I love that she believes in herself. I love that she believes in me. And Maggie? I don't even know if I love her. I crave her. I need her.

I want to stop waiting. I want to start living my life. Only one woman can do that with me. And only one wants to.

But as I wrap my hand around my dick, she's not the one I'm thinking of. Instead, my mind conjures the memory of a feisty redhead in my little apartment by campus. It's a go-to memory for me. I was finishing up my first semester of graduate classes at Sinclair and Maggie was a freshman.

She sat cross-legged on my couch, scanning the music collection on my phone while I pretended not to be mesmerized by her smile.

"How's the love life going?" she asked, suddenly bored with my phone and tossing it next to her on the couch.

From my spot on the floor, I ran my eyes over her face. Those big eyes, the sprinkle of freckles across the bridge of her nose that contrasted so sharply with her wicked smile. "There's not much of a love life to speak of."

She rolled her eyes. "You're a big, bad graduate student now. A TA. An ar*tist*. I see the girls swoon over you. Pick one."

I remember studying her, wondering if she really didn't know. "Maybe I already have."

"So, what's stopping you?" She slid off the couch and sat in front of me on the floor, taking my face in her hands. "You're amazing."

I wanted to lower my mouth to hers and kiss her, but I knew that would scare her off. I'd wanted to kiss her since she showed up in my dorm room at Notre Dame and asked me to. But at Notre Dame she was too young, and there in my New Hope apartment I was too afraid of losing her to make that move. So I said, "Maybe

I doubt my skills."

She laughed. "What skills? Kissing?" When I didn't reply, she frowned. "Fucking?"

"No." My cheeks warmed. Maggie used sex as a shield, and as a result she could talk about it—any part of it—without batting a lash. "Why is it that some girls don't like oral sex?"

Maggie snorted. "Because having a cock shoved down your throat isn't all it's cracked up to be?" She lifted a shoulder, shrugging. "But then I can't really talk for them, I kind of like giving head. It's"—her gaze dropped to my pants then quickly returned to my face—"a power trip."

Oh, hell. The image of her mouth sliding over my cock slammed into me so fast and hard, I had to shift on the floor to ease my discomfort. "I'm not talking about that kind of oral sex."

Her eyes went big and she grinned. "Going down on *her*? That's what you're talking about? What girl doesn't like that?"

I shrug. "Some girls don't."

"Really? Why not?" She frowned. "Are you doing it right?"

I grunted. "Yeah, I'm pretty sure I know what's going on down there."

She lifted a brow. "You sure about that? Maybe you need a second opinion."

"Maggie, what are you doing?" My breath clogged in my chest because suddenly she was shifting on the floor, slipping her panties off from under her skirt. They were white cotton with little rainbows, and as she slid them down her legs, I wanted to touch her so badly my hands nearly burned with all the live-wire nerves. When she pulled them off and tossed them on the couch behind her, I thought I might suffocate from the weight of the desire in my chest.

"Where do you want me? The couch? The floor? Your bed?"

"I'm not just going to use your body like some sort of dummy I can practice on." But even then Maggie was my kryptonite.

When she lifted her face, her expression softened, and I was torn in two by what I saw in her eyes. First, I saw her old need to validate her worth with her body, the reason I refused to touch her when she came to my dorm as a fifteen-year-old. But there was more. I wouldn't have touched her if I hadn't seen it—the lust sparking in her eyes, the way her breathing grew uneven.

The air between us was tense with everything we never said, heavy with the knowledge that this was it for us because we were too different in one way: I loved her. And Maggie? She hated herself with such an intensity that no one she respected could get close.

And now, as my shaft pulses thick against my palm, Maggie fills my brain so completely, there's no room for the self-disgust I should be feeling. In this moment, hanging in the web of the memory, there's no room for guilt. I let myself remember the way she looked as she sat on the edge of the couch and parted her legs, my veins zipping with the forbidden heat of putting my mouth on a woman I'd never even kissed. I let myself remember the first brush of my lips against her inner thigh and the shudder that went through her. Finally, I let myself remember the feel of her against my lips, the taste of her on my tongue, and the sound of her moans as I loved her in the only way she would let me.

As my cock grows slick, the memory moves forward sixteen months in time, her hair spread out around her on the wet grass by the river, her face framed by my hands as I dipped my head for a kiss so long-anticipated that it's the most erotic thing my mind can conjure in this moment, as I tighten my grip and push myself into release.

After, the self-loathing settles in, as it should. I stare up at the ceiling, hating everyone who ever made me believe that love was simple, that it was easy.

If love were simple, my love for Krystal would be enough to wash away the memory of Maggie's kiss.

Maggie

THIS NEW bridesmaid dress is more hideous than the first.

"What do you think?" Hanna asks as I step from the dressing room.

"It's…" *Hideous.* I search for another word. "So unique!"

"We hate it too," Hanna whispers.

I frown. I don't *hate* it, not exactly. It seems cruel to hate such an ugly dress. Akin to hating an ugly child.

The first strike against the dress is its color: maize, a fancy way of saying "sweet-corn yellow." The hue washes me out and makes me look a little malnourished.

The second strike against the dress is the skirt. The base is tea length. I can go for tea length. I even thought the skirt looked cute landing just below my knees. But it has a removable floor-length skirt that wraps around three-quarters of the dress, exposing only a small triangle of the shorter skirt beneath.

The third, and biggest, strike against the dress is the big ass bow sitting right at my hip.

No, I don't hate the dress. I just find it to be a little schizophrenic. Sexy casual here, formal there, little-girl cute there. The combination is disturbing.

Krystal flounces into the dressing room and pretends I don't exist. "Aren't they the best?" she asks Hanna and Lizzy, looking them over. "You are the loveliest BMs ever!" And with that, she leaves the room, calling for the bridal shop's dressing room attendant.

I bite my lip. *BMs?*

"I've been called a lot of things…" Lizzy mutters.

"She's spending too much time on online wedding planning

forums," Hanna explains. Then she drops her voice to a whisper. "You'd think she wanted us to look ugly."

Not sure what else to do, I turn to study my dress in the mirror. Goddamn it's ugly. This is a dress that needs someone to take pity on it and put it out of its misery. Bridesmaid dress euthanasia should be a thing.

"Maybe it's just missing something," I try.

"Yeah," Lizzy agrees. "Like a brown paper bag."

The dressing room attendant returns without Krystal. She's wringing her hands and cringing. "Um, I think your sister needs you."

That's when I hear it. Ever so faintly, I hear the hiccoughing sobs of my big sister in her dressing room.

Hanna, Lizzy, and I exchange worried glances before turning toward the door. I think about staying away, I think about letting the twins comfort her, but there was a Maggie-and-Krystal long before there was a Maggie-and-Will, and right now she needs her sisters. All of us.

My breath catches in my throat as I step into her dressing room. Krystal looks drop-dead gorgeous in white. Her long dark hair contrasts sharply against the fabric and makes her look exotic. Not to mention the things the corseted waist and low-cut neckline do for her cleavage. Even collapsed into a pool of white satin, she's beautiful.

And she's crying like I've never seen her cry before.

"I want to talk to Maggie."

Lizzy and Hanna look at each other and then at me.

I nod, letting them know it's okay. When they're gone, I close the door to give us some privacy. "Krys?"

She sniffs and peers up at me through her lashes. "Do you hate me?"

"No," I say, but the word breaks, catching on something in my throat. "I could never hate you, Krys."

"You should."

I sink down onto the floor next to her, careful not to snag my dress. "I left *him*," I say softly.

I wonder again if Will ever told her the truth about our wedding—what little of the truth he knew, that is.

Krystal's shoulders tremble with her inhale. "You were too young."

"I was," I agree.

"We all knew you were terrified of getting married. It was right there in your eyes every time we brought it up. You didn't run away from Will. You ran away from marriage." She sniffs and wipes her cheek with the back of her hand. "And I swooped in and took him before you had a chance to come back to him."

I look at my hands. How can I deny what she's saying when I've thought the exact same thing?

"I told myself I didn't care what you thought," she says. "I told myself you could hate me if you wanted, but I deserved to marry the man I love. But I was lying to myself."

"It doesn't matter. He's in love with you now. You're in love with him. Nothing else matters."

"We both know that's bullshit. We both know love is never enough."

Her hand is tucked into the pools of satin around her. I find it and slide my fingers through hers. "It is if you let it be."

She lifts her head to look at me. Tears have clotted in her lashes, and there's a faint line of mascara down each cheek. "I'm sorry, Maggie."

"I'm okay," I whisper. Even if it's not true just yet, there's something blossoming inside me that believes some day it might be.

"No marriage is worth losing you. No man is worth that."

"You aren't going to lose me, Krys. I came home, remember?"

Her eyes leave my face and settle on our joined hands. She turns mine over and runs her fingers over the gauze at my wrist.

I snatch my hand away. "That was an accident."

Her brows draw together. "You'd tell me, wouldn't you? If you just couldn't handle me and Will, you'd tell me?"

I take her face in my hands and wipe away her tears. "Of course," I promise, but I don't know if the lie is for her sake or mine.

chapter nine

Maggie

I HAVEN'T been back to my studio since the accident, and I expect to find a bloody mess waiting for me, but someone's been here in front of me. I know, without asking, that it was Will. He wouldn't have wanted everyone else to see it, wouldn't have wanted me to have to endure the questions.

I don't let myself think about last Friday morning at all. Instead, I dive into my work. Or attempt to. With my left hand immobilized, there's not much I can do but bust up some more glass.

There's a knock outside my office, and I bring the mallet down one last time before I answer it—leaving crystal shards behind as I cross the tiny room.

When I open the door, I'm surprised to see Asher standing on the other side, hands tucked in his pockets, eyebrow quirked. He's wearing jeans and a fitted gray t-shirt that pulls across his chest. Tattoos peek out from where the sleeves strain around his biceps, and I want to take a bite of him he looks so delicious.

"Sounds like a herd of elephants in a china shop in there," he says.

"Something like that." I cross my arms. He should probably be pissed at me after the way I kicked him out last week. Or about the fact that I never called to apologize.

But I didn't want to talk to him. I didn't want to remind myself that he knew.

"Are you going to invite me in or should I just make myself comfortable out here?"

I grin. I can't help myself. "There's hardly enough room for two, but come on in."

He steps into the studio and I take a step back to give him space, but he follows me, backing me into a corner until he's leaning over me, his hands pressed into the wall, the heat of his body warming mine.

His eyes are on my mouth, but something hard and angry ticks in his jaw.

"Okay," I say, sighing dramatically. "I guess you can do me against the wall."

That earns me a smile. "Tempting, but that's not why I'm here."

No shit, I think, but I say, "That's disappointing." I cock my head. Pretending to be unaffected by his nearness is too damn hard. Asher is heat and passion and wicked indulgence. He makes me unsteady. "You wanted to help me work?"

He shoots a glance over his shoulder to my growing pile of broken glass and ceramic. "Is that what you were doing?" He steps away to examine my worktable. "What is this stuff?"

I catch my breath and find my footing. "Tesserae," I explain. "I'll use them to make mosaics."

"Wow." Glass tinkles as he sifts through the piles of raw material. "What kind of design are you going to make with all of this?"

I shrug. "I don't know. I only know there's something beautiful there. I'll find it."

He studies a piece of pink-streaked crystal against the midday light coming in the window. It clatters as he settles it back onto the tray and turns to me. "When I found you at the river—"

I cut him off with the shake of my head. "I want you to forget about that day. Please."

"You were wearing a ring. You were alone but you were wearing someone's ring." His gaze drops to my hand and his breath catches. "Jesus, Maggie. What happened?"

I lift my bandaged hand and shake my head. "It's no big deal. I just had an accident with the glass."

He takes my hand in his and examines the bandage. "Stitches?"

"A few."

He nods, satisfied, then surprises me by bringing it to his mouth and pressing his lips against the bandage. This man looks so rough and continues to surprise me with his sweetness.

"Who is he?"

I blink, lost in my contemplation of Asher. "Who?"

"Whose ring were you wearing, Maggie?"

"Oh, we're back on that." I shake my head. "I'm not involved with anyone if that's what you're worried about."

"It was that guy who married your sister."

"They aren't married. Engaged. The first wedding was botched, remember?"

"He was engaged to you first." It's not a question

I back into the wall, trying to get away from the conversation, from his frightening perceptiveness. "We were engaged last spring," I admit. "Whirlwind romance between old friends followed by a brief engagement. I called off the wedding when…"

"Because of the miscarriage," he says, piecing it together.

I don't correct him.

"But he's with your sister now." In only two steps he's against me again, but this time his leg is between my thighs, his hands at my waist.

"He's with Krystal," I manage, but I don't want to think about Will or Krystal.

I want to think about the way Asher's hands are curling into my ass, those eyes hot on me. I want to think about releasing him from his jeans and putting my mouth on him again. I want to think about him fucking me against this wall, hard and long, until I forget.

He presses closer, shifts my weight so it's almost entirely against his thigh. My eyes nearly roll back in my head from that simple, delicious pressure.

"And what about you?" he asks. "Are you over him?" One hand snakes up my shirt to graze the underside of my breast, the other knots in my hair. He tilts my head up until my eyes connect with his.

There's a quiet tap on the door, and I realize I've left it open at the same moment I see Will walk into the studio.

I push Asher's hands from my shirt. He steps back, eyes narrow, jaw ticking.

"Sorry to interrupt." Will runs his eyes over me, but he doesn't look sorry at all.

Asher's face has gone stony. Mine is hot, and my breathing is uneven.

"I wanted to check on you," Will says. "How's your hand?"

"Better. It's making working difficult, but there's plenty I can do with just my right hand." That's a lie. I can't do shit with my right hand, but I don't want him to worry.

Will nods and starts to leave, but he stops himself and turns back to us. "Maggie, take the internship." His eyes flick to Asher then back to me. "I never would have had the courage to take the leap to start the gallery if you hadn't given me permission to dream big."

Asher slides his fingers through mine. "Of course she will."

I blink at him.

Will nods, his jaw set in a tight line. "Great." Then he backs out of the too-small studio.

Once we're alone, I spin on Asher. "You don't get to speak for me."

"Do you want to work in the gallery?"

"Yes, but—"

"Take the internship. Don't let them take your dream. Be part of it."

My shoulders drop and I close my eyes. "It's not that simple."

"Because you still want him?"

My eyes fly open. "Why would you say that?"

"He still wants you," Asher growls.

"He's marrying my sister."

He lifts a dark brow. "That doesn't change the way he looks at you. Or the fact that he'd like to kill me."

I step forward and grab a fistful of his shirt, pulling him toward me.

He leans down obediently, until his mouth is a breath from mine.

"I like you, Asher. But if we're going to keep this up, whatever *this* is, you need to know my life is a little fucked up. *I'm* fucked up."

His eyes search mine. "Then we're a great match."

Asher

SHE PUSHES me away before I can kiss her. "You don't know what fucked up is." She turns to the window, and the sunlight splashes across her freckles, making her look as young as she is.

"Try me."

She whips around and, for a second, I think she might tell me—something, anything other than the shit she shovels to everyone. But then she pastes that smile on her face and shrugs. "Nothing you couldn't hear from the magpies down at the beauty shop."

"And the story they'd tell me, does it involve your ex-fiancé?"

"Of course." Her smile is so manufactured her face looks almost plastic. "A rush to the altar and a runaway bride? Does it get any better than that?"

"But would it be the truth?"

That clears away her smile.

My gaze drops to her bandaged hand and wrist. "Was that about him?"

"What?" She pulls her hand against her chest. "This was an accident."

"Yeah?" I take her hand. She doesn't protest, but she watches me with a tight jaw as I remove the splint to find the swollen, neatly stitched wound.

My heart pounds at the sight of the stitches that run from the base of her palm right onto her wrist. I want to scream, to rage, to punch the asshole who drove her to this. Instead, I re-secure the splint.

"Someday," I say softly, "you'll tell me the whole story. I'll wait."

"When you know the whole story, you won't want me anymore. I'm that kind of girl."

"Don't count on that."

When I lift my eyes to her face, she's watching me with something like wonder. "What?"

She shakes her head. "I can't figure you out."

"Good." I cup her face in my palms and trace her bottom lip with my thumb. "Then maybe you won't be able to figure out how to push me away."

Maggie

I CAN'T create shit with my left hand immobilized, and the doctor wants me to keep the splint on any time I'm working until the wound has a chance to heal more. After Asher left, I was determined to lose myself in my work, making sense of little shards of glass and ceramic, but I'm so damn frustrated at my limited fine motor skills that I'm ready to throw something.

Whatever. I'm a mess anyway. There's some mysterious flower growing outside my art studio window that doesn't agree with my allergies, and at this point there's nothing but a drugstore for some allergy meds in store for my evening.

I lock up my studio and I sneeze for the tenth time in as many seconds.

Asher wants me to open up. I get that. He wants to know me. With any other girl, it would be the logical thing to want, but he doesn't understand what he's asking from me. Not even Will knows the whole truth. He doesn't understand that he doesn't *want* to know the real me.

As I turn toward the exit, I smack right into Ethan Bauer.

We jump back simultaneously.

"Maggie." His lips curve into a smile on my name.

Damn, damn, damn. I have no desire to talk to him.

"Ethan."

His eyes skim over me, and the hot gaze that used to make me wildly reckless with need now only makes me feel disgusted.

"There are nubile undergrads to seduce down this hall today," I say with my sweetest smile.

He winces. "I'm heading to the bathroom."

"Well, there it is," I say, pointing. Again. A smile.

"Nubile undergrads? You really think that little of me?"

Déjà vu.

"*You really think that I don't love you? With all my heart I love you. I want to be with you. I want to wake up next to you in the morning.*"

All lies, of course.

I want to turn on my heel and leave, but I stand my ground.

"You never did have a very high opinion of me." Then he disappears into the bathroom.

He doesn't know how wrong he is. Once, I had a very high opinion of him. Too high.

The first time I posed nude for Dr. Ethan Bauer, I was so at ease, he'd asked me to return. So many models, he explained, were too modest to do some of the more earthy and sensual poses he'd been itching to capture on canvas. *I* would be perfect.

So I posed for him.

"I'm going to ask you to do some things, Maggie, to get you where I want you."

"Okay." I flashed him a daring smile. "I'm not modest, Bauer. I don't know what you're so worried about."

"You're lovely."

I peeled off my dress and he handed me a man's dress shirt. "Put this on?"

"Should I be worried that the artist who was supposed to paint me nude wants me to put clothes on?" I laughed as I slipped the worn cotton shirt over my shoulders.

It smelled like him. And that day, as I inhaled that musky scent, I admitted to myself that I had a crush on him, the notorious womanizer Ethan Bauer.

My fingers moved to the buttons and his gruff voice stopped me. "Don't," he whispered.

"Ah, I see," I said.

"Do you?" He led me to the small couch. "Because I want to see you, Maggie. And if that makes you uncomfortable, I want you to tell me. You need to be comfortable for this to work."

I laughed. "I've already laid myself out naked for you. I can't imagine what you think might make me uncomfortable about posing with a shirt half on."

He didn't reply but situated me so I sat sideways on the couch, legs bent slightly, the shirt covering my breasts.

"Look to the left," he said, clicking on a new light.

He returned to his canvas and studied me. "Beautiful. Are you okay?"

"Maybe you're the one that's too modest, Ethan," I laughed. "I'm fine. Paint, already."

"I'd like you to move your right hand, Maggie. As if you were about to touch yourself."

His words buzzed through me and sent heat to pool in my belly. My nipples tightened under the soft cotton of his shirt as I cupped myself between my legs. "Like this?"

His chest rose, fell, rose again. "You're perfect." He crossed to me, spoke in soothing tones. "We don't want to give it to them. We want to taunt."

He moved my hand, pulling it up so that my palm lay against the flat of my belly, my fingertips just above the thatch of hair between my legs.

"This isn't really my style," I said, eyes on his. "I don't exactly need to sneak up on it."

He chuckled, his face inches from mine, his smile sending that heat circling lower.

If he had moved in first, I may have been turned off. If he had closed the distance between our lips, the next year would have unfolded differently. Maybe I would have gone to more parties. Maybe I'd have followed Lizzy to Brady's a little more often and had a harmless affair with a young townie—maybe some guy I went to school with or a recently divorced physics teacher from New Hope High School. Maybe I'd have given William Bailey the chance he deserved instead of cornering him into a marriage neither of us was ready for. But Ethan didn't make a move toward me.

I recognized the heat in his eyes, and it made me hot, made me feel powerful. In that moment, I wasn't so foolish as to think he might someday leave his wife for one of his students. That would come later. After hours of lovemaking, hundreds of paintings he would never show. His secret obsession, he called me.

At that moment, it wasn't about anything but hot, thick, blood-pumping feminine power. I lifted my head just enough to brush my lips across his. I kissed him, this man I thought so highly of, I was willing to overlook the wedding band on his finger.

I take a deep breath and exhale deliberately, as if to blow away the memory.

Regret holds me in its claws for a few stuttering heartbeats.

Ethan emerges from the bathroom and I freeze. When our eyes lock, the warmth I once felt for him is gone. Those soft gray eyes seem to be pleading me to deny it, to validate his always-faltering self-worth.

"What do you want from me, Ethan?"

"Honestly?"

I let out a puff of air. "I asked, didn't I?"

"Let me take you to dinner. There's so much we never said." His gaze does that roaming, conquering thing again. I want to tell him to keep his eyes to himself, but that would mean admitting I notice.

My eyes began to water, another sneezing attack coming on. "I'd rather not," I say, but it sounds more like *Ud wathur wot.*

Ethan steps forward and reaches for my face. "Don't cry."

The pressure builds further in my head. I grab his wrist to push him away, and William Bailey turns the corner.

Will takes in my face, my tears, Ethan's hand. "What's going on here?"

Ethan drops his hand as if my face was suddenly burning him.

"Maggie, I don't want you seeing him," Will says, hard eyes on Ethan. "He's trouble."

Ethan nails me with the intense gaze that once got me in so much trouble. A moment later, Will's eyes lock with mine. If Ethan's gaze says, "I want you," Will's says, "I need you. I'm incomplete without you."

chapter ten

William

MAGGIE WALKS into the gallery dressed in cut-offs that show more thigh than they cover and a tiny tank top, and I nearly drop a piece of stained glass off my ladder at the sight.

"I'm ready to work," she announces, spreading her arms. "Use me and abuse me."

Having her here is a really bad idea.

I shoot a guilty glance over my shoulder toward the back office, but Krystal's not here. She went over to campus to talk to someone about another painting that she seems to think we need for the opening.

"I'll be done in a minute," I call down from the ladder.

"You mind if I take a look at what you have here?"

"Knock yourself out."

I carefully hang the piece of stained glass from the wire line, pretending I'm not completely shaken by her presence. Floor-to-ceiling windows overlook the river and flood the gallery with light. The stained glass will draw everyone's eye here. I center it carefully before climbing down to greet her.

When I reach the bottom of the ladder, I wipe my damp palms on my jeans.

With a slow spin, she smiles. God, she's practically glowing today. Did Asher Logan do that?

"This photography is amazing." She sits by a box in the middle of the gallery, folding her legs under her as she sorts through artwork.

"He's out of Chicago," I say, motioning to the photos. They've been mounted to stainless steel and make for perfect additions to sleek, contemporary interior designs. They are made to be displayed in panels of three. But which pieces to display at the opening? I haven't decided yet. Maggie was always better at finding themes in collections of art. I'm better off behind the camera.

"What are you thinking for prices?"

I hand her the pricing binder and she scans the columns. "These are really reasonable rates for this kind of talent, but I don't want to scare people away either. We always said we were going to have art for everyone, right?" She tilts her head to look at me and a red curl falls in her face. I make a fist to resist the urge to tuck it behind her ear. She blinks, as if realizing her error. "Of course, maybe you and Krystal weren't worried about that. I'm not trying to make my position more important than it is, I just—"

"Maggie." I hold up a hand. "Stop being so self conscious. We want you here because we value your ideas."

She grins and my shoulders relax. It's such a damn relief to have some of this tension gone between us. "Okay," she says, "because I was thinking we could do a sampling of his different sizes for the opening—that way someone on a budget might still be able to take some of his photography home. Not to mention we could make a nice balance of small and large pieces along that wall."

"Sounds good." Tucking my hands into my pockets, I step closer to examine the photographs she's chosen. "Listen, the house is done."

Her head snaps up and she looks at me with wide eyes.

"Our house. Krystal's and mine," I say hastily, then wish I could pull the words back. I hired the contractor to build the house when Maggie and I got engaged and just never stopped the process when she left.

I study a painting because I can't bear to watch her. "We've been living there for a while, but I think the finishing touches are finally all in place. We're doing a housewarming party this weekend. We wanted to invite you."

"I'll see you then," she says, and I can hear the forced smile in her voice. "What were you going to do with the little room off the front?" She hops off the floor and wanders over to the paintings leaning against the far wall. "I *adore* this watercolor series, and I think it would look great with the lighting in that room."

I swallow. Hard. "We promised to feature Professor Bauer in that room."

Her hands freeze on a watercolor of a little girl in white. "Oh." The tremor in her hand is barely perceptible, but I see it.

"It's just that he helped us get the grant to open the gallery," I explain.

She tucks her hands in her pockets—to hide that they're shaking? "Of course! And, gosh, with that talent why wouldn't you feature him?" She turns a small circle. "Where is his collection?"

You can't protect her, Will. "He's going through his paintings now. He's going to make his own selections."

She gives a tenuous smile. "I would expect no less from the illustrious Ethan Bauer."

I swallow and step away from her. She smells too damn good today. "He's being really damn secretive about his collection. He insists he can't set it up until the morning of the opening, and he wants to stage it himself."

That happy glow seems to slip right off her face. "Why would he do that?"

I lift a shoulder. "Krystal's chalking it up to his artistic temperament, but I don't like it any more than you do." I watch her carefully as I ask, "Do you have any idea what it might be?"

She shakes her head. "I'll talk to him, see what I can find out."

I know that costs her. She doesn't want to talk to Ethan Bauer any more than I do, but I also know he's more likely to talk to her than anyone else.

"It's just so hard to believe," she says as she scans the walls. "This is really happening. When we talked about it, I don't know if I ever really thought we'd do it. But you made it happen." She sets her eyes on me and pain slices across her features so damn clearly I feel like I've hit her. "You and Krystal, I mean."

The silence is awkward and unnatural between us, and I search for something to fill it. "I don't know if we're going to make it," I blurt before realizing I plan to share my problems with Maggie at all. "Me and Krystal? Our relationship is broken. I've done everything I can think but—Jesus, we're not even having sex and that was fine but it's like she doesn't even want me to touch her anymore."

Maggie dodges my eyes. "We shouldn't talk about this."

I release a bitter laugh. "I used to talk to you about all my girl problems."

"Will…"

"I'm thinking about calling off the wedding." Saying the words makes them more real, and as they slip from my lips anger and frustration and regret all rush through me in a flood so intense I can't tell them apart.

She blinks at me. "You are?"

"Yeah."

"What do you want?"

The only sound is the hum of the air conditioner as we stare at each other, and I feel that old addiction surge up, that need for a fix that silences every reasonable thought and makes me reckless until all I can hear is my blood in my ears and all I can think is of tasting her again.

Her tongue darts out to wet her lips before she pulls the bottom one between her teeth.

In two strides, I close the distance between us and pull her against me. Hard. It's stupid and impulsive, and I feel like I might die if I don't do it. But I do. Because last week's brush of lips did nothing to squelch this craving. It only left me wanting more.

I bury my hands in her hair, holding her tight as I slip my tongue between her lips in a kiss that's fueled by this mess of emotion pumping through me. Anger. Frustration. Regret. Her hand curls into my chest, and I pull her closer. I want her curves against me, need her under me. In this moment, my future and my plans mean nothing next to the pulsing need to *possess*. To take.

My hand slips under her shirt. When my mouth moves to her neck, I feel a shudder pass through her, and my dick aches from the unaccommodating confines of my jeans. God, I'd forgotten the rush of making this woman tremble.

"Don't," she whispers.

"It okay," I promise, snaking my hand up to her breast. Even to my own ears, I sound like a manipulative asshole, but only part of my brain registers what a scumbag I'm being. The rest of my mind is four steps ahead, getting her naked and getting inside her. Fucking her until I don't care anymore what a mess my life has become.

I can't register anything that doesn't get me to that goal. So my fingers are working their way to the clasp of her bra before I realize the hand on my chest isn't encouraging. It's pushing me away.

I loosen my hold on her a fraction and she takes the opportunity to shove me, harder this time, until I stumble back.

Her eyes blaze with anger as she lifts her hand to her lips. For a minute, I think it's heat I see there. Passion.

"*Never* do that again," she says. And it's the shaking in her voice that brings me to my senses. It's a shaking that has nothing to do with arousal.

"Oh, Jesus." My breathing is heavy and labored, and I stumble back a couple more steps as I struggle to get the air I need. "Jesus, Maggie. I'm sorry. I didn't think—"

"Didn't think I'd mind being your *whore*?" Her eyes glisten with tears. "Didn't think I'd mind you feeling me up while my *sister* wears your ring?"

"It's not like that and you know it." My jaw tightens. How dare she treat me like one of her asshole ex-lovers when I'm talking about giving up everything for her?

"It's not? Because that's what it feels like, Will. My sister won't fuck you so you came to me for a little something the first chance you got."

I throw up my hands. My dick aches and she's making me out to be trash when I haven't done a damn thing wrong. "Krystal and I are *broken*," I spit out between clenched teeth. "Broken because of how I feel about *you*."

"I don't care," she hisses. "I don't want you to touch me as long as your ring is on her finger."

"That little detail never seemed to bother you with any of your other men." The words are ugly and cruel. The second they're out of my mouth, I regret them, and when she flinches, I hate myself for them.

"Men?" she says softly.

I wince. Jesus, I'm an asshole. "What happened when you were in high school," I say slowly. "I know that wasn't your fault."

She crosses her arms and stares at me, eyes glistening as she waits for me to confess that I know more than she thought I did.

"But Maggie, you have to admit you have a pattern. The sheriff—"

"Fifteen, Will. I was *fifteen*."

I nod, slowly. I'm in dangerous territory here and I know it. "You weren't fifteen when you slept with Ethan Bauer," I say softly, and at her sharp inhale I realize she thought it was a secret. She really believed no one knew she was fucking her married art professor, her mentor, for most of her sophomore year at Sinclair. "And now Asher."

"What about Asher?"

"Well, for starters, he's a no-good piece of shit that only wants one thing from you."

"What?"

I don't repeat myself. I can tell by the anger in her eyes that she heard me just fine.

"You don't get to choose who I'm with, Will. You gave up that right when you shacked up with my sister."

Anger pumps through me at that. Thick and pulsing and hot. "Don't throw that in my face like I betrayed you. *You* called off our wedding, Maggie. *You* left town. What? Did you want me to run after you? Did you want me to *beg* for you to give us another chance? Because I tried, remember? I would have done whatever it took to keep you if I had thought it would work, but you shut me out. Stop making me out to be the villain. *You* left *me*."

"I had my *reasons*," she shouts.

"Yeah? Care to share those?" I wait for an answer I know she won't give me, my heart pounding. When I speak again, I lower my voice. "You don't have to be with me, but I'll be fucking damned before I let you lump me in with all the other assholes you've been with." I drag my hands through my hair. "Damn it, Maggie, why do you give so much to men like that?"

"Men like *what*?" Her arms are crossed tightly over her breasts, as if she has to protect herself from me. *Me.*

The notion is so absurd I almost laugh. I look her over—the thin tee, the short shorts, and for the hundredth time since she developed breasts, I wish I could mandate her wardrobe. I can't stand the things men in this town think about her, but worse is the way she does everything in her power to perpetuate the reputation.

"Men. Like. *What*?" she spits.

"Men who want you as their fuck toy and nothing else."

chapter eleven

Maggie

I AM in hell.

Krystal and Will's housewarming party is over the top. It features all the luxuries that most women only dream of having for their weddings, and only a very elite few enjoy for the sake of showing off their excessive wealth to anyone they can con into attending.

Everyone is dressed to impress, the silver is polished, and the conversation is delightfully polite.

Asher is the evening's only saving grace and right now he's off playing nice with Aunt Kathy who was, apparently, a big fan.

Lizzy and Hanna are keeping me company and not attempting to keep their greedy little eyes off my date. They both look stunning tonight, dressed in matching dark red dresses with halter necklines. They may not look like twins, but from time to time, they like to dress the part anyway.

Personally, I went for the strapless look. I like wearing dresses around Asher. I like the way he can't keep his eyes off my legs. I can practically hear his thoughts as he talks himself out of dragging me to a dark corner to investigate what's underneath. I wish he didn't have such damn good self-control.

I peel the fondant icing off a piece of cake. "God, whatever happened to good, old-fashioned butter cream frosting?"

Lizzy snorts. "They got rid of it when cake stopped being about taste and started being about appearance."

I hold a piece of yellow fondant against the flickering light of a candle. "It looks like plastic. I can't eat anything that color."

"Don't talk to me about food to me," Hanna grumbles. "I'm on a diet."

I roll my eyes. "Why?"

"Three words," she says. "Red. Leather. Pants."

"The ones you wore to Melinda's Halloween party two years ago?" I ask. "Are we talking about the ones so tight that I had to help you put them on *and* take it off?"

"I'm sorry. It sounds like I'm interrupting." Asher grins at the girls as he settles into the seat next to me.

"Kinda," I say, and at the same time Lizzy says, "Not at all."

Asher looks at me expectantly. "Don't let me interrupt. You were talking about peeling leather pants off each other?" He rests his chin on his hands. "Go on."

Lizzy beams. "Asher Logan," she says, offering her hand. "I'm Lizzy Thompson, and I hear you're a little freaky."

"Lizzy!" I swat her arm.

Asher quirks a brow. "I didn't figure your sister for the type to kiss and tell."

"I didn't tell her about the kitchen," I hiss.

"No, just about the night you met." Lizzy wriggles her eyebrows. "But tell me about the kitchen." She leans forward, leering just a little. "Please?"

Asher chuckles but my cheeks are an inferno of heat. Which is ridiculous because I'm not the type to be embarrassed about sex.

Hanna hums as she studies us, a crooked smile on her face. She tugs at Lizzy's arm. "We'll leave you two love birds alone for a bit."

When they're gone, I turn to Asher. He looks so damn sexy

tonight. "You're coming home with me to attempt to redeem this night, aren't you?"

He grins at me. "I thought maybe we could make some coffee. You know, really talk and get to know each other." He winks and I melt a little inside.

"Asher Logan, if you think I'm going to walk around in these heels all night and not get anything out of it, you are mistaken."

He chuckles and kisses me on top of my head. "Maybe we can compromise."

"If your idea of compromise involves a lot of naked flesh, I'll consider it."

I don't get to hear his reply because Will has made his way to us. "Thank you for coming tonight. I told Maggie she didn't have to bring a date, but I suppose someone needs to keep her out of trouble."

Asher nods but murmurs so only I can hear, "I was more interested in getting you into it."

"Love the house," I manage. "Congratulations."

Will's eyes soften as he looks at me, and something tugs in my chest. Regret? Longing? Anger?

Next to me, Asher stiffens. He's too perceptive. As much as everyone else seems blind to it, he sees the way Will looks at me. Asher's seen it from that first night, and now tension rolls off him in tangible waves.

"I hope you're taking good care of Maggie," Will tells him.

"Maggie's not a child," Asher says stiffly. "She doesn't need to be taken care of."

"Everyone needs someone to take care of them," Will counters, eyes hard.

Asher folds his arms, refusing to take the bait.

After a couple of beats of awkward silence, Will says, "Let me know if I can get you anything."

Asher's jaw ticks, and we sit in silence for a minute after Will leaves us.

"I guess it's still a little awkward," I say.

"Because he still wants you."

William

ASHER'S HANDS are all over Maggie. In my house. He touches her at all times. A hand at the small of her back as they tour the house, his fingers laced through hers as they chat with guests by the bar, a finger along her jaw as he whispers something into her ear. And when they are pulled apart, it's worse. The looks she casts him across the room are charged with sexual tension. Want, need, and something tender.

I need a drink.

A soft smile curves Lizzy's lips. "I've never seen her so happy. They're adorable together."

I lean against the wall and watch the couple in question. *I want that.*

But even as I think it, I'm not sure which part I want. Do I want that easy chemistry between them? Do I wish that base attraction was part of my relationship with Krystal? Or do I want Maggie?

"Twenty says they sneak to the bathroom to do the dirty before the night's through," Lizzy says with a grin.

I force myself to return her smile. "That's a sucker bet."

"Maybe." She studies them, sipping at her glass of wine. "But Maggie's turning over a new leaf. I don't think fast and furious bathroom fucking is part of the New Maggie plan."

My silent questions are answered by the image that flashes fast and vivid through my mind. Maggie in the bathroom, her hips propped on the porcelain sink, her skirt bunched around her hips, head thrown back as she bites back a moan, her lover's fingers curling into her hips. But in my vision, they're not Asher's fingers. They're mine. And it's my name that slips from her lips as I press her up against the door and slide into her.

Fuck. What am I even doing?

Krystal comes into my line of vision and I feel like the piece of shit I am.

She's been avoiding me. We don't touch. We hardly talk.

If things hadn't already been finished between us, the receipt I found in her drawer tonight would have been enough to end things.

When I meet her eyes, I realize for the first time that she already knows it's over.

Maggie

I NEED some air, so I slip out the oversized French doors to the back of the house.

Just off the patio, lanterns line the cobblestone path to a lush garden. The thick air of Indiana summer weighs hot and heavy in my lungs.

I follow the path to a burbling fountain and find Will tucked in a corner, an unlit cigarette between his fingers.

"Aren't you going to go inside and mingle with your fiancée?" I ask softly, sinking into the wrought iron chair beside him.

"I needed a break from"—he waves a hand—"you know, everything."

I nod because I do know, and the silence stretches between us, comfortable for the first time since I came back.

He takes a breath. "Have you ever told anyone about the baby?"

Oh, Will. And it hurts so much—the words, the memory. The hurt never goes away, but this moment wrenches it to the surface like someone tore off the bandage and dug dirty nails into my wound.

I blink at him, but I can only think of the morning after

my miscarriage scare. The ER doctor had done an ultrasound and shown me the baby's steadily beating heart. *Sometimes this happens. A blood clot. Baby's fine. No miscarriage.* Just a clot in my uterus and enough blood to keep me terrified for weeks.

The next morning, I woke up and stared at my wedding dress, as if it could make everything okay. As if it could make the lie I told Will true. As if it could make the decision I had in front of me any easier.

"No, I haven't." I meet his eyes—blue, soft, a little haunted. "Have you?"

"I think about him," he whispers.

Her, I think, and my heart breaks, shatters right there on the dregs of my own misery. He deserves to know the truth, but it would only hurt him more. "Me, too," and it's true. I think about *her* every day. "Asher...he also knows."

Will's brow wrinkles. "He does?"

"Yeah. He found me the day I went to the hospital."

"Oh." Hurt flashes in his eyes. "And you two have kept in touch?"

"No. I met him again at Krystal's wedding. We just put two and two together last week." Or Asher did. I didn't remember him. That morning at the river, he'd been inconsequential. I'd been too focused on my own fear.

"Oh. Right." He stares at the fountain. Thinking? Avoiding my gaze? I'm not sure. But then he says, "You know that I wasn't just marrying you for the baby, right?"

I swallow back that thickness in my throat. We'd been together for barely three weeks when I told him I was pregnant. I never would have accepted his ring so young if I hadn't been pregnant.

"I always wonder about that. If you understood how much I cared for you. If you just thought that you were saving me by ending it, leaving town."

"It was for the best."

He finally meets my eyes again. "I'm still in love with you."

I jump out of the chair. I don't want to hear this. "Don't."

I put several yards between us, pretending to examine the fountain. My fingers graze the water-slicked stone of the angel's face.

"Maggie. Is there something more I could have done? To keep you?" His voice is close, and I'm not surprised when I feel his hands on my shoulders, turning me. "It's over between me and Krystal. It will be over. Tonight."

My heart trips. Stumbles. Aches.

"You were right. I had no right to kiss you before I ended it, and I have no right to do it now."

I open my mouth to respond, to tell him he can do better than me and my lies.

But then his lips are on mine and he's kissing me.

It's not the hungry, demanding kiss from the gallery. It's nice. Soft. Gentle. If Will is anything, it's gentle. Maybe I need someone tough, someone hardened like me.

His lips brush mine once, twice, then he retreats. His fingertips trace down the side of my jaw. And I should be angry, but I'm not—not when his kiss makes me feel so safe.

When I pull back, Asher's standing five yards behind Will, his gaze locked on me.

"I thought I'd find you out here." His expression is guarded. "I'll be inside when you decide this is a bad idea."

My heart sinks and my stomach lurches. They collide inside me, my lungs a casualty, torn apart by the wreckage.

Why couldn't he look hurt? Crushed by my indiscretion? Anything but that guarded, you-can't-hurt-me look I understand so well.

He walks away and I ball my fists to resist running after him, resist the instinct to explain what can't be explained.

"He's no good for you, Maggie," Will says softly.

"That's not fair."

Will puts his finger to my lips and studies me. "I'm sorry." Does he mean for the kiss? For what he said about Asher? But he says, "I'm sorry I couldn't be what you needed. So sorry. You'll never know." And then he walks away.

And I'm alone with nothing but the taste of my regret and the weight of my lies for company.

Asher

I WANT to put a hole in the wall of William Bailey's fancy-ass house. I want to break his porcelain serving platters and shatter his crystal.

I want to *drink*.

It's the last that has me so damn unsteady, licking parched lips and watching the door as I wait for her to return. I'm not leaving without her. I'm not running from here with my tail tucked between my legs like he wants me to. He saw me coming and he kissed her to prove he could.

And she let him.

His lips were on Maggie, and I wanted to throw him across the yard, wanted the satisfaction of feeling my knuckles connect with his skull.

God. Damn. It.

Will approaches, his hands tucked into his pressed black dress pants. I hate him so much in this moment I have to ball my hands into fists to keep from decking him.

He runs a hand through his blond hair as he looks distractedly around the party.

Jesus. This guy is class and style and reeks of old money.

I follow his gaze. Maggie has returned. She's twisted that flaming red hair off her neck, revealing the tender spot I know makes her crazy.

Will stares at her, naked longing in his eyes.

Maggie spots me and freezes, deer-in-the-headlights terror on her face. "I need a minute," she says, backing up a step. She looks to Will. "May I use your restroom?"

Will casts a glance over his shoulder. "I think Aunt Shirley's in that one. You can use the one off the master down the hall."

Will and I watch her leave. The tension between us angry enough to bruise.

"Stay away from Maggie," Will warns softly, his gaze on Maggie's retreating form. "She deserves better. Does she even know about Juliana?"

I don't give him the satisfaction of looking at him. My skin across my knuckles burns from my fists being balled so tightly. I force my hands to relax and walk away, going after Maggie without a word to this man who thinks he has some sort of hold over her.

I find her in the master bath. She's standing at the counter, hands pressed against its edge, head hanging. She doesn't look up. "Go away."

I flip the lock on the door before putting my hands to her waist. Our eyes meet in the mirror.

Her eyes blaze. *"I'm fucked up,* Asher. Don't you see that? I'm a fucking home-wrecking *slut."*

I watch her in the mirror as I trace the edge of her jaw with my thumb, leaning in to brush my lips against the smooth, exposed column of her neck.

Electricity.

It's there every time I touch her, and it whips through my veins in a violent, hungry rush. She feels it too. I can see it in her eyes. I can feel it in the way her body instinctively presses closer to mine.

She reaches back and threads her fingers through my hair. "Why are you even still here?"

Our eyes meet in the mirror again. I dip my fingers into the top of her strapless dress and feather them across her breasts. I want to peel it off her, spin her around and graze my teeth over her nipples, set her on the vanity, and open her legs to my mouth. "I care about you, Maggie."

She flinches, as if the words offend her. "You don't know me."

"Maybe not. But I understand you." I let my mouth hover over her ear. "Are you calling yourself a slut because you kissed him or because you know you're going to let me touch you in here?" I pause a beat to let that settle in. Blood pulses hot and thick into my dick at the catch in her breath. "I think you want me to. You want me to make you come in the house of the man you were going to marry."

I am insane with wanting her. I don't care where we are. I don't care that she's just kissed another man. I need this woman despite that.

Fuck all reason, I need her because of it.

I slide my hand up her dress, tracing the edge of her panties with my fingers.

Her hips buck and her back arches as she rocks toward me.

"Tell me you don't want me to take you here," I whisper. "Tell me you don't want me to bend you over this vanity. Tell me you don't want to watch in the mirror as I take you in his bathroom." I slide my fingers down the seam of her ass and cup her from behind.

She gasps and licks her lips. She's struggling to maintain control. "Yes," she breathes. "Please."

I press my lips to her ear. "Tell me that you care about me."

In the mirror, I watch her eyes flutter open. "What if I don't care about anyone?"

I move my hand, rub her, and I'm rewarded with a throaty moan. I could touch this woman for hours if she'd let me. I want to make her lose hold of that control she holds so close. I want to break down her walls.

I slide my fingers into her panties from behind. "You're so damn wet," I murmur, touching her clit.

She moans softly.

A knock sounds at the bathroom door.

"Maggie, are you okay in there?"

Maggie pushes my hand from between her legs and spins around. She grabs my shirt, holding me still.

"My mother," she whispers.

"Yes, Maggie, we're worried about you," another voice calls.

"And Granny," Maggie whispers.

I groan softly. *Nothing* could kill my hard-on right now, but the word *Granny* certainly kills the mood.

"Yeah, I'm okay. I just needed a minute alone."

"Maggie, are you sure that this isn't all just a reaction to seeing Will marry someone else?"

Good question, Granny.

Maggie shakes her head.

"Or maybe you're feeling bad about yourself because you see Krystal starting this great life and yours is in shambles."

"What about that nice man she's here with tonight?"

"Oh, let's not get ahead of ourselves," the other voice protests. "I can hardly see that working out."

"Maggie, even if it doesn't work out, I'm glad you're getting yourself some tail."

"Granny!" Maggie screeches, breaking her silence.

I chuckle silently and Maggie thumps me in the chest.

"I'm sorry, but a girl that young shouldn't keep herself cloistered."

Maggie rubs her hand over her eyes in obvious distress.

"So, what? You want her to tramp all over town?"

"Gretchen, sex is natural. God gave your daughter those parts for a reason."

"Yes, so she could get married to a good Catholic man and make good Catholic babies."

"But until she finds that man—"

"Mom! Granny! Please!" Maggie begs.

She shoots me a death glare when I have to bite back laughter.

Maggie turns on the sink and calls over the running water, "Give me a minute to wash my face, and I'll be out."

"Okay, dear."

"If there isn't anything we can get you."

The women's voices fade as one asks the other, "Where did her delicious-looking date run off to?"

As the sound of their steps fades, I let myself laugh. "They're quite a pair."

Maggie splashes water on her face. "They mean well. We should get back."

With a sigh, I nod toward the door. "Go ahead. I'll meet up with you in a few."

"Rumors are already probably flying that I ran in here in despair and I'm desperate to get Will back to fix my broken life."

A fist tightens in my chest at her words. "Are you?"

She closes her eyes. "No one can fix me, Asher. That includes you."

I let her leave. I let her shut me out. For now.

A few minutes later, I return to the party, but when I survey the room, I don't see Maggie anywhere.

"She left."

I turn to see Maggie's sister Krystal. "Left?"

She shakes her head. "Leave it to Maggie to leave a party without telling her date."

"It's kind of a kick in the balls," I admit.

Her face relaxes a little. "I'm a big fan, by the way, and that's kind of an awkward thing to admit to my little sister's boyfriend."

"Thanks." I arch a brow. "Did she call me her boyfriend?"

Krystal snorts. "Are you kidding? She's hardly talking to me. I stole her man, remember?"

"Hmm. That's not exactly how she explained it to me."

Silence stretches between us for a few beats before Krystal says, "I am sorry, you know. Everything's just so screwed up." She swallows and tears well up in her eyes. When she speaks again, I can hardly hear her. "Will's always been in love with Maggie, and I've always been in love with Will."

"And what about Maggie?"

Krystal frowns. "Maggie? Maggie's too busy hating herself to love anyone."

chapter twelve

William

"You should have told me that you didn't want to marry me," I tell Krystal.

She freezes in the middle of sliding a diamond stud from her ear. "What?"

Her lips part. For a minute I think she might feign ignorance, but instead, she sinks into the chair at her vanity and looks at her hands. "I do want to marry you."

Everyone's left for the night, and I can't put this conversation off anymore.

I study her in the mirror and feel hollow. She looks beautiful tonight. Her hair is pulled off her neck in some sort of twist, and she's wearing a long black dress that makes her look jaw-droppingly elegant. Under the dress, the bra and panties I bought her for Valentine's Day.

On paper, we are so good for each other. We're well-educated, like-minded, and we want the same things out of life. We love each other.

Why isn't that enough?

"If you want to marry me," I say slowly, "why did you sabotage our wedding?"

A teary streak of mascara runs down her face. Her lashes are damp with tears when she looks up at me. "Because you still love her." The words are matter of fact, not thrown like an insult or accusation, simply delivered like an unfortunate truth.

"But I love you too." My voice breaks on the words.

"I know you do."

"Then *why*?" I sink to my knees and take her hands in mine.

She threads her fingers through my hair. "I didn't want to live my life wondering if the man sleeping next to me would rather be sleeping next to someone else."

I squeeze my eyes shut, guilty of the crime. "I needed you to believe in me. In us. The wedding...it made me question everything. It made me question us."

"I needed time."

"Time for what?"

"To prove to myself that things were over between you and Maggie." She gives a sad smile. "But that's not what happened, and I realized I wasn't even living my own life. I was living the life you and Maggie had planned."

"Why didn't you just ask to postpone the wedding?"

"I was afraid you would think I was running away. Like she did."

Her hands are so soft. I kiss each knuckle, then I open her hand and press her palm to my lips.

"It's over, isn't it?" she asks.

"I never thought it would end like this."

She squeezes my hand. "We can't pretend that this is enough anymore."

The silence cracks with a ragged sob. Hers? Mine? I wrap my arms around her waist and lay my head in her lap. She combs her fingers through my hair as she cries.

I know she's right, but that doesn't make this hurt any less. "I'm sorry. I'm so sorry I couldn't let her go."

Minutes pass with nothing but our breath and her tears filling the silence, then Krystal gently pushes me back and pastes on a smile. "We're both going to be fine."

I stare at her, the reality of what has just happened settling in further with each beat of my heart. "Will you stay on? Continue to be a part of the gallery?"

She gives a sad smile. "I'll be there through the opening. After..." She shakes her head. "It was never my dream. It was yours and Maggie's. I was just the understudy."

Maggie

SHE WON'T stop crying and no one can calm her down.

"He was so perfect. Why do things have to fall apart like this? Why can't people just live happily ever after?" She draws in a long, shaky breath and wipes her snotty nose.

Lizzy casts a pleading look at me over her shoulder before returning to patting and cooing. "Everything happens for a reason. Krystal's going to be okay, Mom."

I drag my hand over my face. Sunday morning brunch has been hijacked by the announcement of Krystal and Will's breakup. They delivered the news together, holding hands, and I thought how much stronger she is than I am.

When I called off my wedding, I didn't want to look at anyone, and I left town as quickly as I could. Not Krystal. She delivered the news with her shoulders back and her chin high. Then she and Will hugged before he left.

It would have been relatively painless if my mom wasn't so beside herself.

I turn away from mom's tears and run into Krystal. I've been avoiding her all morning, afraid she'd blame me.

"Can we talk outside?" she asks softly.

I nod and follow her out back. The sky is gray and it's drizzled on and off all morning. A year ago, when I told Will I couldn't go through with the wedding, the weather was like this. We walked by the river, letting the rain disguise our tears as I fed him small pieces of the truth.

I told him about how much I bled at the river and that I went to the hospital. I didn't tell him it wasn't a miscarriage.

I told him it was okay because I wasn't ready to be a mom anyway. I didn't tell him I would be giving my baby to someone else.

I told him I felt like I'd pushed him into marrying me. I didn't tell him that the baby wasn't his.

The memory makes me cold and I freeze in my tracks at the deck steps.

Krystal's halfway down the path to the river before she realizes I've stopped. She turns and waves me down. "Come on, Mags."

I swallow and push myself forward to catch up. When I reach her, she doesn't say anything but continues walking. Neither of us speaks until we're stepping onto the dock.

"I was always so jealous of you," she says softly.

"What?" My oldest sister is about as perfect as a person can get. I can't imagine why she would have ever been jealous of me. "Why?"

She shrugs. "You were the fun one, the cool one. Even when you were young and Will didn't see you as anything more than a kid, he loved to be around you."

"He hung around all of us," I object. "Not just me."

"I was the boring one."

"You're not boring."

Her eyes connect to mine. She looks so tired. "It's okay. It wasn't your fault you shined so bright."

I swallow hard. "You think I shined bright?"

"Brighter than the sun since the day you were born," she whispers. "It's not your fault that Will's still in love with you."

"Oh, Krys."

"I don't blame you anymore." She takes a breath. "I used to, but I don't anymore."

My heart squeezes in my chest and I don't know what to say.

"I blame myself. I knew he was in love with you, but I wanted him anyway. I told myself it was okay because you left." She shakes her head. "But it wasn't okay. He's always been yours."

The forgiveness is in her eyes, and it hurts too much. I walk to the end of the dock and look out into the water. A raindrop hits my cheek and another hits my shoulder, but I don't turn back to the house.

"Will you try to go back to Will?" she asks. "Once everything settles down?"

I watch the rain hit the water, watch the tiny drop get swallowed up by the water. My tongue is heavy, as if it's weighed down by wet sand from the river's bottom.

"You don't have to tell me, obviously," she says, "but I know he'd take you in a heartbeat."

Krystal is offering me a gift that I can't take. Being with Will would mean I would have to tell him the truth—and the secrets I've kept from him, I don't think he could ever forgive.

chapter thirteen

Asher

A KNOCK at my door pulls me from sleep. I roll over and look at the clock.

Five a.m. is way too damn early for company.

I drag myself from under the covers, grabbing a pair of jeans off the floor and tugging them on as I make my way to the door. I'm in my apartment in New York, a place I keep for the sole purpose of the one week a month I get to keep my daughter. If it weren't for her, I'd get rid of the damn place. New York is toxic to me, but I won't spend the little time I get with Zoe in a damn hotel room.

The knock sounds again.

"I'm coming," I mutter, pulling the door open without checking the peephole.

Juliana stands on the other side, her mouth drawn into a pout, annoyance coloring her features.

I cross my arms. "Do you have any idea what time it is?"

"Sure, I'd love to come in. You're such a gentleman." She pushes past me and into the apartment, and my mind is filled with flashes of memories from the days we lived here together. We'd party and roll in about this time and barely make it through the door before we fucked.

Now I never bring women here, and instead of weed and beer bottles, the living room is littered with pink toys.

Suddenly, she turns her appraising eyes to me, my bare chest. Her smile is approving. And a little lopsided. "What do you know?"

"Not much before a decent cup of coffee," I mutter, ignoring the heat in her eyes and the suggestion of her smile. If I'm guessing right, Juliana is drunk or close to it.

Her eyes drop to my crotch. "You're looking good, Asher. So good I haven't stopped thinking about you since you came by the house this afternoon."

I sigh and point to the clock. "That would be yesterday."

"Such a stickler for details."

"Where's Zoe?"

"At home in bed."

My jaw ticks.

"What? The nanny's there. She's *fine*."

"Juliana, you need to understand something."

Her eyes are on my lips as she closes the space between us and trails her fingers over my bare chest. "Yeah? Is it something good?"

Bile rises in my throat as I remove her hand. "I don't come to town to see you."

She rolls her eyes. "Come on, I know you get a little randy in the mornings." This time, both her hands are on me and she looks up at me through her lashes. "Let's have a little fun." She shimmies her body closer and presses her breasts against my chest. "I miss the way you fuck me."

I clench my jaw and fist my hands at my sides. My brain wants nothing to do with this woman, but Mr. Balls For Brains down south has other ideas.

"Come on," she whispers. "Remember how good it used to be."

"Stop," I snarl, stepping back. "I don't remember, and neither do you. We were too goddamn wasted to remember shit. You're with Chad now, remember?" *Chad.* I can barely speak the man's name without spitting. I've come a long way in the last year, and I take responsibility for my actions. But I still hate that man's guts.

She drops her hands and scowls. "Jesus, you've become such a buzzkill."

I don't respond. I don't care enough to argue any more. "My lawyer sent you papers."

She's weaving her way toward the door. "I'm going to pretend he didn't," she says. "You'll change your mind."

"No, I won't." But she's already out the door.

THE SUN blazes hot in the morning sky, and I slip my sunglasses on as I ring the doorbell of the brick monstrosity. The yard is well tended, the gardens lush. Hell, the inside better be in great shape too, since I pay for it all.

Juliana opens the door with a smile that drops from her face the moment she sets her bright brown eyes on me. She's hardly the same woman who stumbled into my apartment this morning. "What are you doing here?"

"I'm here to see Zoe."

Her face turns icy, and she throws a worried glance over her shoulder. Looking for her little guard dog of a boyfriend, no doubt. But I checked to make sure Chad's car wasn't here before I came up to the door. That little protective order he has against me makes it tricky to see my kid.

"You know you aren't permitted—"

"Juliana—"

"No, Asher. Don't. You're the one who screwed up here."

"I don't—"

"Daddy?"

Zoe's standing at the bottom of the staircase, tugging on a pigtail.

The jagged edge of something broken snags my breath from my lungs. I drop to a knee and open my arms.

She gives me a tentative smile before scurrying toward me with a shriek of delight. She throws herself into my arms and clings to me and that jagged edge rips through me and tears away the rest of my numbness.

"Just look at your beautiful new house," I whisper. "I bet you haven't even seen the whole thing, it's so big!"

She giggles. "Have too!"

"I think it's a castle."

"Nuh-uh!" She puts her hands on her hips.

"Sure it is! A big house where a princess lives is a castle."

"It's not a castle, silly!"

"Zoe, why don't you go play in your room?" Juliana says.

"Do you wanna see it, Daddy?" Zoe asks, those milk-chocolate eyes widening.

I kiss her forehead. "Not today, sweetie."

"When do we get another special day?" my daughter asks, backing toward the stairs.

"Tomorrow after piano lessons. I'll pick you up."

She grins and hurries up the steps, taking half of my heart with her.

"Why do you do this?" Juliana demands.

I watch Zoe until she's out of sight then turn to Juliana. "Do what, exactly?"

She frowns and softens the edge in her voice. "Show up here when you know it's against the court order? Get your daughter excited about seeing you before it's your visitation time?"

"Because she's my daughter," I growl. I take a step back. My fists clench at my sides and I feel the old anger rising up in me. "I have a right to see her."

"You do. One week a month."

I take another step back and shake my head. "She's my daughter."

"What if Chad had been here?" She lifts her palms. "Asher..."

But I don't want to hear what she has to say, and I head to my car before I say something I'll regret.

chapter fourteen

Maggie

"I'M GONNA need another," I sing as our waitress comes by our table.

Hanna and Lizzy exchange a look.

"What about you two?" the waitress asks.

"We're fine," Lizzy says, eyeing my nearly empty glass.

"What?" I ask, leaning forward on the table. "Are we having a good time tonight or not?"

"Just take it easy, okay?" Hanna says.

The Friday night crowd is an odd mix of townies and college kids who stayed in town for a job or summer classes. I'm not even sure which category my sisters and I fit into. Are we townies because we grew up here or did we start to get lumped in with the pretentious assholes when we started at Sinclair?

"I'm not spending my Friday night holding your hair while you barf into Brady's toilet."

I roll my eyes. "Lightweights."

I talked my sisters into moving martini night to Brady's, where we're dancing instead of gossiping and drinking cheap margaritas instead of martinis. I almost canceled in favor of some vodka and solitude in my studio, but I thought better of it when I remembered how that ended last time.

I want to talk to them about Krystal and Will's breakup. I want to show them the pictures of Grace that came in the mail this week. I want to ask if they know why Asher wasn't pissed at me when he saw Will kissing me last week.

I want to talk to them like a normal girl talks to her sisters. Maybe, if I have one more drink, I can.

"Maggie," Lizzy calls, waving a hand in front of my face. "Don't leave us, girlie."

Hanna's frowning. "What's on your mind, Mags?"

I blink at her and smile. "I need to know how to seduce a rock star."

I've begun thirty-two text messages to him this week. Thirty-two times, I picked up my phone and pulled up his number. Thirty-two times I deleted the message before sending it.

I want to end whatever this is between us. Other than Will, Asher is the only one in New Hope who knows about my pregnancy. And then he saw me kiss Will and he didn't get pissed. I'm terrified of how much he knows about me, how much he *sees* when he looks at me.

But no matter how many times I tell myself that his disappearance from my life is for the best, every thought circles back to him.

Hanna and Lizzy are staring at me with wide eyes.

"What? Can you blame me?"

They exchange a look. "We just thought..." Hanna begins.

"...Based on the way you two *look* at each other," Lizzy says before Hanna chimes in with, "We assumed you already..."

"You know," Lizzy finishes.

"He won't," I whine.

"Well, there's been plenty of eye-fucking between you," Lizzy says. "We can attest to that."

I groan. "Lotta good that does me. But, hell, I probably

screwed up my chance when I abandoned him at Krystal and Will's housewarming. He hasn't called or anything."

Lizzy chokes on a sip of margarita, her eyes watering. "You left him there?"

"Why would you *leave* Asher Logan?" Hanna asks.

Lizzy scowls at me. "We are living vicariously through you right now. I cannot stress how important this is. Don't screw it up for us by acting like that."

"I panicked," I admit.

"About *what*, exactly?" Lizzy asks. "Because that man *wanted* you."

I think of Asher's penetrating gaze, his attempts to knock me off balance, the way he sees more than anyone else. I wave away the question. I don't know if I could explain *sober*, let alone now while words elude my grasp.

"Wait," Hanna says. "You said *he* hasn't called *you*? Have you tried to contact him?"

I cross my arms. "I thought he might be pissed."

"Yeah, and that's why you start with an apology." Lizzy snorts and extends her hand, palm up. "Give me your phone."

"No," I say, but Hanna is tossing something to Lizzy across the table. "Hey, give it back!"

"If you can't be trusted to do this right, then we'll do it for you." Her fingers are already flying across my screen, and as hard as I try, I can't scowl enough to stop her. "There," she says, handing my phone back.

I snatch it from her hand and open my texts to see what she's done.

I'm at Brady's. Wanna fuck?

Hanna peeks over my shoulder and bursts into laughter as my jaw drops.

"I thought you said I need to *apologize*?"

"Bet you it works," Lizzy says with a smirk.

"I could kill you," I mutter.

She grins. "You could text him again and let him know

your sister stole your phone or you could wait and see what he says. Either way, you're contacting him *and* dealing with the sex question. It's a win-win."

The murderous rage I'm feeling must be showing on my face because she hops out of the booth. "I love this song! Han-Han, let's dance!"

They scurry off to the space in front of the jukebox that we treat as our dance floor, and I'm left smiling despite myself.

The margaritas are catching up with me, and I can't ignore it much longer, so I head to the restroom. Krystal made sure her little sisters knew early on about the assholes who took advantage of girls' neglected drinks at parties and bars, so I'm sure to take mine with me.

I weave my way through bar patrons and back toward the dark hallway that holds the bathrooms.

"Hey, Lucy," a deep voice calls.

I ignore it at first, but the hand on my ass has me grabbing a wrist and spinning around.

A chill spreads over my skin and sweet and sour mix rolls in my stomach. I release his wrist and step back. "What do you want, Kenneth?"

"Nothing," he says, raking his eyes over me and making me feel exposed in my tank and jean skirt. "Not right now at least."

I curl my lip—"Not ever."—and turn toward the bathroom.

I take care of business, wash my hands, and then turn the water cold before splashing my face to cool it, to wash away the memories of being the fifteen-year-old girl the high school boys nicknamed "Lucy." When I close my eyes, I can still hear them calling out from their lockers, can still feel their knowing eyes on me as I walked down the hall. I can still remember my dad learning about it and telling me, *"You get the reputation you earn."*

When the shaking in my hands settles, I pour my drink down the drain. With assholes like Kenny around, the last thing I need is to be blurry-eyed by booze. Or *more* blurry-eyed, as the case may be.

Guys like Kenny made my high school years hell, and I'll be damned if I'm going to let them have that much control over me as an adult.

I exit the bathroom cautiously, worried Kenny might be waiting. But the hallway is empty and I have to laugh at myself when I see him leaning over the pool table. He's not a threat. And if he tries to touch me again, I'll just remind him what I do to the balls of men who grab my ass without permission.

It's a speech I save for special occasions, but it involves scissors, origami, and a staple gun, and it works like a charm.

The twins are dancing, and I almost want to sneak out, too afraid my mood will erase those beautiful smiles from their faces. I make my way to the dance floor anyway, and force a smile as I sway to the beat.

My eyes are closed when I feel someone press against me from behind. After my interaction with Kenny, I'm jumpy and I stiffen immediately.

"It's just me, gorgeous."

My shoulders relax at the familiar sound of Asher's deep voice, and I melt into him and the music, letting his arms wrap around my waist.

I turn in to face him and wrap my arms around his neck and his hands drop to my sides and tighten on my hips.

"Now isn't *that* something," Kenny calls from the pool table. He's looking us over and shaking his head. "Fucking rock star millionaire and he's sleeping with the easiest lay in town. You like 'em loose, Asher?"

Asher freezes and his body goes so stiff against me, I might as well be dancing with a piece of granite.

"Ignore him," I whisper. "He's nobody."

Asher brushes my hair back and presses a kiss to my forehead. "Be right back."

I wrap my fingers around his biceps and squeeze. "Please. Don't. For me."

His jaw is hard as he glares at Kenny across the bar.

"I gotta bounce," Kenny announces, pulling on his coat.

I tighten my hold on Asher's arm. He could escape me if he wanted. I know that. But I don't want him talking to Kenny. I don't want him giving Kenny the satisfaction of the fight he's itching for.

Asher's body is tense and he watches Kenny until he's out the door. Only then does he turn back to me and pull me into his arms.

I peer up at him through my lashes. "I'm sorry about that."

"It's not your fault." The words are ground out through clenched teeth, and his muscles are still tense under my fingers.

"My reputation comes from the choices I made. I'm responsible."

"No one deserves to be treated like that."

There's nothing I can say, so we dance together in silence until the tick in his jaw lets up and his rigid muscles soften.

When the song changes to something slower, he says, "I was a little surprised to get your text. I hope you haven't been looking for me. I've been out of town all week, just flew back in tonight."

"I thought you might be angry with me," I say softly.

"For abandoning me with your family, people I hardly know? What guy doesn't love that?"

I laugh. "Okay. It was pretty shitty of me."

"You're forgiven," he says, brushing my hair from my face.

"So, do you always come when summoned?" I grin. "Or are you finally going to sleep with me?"

His eyes drop to my mouth. "You only summon me when you're drunk."

"It was actually my sisters this time." I lean my head on his shoulder. "Are you going to use that as an excuse again? Because I'm actually not drunk at all. Just...well lubricated."

"You know that's not the only thing stopping me."

"You know too much about me," I whisper. "I don't blame you for not wanting me. You've seen too much of who I really am." Oh God, that sounds like such a pathetic plea for attention that I don't even have to wait till morning to hate myself for it.

He groans, tugging me against him until I can feel the hard

ridge of his erection against my belly. "Maggie." His mouth is at my ear, a rush of heat as he breathes my name. "Do you think I don't want the same thing you do?"

His voice is low, for my ears only, and it sends a wicked whip of pleasure through me.

"Do you think I don't close my eyes and remember exactly what it feels like to slide my hand between your legs? To feel you, wet and swollen for me?"

My breath catches on his words and my heart pounds. I have to avert my eyes. Looking at him while he says these things is too much, too intense.

"Do you think I haven't thought about what it's going to be like to spread your legs and taste you?"

My breath hisses out of me, and I look up to see his hot eyes watching me.

"I want to be inside you, Maggie. I want you in my arms and in my bed, and I'll have you there." He twirls a lock of hair in his fingers and tugs gently until I lift my chin and look into his eyes again.

I swallow. "What's stopping you?"

His eyes drift across the bar and I'm not surprised to see them land on Will. This is Will's favorite place. Is that why I keep coming here? Because I know he'll show up?

"You saw him kiss me," I say. "Why don't you hate me?"

The sway of Asher's hips stalls for two heartbeats before he resumes our dance as if I've said nothing.

"I kissed him. Didn't you see that? I was there with you and I kissed him."

"Why do you need me to be angry with you?" He trails his fingers down my sides, brushes his thumbs over my belly, his fingertips over the curve of my hip.

"You know things." I step back away from his touch to make sure he's hearing me. "You know things that no one else knows. That no one else *can* know. Do you understand that? You shouldn't want to be with me. You should want to be with someone…better."

"Fuck *should*. I want you." His hands are on me again and I feel like I'm walking along the edge of a steep precipice, like I might slip over the edge and lose control.

"I keep waiting for you to stop showing up," I say. "To give up on me."

"Do you want me to give up? Because I saw the way he was looking at you last week, Maggie. If you want him, he's yours."

I blink. Krystal had said the same thing, but they don't understand that it's not that simple. "And what if I want you?" I ask softly.

"I'm here, aren't I?"

"You are. You keep coming back. For what? What is this between us?"

He slides a hand into my hair and leads me to lean into him again. "It's whatever you want it to be, gorgeous. With one exception."

"What's that?"

"It's not just sex. *That's* why I won't sleep with you. I won't *let* this be just sex."

That makes me smile. "Why me, Asher? I'm just some small-town slut with too much baggage. You could have anyone." I can feel his heart beating against my cheek and its steady pace increases at my question. "Why me?"

"Sweetheart, when you know the answer to that question, we won't be talking anymore."

I pull back and blink at him. "You'll be gone?"

His lips quirk. "I'll be inside you."

Asher

Maggie feels so amazing in my arms. I don't want to let her go, even if we are dancing in the middle of a rundown bar. I bury my nose in her hair and inhale deeply. She has me so addicted to her scent, I'm surprised I haven't tracked down her shampoo for a daily hit.

"We're getting another round," Lizzy calls from the bar. "You need one, Mags?"

Maggie cuts her eyes to me before shaking her head.

"You don't have to stop drinking for me," I say softly.

"I know. But it's okay. I'm done."

"What about you, Asher?" Lizzy asks.

"I've got everything I need right here," I call back, tightening my arms around Maggie.

"Want to sit?" Maggie asks.

I nod and follow her to a booth. She grins when I slide into the same side with her, thighs touching.

When I wrap an arm around her, she settles into me, and I see her ex watching us from across the bar. For the first time, though, Maggie doesn't seem to notice or care.

"Why don't you drink?" she asks, peering up through her lashes. "If you don't mind me asking."

"It's a condition of my probation."

She inhales sharply.

"What, like it's a secret?"

"I…" She licks her lips. "I didn't think you'd want to talk about it."

"My past is ugly, and I'm not proud of it, but it's part of who I am. It made me who I am. I'm not hiding from it."

She ducks out from under my arm and wraps her arms around herself. "No one's asking you to."

I squeeze my eyes shut. "I'm doing a fine job of fucking up an otherwise perfect night, aren't I?" I open my eyes again when I feel her fingers on mine.

"I won't judge you for your mistakes, Asher. I'm the last person who would do that."

I intertwine my fingers with hers and squeeze her hand. My heart knots painfully in my chest with something I can't name. "I did it," I say. "I'm not some innocent dude being punished for a crime he didn't commit. I did it."

"Were you drunk?"

"Yes. Drunk. High." The silence grows heavy between us as I let the ugliness rise up. I examine it with such detachment now. "You've read the reports, I'm sure. I was drunk and out for blood."

"I haven't read them." She shrugs. "I don't care to. You aren't that guy, Asher."

Her confidence shakes me, and I have to swallow back this feeling in my throat I know she wouldn't like.

"So, probation? What does that mean?"

"For me it meant anger management classes, and weekly drug and alcohol screening." And a protective order that keeps me from seeing my daughter any time I want.

She blinks. "Wow. That sucks."

I lift a shoulder. "It beats the alternative."

"Which was what?"

"A year in prison for aggravated battery."

"A year?" she says softly. "But you definitely don't have to serve time, right?"

I shrug. "Assuming I can stay on the right side of the law for another month, sure." I force a smile. "But that's why I'm in New Hope and not at my house in the city. Easy enough to stay out of trouble here."

She snorts. "Depends who you talk to."

I squeeze her hand.

"What happens if you get in trouble with the law while you're on probation?"

I take a breath. "I have to serve my year sentence." And worse, I'd miss a whole year with my daughter.

She's silent the entire drive home. I pull into the driveway of her rental and shut off the ignition.

I want to stay with her tonight. I want to kiss away the memory of Will and any other man who hurt her. I want to take her slowly and softly in her bed. I want to hold her, because—whether she'll admit it or not—that's what she needs.

She's looking out her window, not at me, and the soft tension of unspoken secrets hisses like steam in the silence.

"I have a daughter," I say into the darkness. "She's four years old, and smart and amazing, and because her mother is living with the man I assaulted, I can only see her during my one week of visitation a month."

"A daughter?"

"That's why I wasn't around this week," I explain. "I flew to New York for my week with her."

"I had no idea."

I swallow, not entirely sure why I'm sharing all of this. "I want primary custody, but my lawyer said going after that while I'm on probation is asking to lose. So I'm waiting, but she's my world."

She's still not looking at me, but if my having a child scares her away, so be it. Zoe has to come first.

"You're not the only one who's made mistakes. I have too. But I believe we're more than the sum of our mistakes. I didn't used to. I thought I was a piece of shit. I thought I was nothing." I take her hand and lightly brush my thumb over the gauze wrapping her wrist. "I used to drink to feel numb, but then I sobered up and a different kind of numbness followed. It was Zoe who made me feel again, and who made me believe I was more than the sum of my mistakes."

"You're lucky." Her voice shakes. I wonder if she's cried since that day at the river. I wonder if this might be the moment she breaks. What does it say about me that I want her to? I want her to break so I can find her in the pieces, just like she does with her mosaics.

She laughs but it sounds crazed, maniacal, but then she looks out the window and whispers, "Oh, my gosh," and there's a smile in her voice.

The streetlight slants in the window, giving me just enough light to make out her changing expression.

"What is it?"

"That's Krystal's car." She slumps down in her seat, and the light catches on her earring, making it flash in the darkness.

I follow her gaze to the red Mini Cooper parked down the block. "Is she visiting you?"

"Not me," Maggie breathes. "That's Tyler's house."

"Who's Tyler?"

Maggie chews on her lip, masking her smile. "Tyler was her first love."

Krystal steps onto the softly lit porch, dressed in a tank and shorts that show off her long legs. She's quickly joined by a tall man in a dark t-shirt and jeans.

We watch as Tyler cups her jaw in his hands and kisses her softly.

She follows him in the door, and my chest is heavy with the implication of it.

"What will you do?" I ask.

Pulling her eyes from the illuminated scene, she turns to me. "What do you mean?"

"Will you tell him?"

She straightens. "Will and Krystal broke up the night of the housewarming. There's nothing to tell."

Will isn't engaged to her sister anymore, and she's here with me? "They broke up? For good?"

"Yes."

"And you're not with him?"

"No."

I lean across the seat and pull her against me, kissing her hard and hungry, because if she wanted her ex-fiancé back, she could have him. I slip my tongue between her lips and she opens to me, sliding her hands into my hair and kissing me back. Her lips are soft and her tongue hot, and I want so much more.

When we finally separate we're both breathing hard and the porch down the road is dark.

We get out of the car and hold hands as I walk her to the door.

"You want to come in?" she asks, and the need in her eyes is more than a physical reaction.

I brush my lips across hers. "Go let Lucy out. You're coming with me tonight."

chapter fifteen

Maggie

"Do you take all your girls here?" I ask Asher. But the humor fizzles out of my voice when I see him spread a blanket on the grass.

He brought me to his house and led me through the backyard and down to the river.

With most men, this wouldn't make me uncomfortable because knowing what they wanted, knowing where it was going, would give me a sense of control. Not with Asher. "I don't know what you want from me."

"I want you"—he tilts my chin toward the sky—"to look at these stars."

So I do. I turn and lean into his chest and look at the New Hope stars. The bright ones. The ones that are so faint they look more like a hint of light than a dedication to it. I find the big dipper. The little dipper. I listen to the soft rushing of the water and feel my shoulders relax and my breathing slow.

The silence stirs between us for a long time, intense with what hasn't been said, heavy with what I know I can't say. I wish to be someone else, a woman with an untainted past, a woman who could whisper secrets about her life with no real shame.

Finally, Asher speaks. "I'm not asking anything from you, Maggie. I'm a patient man. I know you've been hurt and don't feel like you have much to give."

And there it is again. That ache. That burn to explain. And maybe I would. If this were a different world or I were a different person. If I weren't so very afraid of what it might mean to trust him with the most fragile pieces of myself.

"Normally, I back off when I start to feel something for a woman. But the thing is"—he whispers now—"it's too late. I've already fallen for you."

My eyes fill with hot tears, and I duck his embrace and put space between us. I tell myself I'm not running away. I'm giving myself some much deserved space from a man who wants more from me than I can give.

I step closer to the river and slip off my shoes. Calm rushes through me at the slight give of the earth beneath my feet. The air is heavy with the smell of river. The scent of fresh water mixes with mildew and slowly decomposing earth. I love the smell, love the promise of it. That everything, no matter what its beginnings, has a purpose and will break down and become a part of something new. A tree limb will become part of the riverbed; a frog will become part of the rich soil that will nourish a baby tree until it grows into a great oak.

I sense Asher before I hear him. His fingers slip into mine before I acknowledge him. His big, solid hand warms my smaller one. I have to fight the temptation to pour all of my troubles out to him, to share my worries with this man.

I pull my hand away.

"I don't want to scare you away," he says. "But I'm not the kind of guy who keeps quiet when he feels something. Not anymore." His voice is soft, soothing. A balm to my frayed nerves.

"I'm just not there, Asher. I don't fall in love that easily." *And you don't want the likes of me loving you.*

"Not since Will?"

I don't know how to answer that.

"So many secrets." He sighs heavily. "Love isn't a bartering tool. I just wanted to tell you. I don't expect anything in return. Nothing at all."

I lean against him in the darkness and wrap my arms around his waist. "I didn't say I can't give you anything," I say, pressing my mouth against his chest, kissing my way down.

He draws in a breath. "The girl may be stingy with her love, but she's free with her sexual favors."

I freeze at his words, and he stiffens, seeming to register what he said.

"I'm sorry, Maggie, that was uncalled for."

A sharp stab of pain—of shame—darts through me.

I look out over the water. "Maybe. But it's true. But maybe I'm cheap. Easy."

"Maggie—"

"Don't. Don't say it's not true. Don't rewrite history to make me feel better about myself."

His hand settles on my shoulder. "You give your body freely. That may be true. And you may do your damnedest to keep that heart hidden from the rest of the world. But it's not cold. You've got a great big heart, Maggie. So big that it peeks out from that place where you try to hide it."

A hot tear streaks down my cheek. "How can you believe that?"

He pulls me into his arms, presses my cheek into his chest. "Because I've seen it."

I run my thumb along the faint stubble covering his jaw, and he stares at me, like he's waiting for me to say something, like he needs me to say something. I lift onto my tiptoes and press my lips to his.

The contact is brief but electric. Does he know how badly I want to let him love me? How badly I wish I could love him in return? Once I believed myself incapable of loving. I thought it my sacrifice, the payment for my sins. But I feel it inside me—transformation. Something that was once so hard bending into something pliable. Something that, like the sandy earth beneath my feet, is flexible, can give a little.

Nervous with possibility, I shiver.

"Do you want to go inside?" he asks, running his hands over my bare arms. "Are you cold?"

I'm perfect. The Indiana heat dances in the night air. I let my cheek find his chest again. "Can we stay for a while?"

"Absolutely." Then he dips to take my mouth, and this time we linger.

His touch is soft, gentle. He runs his tongue along my lips, and I open under him. He tastes me, moves into my mouth, slants over me. His hands settle on my back, pressing our bodies closer. I feel utterly cherished.

When he breaks the kiss, a small cry slips from my lips. The river rushes by, the crickets sing, occasionally the hoot of an owl joins the melody, and Asher kisses my neck like he was born to do it.

I lace my fingers through his hair and lead him back up until his mouth meets mine again.

Dear God, this man tastes good. Like the warmth he puts in my belly and the spice he inspires lower. And he kisses like a god. His thumbs caress the small of my back until my head spins and my knees weaken.

He pulls away and takes my hand. Wordlessly, he leads me to the blanket and pulls his shirt off over his head.

"What are you—"

Before I can finish, he turns to me and removes my shirt, unbuttons my skirt and slips it from my hips.

I reach for the button on his pants, but he stops my hands, lifting them to the sides as he admires my body in the faint light of the quarter moon. The smartass comment dies on my lips, and I let myself enjoy his admiration. Unclasping my bra, I let it fall away.

His breath rushes out of him, but instead of the cheap thrill of sexual power, more of that insane liquid warmth fills my belly.

His thumb brushes across a hardened nipple before he peels

away my panties.

He drops to his knees in front of me and finds me with his fingers, rubbing my clit and making me rock unsteadily on my feet.

He replaces his hand with his mouth. The wet flick of his tongue, light at first, then firmer, more insistent. A moan escapes my lips, mingles with the owl calls, and dissipates in the thick, humid air. When I think my knees can no longer hold me up, Asher scoops me into his arms and pulls my naked body against his bare chest.

At another time, in another place, I might have mocked him for this old-fashioned gesture, but right now—as he slowly lowers me onto the blanket, and I can feel the dampness of the earth seep through it—it's perfect. It's exactly what I need.

He discards his shoes and pants, never taking his eyes from me. Never ceasing his exploration of my body with his gaze, he rolls on a condom.

When he lowers onto me, I welcome his weight. I spread my legs so he can settle between them. Eyes locked with mine, he slides into me, and the air leaves my lungs as he fills me. Pleasure stretches its long fingers through me—strokes, caresses, awakens my hardened heart in the hot palm of its hand.

We find our rhythm like that. Asher, never taking his eyes from mine as he moves with me under the light of the waxing moon. Me, flooded with emotion spilling from my newly wakened heart.

Because I'm not a virgin. But this is all new to me. Here. With Asher in the moonlight, rough and hungry and dangerous. Exposed. This is making love.

Asher's fingers thread through my hair, and he pulls my body against his. We've moved into his bed, and we're tangled in his silky satin sheets, tangled in each other.

"I've never been any good at this part," I whisper.

Asher releases a contented sigh. He doesn't share my aversion to post-coital snuggling. "What part?"

"Cuddling. Pillow talk."

"There's nothing to be good at, Maggie," Asher whispers, nestling his nose in the crook of my neck. "Nothing to do. Just be."

I've never felt as exposed during sex as I felt tonight, and yet I'm finding myself less afraid to share in the aftermath. Less afraid the man I just gave myself to might really see me. Usually, I find myself lying there in awkward silence mentally battling the words of my father's ghost.

Whore. Slut. Loose woman.

That's slow coming tonight, but I'm waiting for it.

I inhale. Exhale. Repeat. My muscles relax incrementally. Asher's arm wraps around my waist and I feel his breath against my ear, feel his chest rise and fall against my back. I melt a little.

"I have you," he murmurs. "You're safe with me."

"Of course, I—"

"You don't need to pretend to be strong with me, Maggie. Just *be.*"

I close my eyes and brace myself to fail at this simple task.

Asher's knuckles brush over my belly.

My father's voice isn't here, condemning me. Nothing echoes in my ears. No images of blood-stained hands flit behind my eyes. No memories of my baby being taken from my arms in a suspended moment that feels like I'm being robbed of my soul.

I'm right here with the steady rhythm of Asher's breath and the soft brush of his fingers against my skin.

"You're good to me, and that scares me. I don't deserve you."

"You deserve better," he growls.

I'm surprised to realize how much I like this. How good it feels to have the warmth of his body against mine, his breath against my neck.

His arm tightens around me. "Why do you call yourself a slut?"

"Because I am," I say softly.

He doesn't reply, and his silence is a challenge I can't refuse. Not with this man.

So I explain. "You can only swallow ugly words about yourself so many times before they become part of your DNA. Some girls are told they're important, so it becomes part of them. Some are told they're talented or ugly or fat or special. It's a self-fulfilling prophecy. Me? I'm a slut."

"Tell me who made you believe that."

The room is quiet, save for the whir of the air conditioner and the soft slide of skin against satin sheets. I feel safe here, and for a minute I wonder how my life would have been different if tonight with Asher *had* been my first time.

"I started sleeping with my father's best friend when I was fifteen."

As if I flipped a switch, Asher stiffens against me. "What?"

I find his hand with mine and thread my fingers through his. "Dad was strict with all of us. About the way we dressed, about the music we listened to. The only difference was that I disregarded his rules. I liked tight jeans and low-cut tops. I liked *boys*."

Dad's voice is in my head again, so I focus on the heat of Asher's skin, the feel of his fingers in my hair. "I know now what I didn't understand then. That first time…" I draw in a ragged breath, exhale slowly. Asher's fingers comb my hair. "I didn't understand what was happening. Not really. I mean, I liked this guy, trusted him. Everyone did. He was the county sheriff and a family friend. He was my father's best friend. And I liked him so much that I would find excuses to go to his house. It wasn't all that uncommon for me to hang out over there, and his wife was gone a lot. She's a lawyer, and she was ambitious and worked all the time. Then one day we were watching a movie and he poured me a glass of sweet wine. I drank and we watched. I remember we were laughing about something, and suddenly he was doing things and whispering things, and I knew it was wrong but I also knew he was…in charge? And when it was over, I cried. I cried so hard I made myself throw up."

"Maggie." Asher's fingers curl into my waist but he doesn't pull away. Outside of a psychologist's office, I've never told anyone this story. I've never wanted to. Who would want to be involved with someone as broken as me?

"He was so mad at me. Why was I crying? I was acting like a child and he was sorry he'd made the mistake of treating me like a *woman* when I was going to act like no more than a girl. I was the one who kept coming around in tight jeans and low-cut tops. I was the one who flirted with him. I'd *wanted* it."

"Fucking. Bastard." Asher sits up in bed and pulls me against his chest. I lean into him, soothed by the searing heat of his anger.

"I knew he was manipulating me. Partly. But he was also partly right."

"No."

I shake my head against his chest. "He wasn't lying, you know? I liked him. I liked the way he looked at me. It made me feel… special. I knew what outfits he liked—he told me—and I'd wear them when I'd be around him. I *did* flirt with him. But I was just a kid and when he told me that wanting that attention meant I was asking for sex—meant that I *owed* him sex—I believed him." I have to stop. I have to breathe and remember that it's over. Remember that Toby is gone.

Asher doesn't push me. He holds me and waits.

"I knew he'd forced me to have sex. I knew I told him no. But I didn't understand it as rape. Not then. Not when this was a man I'd never been afraid of. It wasn't rape, it was me being a stupid girl."

"Did you tell your parents?"

"I was terrified of them finding out. Terrified what they'd think of me." I shake my head. "Considering I'd driven him to do it, I didn't know how to tell them. "

"You didn't drive him to do anything. He was a grown man in control of his own actions."

Hearing those words feels so good.

For years, I have told myself I knew what was right and wrong. I didn't need anyone's platitudes. But that was a lie. I need this. I need to tell Asher. "The next time—when he said he needed me, when he said it was our secret, when he said I made him lose his mind and he couldn't help himself—I cried the whole time. I just lay there with my hands fisted in the blankets and I thought—if I can just let him do this to me, if I can just pretend it's okay and make sure no one finds out, everything will be all right." I take in a shaky breath. "I've always been lonely. I don't fit in with my family, and I was afraid of losing this man who had become a friend."

Asher is holding me so tightly it almost hurts, but it's the good kind of hurt. It's a pain that reminds me I'm alive and I'm *worth* something.

"It went on for a few months before my dad caught us. I would find excuses not to go over there. Toby would find excuses for us to be together. When my dad caught us, for a minute I thought everything would be okay. I was *relieved*. My daddy was strict as hell but he loved me, and I thought he was going to make everything okay."

"But he didn't."

This is the part that hurts the most, and I close my eyes against the pain and concentrate on the rise and fall of Asher's chest. "Dad wanted to believe it was my fault. He needed to believe it. He needed to believe his little girl hadn't been raped, needed to believe his best friend wouldn't do that. So he told himself Toby's story was true. I'd taunted him. I'd begged for it. I'd seduced him. Everyone in town loved Toby. He could have had his pick of grown women, so who would believe that he'd force himself on a fifteen-year-old?"

I stop the flow of words tumbling from my lips to take a breath, to focus on the here, the now, the feel of Asher's arms before I continue. "Somehow the story got out. His wife left him and he left town, and everyone thought it was my fault."

"You were fifteen." When Asher says it, it sounds so simple. There's no way he can understand how much I need his faith in me. Even six years later.

Again I find myself wishing I could send him back in time to my teenage self. She needed him even more.

"My dad died later that year." I hate this part—discussing how my mistakes destroyed my father and my family. "He had a heart attack and died. The stress of it all…it was just too much for him. Will was the only one willing to speak up and stand up for me, but he was at college. For months after we buried my dad, my mom couldn't look me in the eye."

He brushes my hair from my face and presses a kiss to my forehead. "It wasn't your fault, Maggie."

"I know that," I whisper.

He slides a lock of my hair between his fingers. "Do you?"

"I'm not a kid anymore," I object. "Of course I know…" I trail off because he's not some therapist I have to convince, and he deserves more from me than the same bullshit I've been shoveling all my life. "I told you I'm fucked up, Asher."

"You're beautiful," he whispers.

"That's superficial. It's meaningless."

"Sometimes. But your beauty? It's the kind that radiates from your heart, Maggie, and it's so damn bright it shines beyond these walls you've erected to protect yourself."

I think of Will's words. *"If you're broken, I'll fix you."* Will didn't even know the whole truth when he made that promise, but he believed I needed fixing. "If I'm not a slut, I don't even know who I am."

Asher rolls me onto my back until his body is over mine, my face framed in his hands. "Don't be afraid to break, Maggie. Stop holding on to the ugliness just to stay whole."

Hot tears slip from the corners of my eyes and roll into my ears. "What if no one can fix me?"

"You don't need fixing." He gives a sad smile and wipes a tear away with his thumb. "It's like your mosaics. The beauty is already there, you just find it. Let go, sweetheart."

"I'm afraid I'll shatter."

He lifts my hand to his lips and kisses along the line of the stitches running down my palm. "If you shatter, I'll find you."

My eyes fill at his words, but he doesn't try to stop it. He doesn't ask me not to cry, he gives me permission to. He lies beside me, pulls me against his bare chest, until I'm baptized by silent tears.

chapter sixteen

Maggie

I WAKE up to an empty bed and the soft sounds of an acoustic guitar.

Asher's bedroom is gorgeous in the morning light. One wall is almost entirely windows looking out onto the backyard and the river beyond, not to mention the beauty within the room. It's sparsely furnished with a walnut king-size bed, end tables, and armoire, and the ceilings are vaulted, adding to the spacious and airy quality, as if it's an extension of the outdoor space.

I pull one of his t-shirts over my head and pad down the hall, toward the sound of the soft notes and low murmurs of song.

I find him with his guitar on the other side of the house, watching his fingers as he thrums the strings and sings softly under his breath. I can't make out the words, but I know they're beautiful because Asher made them.

I don't let him know I'm here at first. He's gorgeous like this. In jeans, his feet and chest bare, the guitar cradled in his arms so natural it looks more like a piece of him than an instrument.

As if sensing me, he lifts his head and smiles. "Hey, gorgeous.

I hope I didn't wake you." He sets the guitar down beside him and stands.

"Don't stop for me." I bite my lip. "I was enjoying watching you."

He shrugs, looking a little self-conscious for the first time since I met him. "It's new, and I'm not ready to share yet. How'd you sleep?"

I grin. "So well. I don't think I've slept that well since I was five."

"Good." He pulls me against him, trapping my arms between our bodies. "Then maybe I can talk you into sleeping here again."

I hum, considering. "Maybe…"

"Can I feed you? I'm not the best cook, but my housekeeper keeps the freezer stocked with some pretty delicious choices and I know how to work the microwave."

"Tempting, but I have to be at the gallery in a little under an hour. We need to finish staging and inventory before the grand opening."

He brushes his mouth against my neck, no doubt leaving beard burn behind.

"How's that going, anyway?" he asks.

I moan, much less interested in talking about the gallery than I am in letting his lips continue their exploration. "It's going fine."

The heat of his mouth leaves my neck, and I open my eyes to find him staring at me.

"What?"

"He kissed you the other night."

I swallow, shifting back half a step. "I've mentioned that."

"Do you want him to do it again?"

I take another step back. I don't want to have this conversation. "Things are over between me and Will."

"You're not answering my question."

I open my mouth to shoot back a smart retort but I can't find one. "Are you seriously jealous?"

Before I can blink, he has me pressed against the wall and his mouth is on mine, rough and possessive. Hands driving into my hair, he shifts me until his leg is between my thighs.

I open under him, wanting his kiss and touch as much as I want to escape our conversation. More. He wraps my hair in his fist and tugs lightly until I open further, press deeper into the kiss.

When I am breathing hard and my legs are shaking, he releases me. I have to lean against the wall for support while I catch my breath.

"What was that?" I ask, chest heaving, my body protesting that there *must* be more where that came from.

"Just a little something to remember me." He winks and walks out of the room. Then, when he's halfway down the hall, he calls, "Tell Will I said hi."

William

SHE'S HUMMING under her breath and smiling while she takes notes in the inventory binder. She's wearing little black pants that stop just below her knees and a flowy tank top. She'd look almost innocent in that outfit if her ponytail didn't show the beard burn on her neck.

I haven't seen her this happy since last spring when I kissed her for the first time, and just the memory of that kiss is enough to make me hard.

"I think it's really coming together," she says, smiling up at me.

I blink at her, too busy thinking about how she got those marks at her neck. For a minute, I don't know what she's talking about. "Oh, the gallery?"

"The gallery." She frowns, studying me. "Are you okay?" She drops the binder on the desk. "How are you holding up?"

I stare at her for a beat. I don't know if she really expects me to answer or if the question is a courtesy. "I'm okay. It sucks, but it'll pass."

I wait for her to ask if I ended it for her, but she doesn't.

I guess we both know I did. At this point, the only question is if Maggie wanted me to.

"I pulled some strings in the department," I say cautiously. "I found a way to get your scholarship back."

Her jaw drops. "Really?"

"You know how I was trying to get you to switch to art education? If you change your major now, you could apply for this art education scholarship that's only available for established students."

The smile falls from her face. "I don't want to do art education."

"I know, you're MFA all the way, but think about the future, Mags."

"I am thinking about the future. I have no desire to spend the rest of my life in a high school."

"You'd be great. Stop letting that old story define you. Everyone else has moved on. It's your turn now."

She takes a step back, her green eyes hard. "Fuck. You. Those were the worst years of my life."

I set my jaw. "So, what? You're going to tinker with glass for a living? Find many job listings for that?"

"Fuck off," she growls. "I know you did the sensible business degree before your MFA, but I'm not you, and I didn't ask for your input."

"I'm trying to help."

"You're trying to fix me," she spits. "You know what? Some people don't think I'm broken."

"Who? Asher? Right, because he's one to judge how fucked up someone's life is."

"Don't act like you know him. You don't."

I laugh. "Oh, and you do? Come on, Maggie. How well can you really know him? What do you know about him? You know his family? Or his plans for the next ten years? Did he tell you what happened with the guy he beat to a pulp?"

"He doesn't have to tell me that."

My lip curls in disgust. "I bet he's found time to fuck you though."

When I register the hot sting of her hand connecting with my cheek, I'm glad. Because I deserve it.

Maggie

MY HAND shakes as I raise it to knock on Ethan Bauer's studio door. I haven't stopped shaking since I left Will and his nasty implications about my relationship with Asher, and to add insult to injury, now I have to talk to Ethan.

I want to pretend that coming here is no big deal, but I have too many memories in this studio. Too many mistakes. I don't want to be reminded how stupid I was to believe the things he told me, how naïve I'd been to hope.

Yet that hope is peeking into my consciousness again lately. When Asher lies beside me. When he touches me.

Is Will right? Am I being naïve?

I stomp down the thought and knock. Without waiting for him to invite me, I open it.

Oh, no.

A young girl's in front of the window, a red satin sheet wrapped around her, her dark hair swept up off her neck, her bare shoulders exposed.

"Maggie?" Ethan calmly puts his brush down.

The girl turns, eyes wide, as if she's been caught doing something much more scandalous than posing for the artist.

I understand. Posing for Ethan Bauer is much more erotic than the touch of most men.

"Ethan," I say. God, I want to be out of here, and soon. "We need to talk." No need to waste time on pleasantries.

"Um, I—" the girl cuts herself off with a quick shake of her head and reaches for her clothes. "I'll give you two some privacy."

I have things to say to Ethan that I don't intend on sharing with anyone else. On the other hand, I don't want to be alone with him. "Stay. I won't be long."

Ethan wipes his hands on the damp towel that hangs from his easel and the smell of paint thinner stings my nose. Red smudges disappear from his hands and stain the towel. Images blip through my mind. My hands covered in paint—the reds and yellows of tulips—and running over his bare chest. Then another blip of my hands covered in red. But blood, not paint.

I push back the unwelcome images and walk to the window where the model had been posing. It has a great view of the wooded ridge that runs along this part of the riverbank—the very best view of any studio at Sinclair.

Only the best for the great Ethan Bauer.

Aspiring artists from all over the country come to Sinclair for the opportunity to paint with Ethan. Some of them probably even make it through without sleeping with him.

The girl sits on the couch, looking uncomfortable as hell in her red sheet.

"What can I do for you Maggie?" Ethan asks. Those blue eyes, usually so hot, so intense, are cold.

"I need to know what you did with the Discovery collection." That's what he had called the paintings of me. And I'd been so flattered.

His eyes narrow. "It's not about you, Maggie. You can't decide you're going to keep art from the world because you're feeling self-conscious. It's not about you. It's art."

God save me from artistic egos. "Are you showing the collection at Will and Krystal's gallery?"

"It doesn't concern you."

Worry, dread, and horror fight for control over my more

sensitive organs. "Where are they?"

The girl stands and scrambles for her clothes. "Maybe I should go."

I shoot her a look over my shoulder. "You need to hear this. Someday you'll be the one wishing you could hide the evidence of your affair with him."

Her cheeks blaze.

A month ago, I would never have said that. But after Will threw it in my face, the pretense seems almost ridiculous.

"Let me take you to dinner," Ethan says. "We'll talk. I want to know what projects you've been working on."

"I'll pass." I back out of the office, glaring at him as I go.

If he won't tell me where the Discovery collection is, I'll find out for myself.

Asher

MAGGIE POPS another grape in her mouth before taking another sip of champagne. She's sitting on the solid walnut monstrosity that is my dining room table, her soft thighs showing beneath the hem of an old Infinite Gray t-shirt. For years, I've thought this space—with its ostentatious chandelier and heavy furniture—a waste, but sitting at the table with Maggie propped before me, I don't think there's a single spot in this house I like more.

"Your house is amazing," she says.

I raise a brow. "What? You didn't let yourself in when you helped yourself to my pool?"

She smacks me across the chest and grins. "Totally different. The pool is outside."

"But the sauna is in the basement," I say, gently parting her legs and positioning myself between them.

"Sauna?" She wriggles forward and wraps her legs around my waist. "How did I miss that?"

I am making myself hold back. I was almost surprised when she showed up at my door tonight, and I gave her the grand tour since we never got around to that last night. As we went from room to room, she was throwing come-hither looks over her shoulder, but I've held back because she's more than that to me, and I won't be like the men who have made her think that's all she has to offer.

So I break a slice of Havarti and pretend I'm not about to lose my mind when she uses tongue and teeth to take it from my fingers. "I think you were too distracted by the Cezanne outside the wine cellar to notice the sauna."

"Oh, I was distracted all right." She locks her feet together behind my back and pulls me closer. "But the painting was only part of the equation."

I offer her a grape this time, and her mouth is hot on my fingers as she takes it with her tongue.

"You like feeding me, don't you?"

"Among other things."

"You have a good eye for art," she says, and I know it's a compliment, considering the source. "Would you be interested in driving up to Chicago with me tomorrow? I need to check out a gallery up there."

I brush my lips over hers. "I'd love that."

She takes another sip of her champagne then frowns at her glass. "You don't drink, but it's not just because of the probation."

"Is that a question?"

She sets her glass on the counter and wraps her arms around my neck. "An observation."

"Do you want to ask a question?"

"Are you an alcoholic?"

I used to deny the label, but I've made my peace with it. The difference a year makes. "Yes."

She runs her thumb along my two-day growth of beard. "Then why do you keep alcohol in your house?"

"Because I won't let it have that kind of power over me."

"But it did before."

"Yes."

"What happened with the guy you assaulted? What did he do?"

I tense. "I told you, I was loaded."

She narrows her eyes. "There was a reason. He did something."

I can feel the hardness in my own jaw from thinking about Chad. "He was sleeping with Juliana. I found out and didn't handle it well."

"Juliana?" she asks softly.

I open my mouth and hesitate before answering. "Zoe's mom."

Her fingers wrap around my forearm and squeeze. "Does it bother you when I drink?"

"No," I say, but she must see something in my eyes because she pulls back.

She drops her legs from my waist and settles her hands on the edge of the table. "It does bother you."

"It bothers me when you get drunk, not when you have *a drink*."

She swallows and shifts her eyes to the abstract painting that covers the side wall. "Do you want me to stop?"

I stand and take her jaw in my hand, turning her to face me. Her big green eyes are rimmed with tears. "I'm not trying to change you, Maggie. I'm trying to love you."

She grabs a handful of my shirt and tugs me close. "Kiss me."

I want to kiss her. Taste her. Cherish her. When she told me about her past last night, it explained so much, and my chest still aches with hurt for her.

"This is more than sex, isn't it, Asher?" she asks softly.

"How can you ask that?" I run my thumb along the edge of her jaw. "I told you last night. I'm in love with you."

Her chest rises with her shaky inhale.

"Do you believe me?"

"I do."

I lower my mouth to hers, and I'm so damn hungry for this,

my hands are on her before I even decide to let this be more than a kiss. I curl my fingers into her ass and draw her against me. I run my lips and tongue and teeth along her neck, and her fingers curl into my hair.

She's so sweet and I could taste her for hours. I want to take her to my bed and keep her there. I test her reaction to my fingers, my mouth, my tongue and my teeth. Lifting her arms, I pull off the t-shirt she donned when we toured through my bedroom. I slip it over her head and toss it across the table.

Her nipples are hard and taut in the cool air.

"You are so fucking perfect," I murmur, trailing my fingertips between her breasts and over her belly.

"Hardly," she whispers, voice weak.

As I lower myself, my mouth follows the path of my fingers, and I circle her navel with my tongue. Tiny silvery scars snake out from here. As I taste each one, she tenses under me.

"Stretch marks," she says softly, dropping her hands to disguise them. "Not so perfect."

I move her hands. "Perfect." And I kiss her there again, mouth, tongue, teeth. When I scrape my teeth across the ridge of her hipbone, she cries out and her moan echoes off the walls.

"I fucking love that I can do that to you." My breathing is choppy, my voice weak.

Her reaction at the other hip is just as gratifying.

Then I slide my hand between her legs and she's so damn wet, my cock jumps in anticipation. I slide her hips forward until she leans back on her elbows.

"I need you," I growl, unbuttoning my jeans.

"I'm yours."

chapter seventeen

Maggie

HE STROKES his thumb down my neck and back up, and it's the innocence of the gesture that makes it so erotic. "You're so blasé about sex, so matter-of-fact, but it's an act. You hide behind blowjobs and hot, frantic fucking."

"There's nothing wrong with those things."

His lips quirk. "Agreed." He lowers his mouth to mine and his lips are so close.

I want him to kiss me. I need him to kiss me. I need him to need me. To use me.

His fingers skim up my arms, sending delicious chills through me before they skim down my body and settle on my hips. "Let me touch you," he whispers. "Let me break down these walls you keep hiding behind."

He's so close, leaning over me, his mouth above mine, but I'm pretty sure I'm shaking. How does he see me when no one else has? How does he know?

When he kisses me, his lips aren't gentle. His mouth is hard and hot and demanding over mine. His tongue invades and his teeth scrape my lips. This isn't a kiss, this is a claiming. And it terrifies and exhilarates me.

His hands squeeze roughly at my ass as he settles me on the edge of the table, his mouth still on mine. The cool air is almost painful against my heated skin, but it's a good kind of pain. I'm feeling. I'm present. I'm alive.

I reach for him, my hand trailing down the hard planes of his chest and below, but he clasps my wrist before I can take him in my hand.

"Let *me*," he growls, trapping my hands under his.

His mouth trails down my neck and between my breasts. He presses his tongue to my navel and licks a trail back up to the pulse at the hollow of my neck. I am exposed and arousal pools between my legs, winds tight and achy and wonderful there.

When I lean my head back and close my eyes, I feel his breath at my ear. "Open them. Watch me."

So I do. He dips his mouth to one breast and then the other, drawing my nipples impossibly tight. Then he sinks lower and opens his mouth against my belly. He hooks his hands behind my knees, the muscles in his shoulders bunching as he lifts them, bending my legs out until they're settled against me on the edge and I am completely and intimately open and exposed to him.

My breath is short and shallow, matching the rapid rise and fall of his chest as he pauses to look. When his eyes on me, on that most private part of me, are too much, I press my knees together. He stops me with the press of his thumbs into my inner thighs.

"You're beautiful," he whispers, finally lifting his eyes to mine. "So beautiful that I won't let you hide yourself from me." He lowers his head and blows a cool stream of air against my exposed sex.

A cry slips from my lips.

"Let me kiss you here. Let go for me."

"Asher," I whisper. His mouth is so close and my body is humming, aching.

He lowers his head and puts his mouth on me. His breath, his lips, his tongue, his teeth, on and against me. And this feels so good, so amazing. The sight of his dark head between my legs, the way his muscles bunch as if his control is this heavy load he must strain against. I watch, and I feel, and I sink into the pleasure of his mouth working and teasing and exploring.

At some point, he releases one of my legs and slides two fingers deep inside me while his mouth closes over my clit. I think I scream and I lift my hips, rocking into his fingers and mouth. His fingers curl roughly against my thigh and he shifts my knee further back, opening me to his fingers and mouth somehow deeper still. And I shatter, my sex pulsing around his fingers, swollen and spent against his mouth.

I've hardly recovered when he's standing, toppling the chair in his haste. He sheaths himself in a condom and slides into me.

Hands holding tight to my hips, Asher locks eyes with me as I rock into him. I want to close my eyes—wash away in the feel of his thickness invading my tender sex—but I keep them open. For him. For me.

Asher

SHE ANSWERS the door in a fluffy pink robe and a smile. "You're early," she says, but judging by the way her eyes skim over my body, she's not disappointed to see me.

I couldn't convince her to stay over last night. She had plenty of excuses, wanting to be at the gallery early in the morning, not wanting to leave her dog alone another night. Ultimately, I decided not to push it.

She backs into the house and waves me in. "I'll be ready in ten minutes. Make yourself comfortable."

As she retreats to the bathroom, I give a few seconds of consideration to following her, untying the robe and pulling it from her shoulders, but I dismiss the idea. I promised her I'd take her into Chicago to visit some art gallery today. When I get her naked again, I'm going to need more than a few stolen minutes, so I settle into a chair and look around.

I want to get Maggie out of this crappy little house. Before this year, I hadn't spent much time in New Hope, but even I know this is an unsavory area more known for meth dealing than the neighborhood watch.

I could put her up in a nice apartment by campus, but she's so drawn to the river, I think she'd be happier at my place by the water.

Who am I kidding? I want her close. After my probation ends, I'm planning on spending a month in New York talking to studios for the first time since Infinite Gray broke up, and I want to know she's waiting for me when I get back.

My thoughts stutter to a halt when she returns to the living room.

"Jesus Christ." I stand and step closer to get a better look. She's in red. A flowing little sleeveless thing that shows just enough cleavage and a whole lot of leg. Her hair is pinned up off her neck, but a few little tendrils hang loose. My eyes trail down to her strappy heels and I'm struck with an image of stripping her down to nothing but her shoes.

Oh, hell yes.

When I return to her face, her cheeks are tinged pink. "I guess I don't need to ask how I look."

Closing the steps between us, I pull her into my arms and press my face into the crook of her neck—to taste her skin, to take a hit of her scent. "How am I supposed to look at you all day and not touch you?" I growl into her soft skin.

My hand slips under her dress almost of its own volition, and I trail my fingers up her thighs.

"Who said you couldn't touch me?" Her breathing is already uneven as I trace the lace of her panties over her hip to the small of her back.

I slap her ass softly. "Don't tempt me."

I DON'T understand the tension in Maggie's shoulders. I would expect her to feel at home in a gallery like this.

The space is large, with high ceilings and track lighting that illuminates the artwork.

A man wanders from the back to greet us, and he takes one look at my tattoos and earrings and dismisses me. Never mind that there isn't piece in here I can't afford. *Asshole.*

"I'm Martin, the gallery manager. Are we just here to peruse?" But then he looks at Maggie and does a double-take, eyes widening.

Maggie doesn't seem to notice. She extends her hand and flashes him that gorgeous smile. "Hello, I'm Maggie and this is Asher. We understand you have some Bauer paintings on display here?"

I thought we were here to check out the gallery. I didn't realize she was looking for a specific artist.

The man's expression is different when he looks at me this time. Being here with Maggie has clearly earned me some sort of art-world street cred. "Of course, yes." He offers me his hand. "It's such an honor. Let me show you to the back."

He scurries ahead and we hang back. When Maggie turns, I catch her eye and mouth, "Honor?"

She lifts a shoulder and shakes her head, but worry creases her brow and her shoulders stiffen even more. There's something she's not telling me.

We follow the man through the large space, the echo of our steps mingling with the soft piano melody playing through the overhead speakers.

He motions to a doorway off the back. "Mr. Bauer's collection has attracted a lot of attention to the gallery in the past months. Just stunning. You should be very pleased."

I frown and Maggie hugs herself, rubbing her bare arms.

Judging by the way she's staring at the door, I'm not sure she's going to enter.

"Shall we?" I say, taking her hand and leading her through the swinging door.

Inside the smaller room is a series of portraits of beautiful women. My eye catches a flash of red in the far corner and I turn to see a portrait of Maggie, her hair lifted by the breeze as she looks at the river. She wears nothing but a thin sheet wrapped under her arms.

Next to me, Maggie's shoulders sag and she starts breathing normally for the first time since we arrived at the gallery.

The studio manager is eyeing her curiously. "Dr. Bauer has such talent. It's true art. Not too sexy. Tasteful." His eyes are on Maggie as he says the last. Those words can't mean much coming from a man who looks at her like he jacks off to the image of her face every night, but I suspect he's nearly as stunned to have her here as I am to see the painting.

"Do we need to go?" I ask softly.

She lifts her chin and smiles at the attendant. "Are these the only paintings of his you have?"

The man frowns. "Yes. Were you looking for something else?"

She shakes her head. "No. You've been helpful, thank you."

I wrap my arm around her waist, half surprised when she doesn't push me away, and we make our way toward the door.

"I'm sorry if that surprised you," the attendant says behind us. "I thought you knew. I thought that was why you came."

"I'm fine." She says, but she doesn't look at him or me as we head to the car. No, all she does is slide her hand into mine and squeeze hard. And it's enough for me.

"WHO PAINTED it, Maggie?"

We're at a little coffee shop down the road from the gallery. I offered to take her to a bar—God knows she looks like she could use a drink—but she declined.

So, here we are. Coffee in hand. The silence of unspoken secrets between us.

I need to know about the painting we saw, but more I need to know about the ones we didn't, the ones she is clearly looking for.

"Ethan Bauer," she says. "He's an art professor at Sinclair." Her voice is clear, strong, as if this isn't difficult for her. I don't buy it.

"When did he paint it?"

"A couple of years ago."

The whirring of the steamer rents through the air as the barista fills an order.

When it stops, I say, "You were a student."

Maggie takes a sip from her cup and avoids my eyes. "A lot of students pose and in a lot less than a sheet. Of course, I wasn't a student of *his* at the time, but he was my mentor."

"Your mentor?"

She nods. "I came to Sinclair for painting. Ethan took me under his wing early on. To foster my talent, he said."

"That's why we came up here, isn't it? You wanted to see if he was showing a painting of you?" I pause for a beat. "You were relieved when you saw it. What did you expect to see?"

She studies her coffee, buying time, and I expect her to dodge the question. I'm surprised when she says, "Ethan painted a whole series of me. A semi-erotic collection of paintings he swore he'd never show."

"And you're afraid he will."

"We had an affair." The words are so soft I almost don't hear them over the soft chatter of the people around us. "He had a bit of a...reputation for sleeping with his models. It wasn't like I didn't know what I was getting myself into." She closes her eyes. "But I don't want anyone seeing those paintings."

"Why the secrecy?"

She's silent so long I don't think she's going to answer. Maggie is such a paradox. On one hand, she's an open book. She doesn't bother disguising the truth when it isn't pretty, and she doesn't seem to be ashamed for her decisions. Except with this area of her life. When it comes to Will, the miscarriage, and the last year, she is closed and impossible to read. She is full of secrets and fighting like hell to protect them.

"You had an affair with him, but you were marrying Will."

Her eyes snap open. "I never slept with Ethan when I was engaged to Will. I may have done a lot of things wrong that year, but once Will and I were involved, things between Ethan and me were over." She lowers her voice and traces a scar in the oak tabletop. "Will deserved at least that much from me."

"What happened to end things between you and Ethan?"

"Ethan was married." She avoids my eyes. "I just woke up. I realized I had fallen into the same patterns as I had in high school. Maybe the sex was consensual this time, but it still wasn't healthy. He was married. He was never going to leave his wife."

"And you were pregnant," I say softly.

Her wild eyes shoot to mine so quickly, I know I'm right. The married man knocked Maggie up, and she hurried and got engaged to an eligible young guy who could play daddy.

Her shoulders rise and fall with her deep breath. She won't look at me.

"Maggie," I say softly.

"I know it sounds stupid coming from someone who had sex with a married man, but I didn't want to hurt anyone."

She chews on the edge of her lip, and I find myself wanting to cup her face in my hands and kiss that abused spot, kiss across her cheeks and down her neck, kiss away the pain and the self-loathing.

She looks like she survived a natural disaster. Worry and concern distort her features.

I try to imagine what that was like for her. Finding herself pregnant with a married man's baby after what happened to her in high school. And I can see it. I can see how a marriage to a willing and available man may have seemed like the answer.

"Would you mind waiting her for a few minutes while I run a quick errand?"

She blinks at me.

"I promise I'll be back in less than twenty minutes."

'

chapter eighteen

Maggie

I AM quickly coming to believe that there is no place in this world I love as much as Asher's arms, talking about nothing and everything in the darkness.

We didn't say much on the drive home from Chicago. He played some music for me, pointing out influences for his new work and sharing his favorite songs. He didn't ask me any more questions about Ethan or Will. He didn't bring up the baby.

And I didn't ask about the blanket-covered backseat holding something that hadn't been there on the drive up.

When we got home and slipped out of our clothes, I caught myself waiting for Asher to touch me, to seduce me, to use me. Then I remembered this was Asher, and it wasn't like that between us.

"Will you go to the gallery opening with me this weekend?" I ask him quietly now.

"Of course."

I watch his expression in the darkness. "Ethan's holding his cards close to his chest, and he won't tell anyone what he's showing in his part of the exhibit."

"You think he might show the paintings of you?"

"I'm afraid he might," I say softly. "I want to prepare myself for that possibility."

"I'll be by your side," he promises.

Warmth blossoms in my chest. I know I can handle this if Asher is by my side.

"Where did you disappear to last year?" he asks.

My fingertips freeze where they'd been tracing the outline of his tattoo. "What?"

He pushes himself up on an elbow. "Last year, you left after you called off your wedding. Where did you go?"

Don't ruin this. Please, don't. "I wanted to get away for a while. I was…more than a little messed up at the time. I needed to get away."

"From Ethan? From Will? From what happened in high school?"

I sit up. "From everyone. From this town." I command my racing heart to slow. Asher is not the enemy. "Why do you care so much?"

"Why are you still hiding from me?"

"You already know. You know more than anyone." I close my eyes, trying to center myself. "I'm going to go to sleep now. I'm sorry if you want to talk more, but this isn't my idea of fun."

I click off the light and move to the far side of the bed. I'm nude but it's his questions that made me feel naked.

Asher's big arm wraps around me and pulls me against his warm, bare chest. "Is it just me," he whispers, "or do you not trust anyone?"

I think about how much it meant to have him with me at the gallery this morning, how he was the only one I could ask to go with me to find the Discovery collection, how easy it was to answer his questions about Ethan. "I don't trust anyone *but* you Asher, but trusting you scares me more than you can understand. I'm fighting it every day."

"Don't shut me out anymore." He kisses my shoulder. "Let me in."

"No one knows about Ethan," I say softly. "It took my family years to recover from the scandal with Toby. This is a small town. People here are cruel and their memories are long. I couldn't tell my mother I was pregnant with a married man's baby. Not after what I put her through in high school."

He presses his lips to my shoulder. "I understand that. And obviously Will did too if he was willing to play along."

I stiffen in his arms, and my heart pounds painfully in my chest until I hear the whoosh of his exhale.

"Will knew the baby wasn't his, right?"

I close my eyes.

Everything had happened so fast. I panicked. It seemed like one minute I'd been hovering in post-coital bliss, running my fingertips through the soft sprinkle of hair on Ethan's chest, and the next I'd been falling hard for Will.

I remember that last morning with Ethan. His studio smelled of sex and stale wine and the sun poked its golden head in between the curtains.

He grabbed my hand, pressed his lips against my palm. "I wish I could stay here with you all weekend, Margaret, but Claudia is going to kill me as it is."

"What will you tell her?" I asked as I explored his body with my fingertips.

"The truth."

"Really?"

"I will tell her that I was working in my studio and fell asleep." He turned, shifting his body so he was on his side, facing me. "I wish I could give you more, Maggie. You deserve more than a bum who's sneaking around on his wife."

"I've never asked for more," I whispered, and it was true. "But I wonder sometimes…" I wasn't sure I could say it.

"About what?" He was already moving, pulling himself off our makeshift bed of sheets and pillows on the studio floor and reaching for his paint-stained jeans.

"What would you do if something happened? If…I don't know. If I got pregnant or something."

His hands froze where they'd been working his fly. "We've always used protection."

I rolled to sitting and crossed my feet under me. "Nothing's one hundred percent," I told the floor. If anyone knew that, it was me. I heard it over and over again from my mother. At my Catholic high school, there'd been no sex talk beyond a brief statement that sex was something sacred that should be preserved for marriage, that contraception was against God's will, and that no contraceptive method was one hundred percent effective. If young women wanted to really protect themselves and please God, they needed to do so with chastity.

"Are you trying to tell me something?" His voice was so cautious, his face so guarded that I felt foolish. It was the first time he made me feel like a kid. But I had to know.

"Hypothetically." This wasn't me. Skirting the issue. Guarding the truth.

"Maggie, I know it takes two. I'd take care of you."

The world contained so much hope at that moment. So much it had poured into me, like the early morning sunshine that warmed the studio.

I raised my eyes to meet his, that golden sunshine filling my most dark and desperate corners. I hadn't taken a test yet, but my period was nine days late and I was like clockwork. My supply of denial was running dry.

"I know you couldn't afford to take care of it yourself," he explained. "I'd take you to Indy or Chicago. We'd get it taken care of there. Discreetly. And I'd pay for it. You don't need to worry about that."

Get it taken care of?

Even now, my hand clutches my stomach instinctively, as if the threat still looms. The golden warmth fled and red-hot terror replaced it.

I remember ignoring his hand and pushing myself up off the floor. The gesture had felt meaningful, and I told myself that it had only been a matter of time before our relationship came to its inevitable end.

I grabbed my jeans and sweater, trying to keep my movements slow and natural—and fearing I was failing. "You better get home to Claudia."

His fingertips grazed the small of my back as I bent to pull on my jeans. For the first time, they weren't a lover's fingertips. They were the enemy's. For the first time, the touch of this married man, my mentor, my professor, made me feel unclean to the core.

I ended our affair that morning. I told him I wanted more from life than to be his mistress. It was so true. I wanted so much more from *him*. But he couldn't give it. And at that moment, as I stood in the soft trickle of morning light and ached inside with a betrayal that cut to the very foundation of my beliefs, I knew I'd never ask him to give me anything else. Not ever again.

Asher brings me back to the present with his lips on my shoulder. "Tell me," he says softly.

"The day I told Will I was pregnant, I was planning on telling him the truth. But he…" I trail off, sickened by my own lies. "He assumed it was his and I let him."

"He deserves to know," he says softly, and I hear something like pain in his voice. "Despite…everything."

"I know."

THE GARAGE is dark, save for the glow of the Jeep's dome light. The concrete floor is cold under my feet.

I move the blanket from the backseat, and my throat grows thick at the sight of the framed canvas. I know he bought it for me.

I stand frozen, hypnotized by that goddamned painting.

There's nothing scandalous about this one, but he bought it. For me.

I hope I deserve him.

I head back into the house and to the couch in the great room. My gaze drifts to the staircase. I should go back to bed. It would be so nice, curling up with a man who wants to protect me, letting him hold me, hiding inside his warmth. Maybe I could even wake him and tell him my story, explain how I let things get out of control. I made mistakes, and I tried to make amends for those mistakes.

Maybe Asher would listen. Maybe if I shattered, he *would* find me.

My hand curls at my stomach.

I didn't give my baby away because I suddenly became a noble woman who couldn't live with a lie. I gave her away because, in the gritty ultrasound image, I saw the blinking beat of my daughter's heart, and I already loved her too much to make *her* live with it.

All week, I've felt something tugging inside me. Like a hidden ribbon unraveling and exposing what I've so carefully kept tucked away.

I want to tell Asher about Grace, but I'm terrified he won't understand.

It *would* feel so nice to have someone on my side. To have a little help carrying the weight of my secrets. And I want to tell someone. I want to utter her name just once. Let just one other living soul in on the secret—screw-up Maggie Thompson created something beautiful.

Asher

SHE'S SLEEPING on my couch with her arms wrapped around herself. She looks so damn lonely it breaks my heart.

"Asher?" She blinks up at me as I lift her into my arms. "What are you doing?"

"I'm taking you back to bed. I can't sleep for shit without you next to me." My jaw tightens against the words. I don't like to think about how much I need this woman. I don't like that, while I need her more every day, she's still pushing me away.

Even as I think it, she wraps her arms around my neck and leans her head against my chest. "Thank you," she whispers. "I forget that I don't have to be alone when you're around."

My heart squeezes, and I take the stairs two at a time. When I reach my bedroom, I don't take her to the bed. Instead, I carry her into the bathroom and lower her onto the edge of the jetted tub while I run the water.

As it fills, I strip off my underwear and help her out of her clothes. She gives me a soft smile and lifts her arms over her head so I can remove the t-shirt. Then she stands and I take my time sliding my hands under the soft, thin cotton of her panties. Dropping to my knees on the heated tile, I take them over her hips slowly. When she's completely bare, I kiss her foot, inside at the arch, the soft curve of her calf and the hot flesh of her inner thigh. Then I hover at the apex of her thighs, a breath away from tasting her.

"You're so gorgeous."

"I like the look of you like that," she tells me with a grin. "On your knees like you're worshipping me."

I lift my gaze to meet hers. "You have no idea."

Standing, I skim my fingers over her. Hips, waist, and breasts that I will never tire of touching.

Then I take her hand and lead her into the tub, settling her between my legs so I can hold her in my arms where she belongs. The hot water pulses around us, and she relaxes into me as I trace an invisible path from her breasts to her hipbone.

"You're the first man I've ever been with that doesn't want to have sex every time we're naked."

I press my lips to her neck, scrape my teeth over the shell of her ear. "There's more to intimacy than fucking," I whisper, sliding my hand between her legs.

I love the sound of her gasp as my fingers slip over her clit, savor the tilt of her hips as my palm settles against her.

"You are so beautiful. I could spend hours touching you."

She draws in a breath as I lift my hand from between her legs and return to tracing lazy paths across her abdomen.

"Are you going to tell me about this?" I rest my fingers over the silvery stretch marks at her navel.

She sighs, but she doesn't tense. She relaxes into me further. "You already know." The relief is in her voice.

"Zoe's mother developed the same thing after her pregnancy. I didn't put it together at first, but today…" I trail off. There's no reason to say more.

"They're my favorite part of my body," she whispers, sliding her fingers between mine. "Because they're proof she was mine once."

My heart squeezes painfully. Juliana had cursed her stretch marks, had hated the way pregnancy changed her body. Maggie is so miraculously different, I want to breathe her in.

"I thought you had a miscarriage." I brush her hair over her shoulder. "That day at the river?"

"A blood clot," she says softly. "I had to believe I was losing her before I could accept that I had to give her up."

"It was a girl?"

She sniffs and leans her head into the crook of my shoulder. "They named her Grace."

I close my eyes, trying to imagine what it must have been like for her.

"I wanted to keep her, but I couldn't do that to my mom. So when Will assumed the baby was his and asked me to marry him…" She releases a long, slow breath.

"Did you ever tell Ethan?"

"He wanted me to get an abortion. I just…I couldn't."

"You did a beautiful thing." I wrap my arms around her waist and squeeze. "You are so amazing."

Maggie

ASHER'S SLEEPING and the steady rhythm of his breathing has me drifting off.

When I came back to New Hope, I imagined a lonely life of grief and secrets, and life stretched out before me like a threat.

I know they think I tried to kill myself the morning I had the accident in my studio, but I hadn't. But when I saw the blood pool at my feet, I hadn't been scared. I'd been grateful that maybe it was over, maybe I wouldn't have to do this anymore.

Asher changed that, and now life stretches before me full of hope and possibility.

I press my lips against his bare shoulder. I close my eyes and feel sleep wrapping me in its cottony grasp.

"I love you," I whisper to this sleeping man. "Thank you for finding me."

He surprises me by rolling to face me and drawing me against his chest. "I love you too."

chapter nineteen

Maggie

"I'm glad you finally took me up on my offer," Ethan says, sliding into the booth across from me.

The upscale Indianapolis restaurant he chose is clattering with the bustle of a healthy weeknight dinner crowd.

Sighing, I look at my watch. He's fifteen minutes late. Some things never change.

He reaches across the table, brushing my hand with his. "How are you, Maggie?"

I pull away. "I'm not here because I want to reconnect."

"That's a shame, though I can't say I'm surprised. I always figured you'd move on to bigger and better things than a small-town art professor. Who is the lucky guy? That rock star fellow, right? Much more your speed, I imagine."

I shake my head. Why hadn't I seen his constant manipulation for what it was from the beginning? "I don't want to talk about my private life. I want to know what you're doing with the Discovery collection. I deserve to know."

He stills and jaw tightens. "Why?"

"Do you really want Claudia to find out about us?" I ask softly. "Those paintings will give you away."

"I'm an artist," he says. "She knows that."

"Ethan, I was pregnant when I left you."

He doesn't move, doesn't offer any response, aside from cutting his eyes to the menu.

"I was pregnant with your baby when I became engaged to Will."

Still no response. I want to smack him.

"But I couldn't go through with it." I'm surprised how easily the words come. "I couldn't go through with the lie, so I called off the wedding and moved to Connecticut where I lived in a maternity group home until the baby was born."

He places his napkin in his lap and lifts a hand to signal the server. "Do you have any wine by the glass?"

"Yes, sir," the server says, producing a leather-bound menu.

Ethan studies it for a moment before pointing to his selection. "Two glasses, please."

"Excellent choice. I'll be right back with that, sir."

I wait, determined to give him time to soak in my confession. He doesn't speak until after the server arrives with the wine and leaves again.

Ethan takes a tentative sip. "It has a lovely, earthy flavor."

My patience snaps. "Do you understand what I'm telling you? I had your baby and gave her up for adoption."

His gaze narrows. "I understood the first time, but thank you for the translation."

"I don't want you trying to contact her," I explain. "She has a good life with a good family, and I won't have you destroying that."

He slams his wine down, making the red contents slosh to the rim. "What, exactly, makes you think that I want anything to do with the child that you allege is mine?"

Fury whips through me. "I don't *allege* anything—"

"Listen, Margaret. I didn't want anything to do with the child when you practically confessed your pregnancy in my studio last year, and I certainly don't want anything to do with it now. Even if it was, as you suggest, my own, it wasn't the product of my intentions."

"Wasn't the *product* of your *intentions*?" The pressure inside me is too much. I want to strangle the bastard. "She's a child, not a *painting*. And what do you—" My breath catches as his full meaning hits me. I'm so angry I hadn't fully registered his words. "You knew?"

He rolls a starched white sleeve and opens his menu. "Contrary to what you seem to think of me, I'm not dense. I knew. I even knew that you gave it up for adoption, though that took a bit more digging. It was in my best interest to know that you weren't going to try anything ridiculous like raising the child on your own."

Flames of anger twisted inside me. "Why would that have been ridiculous?" I have to ask because it's the question that won't leave me alone. Why *would* it have been so ridiculous? Why couldn't I have been a single mom? I could have done it. The truth would have hurt my mother but she would have survived.

Ethan glances up from the menu and smiles sweetly. "Because I didn't need you coming around asking for child support years down the road." He shrugs. "Like I said, I have no reason to believe it was mine. If you'll remember, chastity has never been a virtue of yours."

I force myself to swallow my rage, but it goes down chalky and bitter. "I'm leaving."

"Suit yourself."

I stop, take a breath, and turn slowly. "I sacrificed everything to keep this secret. If you show those paintings, it's hard to say how much of that is going to be brought out into the open."

"Are you worried the truth might ruin things with your latest boy toy? Don't fool yourself, Margaret."

"Some of us are just too cold inside to be capable of real love." He doesn't say the words now, but he doesn't need to. He said them enough in the past that they hang in the air between us.

I used to believe those words, but I don't anymore.

William

I'VE LOST her. I can see it in her eyes. She stands taller somehow, and even when she's not smiling she looks happy. I'm grateful for that, but jealous as hell I couldn't be the one to do that for her.

The gallery gleams. Everything is ready to go for tomorrow night's opening, save the Bauer exhibition in the side room.

Even though she's glowing and standing taller, I can tell Ethan's missing pieces have Maggie worried.

"Did he give you any hint about it?" I ask her when I catch her staring into the empty space.

She swallows and shakes her head.

"He painted a lot of women, Maggie. I'm sure no one will know about the affair if he shows paintings of you."

She doesn't respond, but eventually she turns to me, arms wrapped around herself. "If you knew about the affair, why didn't you ever question whose baby it was?" Her face is lined with grief I wish I could take away.

"You know one of the reasons Krystal and I were such a good match?" I ask, answering her question with one of my own. "She doesn't mind adopting."

Maggie blinks at me. "Adopting?"

"Yeah. We were going to make our family that way." I wait a beat. "I'm sterile. I found out when I was sixteen. Football accident." I wince. "Cleats aren't very forgiving."

"Sixteen?" she whispers. I can practically see her mind piecing together the implications of my confession.

"I would have taken you however I could get you, Maggie." I shove my hands in my pockets. "I still would. I don't think you ever understood that. I don't think you ever believed you were worthy of that kind of love."

Maggie

HE NEVER asked me if the baby was his. I always wondered at that kind of trust. I pegged it for naiveté. I said I was pregnant and he asked me to marry him.

But Will knew he was sterile. Which meant he had known the baby couldn't be his. He knew I was asking him to raise another man's child. And he hadn't said a word because he'd thought that was what I wanted.

"I need to sit down," I say softly.

I head for the patio and Will follows me out. We settle into seats at the stone table, breathing in the fresh evening air.

"I should have told you," he says. "If you'd known I knew the truth, you might not have hated yourself so much."

I look into his baby blues and see honesty there. "You were trying to protect me."

"I'd do anything for you, Maggie." He draws in a shaky breath. "I should have waited for you. I would have if I'd believed—"

"It wouldn't have made a difference." I have to cut him off. I can't make him suffer like this. "Don't beat yourself up for falling for Krystal. I'd already ruined what we had by lying."

He's watching me, pain in those beautiful eyes. "I don't suppose I could talk you into starting over. Starting fresh. With me."

My breath snags on the edge of my healing heart. "I'm in love with Asher."

He closes his eyes as if he can't stand to see my words hit the air. As if looking at me while I say them makes them too real.

"You're going to find someone, Will. I know you're going to get your happily-ever-after."

"And you're sure he can give you yours?"

"I don't think you ever believed you were worthy of that kind of love."

I hadn't believed. Until Asher.

"I'm sure."

chapter twenty

Maggie

"HERE'S TO a new home for martini nights!" Hanna says, lifting her margarita glass.

I grin and take a swig of my beer. I don't know what it is about Brady's—the memories, the neon Bud signs, the clack of billiard balls in the background—but I love being here. "Thanks for meeting me," I say to my sisters. "Tomorrow's the gallery opening, and I wanted to celebrate."

"I can't wait," Lizzy says. "I bought a new little black dress and red heels that make me horny just lookin' at 'em."

The front door opens and Kenny strolls in. It's late on a Friday, and, judging by the way he's walking, he might already be a little drunk. "Lucy!" he hoots when he spots me.

"Get a life," Hanna growls.

He stumbles toward our table. "I'm not hurting anyone."

"I need to visit the little girls' room," I announce, ignoring Kenny. "Either of you want to join me?"

"I'm not ready to break the seal," Hanna says. "I'm going to get us another round. Want another?"

I look at my half-full beer and shake my head. "No. I'm good."

A little bit of a crowd has formed, townies taking advantage of a beautiful June night free of college kids, and I have to maneuver through the crowd to reach the bathroom.

When I see my reflection in the mirror, I almost don't recognize myself. I look…lighter. Happier. It's been a summer, but worth it.

When I come back out into the dark hallway, Kenny's waiting on the other side of the door.

He doesn't let me get far before he has me in the corner, body pressed against mine, hands against the wall on either side of my head.

"Hey, Maggie," he says softly, his eyes on my mouth.

I know I'm in trouble when I hear him use my real name, and I swallow the bile rising in my throat. When the boys at my high school decided I was a slut, I learned quickly they thought this meant I existed for their pleasure, to use when and how they pleased. For a while, I believed them.

Fuck that.

"Kenny, you're drunk. Back off."

He leans closer and my nose is greeted with the scent of beer and onion rings. "Nah," he says, "that's not what you want."

His thumb grazes the edge of my jaw and I struggle to keep my cool, not to panic. I'll get rid of him. He's just a stupid asshole looking for an easy lay, but he's looking with the wrong girl.

"Kenny, you don't want this. What would your wife think?"

"But that's what you like, isn't it? Fucking married men?" His lips curl into a twisted smile. "You act like you've changed, but I know you get around."

I snarl. "You don't know shit."

"Admit it. You're a little wet thinking about me fucking you against this wall and then going home to my wife. You like being the pussy we dream about when we go to bed with our sexless wives."

The moment his hand slides between my legs, I bring my knee to his groin. But I didn't give Kenny enough credit. He presses closer, stealing my leverage at the last minute. His sweaty hand grabs at my inner thigh and I try again, using the very little room I have to draw up hard with my knee.

At first I think I hit him with more power than I have because he flies off me and slams against the opposite wall.

Then I see Asher, fists clenched and eyes blazing as he bears down on Kenny.

"What the *fuck*, man?" Kenny whimpers. "Get your own bitch."

"She told you to *back off*," Asher growls.

"And who are you? Pussy patrol?"

The sick crunch of knuckles connecting with jawbone echoes in the small corridor.

People are gathering at the end of the hall, attracted by the shouts and the familiar sounds of a bar scuffle.

Kenny sneers, his lip bloody. "You can have the cunt," he grumbles. "She was asking for it, but a dick's a dick to her. Mine? Yours? What's it matter?"

Asher's nostrils flare. As I step forward to stop him, he sweeps Kenny's legs out from under him, taking him down.

"Asher," I cry, but he doesn't hear me.

Asher's on the floor, leaning over Kenny when Will appears in the throng and pulls him off.

Asher's eyes blaze as he rounds on Will.

"Let it go, man," Will says. "He's not worth it."

Kenny pushes himself up on his elbows and moans. His lip is bleeding and his right eye is already swelling. His buddy Craig helps him off the floor, glaring at me the whole time. "Why are you getting messed up with Lucy anyway?"

Asher jumps forward at those words, but not before Will can wrap an arm around his waist and hold him back.

I have become that helpless woman who can do nothing but stare as the world moves around her, and before I know it, the police are there, and I want to cry because I recognize both of the uniformed officers who come into Brady's. They both went to my high school. They're both life-long "bros" with Kenny, and they don't ask a single question before they take Asher to the back of a patrol car.

"Wait!" I call, my voice weak. "He was protecting me!"

"We're just taking him in for questioning," one officer promises, but I fucking know this town and I know how the good ole boy system works. Asher won't get to say his piece. They'll hold him as long as they can and record whatever story makes Kenny look the best.

"I was on my way to take a piss," Kenny's saying, "and she kinda pushes me against the wall and presses her hand to my crotch."

My jaw drops. The officer is jotting down notes as if Kenny's story is more than a load of bullshit, and I can't find my tongue.

"I should have pushed her off. I should have, but I've been drinking and I guess I let my dick think for me. Next thing I know her boyfriend's throwing punches right and left, throwing me against the wall and slamming my head against the floor." He wipes the blood from his nose with the back of his hand and a waitress hurries over with a napkin. "I didn't know she had a boyfriend and didn't think to worry about it. I wasn't thinking at all, honestly."

"You weren't thinking because you were too busy trying to force your hand up my skirt to listen to me say *no*, let alone *think*."

"Everyone knows Asher Logan's a hot head," Kenny's buddy says, crossing his arms. "Only reason he's even in this town is so he can stay out of trouble while he serves his probation."

"No. He was protecting me. Asher didn't do anything wrong." My voice trills with the panic that's weighing heavier and heavier on me. My lungs are shrinking and I can't get the air I need.

"Who are the police gonna believe?" Craig mutters in my ear. "Their life-long friend or the slut with a track record for fucking married men?"

I can't breathe. There's no air back here. "Get *away* from me," I scream, pushing at Craig because I know what happens next, I know what this means for Asher.

"Maggie!" Hanna and Lizzy appear at the edge of the throng and push their way back to me.

"We'll need to talk to her," an officer says without looking up from his notes. Kenny's still waxing redneck poetic about my hallway seduction. I have no doubt his wife will know about this before the night's out. Just another person who hates me in this town and for once I don't give a shit what they think. But Asher...

"Maggie," Hanna is saying, "breathe, sweetie."

"She needs air," Lizzy announces, clearing a path through the crowd. For the officers, she tosses back, "We'll be outside when you're ready to talk to us."

"What the hell happened?" Lizzy asks as we push through the front doors.

"Hush," Hanna barks. "Can't you see she's in shock?" She settles me onto a concrete bench in front of the bar and takes my face in both her hands. "Breathe."

"I'm fine," I object. But I'm not fine. I haven't been fine since I was a little girl, since before my body turned on me and ruined my life. I focus on my breathing, expanding my belly until it hurts and exhaling slowly. "I need my purse."

Lizzy hands it over, and I dig out my anxiety medication and pop one in my mouth.

"What's that?" Hanna asks softly, taking the bottle from me. "Jesus, how long have you needed this?"

I blink at her. How long have I needed it or how long have I been taking it?

"I can't believe what they're trying to say about you," Hanna says. "As if that was *your* fault?"

They can't hurt me. They don't matter. I am not the sum of their accusations.

The mantras from my therapist do nothing to soothe my panic when this isn't about me. It's about the man who probably just lost everything protecting me.

"Oh." Hanna pops up and shoves the bottle in her pocket. "Hi, Will."

Will stands a couple of yards from me, his broad shoulders silhouetted by the street lamp and his face masked in shadow.

"Are you okay?" he asks me softly, running a hand through his hair.

I nod. "Kenny didn't hurt me. He didn't get a chance."

"They'll probably keep Asher overnight. There'll be an arraignment in the morning and the judge will set bail. Kenny doesn't need medical attention, so it shouldn't be a big deal. A fine, maybe? It's going to be okay, Maggie."

I swallow hard. *My. Fault.* "He's on probation. He can't have any charges brought against him or he'll lose his daughter. He'll have to serve that old sentence for assault." I'm shaking. "He'll go to prison."

"Shit," Will mutters.

"But who gets to decide?" Hanna pipes in. "Who listens to everyone's side and decides if they should even press charges?"

"If it's the goddamned cops in this town, Asher is screwed," Lizzy says.

I wince and Hanna says, "Liz!"

"The police don't make that call," Will says.

We all look at him, waiting, until I realize what he's not saying.

"The prosecutor," I whisper.

"Oh, no," Hanna cries.

"He's an outsider, Mags," Will says, jaw hard. "This doesn't look good."

Lizzy props her hands on her hips. "I'm so damn sick of this backwards town."

I don't reply because out of the corner of my eye, I see the flashing lights of the patrol car edging around the corner. I stand and let my fingers slide against the glass of the back door as it passes as a crawl.

Asher's head is inclined against the back of the seat, and he winks at me and flashes me a sad smile.

My phone buzzes in my pocket, alerting me to a text. From Asher. They must not have taken away Asher's phone yet.

I love you. No regrets.

I lift my eyes to his as the car pulls onto Main Street, and I watch as the lights fade into the darkness.

"He was just protecting me." But if the prosecutor gets to decide whether to press charges, protecting me may be the worst thing he could have done.

I haven't talked to her since I was fifteen and she was divorcing her husband for sleeping with me.

"Do you want me to go with you?"

I grab a mug and fill it with coffee, shaking my head at Krystal. "I want to go alone." It's barely seven-thirty in the morning, but I'm going to be at the courthouse when the doors open. When I went to the station to give my statement last night, they confirmed what Will had guessed. Asher would be held overnight and bail would be set at the arraignment in the morning.

My stomach churns with anxiety over the price Asher might have to pay for doing the right thing.

"You don't have to do everything alone, you know," Krystal says softly.

Purse halfway to my shoulder, I pause and turn to my sister. I set down my purse, settle my mug and my keys next to it and wrap my arms around her. "I know that now."

She squeezes me hard. "Okay."

I pull into the lot behind the courthouse and cut the ignition by 7:43.

Last night was miserable, giving my statement to those men, knowing they didn't believe me. Knowing they wouldn't care even if they had believed. But I survived it.

I take a last swig of coffee and step out of my car.

"Maggie?"

I turn at the sound of Ann Quimby's voice. "Ms. Quimby."

She's dressed in a smart blue skirt suit and holding a briefcase and looks every bit like a prosecutor should. She narrows her eyes at me. "What are you doing here?"

"I…Asher Logan…last night…" I stutter. I always liked Anna and seeing her again would be awkward under any circumstances, but is especially so under these.

She shakes her head. "Mr. Logan was released this morning."

"Released?"

"I'm not pressing charges. Between your story and Kenny's track record, I have enough reason to believe Mr. Logan used justifiable force to protect you."

My jaw goes slack. "But…Kenny said…" Oh, what I would give for the ability to construct a complete sentence. "Thank you," I whisper.

"You can file a protective order against Kenny," she informs me. "I know Brady doesn't want him in his bar anymore, so you won't have to worry about seeing him there."

I nod. "I will. Thank you."

She turns toward the courthouse.

"Ms. Quimby?" I call.

She stops and turns back to me.

"You don't know how much this means."

She nods. "I'm not in the business of blaming the victim, Miss Thompson." She cuts her eyes away from me and sets her jaw. "I never have been."

We both know she's not just talking about Asher's case.

chapter twenty-one

Asher

WHEN MAGGIE pulls into my driveway, I run outside and pull her against me. She wraps her arms around my neck and cries.

"It's okay, baby," I murmur, stroking her hair. "I've got you."

"I thought they were going to send you to prison," she whispers. "You would have missed a whole year of Zoe's life, and it would have been my fault."

"No." I pull back and hold her face in my hands. "Not your fault. You understand? You didn't ask for Kenny to do that to you."

"But Asher, they could have—"

"I won't let you blame yourself for what some asshole did, Maggie." I kiss her. Hard. When I saw Kenny pushing himself against her last night, I could have killed him. The punches I threw were nothing compared to what I wanted to do.

"I love you," I whisper in her hair.

"I love you too," she whispers back, clinging to me.

Maggie

"ASHER?" I call as I step into the house.

We decided to meet here before heading over to the gallery opening, but I decided to come early. If I take my shower and get ready here, that gives Asher and me time alone before we have to leave.

I call for him again as I walk toward the stairs. The house is quiet.

Neither of us slept much last night. Maybe he decided to take a nap.

A smile curves my lips at the thought of Asher laid out across his bed, his broad, bare back exposed, his expression soft in sleep. The thought sends a flutter through my belly, and I toe off my shoes before heading up the stairs. I'm already unbuttoning my jeans, already planning on stripping bare and sliding into bed with him. I'll wrap my arms around him and let the sound of his breathing lull me to sleep.

But when I step into his bedroom, I don't see the darkened space I expect. Instead, I see candlelight and hear the softly thumping beat of the Infinite Gray album.

Licking my lips, I pull my shirt over my head and follow the candlelit path around the corner into the master suite.

I expect to see Asher waiting for me. I expect to see him reading in the chair by the window or sitting in the bed, that wicked smile on his lips. I expect he'll take over for my hands that are currently unbuttoning my pants.

But I don't see Asher at all.

I see a woman on his bed. A long-legged, blond, surgically enhanced, *naked* woman.

My first thought is that I'm in the wrong place. That maybe I somehow walked through the door, up the grand staircase and into the bedroom of the wrong house.

I stutter back a step. The woman's eyes land on me and flash angry, and I know I'm not where I'm supposed to be. There's no mistaking the feminine jealousy flashing across her features, the condescension on her face as she looks me over.

"What do you think *you're* doing here?" she asks with an upturned lip.

She seems totally unconcerned with her nudity, but I have my arms crossed over my bra and I'm backing away instinctively.

"Hey, babe, what's up with all the candles? Trying to burn my house down?"

The woman's eyes widen and her face is like a flower, puckered and closed at the sight of me and now blooming at the sound of his voice.

"I'm in bed, baby," she calls, her calculating eyes never leaving mine. "But you'll need to take out the trash before we can get started."

Asher comes around the corner and freezes when he sees the woman in the bed.

I'm waiting for him to fix this. Waiting for him to ask her what the hell she's doing here. Waiting for him to kick *her* out.

"Juliana." He looks at her, then me, then back to her.

Juliana? His daughter's mother? Are they still together?

"I'm home," the woman says, sweetness dripping from every word. "Aren't you going to give your wife a kiss?"

"Your wife?" Another step back and I knock over a candle. Hot wax splashes onto my bare feet and pools on the shining wood plank floors. "Shit." I hop away from the candle, the wax burning my foot.

"Juliana, get dressed," he growls. Then he turns to me. "I thought we weren't meeting here for another couple hours."

I blink at him. This has to be a dream. Has to be. A horrible nightmare. There's a naked woman in his bed calling herself his wife and he's looking at me like it's my fault because I arrived early?

"You're married?"

"Of course he's married," Juliana says, coming toward us. Her breasts are perky and full and her hip bones protrude on her painfully gaunt frame.

I shake my head. "Is this a joke?" Or a dream. A joke or a dream. But the cooling wax hardening on my foot feels so real, and this would be too cruel a joke from a man I've fallen for.

"Maggie," Asher says softly. "Juliana is Zoe's mom. I told you about her."

"You didn't tell me you were married to her."

His gaze ping pongs between us and his jaw works for a minute before he says, "It's not even a marriage anymore. Just a technicality."

I feel both like I've fallen and jerked to a stop in midair. Now I'm just hanging here, suspended in time. "But you are married."

Juliana wraps her arm around Asher's waist and he pushes it away. "*Clothes*," he growls.

I can hardly breathe. This is it. This is the proof that I will always be a home-wrecking slut.

I don't know how long I stand there, staring at her as she pulls one of his t-shirts from his drawer like they're her own, staring at him as he repeats, "Listen to me, Maggie."

When Juliana walks back over in the same old band tee I toured this house in last week, I want to vomit. Her arms are crossed under her breasts. "Is she the reason you're leaving me?"

Leaving?

"She's the mother of your child." I'm trying to get this straight, to make sense of it. Oh, God. What have I done?

"We're not together anymore," Asher's saying. "We haven't lived together in over a year. We're getting a divorce."

Juliana sneers at me. "Are you the reason he sent me those divorce papers? Huh? He's leaving me for some teenage country bumpkin?"

I don't tell her I'm not a teenager. I don't tell her I didn't know he was married.

I don't say anything because I've used up all the excuses, and I don't have a single new one worth speaking.

I stagger backward toward the door.

"Don't go, Maggie."

I shake my head. The words "I'm sorry" slip out and I don't even know who I'm apologizing to. Juliana? Asher? Myself?

"I won't let my marriage be ruined by some loose co-ed," Juliana calls. Anger drips from every word. Anger she's entitled to. Anger I deserve.

Asher's calling after me, but I run, and when I hit the stairs I hear him behind me, closer, and run faster. I lose my footing and slide down the last five stairs.

I cry out when I hit the tile floor but I scramble to my feet and reach for the door handle.

"Maggie, don't go, not like this." His hand slams against the door before I can open it. "*Talk* to me."

I force my panicked hands to release the handle and roll my shoulders back. When I turn to him, his face is so close, so agonized, and I hate how much I want to curl into him. I hate how much I want to listen to his explanation. I hate how tempted I am to make excuses. For him. For me.

"I assumed you knew," he says softly.

"Why would I know?" God, it hurts to speak, my throat so thick with jagged bits of my pride. My heart.

"It's never been a secret, Maggie. You never asked and I thought you knew."

"That's not something I should have to ask." My eyes are burning with tears. *Tears*. Fuck him.

"Juliana and I haven't been together in years, but neither one of us was ready to admit it was over." He touches my face. I *let him* touch my face because I am so fucking weak. His thumb tilts up my chin until my eyes meet his. "I was too apathetic to end it. Until you."

A single hot tear rolls down my cheek. "Asher," I say softly.

"Tell me what you need from me, Maggie. You can have it. You know that. *Anything.*"

"I need you to be honest."

"I have *never* lied to you."

"Are you married?"

His face contorts with pain. "Yes, but—"

I put my finger to his lips. "No." I shake my head. "I've heard all the *but's* I can bear. I'm not the gullible child who believes them anymore. I won't be that woman for you. I won't be her for anyone."

"You *aren't* that woman. I'm in love with you. My marriage is over."

"That's what they all say." The laughter that spills from my lips sounds half crazed. "And you know what's so ironic? You're the one who made me give enough of a shit about myself not to believe it anymore."

"Don't lump me in with them." His jaw is hard now. "I'm not like them."

"Let me go, Asher. If you really love me, you won't ask me to stay. You won't make this any harder for me than it already is."

He studies me hard for a moment, as if he could will me to see things his way. Then he drops his hand and steps back, and I rush out the door before I can change my mind.

chapter twenty-two

William

"Jay-sus," Lizzy breathes. "I think everyone in town is here."

The gallery is swarming with locals and out-of-towners, and the crowd spills over onto the patio in the front and the balcony in the back. Wine is flowing, art is selling, and I am fucking miserable.

"You guys should be so damn proud," Lizzy says with a shake of her head.

Krystal's across the room, chatting with Granny, and something tugs long and hard in my chest at the sight of her. We did the right thing. I know we did. But that doesn't keep me from mourning the would-have-beens.

"Oh my God," Lizzy squeaks. "Maggie's here. What the hell happened to her? She looks a mess. Where's Asher? Oh my God, do you think they took him back to prison?"

"No, they didn't press charges."

"But—"

I walk away from Lizzy without excusing myself. Her rapid-fire questions are more than I can bear tonight—even if they're the same questions I have.

Maggie's eyes are puffy and it's obvious she's been crying.

I weave through the crowd and have nearly reached her when Ethan Bauer's assistant squeezes my arm.

"We're ready," she says reverently.

I shift uncomfortably. The side room holding Ethan's top secret collection has been locked up tight since his assistants came to stage it this morning. They insisted the room stay closed until a crowd had gathered.

I nod and the woman scurries over to the steps. "If I could have everyone's attention, we will now open the south room, which features a collection from the illustrious Ethan Bauer."

The crowd applauds and I continue to work my way toward Maggie, who looks lost.

"I present to you," the woman says, "the Discovery collection."

Maggie's head snaps up, and she mouths "No" as the doors open and the crowd files in, their murmurs carrying back into the main room.

I finally reach Maggie's side and she's staring toward the newly opened double doors, her eyes wide. "What is it?" I ask softly. "Are they paintings of you? It's okay, Maggie. No one will know."

She doesn't answer. Instead she says, "Asher is married," and my breath leaves me in a rush. Her eyes meet mine, red-rimmed and vacant. "You knew, didn't you? That's why you said he was just using me for sex."

I swallow and lift a shoulder. "I don't keep up with celebrity gossip, but I knew he used to be. That actress, right? Juliana Weisnith?"

"Yeah. Juliana," she says softly. "God. I trusted him. You're right. I always give myself to the wrong guys. Maybe my dad was right about me. Look at everything I've destroyed."

"No." I take her hand and squeeze. "Don't say that. Your dad didn't even mean the things he said at the end, Maggie. He just… he lost his best friend and his baby girl in one fell swoop, and he said terrible things to try to cope."

She blinks at me and the crowd mills around us, sneaking

glances Maggie's way that tell me all I need to know about the paintings in that room.

She cuts her eyes to the doors and back to me. "Will you go in with me?"

I give another squeeze to her hand. "Of course. I'll be right by your side."

The crowd seems to part as we make our way through the doors, and the moment I step inside, I understand, and my feet freeze beneath me. "My God."

The room features four large canvasses. The painting on the far wall catches my attention first. It's stunning. A woman dressed in nothing but a man's white dress shirt. She's stretched out on a couch, one hand gripping the cushion, the other tucked between her slightly parted legs. Her head is tilted back, her mouth half open, eyes closed, sheer ecstasy shaping her features.

I'd know the shape of that body anywhere. I would recognize her from the pleasure on her face.

Beside me, I hear a small cry and I turn to see Maggie biting her lip, eyes fixed on the painting labeled DISCOVERY.

Her hand covers her mouth as her eyes scan the other portraits.

"I'll get everyone out," I whisper. "We'll close the room back up. It's not worth it."

She shakes her head, eyes brimming with tears. "No. I'm not hiding anymore. Let it be."

I feel completely helpless as I watch her look at the paintings, one by one, as if she's forcing herself to take in every detail, to catalogue her own sins.

"Holy shit," someone says behind us. I think it's Lizzy, but I don't turn to see.

A painting labeled FRIDAY MORNING shows a bed with a fluffy white comforter, a red head peaking out the top, eyes sleepy and seductive.

Another appears to place the viewer from the most erotic position between her legs. The perspective shows her inner thighs and bare stomach, her red hair covering her breasts.

Yet another appears to have been painted from the perspective of the person she's straddling. A yellow sundress is bunched around her hips, and her head is tilted to the side, her eyes closed, mouth parted in ecstasy.

Maggie spins a slow circle, taking in each painting, blood draining from her face.

By the time she looks at the last one, she's pale and unsteady. I hold her up.

"I'm fine." She steps back. "Fine."

She's not fine and we both know it, but she doesn't want to lean on me. Doesn't want to need me. Not anymore.

"I need to go." She turns on her heel and pushes through the crowd.

Maggie

SEVERAL SMOKERS mingle on the front patio and eye me curiously as I exit the gallery. I excuse myself and follow the sidewalk away from the building to a garden area with the solitude I crave.

I should have never trusted Ethan. That is so obvious now I can only shake my head in bewilderment at the girl I was.

"I'm so sorry, Maggie."

I turn to see Will, regret written all over his expression, and my shoulders drop. Funny the difference a month makes. A month ago, I would have thought that exhibition was the worst thing that could have happened. Now, my heart is so torn up over Asher, the exhibit is only another bad bit of luck, but nothing life altering.

"I didn't know what was in there," Will says.

"It doesn't matter." Funny how it took me all these years and all this pain to realize that keeping a secret doesn't change the past. It doesn't correct our errors or mend the things we've broken.

The secret only harvests the hurt next to our hearts, blocking the sunlight from the spot where happiness is supposed to grow.

"I'm sorry about Asher," Will says. "He's not leaving her, then?"

I lift my eyes to his and shrug. "He says he is, but that isn't enough." My voice cracks and before I realize they're coming, tears are streaming down my face and my chest is shaking.

Will pulls me into his arms and strokes my hair as I struggle to breathe around choked sobs.

"I won't be that woman anymore."

Asher

I WANT to rage at someone, anyone. I want to tear these paintings off the walls and burn them.

"We didn't know," someone says behind me.

I spin around to see Will, hands tucked in his pockets, shoulders hunched.

My hands flex into fists and I step back away from the urge to take a swing.

When I got here, Maggie was outside crying. In Will's arms.

"I wouldn't have allowed it if I'd known," Will's saying as he eyes the paintings. "Not in my gallery. But Maggie asked me to leave them."

"Where is she?"

"She went to Brady's with her sisters," Will says, straightening. "You hurt her."

My jaw feels like it might snap it's so tight. I don't want to hear this from the man who just had the woman I love in his arms. But I can't deny it either.

He nods knowingly and slips out the door, leaving me alone to contemplate these paintings.

By the time I got done arguing with Juliana—explaining in no uncertain terms that our marriage is over—I had a long argument with myself about coming here tonight.

Maggie deserved to be pissed at me. With her history, I should have been more forthcoming about the state of my marriage. I'd be lying if I said it never occurred to me that the truth might hurt her, but I told myself it didn't matter because my marriage is nothing but a technicality at this point.

I need to go home and give her space. I need to get on my knees and pray like hell she'll come back to me.

But I have to do one more thing before I can leave.

chapter twenty-three

Maggie

I FINALLY fell asleep some time before dawn, but not before I cried. I cried for the lost young woman I'd become, the woman who'd trusted her shattered heart with a man and had lost it. I cried for the young woman who had placed her baby in a stranger's arms and said goodbye. I cried for my teenage self, the girl who had lost something precious to a man who hadn't been worthy and hadn't had permission.

I'd lain in bed, alone, remembering the only other time loneliness had struck me so deeply.

"Will you tell them that I want her name to be Grace?"

Sister Rose had frowned. *"Maggie, we talked about this. They can—"*

"Will you just tell them?"

Every week, pictures arrive in the mail with a short note.

Thank you for Grace. She is truly a blessing.

Would it be easier if all I'd known of the child I created had been those brief but precious moments in the hospital? Would it be easier if I didn't know my daughter has my red hair and freckles and her dad's dimples?

Would it be easier to sleep in my cold bed when I hadn't known the feel of a man who truly cared for me?

The only place I want to be is curled up on my mom's couch. Right now, I don't mind the doilies and cross-stitched pillows. I don't even mind the oversized golden crucifix that hangs above me.

The cushions shift beside me and I blink up at my mom.

"Here you go, sweetie," Mom says, handing me a steaming mug of tea.

"Thanks."

"Your sisters told me about Asher's wife."

I close my eyes. I can't look at her. Not now. I draw in a shaky breath. "I'm sorry." I shake my head. "I was trying to change."

"It's not your fault, sweetie."

I draw in a shaky breath. "Do you ever think that maybe dad was right about me?"

She gasps. "He wasn't." She shakes her head. "And I'm sorry I let him treat you like he did…after. We were both so heartbroken over what happened to our baby, and we handled it terribly. And I'm sorry for that."

"It wasn't your fault."

"The blame is more mine than yours, Margaret." Her face softens. "I have wished so many times to be able to change the past, to do right by you."

I can hardly breathe; my shattered heart is so painful against my lungs.

She studies me a long moment before nodding and pushing herself off the couch.

"Mom, wait."

My words stop my mother in her tracks. I haven't called her *Mom* since dad died. I never called her by her given name, either. She wouldn't have allowed that. I just haven't called her anything.

My throat is thick with emotion. "Thank you for letting me stay here."

"Of course," she says, her voice crackling on the edges with tears.

I study my tea. "Are you okay?"

She nods. "I like it when you call me 'Mom.' You haven't done that since you were fifteen."

"I…" I was a little shit who blamed her for things she couldn't control. Things that she would have given the world to save me from. Since there's no explaining, I hand her a fat envelope from my purse.

I can hardly breathe as she slides the pictures into her hand. And, as it always does, my heart breaks at the sight of my baby girl with her bright green eyes and wild red curls. Her mother sends me pictures every week. Pictures and gratitude expressed in stories about bath time, bottles, and cooing. I savor the packages like fine chocolate, and they tear me to shreds like razor blades.

I wait for my mother to get angry. For my lying. For my deception. I wait for that moment when she will finally be done with me. I wait but nothing happens. She flips through the pictures slowly, smiling and grimacing alternately, as if—maybe—she's imagining what seeing the pictures must be like for me.

When she makes it through the stack and returns her eyes to mine, she doesn't speak.

"They named her Grace," I say softly, my hands shaking as I take the pictures back.

Tears shimmer in her eyes. I haven't seen my mother cry since my father's funeral.

"I was pregnant when Will and I got engaged," I tell her. "I was pregnant with Ethan Bauer's baby." As the words slip from my mouth, they don't hurt like I expect them to. Instead, the truth is a salve to my abraded heart. "I was going to pretend it was Will's, and I couldn't. I couldn't do that to him. I couldn't do that to her. So I gave her up."

She settles back onto the couch and strokes my cheek. I don't realize I'm crying until I feel her wiping away my tears. I've cried enough in the last twenty-four hours to make up for years of dry eyes.

"I…suspected," my mother whispers. "I didn't know how to help you. I didn't know what you wanted. I should have…" My mom squeezes her eyes shut and shakes away the thought.

"I still hadn't forgiven myself for what happened in high school, and I—"

Mom's breath draws in sharply. "Baby," she whispers.

"I hated letting her go, but I was too ashamed to have a married man's baby. I didn't think I could ever face you again." I squeeze her hand. "I handled it in the only way I knew how."

"I think, Margaret Marie, that you handled it beautifully. And I am proud to have you as my daughter."

My mom wraps her thin arms around me, and I sink into the old, familiar warmth. I can't remember the last time I let my mother hug me, but it feels like returning home. She rocks me gently side to side and kisses my hair.

"What an amazing gift," she says simply, and the words tear me open. I cry into her chest.

When she pulls away, her eyes are wet and there are tears streaming down her face. "I've made a mess of my makeup," she mutters, but her smile says she doesn't really care.

Her hand feels frail in mine. "I'm going to take a walk down to the river."

She nods. "Have you called him?"

I look at the floor and shake my head. No need to say who *he* is. "I'm not ready yet."

"No!" Lizzy shouts. "No regrets about sleeping with Sexy Beast. Absolutely not."

I can't help but smile. She's so flipping cute. "He's married," I repeat softly.

Hanna's scanning through something on her phone, and when she hands it over to me, triumph gleams in her eyes.

She has some sort of gossip site pulled up and her phone is displaying the headline "Infinite Gray Hottie and Actress Wife On the Outs." I scroll through it to see a vague reporting of nothing but a rehashing of the title and a speculation that the couple has separated since the birth of their daughter.

"That was published two *years* ago, Mags," Hanna says.

I roll my shoulders back. "It doesn't matter. I won't be the other woman anymore."

The girls exchange a look, frowning.

"It just feels like Asher's getting a bum rap because of jerks from your past," Lizzy says.

Hanna nods. "Is that really fair?"

I shrug, pushing myself out of my chair. "If he wants to be with me, he can get a divorce."

"I guess," Hanna says softly.

"I'm going to step out for some fresh air," I say.

The girls nod. "We'll be there in a minute."

I'm halfway to the door when Will stops me.

"How you holding up?" he asks.

"I'm okay." And it's true. It's been a week since I walked in on Juliana naked in Asher's bed, and even though my heart aches with missing him, I'm more okay than I have been in years. Ironically, it's all thanks to him.

"I know this handsome blond guy who'd love to take you out sometime...when you're ready." Will gives a self-deprecating grin.

"I appreciate that," I say softly. "But you deserve more than to be my consolation prize."

"I would have settled for that."

I lift onto my tiptoes and press a kiss to his cheek. "And I love you for that."

chapter twenty-four

Asher

SHE CAME *back.*

It's all I can think. I'm consumed by it.

I sent her a text before I boarded my plane in New York tonight. *It's done.*

That was all I wrote. Because I didn't know if the end of my marriage meant the beginning of something new with Maggie or if I'd lost my chance for that.

I came home to a dining room table covered in rocks, scraps, and shards of ceramic and glass.

What did she call this stuff? Tesserae?

There are little piles of it all over the table with note cards labeling each one.

A pile of glass shards, *Crystal serving platter from bridal shower.* A pile of sand, *From the bottom of the river.* Some slivers that glint in the light, *The Infinite Gray album.* A little gravel, *From the parking lot at Cajun Jack's.* Yellow and green chunks of plastic, *Baby bottles I never got to use.* There's even a tiny pile of old guitar picks and one final note.

I think we can make something beautiful with all this. Find me.

Maggie

I PEEL off my shirt and jeans then drop my bra and underwear to the ground and dive nude into the warm water.

I don't like to think what might have happened if Asher hadn't shown up at Brady's that night. I don't like to think what might have happened if he hadn't shown up in my life.

After I left the courthouse last week, I drove to Asher's house, but he wasn't here. I'd sent him a single text.

The text simply read: *Thank you for finding me.*

It wasn't long after that I found out he left town. I assumed he headed to New York to see his daughter. I couldn't blame him.

Then tonight, I got a text from him: *It's done.*

I can only hope that means what I think it does. I am only here because I think it means his marriage is over in every sense of the word now.

I turn through several laps, and I'm not surprised when I see him. I stop swimming and pull myself to the edge of the pool.

"Training for the Olympics?" He's wearing dark blue jeans, but his chest and feet are bare and my mouth goes dry at the expanse of his chest, at the V of muscle that dips into his jeans.

I swallow hard, remembering our first encounter here. "Sneak up on many girls?"

"Only the special ones." His eyes are hot, burning with something more than lust.

When he extends a hand, I take it and let him help me from the water. Then I stand there dripping in the moonlight as he runs his eyes over me.

My nipples harden in the cool air. Without speaking, he dips his head and licks a bead of water off one. My lungs empty, no room for air as the potent tonic of pleasure and love shoots into my veins. It starts cool and runs hotter until it settles between my legs. His big hands settle at my hips, the calluses of his fingertips curling into my ass as he takes my breast into his mouth. My breasts have always been about my lover's pleasure. They're large and awkward but men love them. But when Asher takes my breast into his hot mouth, when he scrapes his teeth across my nipple, when he sucks, I am lost in it. In him. I want him to keep doing this, to keep making me feel this way. I feel my control fracturing under the pressure, but I don't stop him because—for him—I'll let myself break.

I reach for him and unbutton his jeans. I push his pants and underwear from his hips. In a single motion, I drop to my knees and slide them down his legs.

His cock jumps, a breath from my lips, and my heart pounds at the sight of him, the memory of him.

"Stand up, Maggie." His voice is hard, thick with a need I understand.

In the chilly air, my skin breaks out in goose bumps.

Taking both of my hands in one of his big ones, Asher kicks his jeans away and leads me up the steps to his hot tub. I follow him, sinking into the hot, bubbling water.

He cups my face in his hands and stares down at me with those wild blue eyes. I wait for him to drop his lips to mine, but he doesn't.

"If I would have believed a miracle like you could come into my life, I would have ended my marriage last year. I would have been waiting and ready."

I touch his face, his stubble abrading my fingertips. I love this man so much my heart aches with it.

"You're trembling," he whispers against my ear.

I pull back so he can see me shake my head. I'm afraid to talk, afraid to speak the words lodged in my throat. Afraid I might lose it.

He holds me, and I cling to him like I've never clung to anyone. "I found you, sweetheart. You don't need to hold together anymore. I found you."

epilogue

Maggie
Eight Months Later

CAMPUS IS insane with the buzz about tonight's concert. Sinclair students stood in line for days waiting for tickets to Asher Logan's concert—his first by himself, and a kickoff to his fifty-campus tour for his new solo album *Unbreak Me.*

The auditorium is packed, and as the lights go down the crowd explodes in cheers.

The soft spotlights on the stage grow brighter as Asher steps out with his guitar, a fist raised in the air.

The wild shrieks of the girls in the front row fade into the background as I look at him, my heart pounding with pride, my stomach fluttering with nerves.

"Sinclair University, how are you tonight?" he shouts.

They respond with more noise, escalating until the room pulses at the edges with sheer volume and energy.

"Thank you for coming."

As if on cue, the roars quiet as they wait for him to begin.

"This first one's for my girl, Maggie." He turns to where I

stand at the side of the stage and winks at me before returning his attention to the crowd. "It's called 'Unbreak Me.'"

The audience roars in appreciation.

He plays the opening chords of the song he wrote for me, and as he begins to sing, hot tears streak down my cheeks. I close my eyes and mouth the words.

I was nothing but a failure. A fucked-up, broken shame.
I was nothing but this emptiness. A shell ruined by fame.
Don't be afraid to shatter, baby, if that will set you free.
I'll find you in the pieces and that will unbreak me.

When he reaches the end of the song and the crowd's applause dies down, he turns to me again. "I love you, gorgeous."

"I love you too!" I shout back over the audience's screams.

I don't know if he hears me, but he grins, and my chest is so full of love, I might shatter, and I'm okay with that because I know he'll find me. Again and again.

acknowledgements

As always, I owe the bulk of my gratitude to my husband and children. Brian, thank you for playing single dad while I wrapped up this book, but, more than that, thank you for believing in my dreams. With you holding my hand, it doesn't feel like a leap of faith but just another step. To my children, thank you for enjoying PB&J and frozen pizzas and understanding when Mommy needs to work. I love you all more than you'll ever know.

To the fabulous Nina, aka Violet Duke, thank you for believing in this book before I'd even committed to writing it. You saw it for what it could be and helped kick my butt until it became what it is today. You have mad skills, lady.

To everyone else who provided me feedback on and cheers for Maggie's story along the way—especially Marilyn Brant, Adrienne Hogan, Michael Miller, Megan Mulry, and Annie Swanberg—you're all awesome.

Many people helped with the research for this book. A huge thanks to Jim Archer for answering my many questions about the criminal justice system. Thanks to my artist brother Aaron for answering my questions about the art world and to my nurse sister Kim for explaining some ER protocol. Their answers were instrumental to my story. Any errors are my own.

Thank you to the team that helped me package this book and promote it. Sarah Hansen at Okay Creations designed my cover, and it truly takes my breath away. Arran at Editing720, thank you for the fast and thorough edits. Thanks to Giselle at Xpresso Book

Tours for organizing the fantastic cover reveal and release day blitz, and to Julie at AToMR for organizing my reviews. You all earn every cent and more.

To all my writer friends on Twitter, Facebook, and my various writer loops, thank you for your support and inspiration. Lauren Blakely, thank you for featuring *Unbreak Me* in the back of *Trophy Husband*. Thanks to Violet Duke and Lisa Renee Jones for agreeing to share excerpts of their upcoming releases with my readers.

And last but certainly not least, thank you to my fans. I appreciate each and every one of you. I couldn't do this without you and wouldn't want to. Thank you for buying my books and telling your friends about them. Thank you for asking me to write more. You're the best!

playlist

Ani DiFranco—*32 Flavors*
Nine Inch Nails—*Perfect Drug*
P!nk—*Slut Like You*
Cold Play—*Fix You*
The Fray—*How to Save a Life*
P!nk, featuring Nate Ruess—*Just Give Me a Reason*
Muse—*Madness*
Nine Inch Nails—*Hurt*
Ani DiFranco—*Gratitude*
Labrinth featuring Emeli Sandé—*Beneath Your Beautiful*
Rihanna featuring Mikki Ekko—*Stay*
Ani DiFranco—*Amazing Grace*
Josh Radin—*When You Find Me*

stolen
wishes

a Wish I May
novella

stolen wishes

a Wish I May *novella*

by LEXI RYAN

Editing by Rhonda Helms and Editing 720
Cover © 2013 Sarah Hansen, Okay Creations
Interior formatting by E.M. Tippetts Book Designs

For all my readers who loved Will and Cally and wanted to read more. This is their beginning and it's for you.

chapter one

Cally

"COME ON, sweetheart." Kenny Riles edvges forward, his snickering minions close behind. "I'll give you fifty dollars for a hand job. That's twice what I paid your mom."

I wrap my arms around myself, blaming the chill in the early spring night for the shivers running through me. I came to the dark stadium to be alone. Now, I'm wishing I had a friend with me. Hanna to wrap her arm around my shoulders, or Lizzy to crack a joke about the size of Kenny's dick before telling him to fuck off. The guys smell like beer, cigarettes, and a dangerous lack of inhibition.

Kenny's eyes sweep over me greedily. "You ain't out here for nothing. You're looking to suck a little dick, ain't you? Let's see if you're as good as your mom."

The sound of footsteps—a fast and noisy hustle up the bleachers—has me pulling my gaze away from Kenny's hazy eyes.

I can make him out in the moonlight—a figure in a hooded sweatshirt and athletic shorts running up the bleachers and down the steps, up the bleachers, down the steps, zigzagging his way closer and closer to us.

I've never been so grateful to see a jock in my life.

"I'll pass." I try not to let him hear how his words affect me. But fear lodges in my throat, making the words smaller than I intended.

Kenny grabs my hand.

"Back off!"

The clanking of feet on bleachers stops, and silence seems to echo through the stadium. "Get your fucking hands off the girl, Riles," the jock calls, coming toward us.

"What? She your girlfriend?" Kenny asks. "When did you start slummin' it, Bailey?"

Bailey? William Bailey. *Shit.*

Rich kid, golden boy, quarterback. And so very much the object of my fantasies. Really, universe? You couldn't have put *anyone* else here to witness my embarrassment?

"Does she have to be my girlfriend for you to understand what *back off* means?" William asks. He's closer now, his face dark and glowering.

"I'm just giving the girl some business, but I guess if you're her customer tonight, we'll get out of your way."

Hate boils up in my stomach, and I have to close my eyes. I can't look at William when this guy is implying such horrible things about me. I'm too scared to see his face, too afraid he might believe them.

"Come on, guys. Let's get out of here." Kenny and his guys exchange a few grunts and stomp away down the bleachers.

I inhale deeply for the first time in several long minutes and force myself to look at William.

"Are you okay?" He comes closer and pulls the hood from his head. His smile is cautious, worried. I can almost make out the warm blue of his eyes in the moonlight.

My stomach flips. Everyone in this town knows who William Bailey is. He's smart and popular and beautiful. Everything I'm not. "I was just leaving," I lie.

"You're Cally Fisher, right?"

That surprises me. We have one class together—third hour French—but he's always busy chatting with his friends. I never thought he noticed me. "Yeah…"

"I've watched you."

I raise a brow. "You've *watched* me?"

"Wow. Not like that." He chuckles and runs a hand through his hair. He has these unruly blond curls girls go mad over, present company included. "Now I sound like a bigger creep than Kenny, don't I? I've *seen* you. You walk by the river a lot. I worry about you. You're always alone and it's always after dark."

"I like the stars," I answer, then immediately wish I'd kept the childish words to myself.

He shoves the sleeves of his hoodie up to his elbows as he scans the empty stadium. "Me too, but you shouldn't be out here alone."

"And where's *your* babysitter?"

That grin is back, and I feel like the luckiest girl in the world to have it aimed at me. Stupid but true. "Touché."

"Well, thanks for your help with the asshole squad. I appreciate it." I make myself head down the steps. After the day I've had, another ounce of kindness from him and I'm bound to make a fool of myself.

As soon as my feet hit the pavement at the foot of the bleachers, he's beside me.

I shift awkwardly. "You can get back to your workout or whatever."

"I could. Or I could use my chauvinistic concern for your welfare as an excuse to walk a pretty girl back to her house."

My cheeks burn. We walk in silence for a while, cutting across the dewy grass to get to Main Street, where the street lamps illuminate his face and make me feel self-conscious in my ratty old long-sleeve tee.

"So, do you want to talk about it, or would you prefer we continue with the romantic silence?"

I think he might be flirting with me. Which is just… No.

There's no way. This is William Bailey we're talking about. He can have any girl at our high school, and probably a healthy handful of the girls at the university down the street.

"Talk about what, exactly?" I ask stupidly.

"About Kenny? Or the reason you spend more time after dark wandering around New Hope than at your house?"

"Kenny's just a jerk."

"Agreed. And the other?"

How do I explain my nighttime walks to a guy who has everything? The stars winking at me from the sea of black sky, the sound of the river, the whisper of the wind in the trees. In the crisp air, when everything is cloaked in darkness, I feel closer to the stars. No one needs me. No one sees me. No one taunts me. Looking at the stars and wishing for something better isn't just something I enjoy. It's necessary for my survival.

I wouldn't expect him to understand that.

"I like wandering at night." I shrug. I don't want to tell him about what drives me to seek haven in the darkness. Mom, lost in her pills. Dad, nearly as oblivious, lost in his books.

"You don't have to wander alone, you know. I mean, you shouldn't. Guys like Kenny look for any excuse."

My steps slow as we near the turn to my house. "Thanks for your concern. I'll see you around." I turn the corner, and he stays by my side as if I hadn't just dismissed him.

I stop and prop my hands on my hips. I don't want him coming any farther. He lives in one of the restored brick mansions near the center of town, and I'm too embarrassed for him to see the ramshackle doublewide trailer that's barely big enough for my family. "Goodnight, William."

"Oh, so you already know my name? I thought you just didn't care."

"*Everyone* knows your name. And *everyone* cares."

His eyes drop to my mouth. "*Everyone?*"

My heart slams against my chest and I think for one stupid minute that maybe he's going to kiss me, but then he takes my hand and tugs me toward my house. "Let me walk you home, Cally."

We amble slowly, as if neither of us really wants to reach our destination, my body romanticizing every second of this and buzzing with anticipation, while my pragmatic brain frantically denies any possibility that this guy—this *way freaking out of my league* guy—could possibly be attracted to me. He takes me all the way to my front stoop, and I when I turn to tell him goodbye, his gaze is on my mouth again.

William

MY HEART pounds in my chest. I'm nervous. Like a kid on his first date.

Cally has the biggest eyes and the softest lips. This isn't the first time I've noticed. She's in my French class. She's quiet and always looks a little alarmed when Madame Layton expects her to speak.

"Thanks for humoring me," I whisper.

"What?"

"For letting me walk you home. I enjoyed it." I smile and squeeze her hand. Am I the only one who feels this electric pulse of energy when our hands touch?

I wasn't lying when I said I didn't think she cared who I was. She keeps to herself in class, her nose in a book unless she's whispering to the Thompson twins, who sit next to her at the front of the room. I've spent weeks watching the way she bites her lip as she takes notes. I know she lets that curtain of thick, dark hair fall in her eyes when she's trying to hide and which friends make her face light up when she smiles.

And I know the rumors about her mom, which were no doubt the reason Kenny and his crew were harassing her tonight.

My hackles are rising from me just thinking about the asshole leaning toward her on the bleachers, grabbing her hand. "Listen, about Kenny—"

"Don't worry about him. It's fine."

"It's not fine, and I won't let him say those things about you."

She frowns. "Why do you care?"

Because I have a wicked crush on you. Because I've seen you staring up at the night sky like you're looking for something you've lost, and I understand that more than you know. "Because Kenny's an asshole."

She laughs and her whole face lights up. "You can say that again."

I want to make her smile like that all the time. "My friend Max is having a party tomorrow night. His parents are out of town. Any chance I'll see you there?" I hold my breath while I wait for her answer. I shouldn't have asked, but I can't help wanting to see her outside of school. I can't help wanting a chance to make her smile again.

"Cally? Who are you talking to out there?"

I didn't even hear the front door open, but Cally's mom is standing on the porch in a thin white nightgown that's damn near transparent in the porch light.

Cally tenses and pulls her hand from mine. "Mom, go inside. You're not decent."

Her mom looks down as if she needs the reminder of what she's wearing. "He's cute. Is he your boyfriend?" Her words are just slurred enough that I'm not sure if she's drunk or half asleep.

"No, he's not." Cally's so emphatic I wince. She turns to me. "I have to go." Then she hustles to the porch, wraps her arm around her mom and ushers her into the house.

Standing in the quiet night, I can hear their muffled voices inside the house, but I can't make out what they're saying. I'm starting toward home when I hear the porch screen squeak open. I turn back, thinking Cally is trying to catch me, that maybe she wants to say more, but then she sinks to the stoop and looks up at the stars.

She's not out here for me. She's out here to escape whatever is inside that house.

She has no idea how alike we are.

chapter two

Cally

K ENNY 'S WORDS have clung to me like tree sap since he cornered me at the stadium. Thick and sticky and impossible to ever completely remove. No matter how much I try to scrub them away, their residue remains.

"That's twice what I paid your mom."

That's just something mean boys say. I know that. But I also know the looks Mom gets when she goes into town. Women who used to be kind to her now duck their heads and hurry in the other direction when they see her coming.

I told myself Kenny was just an asshole trying to show off for his friends. I told myself he was just trying to get a rise out of me, to see what I would do. But even if that's true, it doesn't mean he's lying about Mom. And even if I want to tell myself he's a liar, part of me already knew the truth about the state of her "massage" business.

And last night when she came onto the porch, barely decent in front of William Bailey, disgust roiled in my stomach. Now every time I look at her, all I can think is, *Did you take money to give*

Kenny Riles a hand job?

"And Frankie said he would do it if she gave him her lunch," my little sister Drew is saying.

I blink at her, realizing I've missed half her story. I try to be a good listener for Drew. Someone needs to be.

"And so she did," she continues, "and on recess, *he did!*"

I fill her bowl with cereal and milk as she settles into her seat at the kitchen table. "Did what?" I ask.

"Ate a *worm*," she squeals.

"That's disgusting!" I wrinkle my nose, and she giggles. She's in first grade and generally a happy kid, despite everything. "Gabby," I call. "Want some cereal?"

Gabby hops up from where she was playing in front of Saturday morning cartoons. She toddles toward me. "With milk," she instructs in her little voice.

I settle her into the chair across from Drew and pour her cereal.

In the living room, Mom is sleeping on the couch, oblivious to our daily early-morning ritual.

"Cally eat?" Gabby asks, her mouth half full of cereal.

I shake my head. I can't handle the idea of food when Mom's purse is staring at me from the kitchen counter, her datebook inside.

My stomach flips when I think about what I might find there, but I have to know.

I leave the girls at the table, giggling about something they saw on a cartoon. The zipper seems to screech as I pull it open. I peek around the corner into the living room, but Mom is still sleeping. With a deep breath, I pull the black appointment book from her purse and leaf through it. Last month, last week. I scan over the scribbled names and I'm almost relieved.

Then I see it. Thursday afternoon. *Kenny.*

I snap the book shut quickly, as if staring at his name next to 4:00 might show me more than I want to know about their appointment.

"Can I have a Pop-Tart?" Drew asks.

I shove the book back into Mom's purse and zip it up, pushing it to the back of the counter where I found it. "No Pop-Tarts. There's enough sugar in that cereal."

"My have Pop-Tart?" Gabby asks. She's talking a lot for her age, but she always substitutes "my" for "I." It's ridiculously cute.

"How about an apple?"

The girls groan, but I grab a knife from the drawer and an apple off the counter.

So what? Kenny got a massage from Mom. That doesn't mean he got anything *more* than that. Does it?

I slice the apple into two bowls, removing the peel from Gabby's half. I'm handing the bowls to my sisters when my father emerges from the bedroom.

"You ladies are up early." He pushes his glasses up his nose and attempts to smooth his bedhead. He probably fell asleep reading in his recliner again.

"This is pretty much the normal time," I mutter.

He rubs his hands together. "I think it's a good day to go book shopping in Indianapolis. What do my girls say?"

"Yay!" the girls chorus.

"I think I'll pass," I say. I'm too preoccupied with the whole Mom and Kenny thing to enjoy a rare day with my dad. The girls will have a good time. Dad goes to these big used bookstores where the girls can get half a dozen new books for under five dollars. Of course, Dad will likely spend too much, buying more books about Taoism and Buddhism and any other -ism that promises to make sense of the universe. But the time with Dad is good for the girls, and the time alone will be good for me.

Mom shifts on the couch. "Cally? Are the girls up? Do they need anything?"

I close my eyes and bite back my frustrations. She wants to be a good mom, just not more than she wants her next fix. "It's okay. Go back to sleep."

"I HAVE a problem."

Lizzy Thompson crosses her arms and looks me over disapprovingly. "That you do. I can't believe you kept this from me."

I shift awkwardly on the steps of her front porch. I don't even know what she's talking about, but I'm freezing out here. "Are you going to invite me in or leave me out here?"

She pulls the door open wider, and I step into the warmth of her foyer. Blood finds its way back to my frozen fingers, making them burn. I pull off my coat, and Lizzy takes it and throws it on the banister before grabbing my hand and dragging me upstairs to her room.

Hanna is lying on her stomach on the floor, leafing through a magazine. When she sees me, her eyes go big. "Is it true?"

"Is what true?" I look back and forth between my two best friends, waiting for them to explain.

"She would have told us," Hanna says to Lizzy.

"Not necessarily," Lizzy replies. "Maybe it was an impulse thing and this is the first chance she's had."

"*She* is standing right here," I mutter. "Tell me what you're talking about."

"We heard you and William Bailey were together at the football field last night," Hanna says, pushing herself off the floor.

"That's true, I guess." I shake my head at the worry on my friends' faces. "I don't understand. What's the big deal?"

The girls exchange another one of those knowing looks. They may not look like it—Hanna with her long, dark hair and Lizzy with her blond curls—but they're twins, and it can be a little creepy how much they can communicate with each other without speaking.

"People are saying you were *together*. In the bleachers," Hanna says.

Lizzy rolls her eyes. "No, they're saying you were *fucking* in the bleachers."

My jaw goes slack, and I stumble back and lower myself to sit on the edge of the bed. I should have seen this coming. William was just trying to protect me, and what does he get in return? A bunch of rumors that he's nailing the poor chick with the slutty mom. God, he must hate me.

"Do you look so horrified because your secret's out or because it's a lie?"

"Lizzy!" Hanna screeches.

"What? Tell me you haven't thought about it. How many times have we placed him in the top five hottest guys in New Hope?"

Hanna's cheeks flare red, and she sinks next to me on the bed. "Ignore her. You don't have to tell us anything, but we thought you should know what people are saying."

I shake my head again. It hasn't even been twenty-four hours, and rumors are already making their way back to my friends. "Who told you that?"

"Krissy told Meagan who told us," Lizzy answers. "But Krissy won't say where she heard it."

"Kenny Riles, no doubt," I mutter.

"Why do you say that?" Hanna asks.

"Kenny's gotta be mad. Will put him in his place last night."

Lizzy narrows her eyes. "Put him in his place before, during, or after he made hot monkey love to you?"

"He didn't—"

"Don't!" She puts her finger to my lips. "Please don't tell me it didn't happen. Not yet. Not while I'm still looking forward to living vicariously through you."

"You're ridiculous." Hanna giggles. "But not wrong. I'll admit to having a stray fantasy or two about William Bailey myself."

"Just *one or two*?" Lizzy says. "He pushed up his sleeves in French the other day, and just looking at his forearms inspired at least seventeen different fantasies that day alone."

"He's taken!" I hear their older sister Krystal holler through the wall.

Lizzy shakes her head. "Don't mind her. She's had a crush on William since they were in eighth grade and thinks he's hers, but he's not into her."

The girls make me chuckle, despite myself. "I'm sorry to say you won't be living vicariously through me today. Nothing happened between me and William on the bleachers."

With a sigh, Lizzy sinks to the bed on the opposite side of Hanna. They lean their heads on my shoulders, squishing me into a twin sandwich.

"Kenny was out with his friends," I explain. "They were drunk, and he was trying to...proposition me, I guess? He said he'd bought a hand job from my mom and wanted to know what *my* going rate was."

The girls gasp in unison.

"He didn't!" Hanna whispers.

Lizzy growls, "What a fucker."

"It was actually kind of scary," I admit. "But then William was there, and he told them to leave me alone. They left, and Will walked me home. End of story."

"Kenny is such a creep," Hanna mutters. "But you need to tell Will so the rumor doesn't take him by surprise."

I nod. Talk about an awkward conversation. *"Hey, when you go back to school on Monday, everyone's going to think you shagged me on the bleachers. Sorry 'bout that."*

"It won't change anything," Lizzy warns. "But I agree it's better if he knows."

"I'm sorry he said that about your mom," Hanna whispers. "He's such a nasty liar."

I swallow hard and nod, remembering Mom's appointment book. *Had* Kenny been lying?

Time to change the subject. "I guess I need to talk to William," I say. "You know, he mentioned a party at Max Hallowell's tonight.

Would you two be up for that?"

Hanna claps gleefully. "We'd love to come with you!"

"Han!" her sister says. "We can't be there when the *obvious* solution is for Cally and Will to do the nasty so the rumor is the truth."

chapter three

Cally

"THANKS FOR coming with me tonight," I say to the girls as we walk up the steps to Max's house.

Hanna smoothes her hair. "Yeah, going to a party at Max Hallowell's house is such a hardship."

"We aren't staying long," I promise, more to give myself courage than because it's what they want to hear. "I want to give William a heads-up, and then we can get out of here."

"Oh, let's not rush away," Hanna says. "We don't want to insult the host."

"Do I sense a crush?" Lizzy asks.

Hanna's cheeks pinken as she knocks on the door. "No crush. He's a nice guy, end of story."

"A nice guy who just broke up with his girlfriend," Lizzy singsongs.

The door flies open, and a sleek-haired blonde stares at us skeptically. "Can I help you?" No, she's staring at *me* skeptically. I think her name is Kristen if I remember correctly. We had gym class together last semester, and she made a few cracks about my cheap wardrobe in the locker room. I might have *thought* a few cracks about her slutty wardrobe.

"This was a bad idea." I turn to leave. This isn't the place for me.

"Cally."

The sound of William's voice calling my name has my feet stalling on the steps. Lizzy squeaks beside me as I turn around. No one ever made jeans and a T-shirt look as good as William does. The dark denim hugs his hips, and the white T-shirt shows off his sculpted chest and shoulders.

"You came." He steps outside and grabs my arm, ushering me into the house.

"Um, yeah. These are my best friends, Lizzy and Hanna," I say awkwardly.

"Yeah, I grew up with all the Thompson girls. They lived next door to my grandma until their mom built that house on the river." He gives them a polite smile before turning back to me. "I'm glad you decided to come. You can throw your coats on that couch over there."

The girls and I peel off our jackets and toss them on the couch, and when I turn around, William is running his gaze over me. I'm wearing jeans and one of Lizzy's sweaters. It's black and fitted and shows more cleavage than I'm normally comfortable with, but Lizzy talked me into it. She also did my makeup, defining my eyes with dark liner and mascara and topping the look off with a swipe of lip gloss. Now I'm glad I let her fuss over me. I like the way his eyes linger on my curves and lips before returning to meet mine.

"You look gorgeous."

"You—you too." Damn. He's so sweet, and I'm just so... awkward. "Hey, can we talk?" Better to rip off the Band-Aid.

He smiles. I'm dazzled by that smile. It shoots something electric through my veins and back to my heart.

I look to my friends, not wanting to leave them before they find their place here. New Hope parties can be cliquey, and not in a good way.

"Go!" Lizzy urges. "We're fine."

I sink my teeth into my lip and nod.

William takes my hand and leads me to the stairs. A few catcalls go up as everyone watches us climb them together. Great. This is the exact opposite of what I came here to accomplish.

"You do fast work, man," someone calls, and someone else says, "Protection is in the bathroom."

By the time we're on the second floor, my cheeks are burning with embarrassment and shame. Embarrassment over the things those guys probably think we're doing up here. Shame for bringing that down on Will.

William leads me into a bedroom just off the stairs and shuts the door behind us. "I'm sorry about Sam and Max," he says softly. "They don't mean any harm. They're just jealous because they couldn't get a girl alone upstairs if they tried."

I shake my head. "I'm the one who's sorry. They're all going to think we're having sex up here."

He chuckles and brushes my hair from my face. His callused fingers set my skin to life, and I want to feel more of them. I imagine them tangled in my hair as he lowers his mouth to mine. I imagine the way they'd feel skimming over my neck. Lower.

"I don't think any of my friends really believe I'm that lucky," he says with a wink.

"You haven't heard yet, have you?"

His face turns serious. "Heard what?"

"Kenny Riles is telling everyone that we—" I swallow hard, my cheeks blazing with a new wave of embarrassment. "He's saying he saw us having sex on the bleachers." Then I add the new detail the girls learned before we left their house tonight: "He's saying you paid me."

Will steps back, his hands balling into fists, his jaw going tight.

"I wanted you to hear it from me first. I'm so sorry."

"Why do you keep apologizing? It's not your fault Kenny's a piece of scum who has to make shit up to feel like he serves a purpose in this world."

"I don't want to hurt your reputation."

He narrows his eyes, then his whole face softens and he steps close again. "You're serious, aren't you? You're worried about *my* reputation? What about yours?"

I lift a shoulder in a half-shrug. "My mom pretty much screwed up any chance I had of having a pristine rep."

He draws in a breath, like he's shocked I said it out loud. I guess I'm a little surprised too.

"I'll do whatever you need to fix this," I promise. "But we should probably start by getting back downstairs so we're not fueling the gossip mill."

"Maybe we should start by getting down there and dancing."

"Dancing?" I can't think straight when he's this close to me. The only thing dancing with William is going to accomplish is making me crush on him that much harder. "How is that going to help?"

He takes my hand and squeezes my fingers. He draws me toward him until my mouth is just a breath from his. Then, his lips curving into that charming, knee-melting smile, he reaches around me and opens the door. "Follow me."

Almost everyone is too preoccupied with their own conversations to notice our return, but Will's buddy Max spots us and shakes his head. "Stamina, man. You gotta work on the stamina if you want the beautiful ones to stick around."

"Cut it out, Max. Cally, this is my idiot best friend, Max. Max, this is Cally, my *guest*." He says the word like it has some sort of secret meaning then slides his hand around my waist and tugs me close.

Max's brows shoot up and he gives a knowing nod. "Say no more." He has a nice grin and he shows it off as he offers me his hand. "Nice to meet you, Cally."

"You too," I say, but the words come out as a whisper. I'm still tangled up in the sensation of Will's arm around my waist.

"I saw you brought your friends." Max nods to Lizzy and Hanna. They're at the island in the kitchen, laughing about something.

"I hope that's okay."

He lifts a brow. "Are you kidding? Beautiful girls are always welcome in my house."

"Max has a thing for Lizzy," Will whispers in my ear.

Max punches him lightly in the stomach. "Hush it, man." Then he turns to me, serious. "But do you happen to know if she's... available?"

Crap. Hanna's the one who likes Max. "Um. I don't think so. I mean, she doesn't seem really interested in more than just, you know, friends and stuff."

"Figures," Max says with a heavy sigh.

William takes me to the makeshift dance floor at the back of the living room and pulls my body next to his. I recognize the song as Nine Inch Nails' "The Fragile." I love this album. Hanna and Lizzy tease me for listening to it, but something about it has always spoken to my heart.

"You don't mind, do you?" His words are lazy puffs of air at my ear.

"Don't mind?" Wow. His presence seems to take away my ability to construct complete sentences. *Real attractive, Cally.*

He pulls me closer and settles a hand at my hip. "Dancing with me," he whispers. "Pretending to be my girl?"

I pull back so I can see his eyes, but they're all serious and expectant as he waits for my reply. God, he's gorgeous.

I don't know what to say, so I don't answer at all, just move with him to the music. His hand slides from my hip to under my shirt, his thumb against the sensitive skin above the waistband of my jeans.

"Hey, William," a girl calls from the kitchen. "Why don't you come in here and take a shot?"

I hardly have a chance to tense before Will pulls me closer. "Can't do that, Meredith. My date's here."

Lizzy and Hanna both turn to us at his words, and I feel my own eyes go wide.

"I'd consider it a personal favor if you could roll with this," he whispers into my ear. "Meredith has been trying to get me to do body shots since she got here two hours ago."

"You don't drink?" I ask, not that it's my business. I've just never been to a party with alcohol before, and I'm not sure what to expect. From the stories I've heard, I half expected everyone to be wasted by the time we got here.

"It's not the drinking that I mind. She's just not my type." When I frown at him, confused, his lips quirk in a half-smile. "You do know what a body shot is, don't you?"

I shake my head.

"Want to find out?" His fingers trail over the sensitive dip in my spine as he asks, and I nod. I would probably agree to anything he asked me right now.

He takes me to the kitchen, his hot hand never leaving the small of my back.

Lizzy and Hanna step back and study us as he leads me to the island. I'd feel guilty about abandoning them tonight, but they seem to be having a great time.

"Where's the tequila, Max?" Will calls.

Max hoists a bottle of amber liquid in the air and snags a shot glass off the counter.

"Do you know what a snakebite is?" Will asks me quietly. He's standing close so only I can hear him when he talks.

I bite my lip. "I don't really go to many parties."

Next to us, Max fills the shot glass with tequila.

"A snakebite is a shot of tequila that you take with salt and lime," Will explains to me.

"What makes it a body shot?" I ask.

His throat moves as he swallows, and his blue eyes go darker somehow, his pupils getting bigger. His lips part as he studies mine. "It's a body shot if you take all the parts of the snakebite off someone else's body."

That makes my pulse kick up a notch. I'm still trying to puzzle out the logistics when Max calls, "No hands, Bailey."

Will winks at me. "And I can't use my hands for anything but putting the salt on you. Are you still game?"

I nod wordlessly, and I'm rewarded with one of Will's full-out grins. I don't need to know details to understand his mouth is going to be on me, and I like the idea of that. A lot.

Will's hands slide to my waist and tighten, and before I realize what he's doing, he's hoisting me up on the counter. I squeak, and the girls cheer. All of them except Kristen and Meredith, that is. They're leaning against the fridge, scowling at me like I killed their puppy.

Max hands me the shot glass and looks at me expectantly.

"Do I hold it?" I whisper.

"If you want," Max says. "But I think you shouldn't make it so easy on my boy here."

Will shakes his head. "Whatever you're comfortable with."

Lizzy rushes over and cups her hand around my ear. "Slide it between your breasts. Trust me."

I gape at her, and she shrugs innocently before joining Hanna at the edge of the kitchen.

I may be inexperienced, but I'm not naïve and I get what this game is about. My cheeks heat as I slide the glass into my cleavage. It's cool against my hot skin, and Will's eyes burn into me as he watches me position it.

Max offers me a lime wedge.

"Do you need your friend to tell you what to do with that too?" Kristen calls.

"Shut up, Kristen," Will says. "You didn't know what you were doing your first time either."

But she's right. Lizzy shouldn't have to tell me what to do. I take the lime and put it between my teeth, facing out. The citrusy pulp presses against my lips, making them tingle. Or maybe the tingle is from the idea of William's lips close to mine.

Will grins and brushes my hair off my neck. "Ready or not."

When his hot tongue hits my neck, I'm assaulted by shivers of pleasure so potent I'm embarrassed to have all these people watching me. Instinctively, I tilt my head to the side to give him better access to my neck.

He nips the skin before lifting his mouth to my ear. "Still good?"

I can only nod.

"Good." He sprinkles salt onto the spot he just wet with his tongue, then licks it off and brings his mouth to the tequila. Since I'm on the counter, he doesn't have to lean down far, but he takes his time wrapping his lips around the glass. His face is practically buried in my cleavage, his breath hot against my breasts, and my cheeks burn with embarrassment and arousal.

When he comes up with the shot and tosses it back, I offer my open palm to take the glass. His mouth closes around the lime, and he holds there for two heartbeats, his eyes closed.

When he pulls away, he takes the lime out of his mouth and licks his lips. "Thanks for that." He brushes my cheek with his thumb, eyes locked with mine.

We hang there for a moment, not moving or breathing, time suspended as our eyes lock. It doesn't matter that there are at least a dozen other people in the room. For that moment, with his gaze equal parts hot and tender, I don't even care what they must think of me or what rumors might or might not be circulating when I return to school on Monday.

"Shit!" someone says. "Did you hear that thunder? It's going to rain!"

"Bailey," Max murmurs by Will's side, "can we get a little help moving the couch back into the house before it's destroyed?"

"I'll be right back. Don't go anywhere." He winks at me, then disappears out the back door.

"Well, *that* was hot," Lizzy says, offering her hand to help me off the counter.

"So hot," Hanna agrees as I hop down. "I'd be jealous if I weren't so happy for you."

"Same here. Crap." Lizzy winces. "I shouldn't have broken the seal earlier. I need to pee again."

"I'll go with you," Hanna says before turning to me. "You

okay?"

"I think so." I put my hands to my blazing cheeks. "I just need a cold drink."

Lizzy snorts. "I'll bet you do. We'll be right back." Then the girls are gone.

For the first time, I look around the kitchen and living room to survey the other party guests. Several of the guys rushed outside at the threat of rain, but the house is still pretty crowded, more so than when we arrived. There's a couple not two feet to my left who may need protection if they dance any closer, and another in the corner practically dry humping.

I look around the kitchen and find a cooler with bottles of water. I really just want to stick my face in the ice for about ten minutes, but this will have to do.

"Look who decided to close her legs for a few minutes," someone snipes as I come up with a bottle. It's Kristen, and she's scowling at me.

"Excuse me?"

"Listen. I know you're just trying to climb on up the social ladder. Heck, if I were a social pariah, I'd do the same. I'm just gonna do you a favor and spell this out for you before you have to learn the hard way. William Bailey can have any girl he wants. Money, good looks, status, Will's got it all. There's only one reason he'd go out with a girl like you. And I'm pretty sure he just showed you what that was."

Anger surges inside me. "You don't know anything." When are Lizzy and Hanna going to be back from the bathroom? I could use some reinforcements about now.

Kristen shrugs and pours herself a shot of tequila. "I'm not judging you for doing it. Hell, I'd fuck him until he couldn't see straight if I had the chance. But I can work in his world, whereas you'll just get hurt if you try. But maybe I'm giving too much credit to a girl who gives it up on the bleachers."

"Who told you that?"

She smirks. "Will was bragging about it to his boys right before you got here."

chapter four

William

"So, CALLY Fisher, huh?" Max says for my ears only as we push the couch back into position in the living room.

I shrug. I like Cally. A lot. But I'm not about to say anything definite to Max until I know the feeling is mutual. It's gotta be, though. The connection between us it too intense to be one-sided. Damn, my blood still runs hot in my veins when I think about the smell of her skin and the little shiver that ran through her when I pressed my tongue to her neck. I want to think she enjoyed that as much as I did. "I don't know yet," I say, scanning the crowd for her face.

Meredith sidles up to me and rubs against me like a cat. "You can do better than her," she purrs in my ear. "Come upstairs with me and Kristen and we'll show you just how much better."

"Give it up, Mer," I say, nudging her away. The last thing I need is for Cally to see one of these drunk girls throwing themselves at me like they give a shit. All they care about is what I can do for their reputation. Or worse, what my money can buy them. I'm so over that kind of girl.

I go to the kitchen, but Cally isn't waiting for me there. She's not in the living room, and she's not dancing.

I glance down the hall and see a long line of girls waiting for their turn in the restroom. Maybe that's where she went. I wonder if I can get her back upstairs. I want to talk to her without all these people watching us. I want to put my lips on her neck again without the excuse of alcohol.

I hated leaving her, but Max's parents would shit if they found out about this party, and how else would he explain a couch left out in the rain?

The feel of a small, cold hand under my shirt has me spinning around. *Cally.*

But it's not her. It's Kristen, and she's grinning up at me like the cat that ate the canary. "Guess your little date couldn't handle partying with the cool kids?"

"What?" I push her hands out from under my shirt. "What are you talking about?"

Kristen rolls her eyes. "Cally and her friends left while you were out back with the guys."

Left? *Shit.* "Where'd she go?"

"Maybe her mom needed help jacking off a client."

"Grow up," I growl. I rush out the front door and down the steps before Kristen has a chance to say more. Cally is walking down the sidewalk with the Thompson twins.

For a split second, I'm torn between following and letting her go. If she doesn't want to be here, I'm not going to make her. But the look in her eyes after I licked her neck has me jogging down the steps after them.

"What's going on?" I ask when I reach them.

The twins exchange a look, then turn to Cally. "Do you want to talk to him?"

She bristles, but nods slowly. "I'll catch up."

The girls nod and cross to the other side of the street, tossing worried glances over their shoulders as they walk away.

What the hell did I miss?

Cally

"Were you just going to leave without saying goodbye?" William tucks his hands in his pockets, and there's something more reserved about his body language. As *he's* the one who's been hurt here.

I thought William was better, different than other guys. But what do I know? Just because I'm attracted to him and he has a sexy smile doesn't mean I should assume he's better than the average horn dog. Heck, maybe that's why he isn't worried about the rumor. How do I know he didn't start it?

Even as I think the question, I know the answer. I know he didn't start the rumor because there's a goodness in his eyes that can't be faked. But is that enough of a reason to trust him?

I want to erase the last twenty minutes, to go back to the dance floor when I believed he might actually want me for me. But I'm not that stupid, and I can't let myself be.

Suddenly, in the war between my body and brain, my brain wins. And my brain is furious.

"I'm not a slut." The words drop like mini-grenades from my lips, detonating the minute they register with him and obliterating that invisible pull between us.

"Excuse me?"

I shrug. "I'm not stupid. I know there's only one reason a guy like you wants to spend time with a girl like me, but you have the wrong idea. I'm not like that."

"A guy…" He draws in a long breath, his jaw ticking. "A guy like me?"

"Money, good looks, status?" I say, using Kristen's words. "But I'm not going to be your easy lay. If that's what you're after, you should go talk to the girls inside. I'm sure you'll find some takers."

He steps back, pain flashing in his eyes. "I would think that someone who struggles with people's assumptions about her would be more careful about making them about others."

"What am I supposed to think?"

He looks up at the dark sky and laughs, a hollow, disappointed sound. The clouds obscure the moonlight and only the distant streetlight reveals his face.

I feel the icy rain hit my cheeks before I see it. Then it's coming down faster, stinging my face as we stare at each other.

His jaw is hard and he shrugs. "Forget it."

My stomach tightens in disappointment. What did I expect him to do?

"Catch up with your friends before they get too far," he mutters. "I don't like you walking alone in the dark." Then he turns and jogs back to the house, and I'm left feeling like a world-class bitch.

William

"You ready to talk about it yet?" Max asks me as we head to the cafeteria for lunch on Monday.

"Talk about what?" I've been in a shit mood since Saturday night, so I can probably guess.

"Who pissed you off, for starters? Or maybe why you skipped out on my party so early?"

I feel my jaw go hard at the mention of the party.

"Ah, so it *is* girl trouble," he says.

"You're worse than a woman. Mind your own business."

"Didn't work out with Cally?"

I scan the notifications on my phone, buying time while I think of how to reply, how much to share. Cally and I are from different worlds. There's a division between the Haves and Have

Nots. Even in a place as small as New Hope—*especially* in a place as small as New Hope. And especially in this school. But maybe that's part of the appeal. Maybe I like Cally so much because she's outside my typical circle.

"It wasn't because of what Kristen said to her, was it?" Max asks. We stop at his locker, and he turns the dial and yanks it open before shoving some books inside.

I scan the lunchtime crowd gathering in the space between the cafeteria and the glass enclosure around the pool. Cally has the same lunch period as me, but she doesn't always come down. "What did Kristen say?"

Max shrugs. "You should probably ask Cally. I wasn't there so I didn't hear it, but Ally said Kristen was feeding Cally shit about you only wanting her for one thing."

I wince. "And she didn't say anything?"

He shifted uncomfortably. "She didn't know what was up with you and the Fisher girl, so what could she have said?"

"Nothing is *up* with her. We're friends."

Max grunted. "You looked like a lot more than friends when your face was buried in her tits."

"Fuck off." The suggestion doesn't carry much weight when my heart isn't in it.

"So, you didn't leave with Cally, I'm gathering?" He slams his locker shut and we start toward the cafeteria again.

I sigh. "She took off. Told me there was only one reason a guy like me would be interested in a girl like her." The words have an entirely different meaning now that I know Kristen was talking shit.

"And you let her go?"

I take a deep breath and stop, leaning against the wall. I'm not up to eating today, though my football coach would be on my ass if he knew I was skipping meals. "It was a bitchy thing to say."

Max nods. "Can't argue with you there. But given her mom's reputation and what Kristen said to her, you can't blame her for being cautious."

"I guess."

"Goddamn Kristen," I grumble, my eyes still scanning the crowd for Cally. "What was she thinking?"

"Probably that if you were going to be using someone for sex, she wanted it to be her."

"Well, she's already given me that opportunity. I passed."

Max shoves his sleeves up his arms. "Damn. Must be tough to be you."

I shrug, not about to explain the truth—that I don't want to be the guy girls like Kristen pursue so viciously.

"There are rumors," Max says, averting his eyes. "I don't know if you've heard them. Rumors that you paid Cally to have sex with you."

I drag my hand over my face. "Yeah. I know."

"And if she's not even talking to you anymore, it's only going to fuel the gossip."

"Do I look like I care about rumors?"

"That's why you're better than the rest of us." He slaps me on the back and pauses a beat. "You're not going to tell me if they're true, are you?"

My head snaps up. "Cally is not a fucking prostitute. Jesus."

"Easy, killer!" He holds up both hands and shakes his head. "I know you didn't *pay* her. I'm just wondering about the other part. But you're too classy to tell me. Never mind."

"We didn't have sex. She's not like that." I spot that long, dark hair at the entrance to the auditorium. And Kenny. "Damn it."

"Good luck with the girl," Max calls as I rush away.

"He's done with you," Kenny's saying when I get close. "I'm just waiting my turn."

Cally's arms are wrapped around her middle and her face has gone pale. "I don't have sex for money."

"So you're trying to say there's something between you and the rich boy? Because it's pretty clear to the rest of us what you are to him. And when he—"

Kenny doesn't get to finish, because I'm spinning him around and slamming him against the wall, my forearm pressed into his neck. "What's that you're saying, Riles?"

Kenny scowls at me. "Thought you were done with her, man."

Fuck. No wonder Cally thinks the worst of me. That's what everyone is telling her to think.

"You're lucky I don't beat the shit out of you," I say in his ear.

"Bailey!" I hear the teacher's voice and back off Kenny, dropping my arm and releasing him. "What's going on?"

"Nothing." I force a smile. "Just having a little chat."

"Let's keep it that way," she says, but she walks away, too sure of my reputation to stop her patrol.

Kenny shakes his head. "She's not worth it." Then he walks away.

When I turn back to Cally, she's staring at me. "Thank you," she whispers. "I guess you're kind of my knight in shining armor lately."

I nod. "No problem." I start to walk away.

"William."

The sound of my name off her lips stops me in my tracks, and I turn back.

"I'm sorry," she says softly. "I should never have believed what that girl told me. You're a nice guy, and it didn't add up. I should've known better than to think the worst."

She looks so sweet standing there, guilt all over her features, and my heart is still slamming in my chest from seeing Kenny bearing down on her like that.

"Let's put a stop to these rumors," I say without thinking. "Go on a date with me this weekend. I won't let everyone think I just used you for sex." Or worse, paid her for it.

"Oh. Um…" She sinks her teeth into her bottom lip, then nods as her cheeks flame red. "Right. Sure."

"I'll pick you up on Friday at six."

Cally

I DON'T feel sorry for myself very often. Maybe I should. My family doesn't have money, and I've never been able to dress like the kids at school. When I was ten, I had to quit dance lessons because we couldn't afford them anymore. I loved dance more than anything, but I understood quitting was a necessity so I never cried about it. Never complained.

My dad taught me to be grateful for the things we do have. A roof over our heads—better than some can say—a family to come home to, and the free will to dream up and go after whatever life we want.

But tonight, I'm thinking of William Bailey and having quite the pity party. I'm thinking about Kenny and his snickering friends and wondering if a pity date with William is really going to solve anything. But mostly, I'm just wishing my mom were different.

She's at the computer when I head out into the living room to confront her. Dad bought a bunch of used components at a sale at the college and pieced together a computer that's supposed to be for my school papers, but Mom uses it more than I do. I don't know what she does on there. I once told myself it was work for her business, but I don't believe that anymore.

"What are you doing?" I step up behind her. She's got some sort of realty site pulled up and is looking at pictures of houses.

"Ever wonder what it would be like to start over?" Her voice is slurred and I spot the glass next to her. Looks like orange juice, but Mom doesn't do OJ without vodka. And she's probably taken her pills since she got home. In other words, it's four p.m.

"Not really," I lie. Because I have thought of it. How could I not? But I don't want to have some fanciful conversation with her while she's like this. I frown at the photos on the screen. She must be drunk. We could never afford a place like that.

"I'm going to make it happen," she says, as if reading my thoughts. "I'm going to find a way for us to start over. To live large for once." She takes in a deep breath, a woozy smile half curling her lips as she lifts her glass for a drink.

I don't normally feel sorry for myself and I don't normally hate my mother, but right now I'm disgusted with her. *Just say it.* "Did you give Kenny Riles a hand job?"

Her glass clatters down on the old desk, and she spins to look at me, blinking. "Who's Kenny?"

I wither right there. Like a flower shoved into a dehydrator. Like a star blotted out by the clouds. Not "What are you talking about?" but "Who?"

"I go to school with Kenny. He said he paid you twenty bucks for a hand job."

She draws her bottom lip between her teeth and chews on it. Her eyes are glassy and she tilts her head to the side. "The name doesn't ring a bell. Is he one of my clients?"

I try to laugh but it sounds wild and crazy, and then suddenly my stomach is crawling into my throat and I can't stand it anymore. I rush to the bathroom and throw up.

I squat hunched over the toilet, listening to the once-comforting sounds of Mom running cold water. My stomach is empty by the time she places the cool cloth on my neck.

"I have an appointment Friday," she says. She hands me a plastic My Little Pony cup filled to the brim with water. "Can you watch the girls? I think your dad has a meeting."

An appointment. She just all but admitted that she does sexual favors for her clients—though I think she's oblivious to what I gleaned from the conversation—and now she wants me to watch the girls so she can meet with one of them? *Fuck no.* "I have a date," I say. "I guess you'll have to cancel your appointment."

She frowns. "A date? Who's the boy?"

"William Bailey." I lift my chin. I know she'll recognize the name, and I want her to understand that not everyone who lives in this house has sold out. I want her to know that nice boys still want to be with me.

Even if it's not exactly true.

"Oh, sweet Cally. What do you think a Bailey wants with you? Don't give it up to him. Your dad was so sweet to me when I was your age and I got pregnant. Look what became of my life. Don't let him steal your chances for a good future."

I clench my fist because I want to slap her. The only one who's stolen my chances is standing right in front of me.

chapter five

William

"MAKE SURE you save room for dessert," the waiter says.

The little restaurant is in a restored brick mansion on the New Hope square. Candlelight illuminates our white-clothed table and reflects in Cally's deep brown eyes.

She's nervous, and it's the most adorable thing I've ever seen. She pushes her food around on her plate and studies me through those thick lashes when she thinks I'm not looking. I noticed her the first day she walked into French class this semester, all that dark hair hanging past her shoulder blades, her eyes guarded when someone talked to her.

Does it make sense to say that I felt instantly connected to her, long before we ever had a conversation? She was a girl who understood loneliness the way I did, who didn't want anything from me.

I picked her up at six, just like I promised, and she was waiting outside for me, no doubt to make sure I didn't go into her house.

I wish she weren't so self-conscious about her home and her family. I don't care that she doesn't have money. I have more than

I'll ever need, and I hate it. I'd trade every penny to have my parents back for a single day.

"Did you want dessert?" I ask.

"No thanks."

I want to reassure her that I'm paying for this and she can order whatever she likes, but the words would only make her more self-conscious. Instead I order the chocolate lava cake, and when it comes, I pull my chair around the table so it's next to hers.

The dark chocolate cake steams, the ice cream on top already melting. I cut into the center with my spoon. Gooey, melted chocolate rushes out.

Her tongue darts out to wet her lips. "That looks amazing."

I scoop a bite—making sure to get cake, melted chocolate, and a bit of ice cream all onto the spoon—then I offer it to her. "Try it."

I slide the bite past her parted lips, and pleasure lights up her face. My breath catches at the sight, and I immediately prepare another spoonful, then another.

When I offer the fourth bite, she puts her hand to her mouth and shakes her head. "It's your turn," she insists.

"I'm good."

She licks her bottom lip but misses the smudge of chocolate just beneath. "Then why did you order it?"

Cupping her chin in my hand, I wipe the chocolate off with my thumb. Her lips part and she's so close I can feel her breath as it rushes past her lips. I want to kiss her. Damn. I can't believe how badly I want to kiss her. Instead, I say, "Go for a walk with me?"

She nods, and after I pay the bill, I lead her out of the restaurant and toward the path along the river, linking my fingers through hers as we walk. The night is clear and the stars shine bright, their pinpoints of light reflecting off the water. Cally looks up at the stars and her whole body seems to soften. I feel the tension rush out of her with her sigh.

"Thank you for tonight," she says. "Most guys wouldn't have gone to such lengths because of a stupid rumor."

"You think I wanted to date you to satisfy the rumor mill?"

She focuses on the pavement in front of us, avoiding my gaze. "Didn't you?"

"You're not that naïve, are you?" That gets her to look at me. Her eyes are narrow and frustrated. "Cally, I took you to dinner tonight because I wanted to. I don't like what they're saying about you, but my reasons for asking you out were more selfish than they were noble."

She stops and leans one shoulder against the trunk of a thick maple as she studies me. "How were they selfish?"

"I wanted a chance to have some time alone with a pretty girl."

She stares at me for two heartbeats. "I really like you, William Bailey."

I tuck a lock of hair behind her ear then shove my hands in my pockets to keep myself from touching her more. "I like you too, Cally Fisher."

Her teeth sink down into her bottom lip and her eyes drop to my mouth.

I fist my hands in my pockets and exhale slowly. "I really want to kiss you right now."

"I really want you to," she whispers, flicking her eyes to mine.

I take a cautious step forward and press my hands against the tree trunk on either side of her head, then slowly lower my mouth until it's a breath above hers. "Has anyone ever kissed you before?"

"Yes."

Jealousy burns in my gut. It's silly, but it's there at the thought of another guy touching his lips to hers. "Who?"

"Davey Mills kissed me on the lips behind the school in second grade." Her eyes flash with mischief and she bites back her smile.

"Lucky Davey," I grumble. "Must have been memorable."

"Yes. He kissed me during a game of truth or dare. I remember he had peanut butter breath."

I chuckle, and her face breaks into a full-out grin. I close the breath between us and brush my lips over hers. Unlike Cally, I have some experience with this, so I'm surprised how much it affects me. Just a kiss. An innocent connection of lips. But the contact is electric and it sends a shockwave of pleasure through me.

I slide my hand into her hair, and she opens under me, meeting the sweep of my tongue with the hesitant touch of hers. She tastes like sweet tea and makes this soft little sound at the back of her throat. I break the kiss before I'm ready because my hands itch to touch her, to slip under her shirt and cup her breasts, to slide around her hips and squeeze her ass. She's not ready for that, and I won't rush her.

Her tongue darts out and skims over her lips. "Come with me."

She takes my hand, and I follow her farther down the path and along the river until there's a break in the trees. She leads me onto the grass and sits on the ground.

I sink to my haunches and settle beside her, the dew seeping into my jeans.

"Lie back." She leans on her elbows and points to the sky. "This is my favorite spot."

We settle onto our backs, bodies aligned, fingers entwined, and look up at the stars. From this spot, the sky is all I can see, and it feels like I'm being swallowed up in it.

"Tell me something no one knows about you," I ask into the silence. It's probably a stupid request, but I don't care. I like her and I want to know more about her.

"Like what?"

"Tell me what you wish for when you look up at those stars."

She's quiet for a long beat, then another. When I hear the whoosh of her exhale, I think she's not going to share anything, but then she says, "Lately, I've been wishing that my parents would get a divorce."

That surprises me, and I roll to my side to look at her as she speaks.

She winces but continues. "They make each other miserable, but instead of facing it or doing anything about it, they both hide. It's the worst possible thing for my parents." She faces me and forces a smile. "Pretty boring stuff, isn't it?"

I trace the worry lines around her eyes until they relax. "It's not boring at all. It's real." The girls I know are so proficient at being fake, they could give lessons. Cally is the opposite of fake. She's authentic.

"I just think they could be happier, you know? And maybe coming out here and making wishes is juvenile, but I like to think of it as throwing positive energy into the universe and hoping it comes back something better."

"You're not like other girls, Cally."

She rolls her eyes. "You say that like it's a good thing."

"It's so refreshing. You have no idea." I slide a hand into her hair and kiss her again. This time, I linger. Our lips brush, our tongues rub, and before I know it, she's on her back and I'm on my side, pulling her body close to mine and resisting the instinct to slide my thigh between her legs.

She keeps her eyes closed for a long time after I draw back, and I'm struck for the thousandth time by how beautiful she is. Dark hair. Pale skin. Rosy lips. "I should get home," she whispers.

I nod, but I stay there looking at her for a few more beats. She doesn't rush me, doesn't seem uncomfortable sitting in the silence.

When walk back to her house, I take her the long way, through town, knowing everyone will see us and talk. Wanting them to.

Cally

THREE WEEKS and six amazing dates, and William Bailey doesn't seem bored with me yet.

The gossip mill isn't giving up on us entirely. There's all sorts of speculation as to why a guy like William would spend so much time with a girl like me. But the worst of it has died down. Apparently, the possibility of us having sex in the bleachers isn't nearly as juicy if we're actually dating.

He showed up to my house tonight and asked my dad if he

could take me on a walk. It was the sweetest thing, though my dad looked a little puzzled by it. We find ourselves down by the river again, the early spring breeze ruffling our hair, the sun loosing its grip on the edge of the horizon.

"This is my favorite time of day," Will whispers.

I lean against him and sigh. "Sunset?"

"No." He reaches over and slides a hand into my hair. "The part where I'm next to you." Then he brings his mouth down to mine and kisses me softly.

I live for these kisses. These happy moments between the craziness at home, the demands of the girls, and the stress of school.

"You are beautiful. You know that?"

"Hmm," I say. "I'm not sure. Tell me again?"

"You." He presses a kiss to the corner of my mouth. "Are." Another kiss right under my earlobe. "Gorgeous." His hand slides up my side until his thumb is brushing the underside of my breast.

That light touch feels so good, and I arch into it, even as my brain screams it's time to pull away. He lowers his mouth to mine and kisses me until I'm breathless. My body wants more, but I'm terrified of what it will mean if we go further. I need to know I'm enough. To know I'm not my mother.

"I'm sorry," I whisper, pulling back. "I can't."

He leans his forehead against mine and closes his eyes. He's breathing heavily, and I like that I can do that to him. I like it too much.

When he pulls back and looks at me, he says, "I didn't mean for that to happen. I'm sorry."

"I'm not ready."

"You don't need to be ready for anything. I just got a little carried away."

"It's not that I didn't like it. It's just…" I draw in a shaky breath and force a smile. "I liked it a lot. I like kissing you, but that's all we can do, and I'd understand if that meant you didn't want to date me."

He stiffens and turns toward the river, resting his forearms on his knees. "Not all guys are shallow jerks who only care about the physical stuff."

"I don't think that of you at all," I protest. "But I want to be fair to you."

"Then give me a chance," he says, turning to me. "Be my girl, Cally. I don't want there to be any confusion about what we are to each other."

My stomach flips at the idea, and I can't figure out what I could have done to deserve someone like him. "Did you miss the memo?"

The breeze floats by, and I can smell him. Boy soap and aftershave. It's a scent I could snuggle into and drift away on.

"What memo?" he asks.

"The one that says the quarterback is supposed to date the head cheerleader?"

"Hmm. I've dated a cheerleader before. It's pretty much overrated. Though"—he drops his gaze to my legs—"I wouldn't complain if you wanted to wear the uniform."

I swat him, and my hand stings when it connects with his solid chest. "Ouch."

"That'll teach you to hit me."

I giggle, then admit, "I like that idea."

"Oh, the uniform."

"No," I squeak. "Of…being your girl. But I need to tell you something first."

He brushes my hair from my face and traces the line of my jaw, his eyes following his finger. "What's that?"

"That night Kenny was harassing me at the stadium?"

His body tenses. "I remember."

I swallow. I need him to know more than the rumors. I need him to know the truth. "He said he'd gotten a hand job from my mom."

"Jesus," he hisses. "He's such an ass."

I pull my lip between my teeth and chew on the corner before confessing, "I don't think he was lying."

"Why would you say that?"

"We don't have much money. My parents are terrible with it, and then there's not much coming in and…" I take a breath, wondering if I dare say the rest out loud when I've never even told Hanna and Lizzy. "My mom's been taking Vicodin since Gabby was born."

"Did she have some sort of complication?"

I shake my head. "No, she just…likes it. She hides in her pills. I don't know where she gets them, but I have no doubt in my mind that her addiction is to blame for at least part of our money trouble."

"I'm sorry."

"She's always had this little massage business, but it's changed in the last couple of years. The ladies don't come to her anymore, and people whisper about her. About what she does. The worst part is that I think the rumors are true. I think she got desperate and…" The truth is too sickening to put into words. "Are you sure you want to get involved with me?"

"I don't care what your mom's done. I only care about you."

"When I say I'm not ready, I don't just mean tonight. I don't know if I'll be ready next month or next year. It's not that I don't want to, but I'm scared I'll become her."

His breath leaves him in a rush. "Never. You'll never be her." He pulls me close, and I move to straddle his lap.

"You seem so perfect. I don't know what being with me is going to do to your life."

"My life is hardly perfect," he scoffs. He holds me close while he lowers himself back into the grass. He's silent for a bit, my head on his chest, his hands toying with my hair. "I was young when my parents died. I have memories of them, but nothing big, you know? My memories are more like snapshots. My dad handing me a big present in Garfield birthday wrap. Mom sweeping me off the ground and kissing my bloody knee. Sitting in the back of the car and watching the two of them hold hands. I wish I had more but it's just not there."

I wrap my arms around him and squeeze because that's all I can do. There's nothing to say to salve the hurt in his voice. Nothing to do but listen.

"I was in kindergarten when they died in the accident, and I don't remember much about that time. I was staying over at Grandma's that night, and Mom and Dad were having 'couple time.' Grandma said it with disapproval in her eyes, so I thought 'couple time' meant something bad until I was older and heard other people use it." He pulls in a breath not much different than the kind I take when I wake up from a nightmare. "They never came home."

"I'm sorry," I whisper. It physically hurts me to imagine little-boy Will waiting for his parents to get home, wishing he'd see them again and learning he wouldn't.

"Grandma didn't like to talk about it. She took me to the funeral, dressed me in a suit and tie, and told me, 'We get one day to cry. After today, we move on. You become the best man you can and you do it for them.'"

"That's terrible. Grief shouldn't have a timeline. And you were just a kid."

"She loves me. I don't want you to think any differently. But her loving me meant that she didn't want me hurting, and if she didn't have to see me hurting, she could tell herself I wasn't."

"What was it like? Growing up without your parents?"

His hands, already in my hair, tighten before he speaks. "I had everything I needed, so I don't want to make it out worse than it was."

"You can tell me."

"It sucked." He forces a laugh. "I love my grandmother, but she wasn't a mother to me. She didn't know how to be, not when she was so filled with grief over losing her own son. She wanted so much for the son she'd lost, and I was expected to fill that void. The grades, the sports, the perfect behavior. I need to get out of here for college. She wants me to go to Sinclair, but I know what that means. She'll want me to live at home. She'll want to control how

263

I spend my days."

"You could go anywhere, do anything."

He hooks a leg behind mine and rolls us until he's on his elbows hovering over me and his lips are a breath from mine.

"What are you thinking?" I ask.

"That I can't wait to tell everyone you're my girl."

Then he kisses me for a long time, slow and sweet. We look at the stars after, side by side, his fingers tangled in my hair. Then we see it. A shooting star, skating across the sky as if it were put there for us.

I can't help but wonder if my time with William will be like that. A precious but temporary gift.

chapter six

William
Eleven Months Later

"OPEN IT!" Cally says, her eyes bright. She's grinning at me, and we both know very well what a fat envelope from a college means.

"I don't want to." I chuck it to the floor and nudge her backward until the bed hits the back of her thighs. She's so damn beautiful when she smiles. Just the idea of not seeing that smile every day makes me want to scrap all my plans for college. Ten months ago, the idea of getting a fat envelope from Notre Dame would have sent me over the moon. When it came today, my first thought was of the long drive between here and there. "There's one more application I'm waiting on." I slide my hands into her hair.

She frowns. "From where? I thought you'd heard from everyone already."

"Sinclair."

She presses her hands against my chest and pushes me back. "No. William. No. Absolutely not."

I hang my head. This is why I hadn't told her. I knew how she'd feel about me sticking around for her. "I don't want to leave you."

"But you need to," she protests. "You need to get away from your grandmother and have a chance to live your life without her constant meddling. You told me that's what you wanted, and I think it's what you need."

I grab her hand and bring it to my lips. "That was before you."

Her eyes fill with tears. "I can't let you do this. I love you too much."

"I love you too," I whisper, then I dip my head to kiss her.

"Don't change the subject," she whispers against my lips.

"I wouldn't dare." Our mouths meet again, and I sweep my tongue across her lips until she opens for me and makes that little kitten mewl at the back of her throat. I nudge her again, and she lowers to the bed, her dark hair fanned against my blue sheets. "You're so beautiful."

She's wearing cut-off jean shorts that show her long legs, and one of my old practice jerseys. Her back arches as she reaches for me, and the jersey slides higher, revealing a narrow strip of creamy skin right above the waistband of her jeans. The part of me that loves her and understands her hang-ups resists, but there's a part of me that's ready to push, a part that wants her too much not to ask for more.

I know my friends think we have sex. Hell, other than Cally and me, I don't know any couples who aren't sexually active. But we have more than they do. We have a connection that I've craved since my parents died.

When Cally's around, I never feel alone.

Cally

OVER THE clothes and above the waist. That was my line in the sand at the beginning of our relationship. Lately, it's a line I want to kick myself for drawing.

When we first started dating, I kept waiting for the other shoe to drop. It's not that I'm a pessimist or something. It's just that William is so much more than I ever would have imagined for myself. He's not just the sexy football player everyone loves. He's smart and kind and thoughtful. And when I told him I wouldn't have sex with him, he took me at my word and has never pushed the physical side of our relationship. We make out, and when things start to get too heated, when I'm ready for him to ask for more, he slows us down and pulls me back.

Over the clothes and above the waist. My rules, followed to a T.

Stupid rules.

I complained to Lizzy and Hanna about my predicament, and Lizzy laughed at me. "So, strip. You show him some bare skin, and I'm sure he'll get the idea."

I was going to wait for our one-year dating anniversary. But lying here in his bed, no one else in the house, my body has other ideas. The way he's looking at me right now gives me the courage I need. I sit up, and before I can talk myself out of it, I pull my shirt off over my head.

His breath draws in with a hiss and his gaze sweeps across bare stomach, my breasts swelling above the cups of my bra. "You don't have to do this if you're not ready," he says, but his eyes give him away. He needs this as much as I do. "Cally, I—"

I unclasp my bra, and he stops talking, his chest rising and falling as his eyes rake over me again and again.

"Jesus. You're beautiful." He wraps his hand around my side and pulls me close, lowering his mouth to mine.

His fingers are gentle. He sweeps them over my bare skin, cups a breast in his palm. I gasp at the brush of his callused hand. He's touched me here before, and I always liked it, but this is different. There's no comparison, and this simple contact makes me want more. Skin to skin, everywhere.

"So damn beautiful." He drops his mouth to my neck. Pleasure jackknifes through me when he rolls my nipple between his fingers and scrapes his teeth over my collarbone. "Let me kiss these. Let me make you feel good."

I'm almost tense, coiled tight and needy, waiting for his mouth on my breasts. I want to feel his tongue against the sensitive flesh of my nipple. He kisses the sensitive crook of my neck and teases me with his thumbs. What will it feel like to have his mouth there? What if I don't like it?

"Relax, baby." He lowers me to the bed and runs his hand across my abdomen. His fingers dip into the hollow of my navel then up between my breasts. He follows with his mouth, hot and wet against my stomach, his tongue skimming under the band of my jeans and sending wild flutters through my belly before he kisses his way back up.

By the time he brings his mouth to my breast, pleasure twists inside me, greedy and impatient and more intense than anything I've ever felt before.

His tongue circles my nipples, one then the other. He closes his mouth over the taut peak and sucks, his other hand pinching the opposite breast.

The spiral of desire pulses harder, more insistent, and I squeeze my thighs together tight as he teases and sucks. I cling to that sensation—the tight, twisting ache. I tug at his hair because I need more, and I'm so close to something but I'm not sure what it is. Suddenly, he sucks again, and that aches twists impossibly tight before shattering and rocking through me in a violent spasm of pleasure.

I cry out, and he sucks harder until the spasm recoils and releases again, and I'm arching into his touch, holding on to his hair and the back of his neck.

Finally, my body lightens and releases, and I drop my hands to my sides. When I open my eyes, William is looking down at me, his blue eyes hot, his face searching mine.

When the realization of what I just did clicks into place in my sluggish brain, my cheeks burn with embarrassment. I held his mouth to me like I was afraid he was going to stop. I—*Oh my God.* Who has an orgasm from a guy touching her above the waist? "I don't know why that happened. I'm sorry."

He smiles but it looks a little pained. "Are you seriously apologizing for the sexiest thing I've ever experienced in my life?"

"I… You thought that was sexy?"

His lips quirk. "Baby, I made you come just by kissing your breasts. Not only was it sexy, I feel like Superman right now."

"Superman?"

"Maybe Houdini is a more appropriate comparison, but yeah." There's so much intensity in his eyes that I can practically feel the weight of his gaze as he runs it over me again. "You've pretty much made my life."

I bite my lip. "It's a little embarrassing from where I'm sitting."

He draws me up against him and nuzzles against my neck. "God, there's absolutely nothing for you to be embarrassed about. The only thing embarrassing here is the way I'm about to come in my jeans without you even laying a finger on me."

"Really?"

He groans. "You have no idea how much I want you. It hurts like hell."

That sobers me, and I pull away. "William, I'm sorry I—"

"Please don't apologize. It's a good kind of hurt."

I guess I know what he means. I've been feeling the good kind of hurt for months. I'm just not sure how much longer I want to feel it. My gaze drops to his jeans before I realize what I'm doing and tear my eyes away. I looked long enough to see some very impressive tightness at his fly that wasn't there earlier.

He pulls off his shirt and snuggles next to me, wrapping his arms under my breasts and pulling me close. "Let me hold you like this," he whispers in my ear.

I breathe in his scent and my eyes slowly drift closed. The sun slants in through the window and warms my skin, relaxes my muscles.

I'm nearly asleep when he says, "I love you, Cally."

I'm getting used to hearing those words. He told me for the first time months ago, and I was in awe that someone as amazing as William could love me. I never doubted his words. They are like him—honest, pure, and easy. But when he first said them, I was struck by the vulnerability in his eyes. I used to think William had everything, but I was wrong. He didn't have love. Not as much as he deserves. And maybe his grandmother's love for him is unconditional, but he can't see it when she puts so many conditions on her approval. My parents might suck at being parents, but I've never doubted their love. I would never have guessed that William needed my love more desperately than I needed his.

"I love you too," I reply softly now.

"If I leave for school, will visit me? Will you wait for me?"

I twist, turning in his arms so I can see him. "Notre Dame isn't that far. A few hours on the bus, and I'll be there."

Relief washes over his face and he slides his hands into my hair and pulls me close for a kiss. When he releases me, I settle into his chest again. "Thank you," I say—to him, to the universe or whatever desperate stargazing wish brought us together.

chapter seven

Cally

He forgot.

I wrap my arms around myself and pace my bedroom. I can't believe he forgot.

My phone rings, and I practically jump across my bed as I scramble to grab it.

I don't bother to read the display. "Hello."

"Hey, chica!" Lizzy says from the other end.

My shoulders sag in disappointment, and I look at the clock. It's after eight p.m. "Hey, Liz," I mutter.

"Any word from lover boy?"

"He texted me to let me know his grandma had roped him into a card game and he'd try to stop by later."

"He's with his grandma!" she howls, outraged.

"No way!" I hear in the background. Hanna, no doubt.

Normally, I wouldn't be bothered by Will playing cards with his grandma instead of spending the evening with me. Because William is just that kind of guy. He plays poker with his grandmother and her friends every week or so. I've never gone (though he's tried to convince me on several occasions), but from what I gather, the women get rowdy drunk and play a cutthroat game.

But it's our one-year anniversary, and I had hoped for more. I'd planned for more. I guess this is what I get for not reminding him of the date. Honestly, I didn't think I needed to, and it hurts, realizing how wrong I'd been.

"You need to call him and let him know how disappointed you are," Lizzy says. "If you don't, I will."

"Please don't." I walk over to the window and look outside, half expecting to see him waiting with roses and a smile. "It's not that big of a deal."

"Liar," she says.

"You know how his grandmother can be. I'm sure she laid on quite the guilt trip, and he didn't feel like he could leave her."

"But it's your *anniversary,*" Lizzy whines.

The sound of dishes crashing echoes down the hallway from the kitchen. Shit. Mom must be cooking drunk again. "I have to go," I say quickly. "I'll call you later."

"You better," she says.

I hang up and slide the phone into my pocket before heading to the sound. I'm met in the kitchen with the sight of my mother putting dishes into boxes. My heart skitters to a stop. "What are you doing?"

"I'm packing." She looks up at me and smiles. It's a real smile. Not one of those Vicodin-laced plastic ones. Her eyes are clear, like maybe she's sober for the first time in months. "You girls and I are about to begin an adventure. A new life in Las Vegas."

"What are you talking about?" Maybe she is high. She's not even making sense.

"In a few weeks, we're moving to Las Vegas. Aren't you the luckiest teen in the world?" She grins at me like she really believes what she's saying.

"I'm not moving anywhere. My life is *here.* You can't seriously expect me to just throw away everything because you want to follow some whim."

Glass clatters as she slams the platter she's holding onto the counter. "This isn't a whim. This is me taking control of my life, making something of it. That's what you told me you wanted, right?"

"I didn't mean—"

"You know, your sisters are excited. Don't ruin this for them."

My sisters are too young to understand what moving away means. "What about Dad?" I manage.

She winces then hides her face behind tissue paper as she resumes packing. "He's the reason this is happening. He wanted to quit his job and go on some spiritual quest in Bali. I decided it was as good a time as any for us to divorce. We haven't been happy together in a long time. This divorce is giving us what we both want."

"Well, I'm staying here." My voice sounds pathetic, desperate.

"You'll love it in Vegas. The lights, the excitement. It will be a fresh start for all of us. Everybody wins." Her smile doesn't look so sure anymore, though.

"Except me," I whisper. "I don't win. I don't *want* a fresh start."

"Well, it's time you grow up enough to understand things aren't always going to go your way."

Fear sits like a stone in the bottom of my stomach. It leaks its toxins into my limbs, making my arms and legs heavy. I can't move. I'm frozen in this spot until she fixes what she's broken. Until she unsays what she just told me.

"Don't look at me like that. I deserve happiness too."

"You're hijacking my life. You get that, right? You're taking something good and destroying it for your own purposes. That's the opposite of what a mother is supposed to do."

Her eyes fill as she stares at me, and I feel like I've just slapped her. "I know I haven't been a good mother, but I've done what had to be done. The girls at the bowling alley told me what the boys at school said about you, the rumors they spread."

"One boy spread one rumor. It's over now."

"I know that's my fault. I'm doing something right for once. I'm cleaning up and fixing my life. I've met someone and I'm ready to move on. So either help me pack or go to your room."

"You're going to change your mind," I say, maybe more for myself than her. "Packing is a waste of time."

I wander back to my room in a daze and shut the door behind me. The soft knocking on my bedroom window pulls my attention from my thoughts. In the darkness, I can barely make out William's face on the other side of the glass.

My chest hurts at the thought of leaving him, but I push the ache aside—there's no way Mom's going through with that—and hurry to open the window. "You have something against the front door?" I ask.

He grins. "I didn't want to wake up your sisters."

Just the sight of him makes me feel better. His smile warms me all the ways down to my toes, and I return his grin as his fingers lace through mine.

"How was poker night?" I ask, determined not to let my disappointment from earlier ruin our time together tonight.

"They're still going, but I excused myself after a couple hands."

"By which you mean you'd already lost all your money to the sharks?"

He chuckles. "Maybe I lost on purpose so I could see my girlfriend."

Oh, God. It's silly and childish, but I don't think I'll ever get tired of him calling me that.

"Do you want to come in?" I ask. I want him to.

"Nope. I want you to come with me."

I squelch my disappointment and climb out the window to join him. I'd been thinking of locking the door and lying with him in my bed, touching, kissing, letting things go too far. I'm ready to go too far.

He helps me hop down from the window and onto the grass. Unlike when we started dating at this time last year, the weather has been warm. And tonight the sky is so clear, the thick crescent of moon is enough to light the night.

"I missed you." He steps closer and places his hands on my hips before lowering his mouth to mine. His kiss starts patient and slow. When I fist my hand in his hair and press my body against his, it changes, growing hungry and impatient. When we break the kiss, we're both breathing heavily.

"You sure you don't want to come into my room?" I say, grasping on to my courage before it fizzles away. "You could lie down with me." *On me.* The idea of the weight of his body on mine sends a shiver through me. The good kind that has my imagination on fire.

He groans, fingers curling hard into my hips. "You're killing me, Cally. If I didn't know better, I'd think you wanted me to break your rules."

"Rules were meant to be broken."

He blinks at me. "Are you sure?"

Am I? My heart slams in my chest. Nerves. Anticipation. Desire, low and heavy in my stomach and sinking to between my thighs. What if this is my last chance? What if Mom is serious about Vegas?

He kisses me hard, his hands tightening their hold. "I don't need everything. I just need you."

I turn to lead him back to my window, and he stops me.

"Not here." He pulls a silky black necktie from his pocket and offers it to me. "Put this on?"

Laughter slips so unexpectedly from my lips that I throw my hand over my mouth, afraid I might have woken the girls. "Aren't we missing some steps between kissing and bondage?"

He steps toward me and takes the tie from my hands, settling it around my eyes. "Trust me." He presses a kiss to my nose, and then he's taking my hand and leading me—somewhere.

"Okay, but I'm just going to tell you now that I don't think we're ready for handcuffs yet."

His soft laughter mingles on the night air with the song of the frogs.

"Where are we going?"

"Patience, grasshopper. You'll see soon enough."

I'm quiet for what feels like forever as we walk. Nerves knot in my belly and every so often he squeezes my fingers. I try to guess where we are from the turns and the sounds of traffic, but New Hope after dark isn't exactly a hopping place.

Finally, we stop. "We're here," he says.

"Hmm. And where's here?"

He releases my hand, and I feel him press a kiss to the top of my head. "Stay right there."

I listen carefully as I wait. I can hear him rustling around with something. Maybe the tinkling of glass. Something clicking. And then, behind all that, I make out the water splashing softly against something. I grin. "We're at the river."

"Don't go ruining my surprise," he murmurs as he releases the tie on my blindfold. When he slides away the fabric, I open my eyes.

"Oh."

We're on an old boat dock behind one of the closed factories on Main Street, and he's laid out a picnic on the concrete. Atop a red-and-white checked blanket sit two fat pillar candles. Their flames wink against two empty wine glasses. A glass serving platter is piled with crackers, cheese, grapes. Next to it sits a bottle of light pink liquid. "Is that wine?"

He grins. "Don't tell Grandma, but I snagged one of her bottles from the basement. It's strawberry." He takes my hand. "Join me?"

We settle onto the blanket, and he takes a slice of pear and tops it with soft cheese. Bringing it to my mouth, he whispers, "Try it."

My lips close around his fingers as I take the bite into my mouth. His blue eyes grow darker, smoky, and he goes for more. I let him feed me. Grapes, olives, cheese, crackers so thin and buttery they melt on my tongue. Every bite is a decadent discovery, and somehow his feeding me seems more erotic than kissing.

When he stops to pour the wine, I look around. I can see why he brought me here. It's the perfect view of the river and, above it, the stars.

"What did I do to deserve this?" I ask.

He hands me a glass. I drink, smiling when the sweetness explodes on my tongue. I've never had wine before, and I like how it sends warmth sinking into my belly.

"This is your reward for putting up with me for twelve months."

He remembered.

My chest tightens, like there isn't enough room to contain this feeling growing there. I don't know what to say, so I kiss him. I press my mouth against his and slide my fingers into his hair. He tastes like fruit and strawberry wine, and I move closer as our tongues touch.

When he moans against my mouth, I break the kiss.

I wait until his eyes open and then lift the shirt from my head. I set it to the side and watch him in the light of the candles and the moon as he takes me in.

"I'm sorry it took me so long to get to you tonight," he says. "I wanted to get everything set up. I wanted it to be perfect."

"It is."

He pulls at my hips, and I lie back on the blanket, bare to the moon and stars and to William's hungry eyes. He sips his wine and gives me a mischievous grin before tipping his glass and spilling a little puddle of it on the flat of my stomach. The liquid runs in cool rivulets over my belly and down my sides, but he dips his head and opens his mouth to the puddle. His tongue is hot, and shivers race through me as he licks away the sticky liquid, leaving my skin damp and hot in the night air.

I need to tell him about mom, about her packing, but I don't want to believe what she told me, and telling him makes it too real. Tonight, being here with him is all I need. Giving voice to my mother's crazy ideas would ruin everything, so instead I say, "Touch me."

William

"Rules were meant to be broken."

I don't think I've recovered from her speaking those words. Because the only thing I've wanted more than to break her rules was for her to ask me to.

Sliding my hands slowly up her thighs, I part her legs and kneel between them on the blanket.

"Come here," she says, reaching for me.

"I'll get there. Be patient." I circle her navel with my thumb, watching her face as the sensation whips through her. Her eyes float closed and she arches toward my touch. Then I replace my thumb with my mouth and trace an invisible path across her belly. She gasps, lifts her hips, and draws up her knees. I love that I can do this to her, love how she responds so completely to every touch.

I slide my hands up her torso and cup her breasts. They're so beautiful and I want her out of that bra so I can suck her nipples into my mouth.

"Cute," I murmur, running my fingers over the soft cotton of her bra. Cally likes underwear, so the Thompson twins bought her a whole load of it for Christmas. Some cute, some silky, some lacy. Watching her pull each piece from the gift bag after Christmas had made me lose my mind as I imagined what it would look like on her. This bra is covered with little penguins wearing top hats. "I'm guessing the underwear matches?"

Her eyes flash as they connect with mine. "Hmm…maybe you should find out."

My heart trips in my chest. I want to take off those jeans and see what she looks like in her panties. I want to cup her between her legs. To feel her there. I want more. "Are you sure?"

She lifts her hips. A tease. An invitation. A request.

Leaning forward, I press my mouth against her collarbone and kiss my way down her body. Placing an open-mouthed kiss over each nipple, I suck at her through the cotton until she cries out. I kiss along her ribs and over her navel. And when I reach the button on her jeans, I watch her as my shaky hands unbutton. I keep my eyes on her deep brown ones and draw the snug denim off her hips and down her legs.

"They match," I whisper, taking in the little penguins decorating the thin strip of white cotton between her legs.

"William?"

I swallow. Hard. I just want to lean forward and kiss her there. Open my mouth against the cotton. I want to explore that sexy strip of skin where her inner thigh meets this private piece of her, and then I want to slide my tongue under her panties and taste her. "You're so beautiful."

I graze my fingers over her stomach and down to her panties, my touch whisper soft as it reaches the apex of her thighs. My patience is rewarded with her cry, so I keep my touch light. "I want to make you come like this." My voice is rough, threaded with need.

She lifts her hips again, pressing into my touch. Then she surprises me by sliding her hands to her hips and pushing down her panties. "Please."

"Oh, damn," I murmur, but I peel off her underwear.

She's bare and exposed to me, and I can hardly breathe. I want to spend hours looking at her, but I can tell by the way she's shifting under my gaze that she's uncomfortable with this. I draw my body up until I'm lying beside her. She kisses me, and I'm lost in it for a moment. The sweetness of her breath, the soft glide of her tongue.

My hand slides between her legs and I gasp, swallowing her breath. I would give anything to know what it's like to feel myself inside her.

She shudders under my touch, and I still.

"Are you scared?" I hate the thought.

"Yes." She smiles at me and tangles her fingers in my hair. "But not scared about this. I just… I think sometimes I'm still afraid I'm going to lose you."

"You have me. I'm not going anywhere."

She closes her eyes.

"Is this okay?" I ask, circling that sensitive spot between her legs.

"If you don't mind."

I press my face into her neck and groan. "Why would I mind touching a piece of heaven?"

chapter eight

Cally

I WANT to touch him, make him feel like he makes me feel, but I have no idea what I'm doing and—

"Let's get you home, beautiful," he says, cutting off my thoughts. He gathers the plates, empties the glasses, and wraps up the food, placing it all back into his backpack.

I swallow back my disappointment. His grandmother is hardcore about his curfew—unlike my parents, who act like they've never heard the word. I fasten my bra and slide into my shirt.

He walks me home, touching me the whole time, like he's afraid I might disappear. At the front door, he kisses me softly. "Goodnight, Cally."

"Goodnight. Thank you for tonight. It was amazing."

He looks down at me and grins. A blond curl falls into his face. "You can say that again."

As I watch him walk away, something nags at me. In my dark house, I make my way to the shower. The nagging remains as I undress and step under the hot spray of water.

I told him I was ready to move forward, to do more, but I

wasn't. I mean, we physically did more together, but I haven't truly moved forward from my previous position, from my fear that my worth to him would be tied up in giving him pleasure. Until I touch him, the fear won't release me from its grasp.

I dry myself off and hurry to my room with my phone to send him a text.

I'm sorry I didn't return the favor tonight. I should have. I think I'm scared.

I send it before I can overthink it and change my mind. I didn't have to wait long for his reply.

I don't want you doing anything that scares you. Anyway, now I have something new to think about while I take care of myself.

For a second, I'm not sure what he means by that, but then I understand, and the realization of his meaning causes something to stir in me. My nipples tighten. I never would have imagined the idea of a guy doing *that* could turn me on, but when I imagine William…

I hesitate, then type, *You…do that?* It's not that I don't believe it. He's a guy with a girlfriend who doesn't put out. Of course he does *that*. But I don't want to change the subject. Not yet.

His reply comes fast. *Don't you?*

My stomach flips and my heart kicks up a notch. I don't know what to say. I've never talked about this with a guy before. The girls joke about it, but this is different. I'm careful with my reply. *I guess. When it's necessary.*

And when's that?

I shift uncomfortably in my bed. If we keep up this conversation, it's going to be necessary very soon. *After a heavy makeout session sometimes. When I'm lying here wishing I were brave enough to do more with you.*

My heart pounds in my ears as I wait for his reply.

Damn. I didn't expect you'd actually tell me.

My cheeks burn, but even embarrassed, I'm not sorry I told him. I want more of this conversation. More of him. So maybe next time he's close to me, I'll find the courage to touch him in return. *Does it make you uncomfortable?* I type. I like that idea—him shifting in his bed thinking about me like I do him.

I grab my phone greedily when it buzzes with a reply. *I want you twenty-four seven. I'm uncomfortable as hell, and it's worth every second.*

Are you sure you're okay with waiting? I type quickly. *Just until prom. Then I'll be ready.* As I hit send, I realize I want him to say no. I want him to tell me he needs me now and doesn't want to wait anymore. I want him to show up at my window again, but this time I want him to come inside.

But his reply is even better than that fantasy. Because I know he means it.

I'd wait forever for you, Cally.

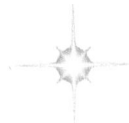

"What are you doing?"

Dad is packing books into a small suitcase when I walk in the door after school. There are two more suitcases at his feet.

"Cally." He looks at me for a long time before saying more. His face is sad, those dark eyes, so much like mine, a little desperate. "One day, you'll be older and you'll understand that sometimes we just have to do things, even if not everyone in our life will understand or approve."

"It's true? You're really going overseas? You're leaving us?" In the weeks since I've caught Mom packing, she's mentioned Vegas a few times, but never with any definitive plans. I've let myself believe that and the half-packed house meant the move wasn't going to happen.

He doesn't answer but drops his gaze to his hands.

"You can't do this." My words sound panicky. Wild. "She's going to make us move, and that's not fair. My life is here. I don't want to leave."

"I'm sorry," he says to the floor.

"Cally!" Drew's voice comes from her bedroom and she shuffles out and wraps her arms around my leg. "Come play Barbies with me?"

"Daddy has to go now, Drew," my father says, nearly choking on the words. He squats to his haunches and opens his arms for her.

Tears burn the back of my eyes.

Drew runs into his arms and wraps her arms around his neck. "Bring me back something cool," she demands. "And maybe next time I can go with you."

"Maybe," he manages, but Drew seems oblivious to his emotion.

Gabby toddles out from the bedroom next, and Dad scoops her off the ground and nuzzles the side of her neck. She squeals with delight.

"I'll call," he says. "And if you want to move back here with me when I get home, let me know."

Drew frowns. "Cally's going to Las Vegas with us. She can't live here with you."

"We're not going to Las Vegas, Drew," I scold, as if it's her fault my parents have lost their minds.

"Yes we are. We're leaving at the end of the month."

My heart plummets, falling far past my stomach, past the floorboards, and deep into the dark and fiery part of the earth. "No."

Mom wasn't failing to say anything about the move because she'd changed her mind. She wasn't talking to me about it because she didn't want to argue. And waiting until the last minute to pack the house? That's just her M.O.

Drew's eyes light up. "But you should come to Las Vegas, Daddy! Mom says it's a super fun place."

She can't comprehend the permanence of my parents' separation. Maybe it's for the best.

"I need to get to the airport," he says quietly, settling Gabby to the floor and picking up his suitcases. "You girls be good."

He heads to his beat-up old hatchback, and the girls rush to the window to wave at him as he goes. They don't understand. Or maybe he's been absent enough in their lives that they truly don't care. I don't know.

I watch his car back out of the driveway, and I feel like he's taking part of me with him. Not because I'm that close to my father, but because he was my last chance to stay here in New Hope. To stay with William.

"Have you packed yet?" Drew asks me. "Are you excited? Do you think we'll get to see the lights in Vegas? How long will the drive take? Can I take my Barbies?"

Her questions nearly shatter me. Even if I could talk my mother into letting me stay here without her, I know I can't do it. Mom's just a couple of orange pill bottles away from being an unfit mother. My sisters need me.

I can't put it off anymore. I need to tell Will.

The birds sing the whole walk to his house. Their happy tune contrasts so painfully with the dull knife sawing through my heart that I just want to close my eyes and listen until their hopeful song fills my ears and my head.

Will's car is in the driveway, and I don't ring the bell. I go to the back of the house and through the mudroom door he keeps unlocked when he's home. His grandmother is in Indianapolis visiting her cousin this week, and he made it clear I could come over any time I wanted. Made it clear that he'd like me to stay over. Why haven't I? What am I waiting for?

The mudroom leads to the kitchen, and I find a banana peel and an empty cereal bowl, milk lining the bottom, on the counter. He must have made a snack after getting home from track conditioning.

I head to the front of the house and find him on the couch, hair wet, bare from the waist up, and sleeping. One hand is behind his head. The other rests on his abdomen, right over that faint trail of hair that marks a path from his chest into his sweatpants.

Between football and track and general self-discipline, Will pushes his body hard, and he exhausts himself in the weight room.

I approach the couch quietly and lower myself to my knees on the floor beside him. He'd want me to wake him up, but I want to look at him first, memorize the shape of his chest and the flat of his stomach, the way his thick blond lashes curl against his cheek, and the untamed curl of his hair.

Before I realize what I'm doing, my hands are on him, tracing down his body, following that path of hair to the waistband of his sleep pants. I've touched Will before. I've given him massages, put my lips to the bare skin of his back, kissed my way down his spine while my hands rubbed at his sore muscles. I like massage. Despite the ugly things Mom has done to her massage business, I admire the art of human touch. With William, massage feels like this gift I can give him.

He shifts, and I lift his hand from his belly and start to work my thumbs into his palm. I work my way up to his forearm, and he moans appreciatively in his sleep. I stroke his arm, kneading the shoulder and the bicep, keeping my touch light and easy. When I finish his arm and he's still sleeping, I straddle him and start on his chest. His pecs are always so tight, and he shifts under me when my fingers press into those muscles.

I shift to catch my balance, and when I settle back down, the hard length of his erection is settled right between my legs. I draw in a breath at how good it feels and flick my eyes back to his sleeping face.

I've wanted to touch him for so long now, and I've been too self-conscious. This could be my last chance. I could be leaving at the end of the month. Will wanted us to keep seeing each other while he went away to college, but the nearly two thousand miles between New Hope and Las Vegas is a far cry from the few hours between here and Notre Dame. We'll be lucky if we see each other a couple of times a year.

The thought tears through me savagely, and I swallow a sob. I'll anesthetize the pain of the future with the beauty of the moment.

I shift back and lower my head to his chest, following the same path my fingers just took with my mouth and kissing my way down that downy-soft hair on his belly. When I reach his waistband, I lift my head to see him staring at me. His chest rises and falls in a rhythm faster than his sleeping breath and his blue eyes have gone smoky. I don't say anything, just lower his pants down his hips with a light tug.

He isn't wearing underwear beneath his sleep pants, and my breath catches at the sight of him. I've felt him before—between my legs and through our clothes—but I'm still surprised at his size. But it turns me on too. Seeing how aroused he is. Knowing he's watching me. That he wants this.

I put my hand around him, a little unsure and awkward at first, but then he groans—long and low—and I'm emboldened and tighten my hold. I lift my eyes to his face again as I stroke him and he's still watching me with heavy lids and parted lips. The pleasure on his face is the most beautiful thing I've ever seen.

I've been afraid of becoming my mother. Afraid that sex with William would destroy everything. I underestimated us.

"Jesus," he hisses at the first touch of my tongue. "Cally."

I might not have done this before, but I've read enough issues of *Cosmopolitan* to have an idea how it's supposed to go.

Before long, his hands are tangled in my hair and his moans of pleasure fill my ears, and I'm saying a silent prayer of thanks to all those *Cosmo* articles.

William

SHE'S CRYING. I'm not sure what I did wrong, but it must have been terrible because one second she was snuggling with me on the couch after giving me the most precious gift in the world, and the next her body was shaking and her tears were wetting my bare chest.

"Sweetie." I tuck her hair behind her ear and dry her wet cheeks with my thumb. "What's wrong?" Jesus. Is this about what she just did? Does she think that makes her like her mom? Should I have stopped her? "Talk to me."

She draws in a shaky breath, rolls off me, and walks across the room to look out the window. I follow her, my stomach churning and sour. I've never seen her this upset.

"I knew this couldn't last, but everything was going so well. Now she's ruining it all."

Her words terrify me. *I knew this couldn't last.* "You're not making sense. What couldn't last?" I already know she's talking about us, but I don't want to admit it to myself. I can't let myself belief she's ending this. Not now.

She presses her palm against the glass. "We're moving."

Those were the last words I expected to hear, and at first they don't even make sense to me. "What?"

"To Las Vegas. We're moving to Las Vegas."

I feel like the earth has just been yanked out from under my feet, but I make myself take a deep breath. Turning her around, I look into her eyes. "Start from the beginning."

"Mom and Dad are getting a divorce, and Mom's taking us to Vegas to live with this guy she met online." Her voice shakes and her eyes brim with tears.

I slide her hand into mine, interlocking our fingers and squeezing. "Can you stay with your dad?"

She shakes her head, and a tear spills onto her cheek. "He's going on some spiritual journey in Asia. He's already left."

"You can stay with me," I blurt. God, my grandmother would pitch a fit, but I ask for so little, and we could make it work. Somehow.

Cally shakes her head. Another tear escapes. "My sisters. You know my sisters need me. Mom's cleaning up, but what if that doesn't last? What if…" She squeezes her eyes shut and her chest shakes with her tears.

I gather her against my chest and smooth her hair. "Shh," I whisper. "Shh."

I guide her back to the couch, where I pull her into my lap and hold her.

I keep my thoughts to myself and let her cry. She needs this as much as I need to hold her, to feel her in my arms while I still can.

My brain is scrambling to come up with reassurances, plans for how we're going to make this work—because there's no alternative. We *are* going to make this work. Anything else would be like rejecting a piece of me. She's my heart, my breath.

We're connected. Tied together by something bigger than ourselves. Like the moon brings the tide back to the shore, the stars will always bring me back to Cally.

chapter nine

William

HER ROOM is empty. Her walls are bare, the posters and knick-knacks taken down and packed into the boxes now filling the moving truck parked in her driveway. Her dresser and bed are gone, and her chair and reading lamp with them.

All that remains is a makeshift sleeping spot on the floor, a small pile with tomorrow's clothes, and a tiny toiletry bag.

The sight tears me right in two, but I don't let on how much I'm hurting. I can't. I've done everything to make the most of our last weeks together, and tonight will be no different.

"You should get home," she says. "Get some sleep."

We've been sitting here most of the night, cuddled into the corner of her room listening to NIN on my iPod. I don't intend on going anywhere without her tonight, and I certainly don't intend on sleeping.

Her mom announced they'll be leaving at sunrise, and I won't miss a second with her.

I stand. "Come with me."

She takes my hand and follows me out the front door. I can't take another moment sitting in that house, watching her eyes scan the bare walls, the empty closet, the spot where the bed used to be. Besides, I have a surprise waiting for her.

Hand in hand, we walk to town and behind the old factory and onto the dock. I have everything set up for us here. We've made a habit of this since our anniversary. Blankets, candles, strawberry wine. From the moment she told me she was moving, I knew this is how I wanted us to spend our last night together.

She gasps when she sees it, her steps slowing. "You didn't have to do anything like this."

Thunder rolls overhead. The whole weekend has been gray and gloomy, only threatening rain. I say a silent prayer that the downpour that's sure to come will hold off until morning. I planned for stars. That's all I wanted for her. For us.

I light the candles and open the wine. The crystal goblets I snagged from my grandmother's hutch glint in the candlelight.

Cally shivers and lowers herself onto the blanket across from me. She avoids my gaze as she sips the wine, and I know she's trying not to cry.

"I have something for you," I say softly. I grab my backpack from where I'd stowed it by the edge of the building and pull out a small red box wrapped in white ribbons.

She takes it carefully. "You shouldn't have."

"Just open it."

She pulls at the ribbons with shaking hands and takes off the lid. I hear the catch in her breath when she sees what's inside. "But I won't be here," she whispers.

"Yes, you will," I promise. "One way or another, I'm going to get you here. I don't want to go to prom with anyone else, Cally. I want to go with you. Tell me you're on board with that. Tell me I can look forward to dancing with you in my arms."

Her face softens and her shoulders sag as she drops her gaze back to the prom tickets in the box. "Of course. We'll make it work," she whispers. And relief rushes through me like fresh air because I know she's talking about more than prom.

Cally

THE NIGHT sky is dark with thick rain clouds, blocking the clouds and clogging up my throat as I try to prepare myself to say goodbye. "I can't see the stars."

He turns my face to his. The candlelight flickers in the wind and casts shadows across his gorgeous face. I've been living a dream with William. Over a year of a life I never thought I'd get to live, receiving love I didn't realize existed.

He presses his lips just below my ear and trails kisses down my face. I melt a little, my defenses falling when I need them most. "We don't need them tonight."

I wish he were right, but I feel like a wish and a dream is all we have. How many high school sweethearts stay together? A few, maybe. But how many high school sweethearts weather the storm of a long-distance relationship and stay together? Maybe in movies. But this is real, and William deserves more than some long-distance girlfriend.

"She's being so selfish, taking us away from our life here. Taking me away from you." I sound petulant even to my own ears, but it's as if I believe giving voice to my frustrations will fix them. Not true.

William's eyes narrow. "Don't give up on us." He smoothes my cheek with his thumb. "She can make you move, but she can't take you away from me. You're mine. In New Hope, in Nevada, in Timbuktu, you'll always be mine."

He rolls over so he's hovering over me, his body on mine, his hips pressed to my hips, and he traces the lines of my face with his fingertips. My jaw, my cheeks, my lips. Despite all his bravado, he knows this is goodbye.

I pull him down to me, press my lips to the side of his neck, his jaw. "Can we really survive a long-distance relationship?" I hate how much I need his reassurances, but I want to hear them. Because even if he's wrong, his belief in us is the only thing that's getting me though this.

"It'll only be long-distance when we're apart. You'll be back for prom. We'll see each other this summer."

"Prom." The prom his grandmother wanted him to attend with some rich friend's daughter. Instead, he's holding out for me. How selfish have I been? He should be with someone better, someone *here*.

He slides his hand into my shirt and brushes my breast with his thumb. The single touch sends shivers of pleasure through me that gather in a needy knot of impatience between my legs.

"Prom," he repeats. "Just like we planned. Then when school starts, you can visit me at the dorms."

And always be scraping for money to buy my next plane ticket or, worse, letting him pay my way time after time. "You deserve better." But as I say it, I part my legs, wanting to feel him there where I ache. He brings up his knee until his thigh is firmly pressed between mine, and I moan against that delicious pressure.

"There's nothing better than you."

I blink back tears. "I don't want to wait for prom night," I murmur. Because I know now what I need to do. What I need to give him. "I'm ready now."

His nostrils flare and his eyes darken. "Are you sure?"

I wiggle under him and wrap my legs around his waist. I feel him pressing into me. I have to do this. I should have done it a long time ago.

A tear slips from my eye and rolls down my cheek, and he freezes. "Not tonight. Not while you're so sad."

I feel like I've already lost him. "So this is what goodbye feels like."

"No," he growls, and his fingers tighten their hold at my sides.

"We have to say goodbye. I leave in a few hours."

With his thumb against my cheek, he wipes away my tears.

"We aren't going to say goodbye because this isn't the end of us. It's only the beginning."

Squeezing my eyes shut, I just lie there while he kisses away my tears. "If we don't say goodbye," I whisper, "then what do we say?"

"Look at me." His voice is firm and strong, but his eyes are soft when I look into them. "This isn't goodbye."

"We can't pretend that everything is going to be the same."

"Hello, Cally."

"William—" The intensity of his love breaks my heart. Because even if he can't see it, I know what's coming. I'll be in Las Vegas and he'll be here. It will be fine at first, but then his grandmother and his friends will pressure him to spend more time out. Eventually he'll meet someone, because that's what happens to amazing people. They fall in love with other amazing people.

"It doesn't need to be the same," he says. "I love you, and I'm telling you hello. Hello, Cally."

The candlelight catches on a tear on his cheek, making it glisten for a fraction of a second before it falls away. Maybe I'm not the only one who understands what we're up against.

Wrapping my arms around him, I pull him to me and he buries his face in my neck, his breath hot and a little shaky. And because I can't bear his sadness, I whisper, "Hello."

wish i may

wish i may

by LEXI RYAN

For my big sisters, Kim and Deb.

about this book

I grew up wishing on stars.

My father taught me to believe...in destiny, in magic, in happily ever after. Dreams were my scripture and the starry night sky was my temple. Then Mom stopped believing, left him, and took us with her. At the age of sixteen, I cashed in my dreams to pay the rent, pawned my destiny to keep my sisters together.

Now, seven years later, I'm returning home, grieving the death of my mother, and settling my sisters back into the life Mom threw away. I never intended to stay. I don't want to deal with my father, who is so invested in the spiritual world he forgets the physical. I don't want to face William Bailey, whose eyes remind me of the girl I was, the things I've done, and the future I lost.

This would all be easier if Will hated me. As it is, I have to hold my secrets close so they won't hurt him more than they've already hurt me. But he wants to be in my life. He wants what I can't bring myself to confess I sold. He wants me.

I find myself looking to my stars again...wondering if I dare one more wish.

prologue

William
Seven Years Ago

CALLY TILTS her face to the starless night sky as if waiting for its kiss. "I can't see the stars." She squints, trying to make them out through the thick storm clouds hanging over us.

I turn her face to mine and trail whisper-soft kisses beneath her ear and along her jaw until she relaxes in my arms. "We don't need them tonight," I promise, though I know it's only true for me. Cally always needed the reassurance of wishes and destiny—a byproduct of a combination of shitty home life and odd-duck father. Tonight, she needs all that more than ever.

"She's being so selfish, taking us away from our life here. Taking me away from you."

We've had this conversation a hundred times since her mom announced their move last month. I know where she's headed with it, and I won't let her go there. Not tonight. "Don't give up on us." My voice is hard and I have to concentrate on not holding her too tightly, but I already feel her slipping away. "She can make you move, but she can't take you away from me. You're mine. In New

Hope, in Nevada, in Timbuktu, you'll always be mine."

Rolling over her, I support myself on my elbows and cup her face in my hands. I rub my thumb over the pale skin of her jaw, the flush of her cheek, the rosy pink of her kiss-swollen lips. She threads her fingers through my hair and pulls me down so she can run kisses along my jaw.

"Can we really survive a long-distance relationship?" she whispers.

"It'll only be long-distance when we're apart. You'll be back for prom. We'll see each other this summer."

"Prom."

I run my hand up her side and brush the underside of her breast with my thumb. "Prom. Just like we planned. Then when school starts, you can visit me at the dorms."

"You deserve better," she says.

Under me, she parts her legs until my knee slides between them. She moans into my neck. "There's nothing better than you." I flick my tongue against her ear.

When I pull back, tears glisten in her eyes. "I don't want to wait for prom night. I'm ready now."

For a year, we've been together and held off on sex because Cally wasn't ready. She feared having sex too young would make her like her mother. Even if the fear wasn't entirely rational, I understood. "Are you sure?"

She shifts under me and wraps her legs around my waist so only our clothes are between us. Adrenaline and arousal pump through me at the thought of making love to her. Then a tear rolls down her cheek, and I know I can't.

"Not tonight," I whisper. "Not while you're so sad."

She lifts her eyes to the clouds again. "So this is what goodbye feels like."

"No," I growl. The apology in her eyes breaks my heart.

"We have to say goodbye," she whispers. "I leave in a few hours."

I wipe away the tears on her cheeks. "We aren't going to say goodbye because this isn't the end of us. It's only the beginning."

She squeezes her eyes shut and more tears roll down into her hair, and I can't do anything but press kisses to the path they left behind. I hate how helpless I feel.

"If we don't say goodbye, then what do we say?"

"Look at me." I don't speak again until her big brown eyes are locked on mine. "This isn't goodbye."

"We can't pretend that everything is going to be the same."

"*Hello*, Cally."

"William—"

"It doesn't need to be the same. I love you, and I'm telling you *hello*." My chest burns with this tightness, but I reign in my emotions, knowing I have to hold us both together. "Hello, Cally."

She wraps her arms around me and pulls me close again. A tear that isn't hers splashes onto her cheek. I bury my face in her neck to hide my own fear, and she whispers, "Hello."

chapter one

Cally

"In one hundred feet, turn left onto Dreyer Avenue," my GPS instructs.

I inch forward, peering out my windshield and scanning the manicured lawn to the left for any sign of a road where there is nothing but grass.

"Recalculating," the computerized voice tells me. Her tone suggests frustration with my inability to follow simple instructions. "In one hundred feet, take a U-turn, then turn right on Dreyer Avenue."

"There is no Dreyer effing Avenue." I pound on my steering wheel. This is the fifth time since I returned to Middle-of-Lots-of-Cornfields Indiana that the fucker has tried to turn me into someone's yard. Thirty minutes ago, she repeatedly directed me to drive right into the damn river. Good thing I decided to drop the girls off at the hotel when we got to town, lest they see their big sister go homicidal on an electronic gadget.

Yanking at the wheel with unnecessary force, I pull the car over and throw it into park. My chest is tight and my eyes burn

LEXI RYAN

with tears I swore I wouldn't shed today. I made it through the last month without crying. I won't cry now.

It's bad enough that I've been reduced to this. Bad enough that I have to rely on my estranged father at all. Bad enough that I have to track his hippie ass down since he's too goddamned paranoid to carry a cell phone. But here I am.

"You shouldn't hate him so much," my mom told me six months ago. *"He hasn't had an easy life."*

"I don't hate him. I'm ambivalent."

But that was before Mom's "heart attack" (code for *drug overdose* that may or may not fool my sisters). That was before the funeral and the grief and the bills. That was before my life disintegrated around me, as if it were built of nothing but dust.

I'm exhausted, one sister hates me and the other isn't speaking, and my ass is sore from being stuck in this car.

Fresh air. That's all I need. Then I'll follow the road back toward the highway and ask a gas station attendant for help.

I unbuckle and step out onto the paved street. God, it feels good to stretch.

I can't get over how *green* everything is. It's as if I've forgotten the color can exist in nature. The scent of cut grass is almost as rejuvenating as a solid night's sleep for my state of mind. The air is warm and sticky, and children are playing in the sprinkler on a front lawn down the street.

I remember doing that as a kid. Before the move. Before the end of our world as we knew it. Is it too late to give my sisters a chance at that childhood?

Doubt lodges like a soggy lump in my throat.

"Can I help you?"

I snap my head up, startled. "No, I'm good. I—" My eyes connect with the owner of the voice, and I lose my capacity for speech.

"Holy shit." The Adonis from my past narrows his eyes. "Cally?"

The sound of my name on his tongue catapults me back in time and suddenly I'm sixteen again, his cool cotton sheets sliding

307

against my skin as his fingertips trace the line of my jaw, the hollow of my neck, the curve of my hip. I'm sixteen again and licking sweet strawberry wine from his lips.

Time has been kind to William Bailey. Bare-chested and glistening with sweat, he has an iPod strapped around his thick biceps and a T-shirt tucked into the side of his running shorts. He's bigger than he was at eighteen, more built, which is saying something since he was New Hope High School's star football player back then. My gaze drifts south but gets snagged at the ripple of his abs and the trail of blond hair disappearing into the band of his shorts.

Sweet Jesus.

The sound of him clearing his throat has me yanking my eyes back up to meet his.

"Look at you. You're all grown up." He grins, and my knees go a little weak. How could I have forgotten the effect this man's smile has on my knees?

"I could say the same for you." I bite my lip. Hopefully no drool has escaped.

That knee-killing grin grows wider. I'm toast.

This isn't what I expected. Not that I expected anything from William. I *hoped* to make it through my few days in town without seeing him, but of course not. Here he is. Looking for all the world like he's actually glad to see me when he should hate me.

"You live here? I mean around—" *Shit.* How am I supposed to construct a coherent sentence while looking at his bare chest? And that's not even taking into account the memories flooding my mind at the sight of him. I may have never had sex with him, but I have enough memories of doing *everything else* to rival even the most creative fantasies.

Shifting my gaze to those deep blue eyes is no better. A girl doesn't forget those eyes watching her as their owner slides his hand between her legs for the first time.

I study the ground and wave a hand to indicate the spot where Dreyer Avenue definitely is *not.* "I'm looking for my dad."

"You're in the wrong neighborhood." His voice has that low, delicious treble that makes my insides shimmy.

When I sneak a peek up at him through my lashes, I catch him studying me with his own assessing gaze.

I can imagine what he sees. We've been on the road for two days, pulling off only for gas and restroom breaks. We stopped in Kansas last night so I could get a few hours of sleep, and then it was back in the car at four a.m. for another full day today.

I would categorize my ensemble as "road trip chic." My snug-fitting black yoga pants end just below my knees, and I'm wearing a T-shirt that says *Peanut butter jelly time!* The outfit is topped off with bright orange flip-flops and the ponytail I threw my hair into this morning.

So, you know, the exact outfit I *wouldn't* have chosen to be wearing for a reunion with my first love.

I lean into my car for the scrap of paper with Dad's address and shove it into William's hand. "Can you help me find this?"

He doesn't look at the paper but frowns at me. "Seriously? You're lost?" He pauses a beat. "In New Hope?" His tone suggests that I've gotten myself lost in a paper bag. And, okay, New Hope *is* pretty damn small, but I haven't lived here in seven years, and it's changed a lot. The good areas are all run down now, the factories are closed, and the vast expanses of open land by the river have been developed into fancy neighborhoods with yuppy McMansions so ostentatious I can practically smell their oversized mortgages.

"My GPS keeps trying to get me to drive into the river."

At least that wipes the scowl off his face. "Yeah, GPS systems haven't kept up with the developments around here real well." He rubs the back of his neck, and the movement sends the muscles in his arm and shoulder flexing. Between his sweaty muscles and my memories, I'm pretty sure my panties have all but disintegrated.

I clear my throat and resort to asphalt-gazing again. How hard is it to put on a shirt? "If you can point me in the right direction, I'll get out of your hair. I'm sure I'm the last person you wanted to see today."

His grunt has me looking up at him again. Those blue eyes, those crazy blond curls. That mouth. "Cally…"

I sink my teeth into my bottom lip as our gazes tangle. He takes a step toward me, and he's so close, I have to lift my chin to keep my eyes on his, have to curl my fingers into my fists to keep from touching him. He's sweaty and solid and so damn gorgeous.

I wait—for him to tell me how horrible I am for what I did to him, for him to ask me why I did what I did. I don't know what I'd say. It's hard to imagine that, once, leaving New Hope—leaving William—seemed like the worst thing that could happen to me. I was so wrong.

But he doesn't ask and he doesn't move away from me. His gaze dips to my lips for the briefest moment, and the way my body responds to his nearness, even all these years later, even after… everything…it only confirms what I suspected.

After seven years. After the lamest breakup in the history of breakups. After breaking his heart and dismissing my own, I'm still very much *his*.

William

CALLY.

I can hardly breathe. My brain doesn't have time for something as trivial as oxygen when it's so busy cataloguing her features, memorizing the exact shade of her mocha eyes, warring with the anger and regret that have sprung to life as if they never left me to begin with.

I never thought I'd see her again. I didn't think I wanted to.

The moment I step closer, I realize my mistake. Being near her is like a sip of water to desert-parched lips. It whips something through me—memories, lust, first love. *Heartbreak*. She tilts her lips up to mine, and I actually think for one goddamned ridiculous minute that I might kiss her, that I want to. That I would swallow all my pride and forgive her for just one taste.

I step back before I can give in to the impulse, and her cheeks blaze to life, her blush as cute as the rest of her. That's the word for her: cute. Sweet smile and peppy ponytail, she exudes cuteness.

Except her ass. Her ass doesn't even land in the same stratosphere as cute, and those tight little pants do nothing to hide its soft, round curves. And her breasts. There's definitely nothing *cute* about the way her T-shirt stretches across their fullness. Or her go-for-miles legs. Not to mention the narrow strip of skin exposed between the hem of her shirt and waistband of her pants. Just looking at the single inch of flesh below her navel, and I practically taste strawberry wine.

Moonlight. Her warm skin under my tongue. The sound of her moan as my mouth dips lower.

The memory grabs hold of my senses and won't let go.

Fuck. I can't even lie to myself. Nothing about her says *cute.* Everything about her says *sex.* And *mine.*

"Directions?" she asks. "To my father's house?"

"Do you want me to walk you there? It's close."

I immediately regret the impulsive suggestion. I should be giving her directions, putting her in the car, and sending her back out of my life. But I want to be close to her for a minute, to prove to myself that I'm bigger than a seven-year-old shit breakup.

Or I want to prove to myself she's more than just a dream.

She worries that plump bottom lip between her teeth because, obviously, she's trying to torture me. How can I want her so much when I thought I hated her?

"I don't bite, Cally."

She mutters something I can't quite make out. It kind of sounds like "Damn shame," but I can't be sure because she's grabbing her purse and avoiding my eyes.

"Are you staying long?" I ask as we start walking. My voice sounds too damn hopeful and I hate that, but what are the chances she'd show up here again, let alone find herself lost right in front of my house?

She's here to see her dad, I remind myself. That shouldn't come as a surprise, but as far as I know this is the only time she's been back since she moved away.

"No. Not too long. Maybe a couple of days. I…my mom died, and I need to get my sisters settled in with my dad."

I stop walking and turn to face her, all my bitterness and aggravation falling away.

She's looking at the ground, those worry lines making an appearance again. I grab her hand and squeeze. "I'm sorry." I don't ask what happened. Having lost both of my parents when I was a kid, I know how quickly that question gets old.

"Me too."

We both know there's not much else to say, so we walk instead. She follows me, and we cut through my yard to the paved path down by the river. I resist the urge to point out my house, to show her how well I've done for myself. It would be mostly a lie anyway.

"So you still live here in New Hope?" she asks softly.

"I came back after undergrad."

"Anybody else stick around?"

I narrow my eyes at her. Does she already know my screwed-up history with the Thompson family, or is the question sincere? "Some of the guys from the team—Max, Sam, Grant. And all the Thompson girls except Krystal. She just moved to Florida with her boyfriend last month."

The mention of her old friends brings a smile to her lips and lights up her face, making her look like her old self. "Lizzy and Hanna are in town?"

"You should see if you can hook up with them before you leave. They'd love to see you."

She doesn't reply, but there's something about the way her face changes that tells me she's not going to seek them out. I wish I didn't need so badly to understand why. Cally didn't want to leave when her mom moved her away. She didn't want to leave her friends or her family. Didn't want to leave the life she had here. She was determined to keep in touch with us all, even talked about coming back here for college. She hadn't been gone but a couple of months when all that changed, and suddenly she would have nothing to do with any of us. Even me.

Arlen Fisher's cabin is along the river just off New Dreyer Avenue. The original road was closed in favor of creating some common green space for the new construction. This, of course, was code for putting some distance between the old rough neighborhood and the ritzy new one.

When I point to Arlen's house from the trail, she frowns.

"It's really...small."

Her dad's a rough man. Simple to the extreme. His cabin sits in the trees just beyond the flood zone. It's small, no-frills, and falling apart.

"Are you nervous?"

She's slowed her steps, consciously or not. "I've only seen him a handful of times since we moved."

That surprises me. Someone would have told me if she'd been back, as there aren't exactly secrets in this town, but I would have expected that her dad took trips to Nevada to see all three of his girls. "Really?"

She shrugs. "It wasn't what we intended, but things just never worked out. You know my dad. He has other priorities."

I remember, vaguely. The man liked books and studying religious texts. He liked to spend his time meditating and his money visiting psychics and spiritual leaders. "That sucks."

"The road goes both ways," she says, and I don't know if she's reminding herself of her own responsibility to the relationship or his.

"How do your sisters feel about moving back here?"

She leans over and picks up a gnarled tree branch. It's as long as her legs, and its beautiful knots stand in contrast to the smooth skin of her hands. I already wish I had my camera.

"He sent me my ballet slippers," she says softly. "After he found out about Mom's death. I didn't even know he had them, and they showed up in this package—these tiny little slippers Mom and I had picked out together before my first lesson." Her lips curve in a smile. "I was only five, and I remember him telling me, 'If you want to be a ballerina, just believe you will be.' It was always that simple with him."

Once, it was that simple with Cally, too. I was drawn to her because that unfettered optimism radiated from her. After spending my formative years in my cynical grandmother's house, Cally was a breath of fresh air.

I look up at the house. The sun has dropped in the sky, and the little cabin looms darkly in the shade of the trees. "Are you ready?"

"I think so."

"Want me to wait here?" Again, I surprise myself. I should be itching to get away from her, from the reminder of what she did to me, but it all seems so long ago and unimportant under the pall of the crappy last couple of years. And next to the news of her mother's death, my old resentment seems downright trivial.

Her shoulders drop with her exhale. She's nervous. "Thanks."

She maneuvers through the trees and up the steep wooden stairs to the house. After knocking on the door twice, she turns the branch in her hands, waiting, fidgeting, while I wait in the trees. This whole thing should feel much more awkward than it does.

She knocks again, leaning forward this time to peek in the window.

Two minutes later, she gives up and heads down the stairs.

"Y'all looking for Fisher?" someone calls when Cally reaches me.

Cally perks up. "Yes. Do you know when he'll be home?"

I recognize Mrs. Svenderson from my grandmother's beauty parlor. She swats away gnats as she moves toward us. "Dunno when," she says. "He just left, so I 'magine it'll be a few days, least. Usually is."

I watch Cally as she digests this. Emotions flash across her face one by one—disappointment, sorrow, frustration, and finally anger, settling in around her jaw and eyes.

"Thanks. I appreciate you telling me."

"I thought you were too good to come visit your old dad," Mrs. Svenderson says. "What's brought you here now?"

Cally gives a polite smile but doesn't answer the question. The old women around here don't beat around the bush. They figure life's too short, I guess, and ask what they want to ask.

"It's nice to meet you," Cally says, as if the woman didn't just insult her. "Thank you for your help."

When she reaches my side, we turn together and make our way back along the river.

"Did he know you were coming?"

"He knew." Again, anger flashes in her eyes, and it looks comfortable there, as if this Cally is angry a lot. The girl I knew wasn't like that, but a lot can change in seven years.

"Do you have a place to stay? Where are your sisters?"

"I dropped them at the little motel back by the highway. I wanted to make sure Dad was ready for us. They've had enough surprises lately."

What motel by the highway? "Wait. The Cheap Sleep?"

She shrugs. "Sounds about right."

Cally and her sisters certainly aren't living large if that's where they're staying. "You know people don't actually sleep there, right?"

She chuckles. I like the sound of it. It's not the girly laugh she used to have, but neither is it an adult's carefully crafted facsimile of a laugh. It's soft. Sweet. Honest. "We'll be fine. It's just for a few nights. Until Dad returns home and I can get them settled with him."

We walk in silence for a few minutes, the only sounds the rush of the river and our shoes scuffing against the paved path.

"Do you live around here," she asks, "or are you in town with your grandmother?"

When we cut back through my yard to her car, I nod to my house. "That's mine."

It's odd, seeing it through her eyes. I'm proud of the home I built—a two-story, brick behemoth with a gorgeous flagstone patio in the back—but as I watch her take it in, I'm almost embarrassed at the excess. Cally and her family never had much. In fact, they rarely even had *enough*. And now they're staying at the Cheap Sleep, and her dad is living in that dilapidated old cabin. Not much has changed.

She forces a smile. "It's beautiful. I'm very happy for you."

She steps away, but I grab her hand fast.

"Cally."

She turns to me, those big brown eyes, those perfect pink lips.

There are a hundred reasons why I shouldn't want anything to do with her, but I have two, maybe three days before she disappears from my life again. Maybe for good this time. I can't handle the idea of this being the end, and I'll be damned if I'm letting her stay at that shitty motel. "Why don't you and your sisters stay with me?"

She snorts. "You surely don't have room for us *and* your wife and two-point-four children."

"No wife. No kids. Just me and way too damn much space."

She shakes her head. "That's sweet of you, but we'll be fine. You've already done more than most would have." She walks to her car, slides into her seat, and pulls away without another glance my way, leaving me alone with my memories of strawberry wine.

chapter two

Cally

STRAWBERRY WINE.

I can practically taste it as I drive away from Will and back to the motel. It's the taste of my old life. Of careless teenage rebellion and first love, of starlit nights on the dock behind the old warehouse on Main. William and I would sit on the cool concrete and sip strawberry wine he snagged from his grandma's wine cellar (an impressive 500-bottle collection of Boone's Farm). We'd watch the moonlight play off the water and drink straight from the bottle. Sometimes we'd just look at each other. On cloudy nights, we could hardly see at all and had to let our hands do the looking—his thumb skimming across my lips, down my neck, under my shirt.

That was where I told him I loved him the first time. Where he splashed wine on my stomach and bent to lick it off. It was where he first unbuttoned my jeans and kissed his way down my body until he pressed his mouth—hot, wet, and so slow I wanted to die—right against the damp cotton of my underwear. And the night before I had to climb into the U-Haul with my mom and two little sisters, it was there on the dock that he kissed me softly, like I was this fragile thing he feared he might break. He ran his mouth down my neck and cupped my face in his hands and whispered, "*Hello.*"

Strawberry wine, William Bailey, and a life so much simpler.

When I get back to the hotel, my fifteen-year-old sister, Drew, is sprawled on one of the two double beds, tinkering with her iPod, earbuds in her ears. She's wearing a white tank and cotton shorts that say "You Wish" across the back and show more of her ass than they conceal. Her long, dark hair falls over half her face like a curtain, hiding the features that look so much like Mom's.

"Did you find him?" she asks, lifting her head and popping out one earbud. "Dad better live in a big-ass house with a live-in cook and on-site spa."

I snort. "Okay, Pampered Princess."

"This so-called *hotel* is disgusting. Pretty sure they're renting rooms by the hour here, Cally."

If Extreme Bitchiness were a sport, my sister Drew has spent the last month training to be the world champion.

She's dealing with losing Mom. It's something I must remind myself of again and again. Instead of spending thousands of dollars we don't have to visit a shrink, who would tell us this is her way of dealing with her grief, I just need to accept it. I need to be patient until my still-bitchy-but-much-more-bearable sister comes back.

"He's out of town," I say. No need to tell her how unequipped the man is for company, let alone to take in and care for his youngest daughters. I couldn't see much through the little window, but my view into the old living room let me know there wasn't much to see. Books, books, books. Not even a fucking couch.

We'll figure it out. It's a mantra I've all but worn out over the last seven years.

"It'll be okay." God, I don't sound the slightest bit convincing. Even *I* am unsure about the wisdom of my plan. But what am I supposed to do? Move them into my crappy little apartment in Las Vegas with my three roommates? Let Johnny teach Gabby how to roll a joint while lecturing Drew on the acceptable price of a dime bag? Or worse, beg Brandon to take me back so he can take care of us all? *Fuck no.*

"Mom worked her ass off to get us out of this crappy little town," Drew says.

"So we're rewriting history today?"

"You really think she'd want you bringing us back here?"

I don't bother answering her. I'm sick of her painting Mom as the martyr she wasn't, sick of defending my decision to track down our father, sick of trying to explain that there's no money tree to harvest in order to allow her to keep living her old life.

"Whatever." Dismissing me with a roll of her eyes, Drew pops the earbud back in and snatches her cell off the end table. Her fingers fly across the screen, no doubt texting her friends back home about what a heinous bitch I am.

If this is what motherhood is like, God can strike my ovaries useless right here and now.

I spot Gabby in the corner, sitting on a battered wooden chair and peering out the window to the parking lot below. She's ten but she was born premature and her tiny frame and baby features never seemed to catch up, so she looks younger than she is. She looks up at me and gives me a sad smile, as if in apology for Drew.

My heart squeezes so hard and tight, my chest hurts and my lungs ache. I need those long, ragged breaths of a good cry and the bone-melting sleep that comes after. Every moment has been full since Mom died, and I haven't given in to the temptation since the funeral. Crying is a luxury I'm saving for a private moment.

"How about we order a pizza for dinner?" I force enthusiasm I don't feel into my voice.

"We had pizza for lunch." Drew rolls to her back, never taking her eyes off her phone.

She's right. In an attempt to lighten their sagging spirits today, I made a lunch stop at Chuck E. Cheese's. It failed miserably.

I ignore her objection—pizza is cheap and something they'll both eat—and look at Gabby. "Pizza and then maybe we'll order a movie on Pay-Per-View, what do you say?"

Gabby nods before returning her attention to the window and the parking lot below. What is she looking for? Or who?

The doctor said that there's nothing physically wrong with Gabby. *"She can talk, she's just choosing not to."* Then she recommended a therapist. Again.

I dig my wallet out of my purse and count the bills, even though I already know exactly how much I have. Or, more to the point, how much I don't have. I didn't anticipate my father not being here, and I'm out of money. All I have left is two singles, a quarter, two nearly maxed out credit cards, and a bank account wiped clean by Mom's funeral expenses. As it is, I'm going to need money from Dad just for the gas to drive home.

I pull out the Visa and grab the phone book.

Where the hell are you, Dad?

William

THE MORNING sun is hot on my back as I knock on the door to room 132 at the Cheap Sleep and hold my breath.

What am I doing? Cally wants nothing to do with me, and she's leaving town in a few days. I should be calling Meredith, the granddaughter of my grandma's best friend since childhood. Meredith has everything going for her—the career, the family, the personality. Fuck, she's even gorgeous, and—judging by some of the texts she's sent me—a little dirty in the best of ways.

But I'm not calling Meredith. I didn't even respond to last night's text—a creative promise of what she'd do for me if I came to her place tonight. No. Instead, I'm here, chasing after Cally. Again.

My thoughts are cut off when she swings the door open. She's dressed in cut-offs and a tank and her hair is tied back at the base of her neck.

She freezes when she sees me. "What are you doing here?"

I lift the box in my hand. "Donuts?"

"Oh, thank Christ!" says a voice behind Cally. "If I have to eat another peanut butter sandwich, I'm going to retch."

A teenage version of Cally appears beside her at the door and snatches the box from my hand. She has Cally's dark hair and is dressed in far too little. Her short shorts and tank reveal more than they cover. I'm tempted to offer her my shirt to protect her virtue.

"Drew, don't be rude," Cally says.

I raise a brow. "Drew? Holy shi—shoot." Of course Cally's sisters wouldn't be the little girls they were when they moved away, but it's still a shock. Drew was in grade school when they left town and now she's got cleavage spilling out of her shirt.

Drew snorts. "You can say 'shit.' We're not babies anymore."

"Drew!" Cally scolds.

"Gabby!" Drew calls, ignoring her older sister and opening the donut box. "Cally's boyfriend bought us donuts."

"He's not my boyfriend," Cally says, snagging a square glazed donut from the box. "Don't eat too many. You'll make yourself sick."

"'You'll make yourself sick,'" Drew parrots.

Gabby's eyes light up as she looks into the box and draws out a chocolate croissant.

"You really shouldn't have," Cally says.

The little girl looks up at me with her big sister's killer brown eyes and smiles, and I know I couldn't regret this morning's impulse if I wanted to.

"Well done, sis. We're in town less than a day and you're already hooking up." Drew pushes her palms to the ceiling in a "raise the roof" gesture. "My sister is a player, man. Don't say I didn't warn you."

"Drew!" Cally says around a bite of donut. "Seriously!" Stepping onto the sidewalk with me, she pulls the door shut behind her. She puts her fingers to her mouth as she chews and swallows. "I apologize for Drew. She's just looking for attention."

"It's okay. I'm glad I could save her from the horror of another breakfast of peanut butter sandwiches."

She smiles at me, a patch of sugary glaze just below her lip. "Why are you here—really?"

Without thinking, I reach to brush away the glaze, and the space between us suddenly pulses thick with awareness.

Her tongue darts out to lick her lip and skims my thumb. "We can't do this."

"Why not?" I step forward, closing the small space between us, and slide my fingers into her hair so I'm cupping her face. It's so easy to touch her like this. Maybe it's stupid. Maybe I should stay far away from her. But I can't. And I don't want to. "Go out with me tonight, Cally."

"You know that's not a good idea," she whispers.

"You're leaving, I get that. I'm just asking for one night. You, me—" I smile because she's already turning her face into the palm of my hand, already as drunk on the memories as I am. "—and some strawberry wine."

chapter three

Cally

I SHOULD not go out with William Bailey. Nothing good can come of that.

I don't know how many times I've repeated these words to myself since he showed up at our hotel room this morning. Yesterday, I saw him and went from zero to lusty in one-point-five seconds, but I blamed his condition—sweaty, shirtless, generally mouthwatering in every way.

I didn't have that excuse this morning when he showed up looking so damn respectable in khakis and a deep blue polo the color of his eyes. With a freshly shaven jaw and those messy curls damp from his shower, he smelled of aftershave and soap. My panties didn't stand a chance.

So I'm still attracted to him. And he's still attracted to me. But that doesn't change what I did. And it doesn't make a date with him a good idea.

This is what I'm reminding myself of again and again as I push my cart through the produce section of the grocery store. This is what I'm repeating in my mind as I sip a cup of free grocery store coffee and catch myself holding the cheek he touched this morning.

"Oh my God! Cally Fisher, is that you?"

I'm getting sick of this reaction from random townies, but I plaster a smile in place and turn to the feminine voice asking the question. As soon as I spot the bouncing blond curls, my smile turns genuine and I screech. "Lizzy!" I throw out my arms and we run to each other, hugging like the BFFs we once were.

Her skinny arms squeeze me tight and she squeals. "I never thought I'd see you again! You disappeared off the face of the fucking Earth, girl!"

My throat grows thick, and I swallow back unexpected tears. As far as my former life here was concerned, I did fall off the Earth, and not for any of the good reasons. "I know. I suck."

Lizzy steps back and shakes her head. "Don't say that. You were entitled to live your own life. You needed to cut ties here in order to move on."

She's probably the only one who saw it that way.

I look around the grocery store, scanning the faces in produce.

"Hanna's not here," Lizzy explains, knowing I'm looking for her twin. "But I cannot wait to see her face when she sees you. We should totally surprise her."

"I'd like that." Again, I'm swallowing, and there's an alarming burning behind my eyes. I shouldn't have worried that the girls would hold my rare and overly brief communication against me. The Thompson girls are the best kind of friends—the kind who never made me feel less-than, never required me to pay my dues, never asked anything of me, actually.

Lizzy's green eyes light up. "Will you be here next week? We're having this giant end-of-summer bash at Asher Logan's place. It's going to be fucking epic."

I choke on my coffee. "Not *that* Asher Logan, though, right?"

She wriggles her brows and grins. "Yes, *that* Asher Logan."

"He lives here? In New Hope?"

"Right next door to my mama," Lizzy says, raising four fingers.

"Girl Scout's honor."

I fold her pinky down, and she giggles. "Christ," I mutter. "I told my mom New Hope wasn't boring."

"And get this! Maggie's dating him. Practically living with him, actually, though she still has her old place by campus."

"Maggie is dating Asher Logan."

"I swear to God! And if she didn't deserve every ounce of his sweet, sexy ass, we'd hate her for it."

"Go, Maggie!" My smile drops away when I see Drew approaching us, arms crossed, a scowl on her face. "Drew, do you remember Lizzy?"

"Vaguely," she says in a bored tone.

Lizzy's jaw unhinges at the sight of my beautiful little sister. "Drew? No way! You're way too grown up!"

Drew rolls her eyes, no doubt sick of hearing those words from everyone we've run into. "They don't have any veggie burgers."

"Don't be rude," I warn.

Lizzy waves away my concern. "You're at the wrong grocery store if you want a good vegetarian selection. Go to Horner's by campus. They'll have everything you need. Fancier stuff for a fancier girl."

I wince. No doubt my picky sister would prefer the swanky high-end grocery, but I came here on purpose. Namely, I don't have cash to waste on designer veggie burgers. I also came for the free coffee but mostly for the prices.

"Thank God," Drew breathes, turning up her nose as she looks around the store.

She's become such a pretentious snob in the last few years. It was one thing when Mom was around to coddle her, but I'm sick of her acting like she used to live some posh life when that's never been the case. Given our circumstances now, I can hardly stomach her attitude. And when I think about the sacrifices I made so she could have the things she did—food, clothes, a roof over her head—I want to smack her.

Lucky for Drew, I'm only a shitty enough sister to think about smacking her and not enough of one to actually do it. I know she can't comprehend our situation. Truthfully, I wouldn't want her to.

"Oh my God," Lizzy squeals. "Is that little Gabriella?"

Gabby scoots to my side and leans away from Lizzy.

"I used to help babysit you, little stinker!" Lizzy says, clapping her hands. "My God, you're all so flipping dark and gorgeous. Where's your mom? How's she doing? Are you just visiting or back for good? So much catching up to do. We should—" Suddenly, Lizzy seems to register the horror on my sisters' faces and she cuts herself off.

"My mom passed away last month," I tell her softly. "I'm here to get the girls settled in with my dad."

"Gabby wants to wait in the car," Drew says, grabbing her little sister's hand and throwing a bitter look at Lizzy. "I'll take her."

"Jesus," Lizzy breathes as they walk away. "I had no idea. Are you guys okay? I mean, considering?"

"It was unexpected," I say, which is true. Mom had really shaped up her life. I can't say she ever let go of her precious orange bottles, but in the last few years she'd at least been a functional addict. Her overdose came out of the blue. "They're taking it pretty hard. The move doesn't help."

"I feel like a total bitch." Lizzy draws her bottom lip between her teeth as she watches my sisters push through the double doors to the parking lot. "I'm talking about rock stars and parties and you're here because you lost your mom."

I try to take a deep breath, but all this aching pressure in my chest keeps it shallow. "It feels good," I confess. "To talk about something fun for once."

"Well, it's next week. Seriously, you can bring your sisters if you want. Or you can come alone and drink yourself stupid. I'm cool either way."

Tempting. It would be nice to pretend to be a normal young twenty-something. I never got that experience.

"Give me your phone." She's already snagging it from where it was sticking out of my front jeans pocket. Before I realize what she's doing, her fingers are tapping buttons, and she's handing it back to me. "I just sent myself a text from your phone. Now we can get a hold of each other."

"Great," I say weakly. I know it would just hurt her if I tried to explain why I hesitate to do that. Keeping up with the people from my old life will only remind me of all the things I can't have. All the ways I've failed. I don't like to dwell on that shit. "I'd better get these groceries and get out to the girls."

As I walk away, I hear her call, "Think about the party!"

I pile my minimal groceries onto the belt at the checkout— peanut butter and off-brand wheat bread, ingredients for beans and rice, spaghetti, marinara sauce, bananas, apples. If my parents taught me anything growing up, it was how to eat cheap. I sprung for the fresh strawberries since they were on sale and Gabby's eyes got that sad, hazy look when she spotted them.

This will all have to go on the credit card, but it should be the last major expense before Dad returns. God, what I'd give to get into that house before then. No doubt it needs a good cleaning, and his piles of notes on the nature of the Universe or whatever else the hell it is he's always poring over probably cover every flat surface in the house.

I've already made long lists of the supplies I'll check his house for before leaving. I brought as much as I could—clean sheets for the girls' beds, some basic cookware, all their clothes and personal items. They weren't exactly living the high life with Mom, so the pickings were slim.

The clerk is ringing up my items when I hear someone call my name again. This time I know who it is and turn to a smiling William Bailey. His gaze is already at my feet, taking in my hemp wedge sandals and inching up my bare legs.

I really have no respect for men who do that elevator-look shit in public. So why is it that when Will does it, I want to strip for him and invite a repeat performance?

I'm trying to play it cool—to pretend the look in his eyes has no effect on me, but I think we both know better. "You're not used to girls telling you no, are you?" I ask with a raised brow.

He grunts, "You'd be surprised," then takes something from his pocket and hands it to me. "I saw Granny downtown, and she told me where your dad is. This is the number for The Center. I was on my way to the hotel to give it to you when I saw your car."

I take a piece of paper from his hand and stare at the number that will get me in touch with my crazypants, absent-minded, insert-twenty-other-shortcomings-here father. "Oh. Thanks." The fact that I'm disappointed Will isn't just here to talk me into that date? Ri.dic.u.lous. "What's The Center?"

"It's a Spiritualist camp a couple of hours from here."

"Spiritualist camp. Of course."

Behind me, the cashier is clearing her throat, trying to get my attention.

"Oh!" I fumble through my purse and pull out a credit card. "Here. Use this, please." The woman takes the card, and I turn back to Will. "Your grandmother knows the number to a spiritualist camp?"

He shakes his head. "No, not my grandmother. Granny—the Thompson girls' grandmother."

That makes a little more sense. I vaguely remember my father going to the woman for readings of some sort from time to time. "Well, I appreciate it."

"It's declined," the cashier says apologetically. "You want me to run it again?"

I close my eyes. That was only a matter of time. "Let's just try this one." I pull out my only other credit card and hold my breath as she slides it through the reader.

"Do you need some money, Cally?" Will asks softly.

The woman bites her lip. When she turns to me, she doesn't say anything. She doesn't need to. Her face says it all: Declined.

I can't look at Will. Mortification is climbing up my neck and into my cheeks, hot and red. "I'll pay you back."

I pick up my three bags of groceries while Will pays, and I want to crawl under a rock and disappear and a hundred other clichés all at once. When he takes the receipt, I head for the door, but he cuts me off and takes the bags from my hand.

"Let me."

"I can carry my own groceries."

"But then I can't show off my manly muscles and charm."

Oh, God. He's too freaking good and sexy, and I have a serious case of *want-what-I-can't-have*.

THE RING of my cell breaks the tense silence of our motel room. A quick look at the screen shows an unknown number.

"Hello?"

"Cally?" It's my dad. I recognize his deep, scratchy voice. I called the spiritualist camp Will told me about and asked them to please have him contact me. I'm impressed it took him less than two hours.

"Dad? Why aren't you here?"

"Tell him he's earned Worst Father of the Year award already," Drew says.

I narrow my eyes at her and slip out of the hotel room so she can't add her two cents to our conversation.

Dad clears his throat. "Where are you?"

I squeeze my eyes shut. He's so absentminded. "The girls and I are in New Hope. Remember?"

"I thought you were coming on the tenth."

"It's the eleventh, Dad."

"No, it's not. It's... Oh." He clears his throat again. "Are you okay? Was the drive okay?"

"We're fine. When will you be home?"

I wait through the long silence. My father is a thoughtful man. Intelligent to a fault. When I was a child, time and again I'd ask a question and just when I'd be convinced he hadn't heard, he'd finally answer me. "I have a class tonight. Is it okay if I get in late?

There's a guest speaker in from Seattle, and I don't want to miss this if I don't have to."

"That'd be fine. But Dad, are you really up for this? Raising two girls? Having them under your roof? Being responsible for them?" I wait. Listen. Wait some more. I hear him breathing and I wonder what he's thinking.

Finally, "It wasn't a responsibility I ever intended to give up. I'm glad to have my girls back."

Tenderness wells in my chest, spilling over, even as anger still boils in the pit of my belly. They crush together and make me feel childlike and helpless. Because despite all his faults, he's my father, and I love him. He means well, even if he falls short. I have to swallow back emotion before I can speak. "I'll see you tomorrow, then?"

"Yes. I'm sorry I wasn't there, Cally. I won't let you down again. I promise everything is going to be fine."

"That's good to hear," I whisper, and whether I should or not, I kind of believe him.

⁂

"HOLY SHIT, Dad. Nineteen seventy-two called and it wants its house back."

Inside and out, the house cries for maintenance, and Dad has an explanation for every shortcoming. From green shag carpet that needs replacing (*"I had it professionally cleaned before I moved in."*), to the gutters that are full and falling off the house (*"With the pitch of this roof, we don't really need gutters."*), to the barely functional kitchen (*"That's what the hot plate is for."*).

I met Dad at the house midmorning, setting the girls up with a movie and some snacks at the motel so I could get their rooms pulled together here.

After Mom left Dad and took off for a "better life" (oh, sweet irony), Dad quit his job at Sinclair University, sold my childhood home, and went all *Eat, Pray, Love* on his life. The girls were young, so I don't think they care that Dad doesn't live in the old house, but they *will* care if they see they're expected to live in a madman's hovel.

"Did you do *anything* to prepare for them?" I ask, peeking into the bedroom the girls are supposed to share. "You've known for a month they'd be moving in with you."

"What do you mean?" His question is followed by a long coughing fit. His third in the ten minutes I've been here.

"We have to move these bookcases out of their bedroom. Little girls don't need their bedrooms filled with *The Gospel of Sri Ramakrishna* and the *Tao te Ching* and whatever else you have piled on those old shelves."

"That's my collection of religious texts signed by spiritual leaders from around the globe. There are over two-hundred autographed books. I think they'll find it cool."

I gape at him. Crazy. Pants.

"You think they'd mind?"

I grab a book at random to prove my point. "*Learning From Your Past Lives: Enlightenment through Deep Meditation.* Yeah, that'll make a nice bedtime story." I prop my hands on my hips and stare at him. He starts coughing again. A violent, angry cough.

"Okay, okay," he says when the fit passes and he's catching his breath. "I can move them to the attic."

"Have you talked to a doctor about that cough?"

He nods. "A healer." Then another coughing fit.

I raise a brow. "A healer or a *real* doctor?"

"I don't like Western medicine. You know that."

"You don't *like* it? You sound like you're ready to cough up a fucking lung, but you don't *like* it?"

"I'm working with a very talented healer. I just need some time to meditate on our healing mantra and—"

"No! Uh-uh. You are not leaving your health in the hands of a fucking *mantra*." He flinches at my second use of the f-bomb, but I don't even care. I need him to hear me. "Jesus, Dad, you're responsible for two girls now. Don't you get that? They *need* you."

"I see your mother's skepticism finally rooted itself in you."

The little girl still living somewhere inside me flinches at those words. I was once so special to my father because I, too, believed in the magical things he did. I, too, believed everything happened for a reason, wishes came true, and good would always overcome evil.

Part of me wants to be his special princess even now. And even though I don't believe any of that crap anymore, part of me wants to, just so my father will be proud.

Fuck. Shit. Damn. "I want you to see a doctor on Monday before I leave. I want you—"

"Okay."

"—to take care of yourself. What?"

"I said *okay*," he says softly.

Maybe I should just pack up the car and take the girls back to Vegas with me. If I thought I could make a life for them, I probably would, but I can see it in his eyes—my dad is ready to do right by his girls. And I know New Hope is a better place for them than my world will ever be.

"Thank you," I say softly. Then I grab a box and start packing up books to take to the attic. Tonight, I'll call my boss and tell her I won't be back until the end of the week. If I'm going to make this house a home for those girls, I have my work cut out for me.

chapter four

Cally

I NEED to get back to the hotel, but instead I'm sitting on my dad's front porch, looking up at the stars through the trees and listening to the river run beyond them. The house may be shit, but I'll give him credit for the location.

When my phone rings, I'm so sure Drew is calling to ask when I'll be back that I don't even look at the screen before taking the call. "Miss me?" I ask with a smile.

"More than you can imagine." That voice is definitely not Drew's.

Cold dread steals through me at the sound of the deep, familiar voice. "Brandon? Is that you?"

"Guilty."

Fuck. I swallow, preparing to tread carefully. "What a surprise. How did you get this number?"

"Baby, you know you can't hide from me."

"I wasn't trying to." Not a complete lie.

"I miss you," he murmurs, dropping his voice to that low whisper he used to use in bed. Four years later and I still remember.

"Surely you've found someone better than me by now." I force a smile to my face as if he can see me.

His low hiss slithers through the phone line and then I hear a hard *clunk*, as if he just threw something against a wall. "Jesus, Cally. You know I don't want anyone else." His voice softens, the anger floating away as quickly as it came. "You're my girl."

I don't reply. There's no response I could live with that won't just piss him off.

"I thought you'd come to me when your mom died. I know you need money. Your sisters need money. Let me help."

At what price? "We're fine," I lie.

"I blame those college classes, making you think you're less of a woman if you take money from your man."

You're not my man, I want to scream. But it doesn't matter. Brandon has only been back in Vegas a couple months, and soon he'll remember I'm no longer his "type" and he'll find someone who is. In the meantime, I just need to let him feel like the one in control.

"Do you have everything you need?" he asks softly. "Whether you're with me or not, I don't want you going without."

"You've already done enough."

"I'd do even more. For you…." Again, that low whisper. "Damn, I miss you girl."

"What about Quinn? Don't you miss her?" God bless that girl. Finding out about her visits with him gave me the perfect excuse to cut ties while he was gone. Or cut them as much as I dared.

"Cally, baby, please."

I look up at the stars. When did I lose sight of mine? My father raised me to believe in magic, in wishes, in beautiful destiny. And then life went to shit and destiny played second fiddle to just getting by.

"Come see me when you get home. We'll talk about what we can do for your sisters. We'll talk about us."

"Okay," I lie. I won't go to him willingly again. Not if I'm left with a choice. But if I say no, he'll think I'm playing hard to get, and that will make him want me more. "Goodnight, Brandon." I end the call before he can reply.

I catch my breath in the darkness, trying to let the adrenaline fizzle out and my heart rate slow. Just the sound of his voice makes me crave a hot shower and a scouring pad. Or maybe just the touch of a man who makes all the ugly go away.

I scroll through my sent texts to find Lizzy's number. I punch it in and hold my breath while I wait for an answer.

"Cally!"

My chest warms with the enthusiasm in her greeting. "Hey, Liz. I was wondering if you had William Bailey's phone number."

William

THE GYM is nearly empty tonight except for Max, who's working behind the counter, and Sam, who's spotting for me as I attempt to channel my frustration into the weights.

My phone buzzes, and I open the latest text from Meredith, detailing exactly what she'll do with her tongue and certain parts of my anatomy.

Our grandmothers have been doing their best to set us up, and I'm beginning to think I made an epic mistake by sleeping with her. I thought we were on the same page, though. We both wanted something casual. Companionship. A good time.

Or so I thought. But these texts are becoming more frequent and when I was at her place last week, she slipped and asked how soon I wanted kids.

I'm about to throw my phone back down when it buzzes again with another message from her.

"Meredith?" Sam asks.

"None other," I mutter. I tap out a quick excuse and toss my phone down.

"Why do you suddenly seem so uninterested? She's fucking hot. And smart. And she's got her shit together."

"She's getting too serious. I think she's going to want something...long-term."

Sam lifts a brow. "So complains the Mayor of Commitment-Land?"

"Shut up," I growl. "That's not what I want right now."

"Hey, I heard Cally Fisher's back in town," Max calls from behind the counter.

"Cally Fisher?" Sam asks. "You shitting me?"

I grab a pair of forty-pound dumbbells. "Yeah, I saw her already."

Max grunts. "Did you tell her to fuck off?"

I drop the weights and turn on him. "Don't."

Max lifts his palms up in surrender. "Message delivered and received, man, but you do remember that she totally burned you, right?"

How could I forget? "It doesn't matter anymore. That was a long time ago."

Sam chuckles. "Who knew she could still have a hold on you, what, six years later?"

"Seven," I mutter, dropping down to the bench to rest my head in my hands. I swear my mind hasn't stopped spinning since I spotted her lost outside my house.

"You still want her," Sam says softly. It's not a question.

Max heads over to join us. "Is she sticking around?"

"Her mom died. She's here to move her sisters in with her dad, then she's heading back to Vegas."

"That sucks," Max says.

One look at my eyes, and Max is backing up. "Fuck. And I thought you had it bad for Maggie."

My phone buzzes again.

"Meredith again?" Sam asks.

"Probably."

Before I realize what he's doing, Sam scoops my phone off the ground and reads my text, his eyes going wide.

"That shit's private," I protest, but I really don't care. There's nothing worth protecting about my relationship with Meredith. But then Sam lets out a low whistle that has me whipping my gaze back up to him.

"'This is Cally,'" he reads. "'Is your offer still good for tonight?'"

I snatch the phone away from him, half convinced he's screwing with me, but sure enough, Cally's message is staring back at me. I punch the *call* button without hesitation.

"William?" I would recognize that sweet voice anywhere.

"Cally?"

"Yeah. I hope you don't mind. Lizzy gave me your number. I didn't want to call in case it was a bad time."

Max smirks, but he and Sam head to the other side of the gym so I have some privacy. We'll give the assholes credit for that much at least.

"Of course it's not. Is everything okay?"

The line is silent for a few beats too long, and I look at my phone to make sure it didn't disconnect. Then finally, she says, "If you seriously don't hate me, I'd like to go to dinner with you tonight. That would be…amazing."

"Can I pick you up in an hour?"

"Okay." *Pause.* "William?" I love the way my name rolls off her tongue. She takes my very corn-fed, middle-America name and makes it sound almost exotic.

"Yeah?"

"Could we go for dinner somewhere outside of New Hope? I just remember how people talk and I don't want that."

There's more to it than that, but I'm not going to push. Not now. "I know just the place. I'll see you in an hour."

Cally

"You look cheap," Drew says from behind me as I take in my muddled reflection in the old mirror. "Do you really have a date, or are you planning to stand on the corner and give five-dollar blow jobs?"

I spin on her. "Watch your mouth, missy! You think Mom would want you to talk like that?"

She lifts a brow, unimpressed by my wrath, and returns her attention to her cell phone.

With a long, deep belly breath, I turn back to the mirror. She's right, of course, which just pisses me off more. I brought clothes suitable for cleaning, unpacking, and sleeping. Nothing for a date with the sexiest man I've ever met. And as much as I tell myself it doesn't matter, that's just a bunch of crap. I was forced to open a box of Drew's clothes and borrow her black cotton dress—a "favor" she only allowed when I promised I would send her money for a new dress. But Drew is shorter than me and less curvy, so something that looks sweet and sophisticated on her makes me look like a floozy showing more leg and cleavage than the showgirls on the strip. I'm tempted to call Lizzy and see if she has a dress I can borrow, but Will's going to be here any minute, so there's no time for that.

Someone squeezes my hand, and I look down to see Gabby giving me a half smile. I don't know if I've seen her smile all-out since Mom died. I miss her smile. I miss the sound of her voice.

Reaching onto her tiptoes and behind my head, she pulls the hair tie from the base of my neck so my long, dark hair falls free, then she places her hand against my cheek and nods her approval. She might not be talking, but most days she communicates with me one hundred times better than Drew does.

I pull Gabby into a hug and take in the sweet bubblegum scent of her hair. When I release her, Drew is staring at us and, for the split second before she can hide it again, there's sadness in her eyes.

"You sure you guys will be okay?" I ask.

Gabby squeezes my hand, and Drew nods, averting her eyes. "You deserve to have a little fun too."

My breath catches with surprise, and that need to cry is back. *Damn it.* I shove it down. "Thank you."

Drew lifts a shoulder. "I can tell you like him. Anyway, he's hot."

I grab a pillow and throw it at her. "Hot and too old for you!"

She laughs and throws it back at me. "Yeah, but which one of us is going to be living here?"

"I don't care how hot he is, if he touched you, I'd cut off his balls."

Something flickers in her eyes, a secret caught peeking from the hidden corner of her mind. Even though I haven't lived under the same roof as the girls since I was sixteen, I've remained their primary breadwinner and been involved in their lives. My role as surrogate mother isn't a new one. And yet there's so much I don't know about her. I want to fix that, but there's a rift between us that I don't know I can heal from a distance.

From the outside looking in, people are probably most worried about Gabby. But me? It's Drew who keeps me up at night. Gabby's going to be okay. I believe that. But Drew is just old enough that she can really get herself in trouble if that's what she wants to do.

I swallow hard, pushing back the fear and sadness and locking it away for another time. "I'm going to wait outside. Slide the deadbolt and the chain behind me. I'll text you when I get back, and you can let me in."

Drew nods and pops her earbuds back in, and Gabby blows me a kiss.

I push myself out the door before I can change my mind and I'm greeted by a night of glittering stars. The stars in New Hope are brighter and more plentiful than anywhere else I've ever been. When I was a little girl, I would look out my bedroom window each night and pick my favorite one and only then would I make a wish. My father taught me to believe in the magic of wishes and destiny, and I was such an adoring daughter that his words were my scripture and the starry night sky became my temple.

When we moved to Vegas, Drew was eight, and she told my mom she felt sorry for people who lived there because weren't enough stars to go around. Mom laughed and said you don't need stars when your wishes had already come true.

She thought Rick was her wish come true. That was why she took us there, away from my dad, away from New Hope. She met some guy online, hooked up with him a few times while telling Dad she had to travel for "trainings" for work. Then she served her husband with divorce papers and took her daughters to live with a complete stranger who she thought was her everything.

We were there less than a month before she realized Rick wasn't the man she thought he was. He was a controlling drunk who liked to put his hands on my mom and sometimes me and the girls. We left his million-dollar home and found ourselves a couple of rent checks away from eviction and a homeless shelter, but it was the right decision. For all the mistakes Mom made, for all the decisions I wish she handled differently, I'm proud of her for leaving that man.

A black BMW pulls up in the spot before me, and William steps out, wearing dark dress pants and a grey button-up Oxford. The sight of him flips a switch in my body and I'm instantly buzzing with awareness.

"Hey, beautiful," he says softly, and with one slide of his eyes over me, all my concerns about this dress fizzle away.

chapter five

Cally

THE LITTLE tapas restaurant north of Indianapolis is the perfect setting for a secret date with this man who makes me forget myself. There's candlelight and soft music, and we're sitting in the corner at a booth that puts us at a little round table sharing the same curved seat.

We're eating brie and fresh fruit, seared ahi tuna, and miniature crab cakes, and already coming to the bottom of our first bottle of wine.

"So, what are you doing these days?" His voice has gone deeper and husky, and for a minute I'm so tied up in the sensual pull of the sound of his words that I don't actually register what they mean.

I blink when I realize he's staring at me expectantly. "Oh, I…I'm a massage therapist?" I hate that the answer makes me uncomfortable. In most contexts, I'm proud of what I do, but William knew my mother. I resist the urge to get defensive and explain that she may have taught me to love her trade, but I don't get big tips she did for the reasons she did. Not that I have any room to judge her anyway. I have my own secrets.

"Is that a question?"

I smile and shrug. "I don't know. I like what I do, but there are always people who assume the worst." People in New Hope. People who have already made up their minds about me and my family. "What about you? Do you still like photography?"

"I do. I teach it over at Sinclair."

"You're a college professor? Seriously?"

He grins. "I landed a fellowship after I finished my MFA. I like teaching, but I'd rather actually be a photographer than teach other people how to be."

"You were always so talented," I say softly. "I'm glad you didn't leave that behind."

"What about you? Did you go to college?"

"I got my massage certification at a community college and I've taken a few classes since, but I haven't managed to finish any kind of degree." I won't any time soon, either. I need to work as much as possible and send money to Dad to help with the girls.

Reaching across the table, William catches my fingers under his. "Why did you call, Cally? What made you change your mind?"

Why *am* I here? Because I want him? Because I'm trying to forget Brandon? Because I'm lonely as hell and needed an adult to talk to?

"I guess that's as much a mystery as why you would want to be here with me. After... Should we just acknowledge the elephant at the table and talk about how I stood you up for your own prom?" I let out a breath, relieved to finally say the words to his face. "I'm sorry. I've always been sorry. I hope you know that."

He drops his gaze to my mouth. "Come here."

Biting my lip, I slide around the booth so I'm next to him. The lights are so low, I can barely make out his expression, but I don't need to in order to feel the heat between us. Is it in my head? Can he feel it too? Whatever it is—hormones, memories, the knowledge that this is temporary and I'm leaving soon—the pull between us is magnetic, and I let my bare thigh press against the soft fabric of his pants.

"That's better," he whispers, his hot eyes on me.

"I think so, too."

He lowers his head and glides his lips over my neck in a movement so sweet, so simple, my breath leaves me in a rush. "I'm supposed to be pissed at you," he whispers. "You broke my heart."

"Then why aren't you?"

"When I saw you again, there was no room for my anger. I want you too much."

Under the table, his hand settles against the inside of my knee, making little circles that send my heart racing and turn my muscles to jelly. "Me too," I admit.

His fingers trace an invisible line two inches up the inside of my leg, and I clench my thighs together instinctively, trapping his hand between my legs.

"I can stop," he says in a whisper.

"No," I breathe. I want the opposite, and I force myself to relax, and my legs open to the exploration of his hand.

"You look amazing in this dress. I love the way it shows off your legs, but it just makes me think of having them wrapped around me."

I bury my face in his neck and moan softly, remembering the way he used to touch me. He smells amazing, and his whisper-soft exploration of my thigh sends tiny shivers of pleasure through me.

His hand slides higher until his fingertips reach the edge of my panties. I almost squeeze my legs together again—not because I want him to stop but because I want his hand there so badly, touching me, exploring me, his fingers sliding into me.

"What do these look like?" He traces down the satin center of my panties.

Oh, God. By some miracle, I'm already ready for his touch. I haven't been this turned on this quickly since...since William.

His knuckles brush over me, lightly pressing the soft fabric against my swollen clit.

He opens his mouth against my ear and draws my earlobe between his teeth, nipping and sucking. My eyes flutter closed. I want to fall into the pleasure that's spinning like a cyclone around every nerve ending, and I'm almost afraid of how quickly he has me falling into it.

I rock into his hand instinctively. "Touch me."

"Tell me," he whispers. He makes wicked little circles on my panties. "What do they look like?"

This desire clawing at me is madness. At this moment, I would do anything to get him to slide under the barrier between us. "They're black satin."

"Mmm, satin. I can tell." He rewards me by rolling his fingers against the fabric in question.

Holy shit.

"What else? How do they look?"

Under the table, I cling to his forearm as if I'm afraid he might escape. "They're string bikinis with a little bow at each of my hips."

His hand leaves that pulsing, aching spot between my legs to explore the string over my hip, leaving me ready to cry out or beg or both.

"God, I bet these are gorgeous on you. If I had you alone, I'd stand you in front of me in nothing these panties and I'd untie them with my teeth."

Yes, please.

I can hardly breathe. I want what he's describing. More. "Have you thought a lot about getting me alone again?" Drawing back a bit so I can watch his expression, I watch his eyes and wait for the answer I need to hear.

"Every second since you showed up on my street."

"Me too. And before."

Heat flares in his eyes. The intensity of his gaze would scare me if I didn't already trust this man with every inch of my being.

He presses his mouth against mine as his hand returns between my legs. It's not a gentle kiss. It's hard—punishing and demanding—and I need it. I could lose myself here, in this kiss that is equal parts desire, anger, and regret. I could forget who I am, what I've done, and become the stroke of tongue against

LEXI RYAN

tongue, become the pleasure of his hand working between my legs as I moan into his mouth.

He breaks the kiss and leans his forehead against mine. "You feel so damn good." His hand moves slowly, smoothly.

How can he affect me so much more than any other man I've ever been with? He's always been the standard by which all other men have been measured and come up short.

I shouldn't be here with him. I gave up my right to this seven years ago. I take a long drink of my wine—seeking courage and permission for this evening suspended outside of time and heartbreak. One night. One indulgence.

I lift my hips off the seat, seeking out his touch.

"Do you want more?" The words are so low they're more a vibration against my ear than a sound.

"I'm leaving in a couple of days. I can't stay." And that's the only reason we can do this at all.

His teeth nip my ear again, suck at the lobe before he speaks. "That's not what I asked, Cally."

Outside my panties, the pad of his thumb is resting on my clit with nothing but the promise of the pressure I need. When his hand leaves me, I hear my own gasp of protest.

"Come home with me tonight."

I squeeze my eyes shut. After weeks of looking after my sisters, I need to be something other than a resented stand-in mother. Even if only for a couple of hours in this man's bed. He deserves the night I once promised him. *I* deserve it. But I shake my head. "I can't."

"Then tell me to stop." The rough pads of his fingers toy with the thin ribbons at my hips. With his free hand, he places a sliced grape to my lips, and I take it, only briefly letting my lips brush his fingertips. His eyes flash—hot and hungry. "Tonight is yours. Whatever you want."

"This," I whisper, rolling my hip into his touch.

Then he tugs, and he releases the tie on my panties. His hand snakes around to the other hip, and he grins at me as he frees that side as well.

"Lift," he whispers, and before I realize what he means to do, he's slipped my panties from under the table and tucked them in his pocket. He flashes me a small smile as he sips from his wine glass.

My panties are in William Bailey's pocket.

"You intending to give those back?"

"Not a chance." But then, instead of heading straight for my newly bare girly bits beneath the table, he cups my face in his big hand and brushes his thumb across my cheek. "Memories have this amazing way of changing on us, and I had myself convinced you couldn't have been as beautiful as I remembered. I was idealizing you."

I can't reply. The heat in his eyes alone is enough to make me want to crawl into his lap. Add the way he's been touching me, and in this moment, I am his.

"I was right about one thing," he whispers.

"What's that?"

"My memory got it all wrong."

"It did?"

"You're so much more beautiful than I remembered."

Our lips touch again and I will myself to memorize every second of this kiss. The soft brush of his lips before he opens his mouth over mine, the patient sweep of his tongue as I open for him, the way he tastes—a potent cocktail of wine and regret.

I don't even realize his hand has left my face until I feel the possessive wrap of his fingers around my thigh. Then, as he slides to points farther north, I have to break our kiss to catch my breath.

"Jesus," he hisses as his fingers reach my wet heat.

I almost cry out when he takes my swollen clit between two fingers.

"You're so wet," he whispers against my neck. "So damn wet."

"I—William…." I have to fight to keep my volume down, to keep from moaning.

He's touching that swollen, sensitive spot in a slow and gentle rub that has me rocking into him.

"You want to know what I'd do to you if you came home with

me tonight?"

I'm weak. I want to know, need to hear. "Yes."

"I'd get you naked because you have too goddamn many clothes on right now. Then I'd start with your amazing breasts. Remember how I could get you off just by kissing your breasts, sucking those beautiful nipples?" He brushes my taut nipples with his free hand and even through my dress and thin bra, the contact is enough to make me gasp. "Answer me, Cally."

"Yes," I breathe. His fingers have slowed their movement under my dress, as if he knows how close he is to getting me off and he wants to wait.

He moans appreciatively. "I'd start there. My tongue and lips and teeth on your breasts until I've memorized every curve and dip, until you're begging me for more—" He removes his hand from between my legs, "until you come for me."

"William."

"I'll get you there, baby. I swear. But not yet." He slides his hand farther up my dress and circles my navel. "Do you want to know more?"

God help me, I do. I want to know it all. And then maybe when I'm back in Las Vegas and wishing I could have him, I'll shape his words into my very own fantasy. My very own souvenir of my *what-if* life. "Please."

"Then I'd kiss you here." He pinches my navel piercing. "Damn, I bet this looks so sexy on you. When did you get it?"

"After I moved."

He draws back, his eyes hot on mine, his jaw hard. "For a man?"

"No. I got it when I was missing you."

He moans into my ear then fans his hand out to my waist. "I'd have to take my time there then. I'd run my tongue from hipbone to hipbone, then turn you over and lick down your spine." He slides his hand across my hip and under my ass. "When I got here," he says, squeezing, "I'd have to see if you're as sensitive here as you are everywhere else. Your ass is so incredible, and I can't forgive myself for neglecting it when I had a chance. I'm dying to bite you *here*."

He pinches my ass, and my breath draws in sharply. I shudder in his arms and feel his smile against my neck.

"Would you be ready for me then?" As he asks, he returns his hand between my legs, and I find myself scooting to the edge of the seat, parting my thighs to give him better access. I don't just want him to touch me. I need it. Like water. Like air. I *need* to feel William's hand between my legs because right now I am nothing but the pulsing ache of my arousal, and it's the fucking best I've felt in months.

No man I've ever touched could touch me the way Will does. It's like he has some sort of ability to intuitively know how I'm feeling.

Even now, sitting at the back of this candlelit restaurant with the wait staff milling around us, he doesn't rush in his movements. His fingers slide over me, alternately teasing and touching, working anticipation in equal measure against the pleasure.

"What else would you do?" I bite back a moan. "If we were alone?"

"I'd drop to my knees," he whispers. "And I'd cup your amazing ass in my hands as I tasted you."

It hurts, sitting here, listening to this, wanting it, knowing I can't let myself have it. Knowing that tonight, this moment, is all I get.

I curl my nails into his forearm, and he groans in my ear.

"But for now," he says, "for now I'll settle for touching with my fingers what I want to taste with my lips." He slides two fingers inside me, curling them as his thumb rubs my clit. "That's what I want you to think about next time you touch yourself."

I shudder, the pressure and pleasure building. "William," I whimper.

"Because next time my dick is in my hand, I fucking swear that's what I'll be thinking about. You. Naked. The taste of your pussy as you come against my tongue."

Dear God.

I have to bite his neck to muffle my moan as my orgasm hits, hard and fast.

chapter six

William

THE CAR is quiet on the drive home, and when I reach for her hand, she lets me take it. I have to remind myself that she's leaving. That this—the sweet silence of our touch, her soft fingers twined through mine—this isn't the new normal. I don't get to keep her. I don't get to finish what I started at the restaurant. She's leaving.

When we pull up to the motel, she doesn't rush from the car, so I turn and press my lips to hers. At first, I think she's going to pull away, but she opens under me slowly, and what I intended to be a brief goodbye kiss leaves me hard and breathless, and her clawing at my shirt and half in my lap.

We lean our foreheads together and catch our breath.

"When are you leaving?"

"Tomorrow? Day after tomorrow maybe? Dad's home. I just want to get the girls settled, but then I need to get back for work."

There's nothing I can say to get her to stay. I'm not even sure I should want her to. Tonight wasn't real after all. Reality wouldn't have let me touch her in in public like that. Reality dictates that I stay away from her, that I hate her for what she did to me. Or, at the very least, that I want nothing to do with her.

But tonight wasn't reality. It was like visiting a memory. And it was perfect.

I walk around to get her door. The moment she steps onto the pavement, I have her pressed against the side of the car, my hands in her hair, my knee between her legs, pressing our bodies as close as possible. Because touching her in the restaurant only made this need for her grow, and now I want her more than ever.

She kisses me back, clings to me, hand fisted in my shirt. Her mouth and hands match the desperation of my own, closer and closer, as if she wants to disappear into me.

I want more. I want to put her back in the car and take her to my house, take her to my bed. Because if tonight is the only stolen moment we get, I don't want it to end.

But despite all that, I'm the one who breaks the kiss. I'm the one who pulls away. Looking at her doesn't make it any easier. She's so fucking beautiful it breaks my heart. Flushed cheeks, swollen lips, thick lashes fluttering as she opens her eyes.

If I'd forgotten who and where we are, if I'd forgotten that she's no longer the girl I once loved, the look in her eyes brings me back. The girl I knew would have had nothing but love and desire in her eyes. But I see pain there now, pain and weariness edging away her desire.

"What happened to you?" I whisper.

"What do you mean?"

Swallowing, I trace the edge of her jaw. "You've changed. There's something…darker about you now."

Sadness washes over her face. "I regret so much. I should have been with you and I shouldn't have…." She shakes her head and looks up at me through her thick lashes. "You should hate me."

Impossible. "I've tried." I force a laugh, but it's hollow. "I don't know how."

Her lips tilt into a ghost of a smile. "You're too damn good, William Bailey, and I don't deserve as much of you as you've given." She grabs my hand and kisses the rough skin of my knuckles.

"Thank you for tonight. It was amazing."

I kiss the corner of her mouth and squeeze her fingers in mine.

"I should go in," she says. "I'll never forget this. Goodb—"

I press a finger to her lips before she can say our once-forbidden word. Because I can't bring myself to hear it. "Don't ruin tonight with that word."

She closes her eyes.

"Sleep well," I whisper.

She slips away, heading toward her room and leaving me feeling empty. "Sleep well," she calls over her shoulder.

I watch her disappear into her room, and then I look up at the moon and stars we once wished on together. They make me feel lonelier than ever. Because she may no longer be the girl I once loved, but she's the woman I want.

Cally

WHEN GABBY was six and Drew was eleven, I pawned a pair of three-carat diamond earrings and took the girls to Disney Land. We didn't stay at the fancy resorts and we couldn't buy all the cool souvenirs, but the girls didn't care. We packed up the car and drove to a cheap motel, setting an alarm so we would be at the park gates right at opening. Maybe it wasn't the smartest thing to do with the money. There were a thousand other ways we could have spent it. There was definitely a voice at the back of my mind that said this was why rich people think poor people make their own problems. But the look in Gabby's eyes when she saw Minnie Mouse for the first time made it worth it. Even Drew teared up as Goofy wrapped his arms around her and spun her around.

At Gabby's parent-teacher conference two months later (where I was standing in for Mom, who was "sick"), the teacher confronted me about it. Was that really the wisest use of our limited funds? Didn't I understand that we were two months behind on our share of classroom supplies? Think how many pairs of shoes I could have bought the girls with the money we spent on our park passes.

I stared at my lap and took every judgmental word from her lips. But it didn't matter what she said because, for one day, I got to show my little sisters that there really are magical things in this world. I got to prove to myself that the entire world wasn't as shitty as it had felt for the three years under Brandon's rule. That was worth a thousand years of school supplies and a hundred pairs of new shoes. Maybe I'm a little bit like my father in that way— willing to sacrifice practicality for a little magic.

As we pull up to Dad's house, I wonder if any of that has stuck with them or if they've lost faith in their world. I throw the car into park and turn to Drew, whose eyes have gone wide and horrified in the passenger seat.

Thunder rolls in the distance and heavy storm clouds hang over the house, making it look even more depressing than it did in yesterday's sunshine.

"It looks worse than it is," I say softly. "A little TLC, and it'll be just fine."

She climbs out of the car and slams the door behind her. The sound echoes through the car.

I turn to Gabby in the back. "It'll be an adventure."

Her bottom lip trembles and she's twisting her hands in her lap. She was three when we left and the couple of times she saw Dad over the years weren't enough to create those bonds a child deserves to have with a father, especially if he's going to be her primary care provider. Of course, she hasn't said a word about any of this, but she doesn't have to. It's all written on her face.

I climb out of the car and open her door, offering her my hand.

We twine our fingers together and follow Drew to the door— Drew, who's decided to take the disinterested tack and is already glued to the screen of her phone.

Dad pulls the door open before we even climb on the porch.

"Welcome home. I was wondering when you'd get here. You girls hungry? I made some chili?" He's speaking too fast—a rare occurrence for my father—and his words trip over each other.

Drew glances up from her phone but doesn't answer. Gabby squeezes my hand.

"Chili would be great," I answer, leading the way in the house.

I'm relieved to see that he's straightened up the place a bit. The kitchen counters and little table are clear of papers and books, and he's set out red disposable bowls at each of the four seats, a metal spoon and glass of water next to each.

Gabby and I sit down, and Drew joins us, her jaw tight.

"Phone," I remind her, and Drew slides it into her pocket with a roll of her eyes.

We sit quietly as Dad serves us the thin, red soup he's calling chili. We stare at our bowls.

"Did you make this?" I pick up my spoon, preparing to set a good example for my sisters.

"Yes. I hope it's okay. I'm not used to cooking for anyone but myself."

"What's in it?" Drew asks, poking at it with her spoon.

"It's…vegetarian." Dad clears his throat. "Tomatoes, beans, onions, green peppers, okra."

Drew drops her utensil. "I'll pass."

"*Vegetarian*," I growl.

"*Okra*," she growls right back. She crosses her arms over her chest and leans back in her chair.

"Thanks for thinking to make us lunch, Dad," I say, attempting to salvage these awkward beginnings. "That was thoughtful." I make myself take a big bite, keeping my face neutral as I chew and swallow.

Next to me, Gabby slowly lifts her spoon to her mouth. She blanches slightly when the soup hits her tongue—the still-crunchy vegetables and slimy beans make for an odd combination of textures—but she's a trooper and smiles at Dad before slowly taking another bite.

"So, what grade are you girls in now?" Dad asks between bites of his own soup. I've never seen him so nervous. For the first time I'm realizing that the girls aren't the only ones suffering a major life upheaval. "Drew, you must be in, what, seventh grade by now?"

Drew shoots me a look, as if our father's cluelessness is entirely my fault.

"She's in high school, Dad. Drew will be a sophomore. And Gabby will start fifth grade in the fall."

Dad looks taken aback by this information. "You've grown up so much," he says, almost to himself. Then he turns his gaze to his soup and we finish our meal in silence.

I make a mental note to get money from Dad to go grocery shopping for some basic foodstuffs. Drew will likely starve before eating okra. She may be a vegetarian, but she shouldn't be mistaken for someone who actually eats vegetables.

After our meal, I show the girls to the room they'll be sharing, and for Drew's sake, I try to see it through her eyes. Old pea-green shag carpet, mattresses on the floor that I've already made with their sheets and blankets from home, rickety little end table between the beds.

"This is worse than the brothel of a motel you had us staying at," she says under her breath.

"It'll be better when we move all your stuff in."

She snorts. "Sure. The lipstick on the pig didn't do it, so let's try some mascara."

"Drew, I need you to *try*." I feel Gabby at my side, grabbing my hand. "This situation will only be as good as you let it be."

"Good?" Her voice shakes and she throws her phone on her bed. "What in the *fuck* is good about any of this? I lost my mom and I have to live with this guy who never cared enough to visit more than a handful of times or, I don't know, *call* on my birthday. I had to leave my friends and my home. I hate this house. I hate this town, *and I fucking hate you.*"

I stagger back as she twists the dull blade in my heart. "What do you want me to do?" Tears roll down my cheeks because I'm not heartless and I hate what I'm asking of them. "I'm serious. Please tell me, because I don't know what to do."

Beside me, Gabby squeezes my hand. Then she speaks. It's the first word I've heard from her lips since I found her squatting on the floor next to Mom's dead body.

"Stay."

chapter seven

William
Seven Years Ago

"SHE'S NOT taking my calls." I throw the phone against the locker room wall. It hits with a sharp *crack*. Brand fucking new phone ruined. I'm not even like that. I don't lose my temper over shit. But Cally left, and I'm not even myself anymore.

At first it was okay. We talked all the time. I sent her a new cell since her mom missed the payment on her old one and it got shut off. We shared the mundane details about our days. We texted. We made plans for prom. I sent her emails with the web links about the little cabin I booked. We traded text messages about the strawberry wine I snuck from Grandma's basement. We whispered late until sunrise about our first night together. And I confessed how I can't stop thinking about what it's going to be like to finally slide inside her.

Those stolen moments weren't enough, but they kept me sane. And now I don't even have that much.

Max and Sam exchange a look. They've been holding their tongues where Cally's concerned, but I can see they're done with that.

"Man," Max says, "you're about to start college. It'll be awesome."

"Maybe you should just…let her go," Sam says. "Be young. Date around."

I set my jaw. "Right. Sure." But they don't fucking understand. I don't want to date around. I want *Cally*.

I drag a hand through my hair. My stomach burns. She's been ignoring my calls, blowing off my texts with occasional vague responses about being "busy." The last time I did get her on the phone, she was distant, not saying much, not bothering to laugh at my jokes and making excuses to get out of the conversation before it even began. "I sent her plane tickets to come home for prom. That'll help. I shouldn't have gone so long without seeing her. Prom will fix things."

"Long distance is hard when things are good," Max warns. "It's no way to fix a relationship that's broken."

"*We're. Not. Broken.*"

Sam shoves his hands in his pockets. "Are you sure she's still coming?"

"Of course she's still coming. She hasn't said otherwise."

The guys both nod and exchange those damn knowing looks again.

"She's not cheating on me," I mutter. They haven't said it, but that's what they're thinking. They're thinking I'll be better off without her. But they don't know Cally like I do. They don't understand how she gets me like nobody else, how she fills the aching hollow places that I've had since Mom and Dad died. "She wouldn't cheat on me."

"Okay, man," Max says.

"Of course not." Sam slaps my back. "Is there anything we can do?"

Their kindness pisses me off. They wouldn't drop the subject so easily if they believed she was being faithful. "Just…leave me alone for a while."

After they're gone, I grab my phone from the floor. The glass is shattered, making a starburst on the screen that reminds me of the girl I'm too afraid to admit I've lost.

William
Present Day

ANOTHER BLAST of thunder rattles the glass in the gallery windows, and I'm fucking glad. Rain pelts the back deck and hits the river with a vengeance. The day is gray and the weather violent. It matches my mood.

Soon, Cally will take the girls to her dad's and then she'll leave town. Maybe forever this time. Or maybe she'll be back often, since her sisters are here now. The hope is almost worse than the despair.

I slam my palm so hard against the glass, it stings. "Fuck."

"Well, hello, sunshine."

I don't bother to turn toward the sound of Maggie's voice. I'm glad she's working today. She can cover the gallery so I can get the fuck out of dodge and blow off some of this steam. A run in the rain might help. Or a bottle of whiskey.

"I'll make coffee," she calls, and then I hear the click of her heels on the stairs as she climbs up to the kitchenette in the loft.

I drop my head and lean against the cool glass. I want to go back to Cally's hotel and beg her not to leave. I want to taste her again, just to make sure I won't forget the flavor of her lips, to touch her one more time so I remember the sound she makes when she comes. I want to drown in the feel of her hair and the softness of her skin until the bad shit washes away.

And at the same fucking time, I want to fight with her. I want to call her out on what she did to me seven years ago. I want to make her understand how much she screwed me up.

Maggie's footsteps sound above and before I know it, she's back down and shoving a hot mug of coffee into my hands. "Drink before I have to put you down," she scolds. "I left a very sexy, very willing man in bed to talk fall exhibition with you. If you're going to be a grumpy ass, I'll go right back out that door and spend my morning screwing his brains out."

"I'm so glad we've reached a point in our relationship where you can be so open," I mutter, though truthfully, I am.

She returns my scowl with a smile. "I know. Isn't it special?"

I watch her sip from her coffee, her red hair flying in loose and wild curls around her face. In the last two months since she worked out everything with Asher, she's been happier than I've ever seen her. I wouldn't have thought it was possible, but she's even more beautiful when she's happy.

I'm so fucking glad we're past those awkward early days after she chose Asher over me. We got there faster than I expected. Not so long ago, I wanted Maggie more than I wanted anything else. Or I thought I did. It's so obvious we shouldn't be together. I didn't want a life with her. I wanted to save her from my screwed up past and save myself from my guilt. There's a big fucking difference. We would never have worked. I think Maggie understood that, but me? I hold out for the dream. Maybe Cally taught me that.

"Who's the girl?" she asks, peering into the dreary day. "Is this about that Meredith chick? She was here looking for you the other day."

Meredith. *Crap.* "Why do you assume there's a girl?"

She lifts a brow and snorts. "Because. You're Will. With you, it's always a girl. Usually a broken one or a forbidden one."

I guess I earned that. "Cally Fisher's back in town."

She whistles, low and smooth. "As in, your high school sweetheart?"

"That's the one."

"And you've seen her?"

I don't answer, but the truth must be in my eyes because Maggie steps back and holds a hand to her chest. "Holy shit, Will.

You slept with her? How fast do you *work*?"

"As if I'd tell you."

"I thought you were taking a break from relationships?"

"I am," I growl, my jaw set tight. Two failed engagements in as many years is more than enough reason to step back from the dating scene for a while. Not that my feelings on the matter have slowed my grandmother's attempts to set me up with Ms. Right.

"So Cally's back in town. You still have feelings for her, but you didn't sleep with her—though, clearly, you did more than have a nice little chat. And now you're trying to convince yourself not to dive headlong into another super-intense relationship. Especially one that's doomed to failure because she dropped you like a bad habit. Is that about right?"

"There's no danger of a relationship. She's not staying."

"Oooh. That explains the mood."

"I guess."

"I remember when she left," Maggie says, looking thoughtful. "She screwed you over. Why would you even want anything to do with her?"

"I know."

"Did she ever explain?"

"Explain what?"

Maggie narrows her eyes and crosses her arms. She's not going to tolerate me being obtuse today.

"Explain why she broke up with me via text message the night she was supposed to come back for the prom? Why she sent back the cellphone I bought her so I couldn't get ahold of her anymore? Why she was fucking another guy when I tracked her down in Vegas?"

Maggie lifts a brow. "Yeah, something like that."

"No," I growl. Thunder cracks and shakes the entire building. "I didn't ask."

"Because you don't want to know?"

I shove my hands in my pockets and walk away from Maggie. She understands me too well, and I'm not sure I want to be understood right now. I just want to be dark and broody and pissed off. And yet I answer anyway. "I didn't ask any of those questions because I knew she wouldn't spend any time with me if I did. I wanted her too much to risk that."

"Oh. My. God. You're still in love with her."

I drag a hand through my hair and avoid her eyes. I don't know what I am. "I see her for the first time in seven years, and I want her back so damn badly—despite all logic. She's here and she's beautiful and she owns a piece of me I'd forgotten I even had." I lean against the wall and sink to my haunches. "She was in town and *lost*. Of all the places she could have been lost, she found herself right in front of my house."

"I can see how that might suck, but…." She trails off.

Maggie doesn't get it. "*Cally* used to tell me that destiny would bring us together again and again, that she was mine. What are the chances of her showing up on my street? In front of the house I built?"

She looks skeptical. "She didn't know you lived there?"

"No. I don't think she even wanted to see me, but there she was. And now…what? Am I supposed to just let her go?"

"Do you really want me to answer that?"

I swallow hard. I wouldn't want to hear it from most people, but I trust Maggie. I nod.

"Yes," she says softly. "You need to let her go."

"Goddammit."

"Listen to me. You are quick to give and quick to love. You want to share your life with someone. I get that. You want marriage and the family you didn't get as a kid. I get *that*. But that's why you need to let her go. Because you need some distance to figure out how you really feel about her. Right now you're flying high on nostalgia. You need to know if you can forgive her before you ask for more."

I drag a hand through my hair and nod. I know she's right.

"I remember what everyone said after she dumped you," Maggie whispers. "I remember the rumors."

"They were rumors," I growl. "Nobody knew."

She shrugs. "But what it they're right? What if the guy you found her with was the reason she broke up with you? What if she cheated on you? What if she was in Vegas, sleeping with some older guy, while you were here, waiting like the good boyfriend you were? Can you really get past that?"

I stare at her. Because this is Maggie and of all people, she knows just how much I'm willing to forgive.

"Not me," she whispers. "I know you forgave me, but that was because you were trying to save me. That's not the case with Cally. Everything is different with her. I'm not asking if you can forgive just anyone. I'm asking, can you forgive *Cally*?"

She's right. There's a difference. I'm not sure it makes sense, but it's true.

"Let her go, Will. As a favor to yourself. If all that destiny crap is real and you're meant to be together, she'll be back. Right?"

I hang my head. Because she's right.

"Just let her go."

chapter eight

Cally

NEW SCHOOL, day one. Drew walked, since the high school is only a couple of blocks from Dad's. I offered to walk with her but she rolled her eyes and accused me of trying to make her the laughingstock on her first day at a new school, so I let her go on her own.

Now it's Gabby's turn, and my stomach is a mess with worry. Aside from her one-word request last week—*Stay*—she hasn't spoken. I already had a meeting with the school counselor and exchanged emails with her teacher. Everyone assures me they'll work with her, but I hate that I can't be at school with her to see for myself. My only reassurance is that at least I'll be here. Here in New Hope, living with Dad for the foreseeable future.

My boss at the spa back in Vegas has agreed to hold my job until the first of the year. I fought so hard to get into a position where I could support myself, and that job is an important part of the equation—great tips, decent salary, benefits. I need the income to help Dad support the girls. I need the income so I don't have to rely on Brandon again.

Would I have quit if my boss weren't willing to work with me? Probably. Gabby needs me, so I'll do what needs to be done. I always have.

We drive to the elementary school. It's only about a mile and we could walk, but it's a hot day and I don't want Gabby feeling self-conscious in sweaty clothes.

I offer her my hand as we approach the building. She shakes her head, reminding me that despite currently having the speech patterns of a toddler, she is in fact ten years old and doesn't need her big sister holding her hand.

We walk through the front and head into the building. Once we get to the heavy oak door to her new classroom, she stops me, her hand squeezing my wrist.

"I have my cellphone," I tell her. "I'll be looking for a job all day, but you call if you need anything."

Worry is written all over her face, and I find myself questioning our move for the hundredth time. I didn't have a home for them in Vegas, so I assumed they'd be better here. I assumed I'd be able to work and send Dad part of my monthly check. But now that part of the plan is gone. What if I was wrong? What if uprooting them from their lives after Mom's death was the worst thing for them? And now that I've chosen to stay, what if I can't find a job?

Finally, Gabby squeezes my wrist again, takes a deep breath, and heads into the classroom.

When I turn around, I see Lizzy Thompson. She's practically glowing, her smile is so bright. "Lizzy! What are you doing here?"

"Student teaching!" She rubs her hands together. "Well, it doesn't actually start for a few weeks, but Mrs. Monroe said I could come meet the kids for the first day of class and I just found out Gabby's one of the students. This is going to be great!"

Relief swamps me. "I'm so glad you'll be in there."

She squeezes me into a tight hug and whispers, "She'll love it. Have some faith."

"I know." I shrug. "This is what parents must feel like, huh? I think I'm more nervous than both the girls today."

"They'll be fine. But you? You look like you need some stress relief, and I know just the thing." She grins. "I'll text you the details."

"Stress relief" sounds like code for "party," and I don't have time for that right now, not with finding a job and working on Dad's house. I don't want to seem unfriendly, though, so I return her smile. I can always let her down after the invitation comes. "Okay. Thanks."

I'm heading out the front door when the secretary from the front office calls my name. She's a tiny little thing with a gray bob and a sweet smile. "You're Gabby Fisher's sister?"

"I am."

She presses an envelope into my hand and drops her voice low. "Your father's textbook rental check bounced."

"Oh." *Shit.* "I'm sorry about that. He can be kind of... absentminded. I'll have him...um...move some funds and write a new check."

Her smile suggests she knows there are no funds to move. "There's paperwork in that envelope for assistance. You just have your father fill it out, and Gabby's textbooks will be taken care of. I also included the application for free lunch."

Of course. Because the Fishers always need handouts. Nothing changes. I force myself to thank her before rushing from the building.

I'm unlocking the car when I hear someone call my name. I pin on my smile before turning.

"Cally Fisher, right?" the woman repeats. I don't recognize her. She's gorgeous and sophisticated in a black pencil skirt and a button-up pinstriped shirt, her long, blond hair pulled into a low ponytail.

"Yes, that's right." I offer my hand. "And you are?"

She drops her gaze to my hand and then brings it back to my face. "I'm Meredith Palmer. Owner of Venus Salon?"

She still hasn't taken my hand. Feeling like an idiot, I tuck it back into my pocket. "It's nice to meet you," I manage. This woman may be smiling, but coldness radiates off her. For whatever reason, she doesn't like me.

"I saw that you were interested in working as my massage therapist."

I shift uncomfortably. I already know where this is going. "I was looking into it."

"Yeah." She straightens her shirt and repositions that plastic smile. "But you see, we're not that kind of establishment, and I would rather watch my business *wither and die* than have someone like you giving—" she lifts her hands and makes air quotes, " —'massages.'"

William

TUESDAY MORNING brings sunshine and clarity. Maggie's right, of course. I need to let Cally go. Not that I have a choice. She'll leave town soon—hell, maybe she's already left—and I'll forget there was ever a woman who owned me, body, heart, and soul, as much as she did.

I turn on the gallery lights and start up the computer. Maggie will be in soon, and she can watch the floor while I take care of some paperwork in my office upstairs. I need to finish the grant proposal for the downtown arts event and hopefully finish the syllabi for my fall classes.

When I unlock the front doors, I find Cally waiting on the sidewalk.

"William?" She blinks at me, as if she can't figure out why I'd be here. I'm wondering the same about her.

"Good morning." God, she's beautiful. She left down her silky, dark hair today and it's like a curtain over half her face. I clench my fists against the temptation to touch it, tuck it behind her ear to reveal the smooth skin of her cheek, kiss her lips.

I should send her away quickly. When she's looking at me, I can't lie to myself about being at peace with letting her go.

"I'm here about some rental space? Do you know the owner?"

"Rental space?"

"Yeah." She raises onto her toes and peeks into the gallery over my shoulder. "God, it's such a gorgeous place. Do you mind?"

I step back and motion her in. "By all means."

Her eyes are wide as she surveys the space and studies the art hanging on the walls. First, she approaches a work done in pastels. A child's face is lit up with laughter as she squeezes a large male hand between both of hers. "Wow." Cally's mouth drops into a perfect circle of awe.

"Maggie Thompson did that."

"Who's the child?"

"Her name is Zoe. She's Asher Logan's daughter."

"Asher Logan has a daughter?"

"Yeah. She lives in New York with her mom most of the year, but she spent most of July here. She and Maggie were inseparable." I shake my head, remembering the look of pure contentment in Maggie's eyes when she brought Zoe around. "Maggie and Zoe might not share any blood, but they were meant to be mother and daughter."

"She loves her. You can see it on the canvas." She moves to the next wall and stops at the five-by-two-foot panoramic of the New Hope River.

I'd taken a photograph from the same spot every week for a year, then I'd digitally merged the images together so they appear to be a single photo. The seasons change by the slightest degrees from left to right.

She lifts her fingers to the placard with my name just below the photo. "You made this. It's amazing."

My heart is pounding. Cally in my gallery. Cally looking at my photographs. Cally close enough to touch.

She spins toward me and sinks her teeth into her bottom lip.

I shove my hands in my pockets, temptation three inches away.

"Good morning?" someone calls from the front door.

Maggie stands just inside the gallery, her brow wrinkled with worry as she takes in Cally and me standing together.

Cally jumps back when she spots Maggie. "I'm just here about a room Lizzy was telling me about."

I shake my head. I already forgot about that. I was so absorbed in watching Cally appreciate my gallery—so absorbed in watching *her*—that I lost focus.

I turn to Maggie. "Can you handle things down here for a bit?"

"No problem. I was going to do inventory today while it's slow, then later I need to talk to you about my schedule for the fall."

"Of course." I turn to Cally. "Follow me upstairs?" I head into the loft, where I feel her watching me as I pour myself a mug of coffee. "Want one?"

"Sure."

"Cream or sugar?"

"Cream if you have it."

Opening the little fridge, I pull out the cream and add a dash to her coffee before handing it to her. "How's that?"

Her eyes close as the first sip hits her tongue and that soft, mewling sound slips from the back of her throat, reminding me of our night in the restaurant and turning me *way* the fuck on. "God, that's good."

"Jesus, I thought I was special for making you moan like that, but now that I know coffee can render the same results, I might need to check my ego."

Her cheeks flush and she shoots a look toward the stairs then back to me. "Hush!"

"Maggie doesn't care."

"Yes," Maggie calls from the showroom floor below, "yes, Maggie does care."

I bite back a grin and motion Cally toward my office, closing the door behind us so we can have some privacy.

"To be fair," she says, "you make a damn good cup of coffee and I've been subsisting on instant crap. Powder creamer and all."

"Instant? Damn, you must have been hard up."

Her eyes connect with mine for a minute, and the heat there clears up any doubt in my mind that she was left wanting as much as me after our date.

Let her go, I remind myself.

"I'm looking to rent a room for massage therapy clients, and Lizzy said there was an apartment above the gallery she thought would work great. Obviously you work here too? Do you know the owner?"

"You're looking at him."

She drops her gaze to her coffee. "I was beginning to suspect as much. Lizzy could have mentioned that."

"I'm glad she didn't." We both know Cally wouldn't be here otherwise. Maybe that was intentional on Lizzy's part. "So you're staying?"

"For a couple of months, yes."

"What changed your mind?"

She crosses her arms and her face turns sad. "My sisters. It was foolish of me to think I could just drop them at Dad's house and they'd magically feel at home." She shakes her head. "And the house is a disaster. Not dirty, really, but a mess and not maintained or updated. I took a shower there this morning and the water pressure was so bad it took ten minutes to wash the shampoo from my hair. So I'm staying, helping get the house in order, helping my father figure out how to be a dad. It'll be okay."

"So you're going to start up a massage business while you're here?"

She shrugs. "I need money, and it's what I do. Lizzy gave me a couple of leads on spas by campus that might be looking for someone, but—" She hesitates for a minute, choosing her words. "Nothing worked out."

"Wouldn't the money be better on your own?"

She shrugs. "Established businesses come with built-in clientele. Kind of a shortcut, which makes sense since I don't plan to stay."

"My friend Meredith owns a salon, and I think she was looking for a new massage therapist." I'll call in a favor. God knows Meredith has made it clear enough that she wants to see me again.

"Meredith Palmer? At Venus Salon?"

"Yeah, that's her."

"She's not interested in hiring me."

"What? Why?" She lifts her gaze to meet mine, and I get it. Meredith knows about Cally's mom. The rumors. "I can talk to her. I'll explain."

She puts her hand on my arm, stopping me from getting my phone. "Please don't." She forces a smile. "It's probably best. Once I have a client list built up, the money is much better on my own. I'll find a space to rent."

"*That* I can help you with."

She sinks her teeth into her bottom lip. "How often are you here?"

"Often enough."

"I think we both know this would be a bad idea so—"

"Hold that thought." I motion back to the hallway.

She follows me across the little kitchenette and reception area to the other side of the upper story that holds a small apartment.

For a few weeks after my second failed engagement, when I was just opening the gallery, I spent a lot of nights here to escape the big, empty house and all my ruined plans. Now the apartment sits unused for the most part.

I pull my keys from my pocket and unlock the door, flipping on the lights as we head in. "There's access from the outside, too, a balcony out back, and a stairwell down the side of the building. Your clients wouldn't have to go through the gallery, though they're welcome to."

She nods, but she's frowning.

"What's wrong?"

She turns a slow circle, taking in the furnished living area and small kitchen. "It's just really nice, but it's too much."

"Would you be living here, too?"

"No. I'll stay with the girls. I just need a space to work."

I motion her toward the bedroom. "I thought this would be a nice space for you," I say, flipping on the lights in the small bedroom. "Honestly, I've become accustomed to using this apartment for a quick shower when I don't want to run home. I'd give you a deal if you wanted to rent only this space, and I'd make sure to stay out of your way when you had clients."

She nods as she looks around the room. Like my office, this room has a set of floor-to-ceiling windows that overlook the river and let in tons of light. "Lizzy was right. This would be perfect."

"Then why do you sound so disappointed?"

"It's not a good idea for us to work this close."

Despite all reason, I can't help but smile. "I can't think of many ideas better. You don't even have to pay me upfront. I know money's tight now. You can pay me once business picks up." I sound desperate. Maybe I am. I want to be close to her, to have her close to me.

She shakes her head and looks at me, bewildered. "I'm not in a position to say *no* to that, so…thank you."

I grin. "You'll take it?"

Slowly, she returns my smile, but hers is shakier, more tentative. "I'll take it." She pauses a beat. "William?"

"Yeah?"

"Thanks for not assuming the worst. About the kind of massage business I'll be running, I mean. Thank you for understanding I'm not my mom."

"You'll never be like her, Cally. You're too good."

A crash echoes off the walls as her coffee cup slips from her hands and shatters on the floor, coffee splashing all over her legs.

"Oh," she whispers. "I'm so sorry."

I run to the kitchen for some towels, and when I return, she's on her knees, collecting shards of coffee mug. Her hands are shaking.

"Hey." I sink to my haunches, dropping the towels and taking one of her hands in mine. "It's no big deal."

A tear spills onto her cheek. "Mom wasn't bad. She just did

what she believed she had to do."

"Aw, shit." I gather her against me, and she cries, big, body-shaking, silent sobs that leave my shirt wet and me feeling like the biggest asshole on the planet.

chapter nine

Cally

AFTER I recover from my little meltdown, I rush from the gallery as quickly as I can without running. I need to put space between me and William. It felt too good to cry in his arms, to have him stroke my hair and murmur apologies he doesn't owe me.

Once I'm outside, I go around the building and sink onto a bench, dropping my head into my hands. I take deep, calming breaths.

Everything's going to be okay. It's all going to work out.

That space is perfect. So perfect. The apartment's tiny kitchen and living room would make a comfortable waiting area for clients. I would set out herbal teas and bottles of water on the kitchen's granite island. Clients could sit with me on the couch and chat about their concerns with their bodies. And the massage room? Those windows overlooking the river give it a unique ambience I would bet nowhere else in town can match. I'd set up the room with minimalist luxury, and my clients could look out those windows as I gave their massages. Not to mention how ideal the location is. What says "high class" more than an art gallery? And even though my business wouldn't be a part of the gallery, people would connect the two in their minds, instantly earning me the respect I'll need in order to escape my mother's reputation.

It's perfect. And I should probably walk away. Because I already want William too much, and I can't have him. If he knew the truth, he wouldn't want me anyway.

Someone sits next to me, and I look up to see Maggie Thompson, her red curls framing her frown. I remember being jealous of her when Will and I were dating. She's a couple of years younger than me, so it's not as if he seemed interested in her *romantically* back then, but I knew how she felt about him. She would have been maybe fourteen when he and I were together. But he was always very protective of her. Of all her sisters. And now she's working for him. Interesting.

I sit up and force a smile. "Hey, Maggie."

"Hey." She toys with the pendant on her necklace. It looks like a piece of shattered glass, and the sunlight dances on its surface. "Do you think renting that space is really a good idea?"

"Probably not." I should see about commuting to Indianapolis. Maybe I could find a position at a spa where I wouldn't be working under the shadow of Mom's reputation. But that would mean gas money, and I'd have more hours away from the girls. I've always wanted to work for myself, but I've never had the luxury of being able to walk away from the benefits of working for a large company. This may be my only chance.

"But you're going to do it anyway?" she asks.

"Sometimes the bad idea is still the best option you have."

She narrows her eyes and studies me as if she understands this. Most people wouldn't. "And what about Will?"

Even in the hot August sun, I rub the chill from my arms. I don't want to talk to Maggie about my relationship with William—despite the fact that she's been here while I've been away. Or maybe because of it. I don't want to talk to anyone who knows that I broke his heart. I'd rather pretend that didn't happen. *Real mature.* "What about him?"

"You're staying in town for awhile. Are you going to get back together with him?"

"I— It's—"

"None of my business?" she asks with a raised brow.

I let out a breath. "Yeah. Pretty much."

She looks out at the river, and I'm relieved to have those scrutinizing eyes off me. "You can't pick up where you left off, Cally. William's not the same person he was when you lived here before. He's been through a lot."

My life, on the other hand, has been a freaking walk in the park. *Right.* "I'm not trying to pick up where I left off. You don't need to worry about that."

"But you slept with him?" Her gaze is back on me now.

"What? No. Did he tell you that?"

Her shoulders drop and she shakes her head. "No, he didn't, but I can tell something happened between you two to get him all hung up on you again."

I push off the bench. Nothing's fucking changed. People in this town still believe Will is a saint and I'm just a dirty poor girl who must have tricked him somehow to make him fall for me. I wonder if Will ever figured out that's why I wouldn't have sex with him. There were some who assumed I was easy, who thought sex was the only reason a good-looking young man like him would be with a girl like me.

Maybe, once, I might have felt the way they did. Although I respected him too much to think he was using me for sex, I didn't understand why Will would want me when he could have any girl in our high school. I didn't understand why he went against his grandmother's wishes and dated me when there were dozens of prettier, smarter girls from better families. Girls his grandmother would have been happy to see him with. Girls his friends wouldn't tease him for loving.

But I'm older now and I know my worth. Funny how low I had to sink to learn it.

"I appreciate your concern," I finally say, choosing my words carefully. "But I think Will can take care of himself."

"I'm just looking out for a friend."

"And that's all he is to you? A friend? You're sure about that?"

She flinches then her face hardens. "Don't pretend you know me or what I'm about."

"Fine. But return the favor." I turn on my heel and walk away, my anger growing with each step. Because I didn't ask for this. If Will is "hung up" on me again, it's certainly not because I encouraged it. And yet, I know I'm not angry with Maggie. I'm angry with myself.

Cally
Seven Years Ago

THE RESTAURANT is a little on the dark and dingy side, but it's close to the apartment, and I wouldn't have to take the bus or use Mom's car to get here. I head straight to the bar to ask the hostess if I can see the manager.

The waitress looks me over and shakes her head but does as I ask.

There's a silver-haired man sitting at the bar, looking me over as if assessing the value of a horse. I'm tempted to ask him if he'd like to check my teeth when a short, stocky woman comes out from the back.

"Hello—" I pause. Her name tag says *Manager*. No name, just *Manager*. "Hello, I'm Cally Fisher." I stick out my hand, and the woman takes it with the enthusiasm of a person picking up a piece of chewed gum. "I was wondering if you had any positions available for servers. I have some experience, and I'm a hard worker."

"How old are you?" she asks, hand propped on her hip.

"Twenty-one," I lie. Because no one wants to hire a waitress who can't serve alcohol.

She snorts. "Yeah, me too."

"I really need a job. My family—" I cut myself off, not wanting to sound too desperate. "I could really use a break. I'll do anything. You won't be sorry."

She crosses her arms over her chest. "I need a hostess. Nights and weekends, minimum wage, no tips. Take it or leave it."

Minimum wage. That won't be enough, but it will have to be for now. Because even a little is better than nothing. "Okay."

"Come back tomorrow and fill out your paperwork. You can start this weekend." Then, as if dismissing me, she turns on her heel and walks away.

"Looks like it's your lucky day," the man says.

I force a smile. "Yeah. I guess so." I don't want to sound ungrateful, but minimum wage isn't going to get me far. "Maybe I can work my way up to server, right?"

He shakes his head and pulls a business card out of his pocket. "I'm not talking about some crummy hostess job. I'm talking about the fact that I'm sitting right here."

I unconsciously step back, away from him, away from his greedy and calculating gaze.

He shrugs and tosses his card on the bar. "You need money? I can help. A little loan. Work it off or pay me back. Whatever. No big deal."

I eye the card, afraid to touch it. "Work it off doing what?"

"Don't worry so much. This is what I do. Help people."

I don't need a flashing neon sign telling me this man is bad news. I already know it. I swallow hard and take another step away. "I appreciate your offer. But I'm okay."

He smiles. Not creepy, not in a leering way, just a genuine smile. He throws some money on the counter and shakes his head. "Your funeral, sweetheart."

What does that mean? I watch him leave the restaurant and only after the glass door floats closed behind him do I pick up his card. *Just in case*, I tell myself, tucking it into my purse.

When I get home thirty minutes later, I expect to find Mom stoned or crashed on the couch. She's been hitting the Vicodin pretty hard since things didn't work out with Rick.

But she's not sleeping. She pacing and antsy and in a *mood*, which is way worse.

"Did you know there's a fucking waiting list to stay at the only decent women's shelter in town?" Mom throws the phone across the room, and I hear a crack as it hits the wall. Her eyes are bloodshot and she's chewing on her thumbnail again.

"I got a job," I tell her, sitting on the edge of the bed. "At that restaurant down the block."

She shakes her head, eyes watering. "It's too late. They're gonna throw us out if we don't have two months' rent by the end of the weekend. Landlord did me a favor letting us move in with nothing, but now he wants his money. We're gonna be on the streets."

I tell myself it's the Vicodin talking. Or rather, the lack of Vicodin. She goes just twenty-four hours without, and the worst-case scenarios start. It's never as bad as she thinks. Though it has been getting much worse, and I'm starting to get worried.

"Let's go home, Mom. Why are we even staying here? We can move back to New Hope."

She laughs but it's not my mother's laugh. It's a frightening, nearly maniacal sound. "You think we'll be better off there?"

"Yes! We'll move back in with Dad."

"Your father is off in India, finding his inner peace or some shit. We sold the house, remember? Aside from your boyfriend and a bunch of judgmental assholes, what's waiting for us there?"

I squeeze my eyes shut. We should have never left. We should have never come here. Dad taught me that all you have to do is believe things can be better, and they will be—*the power of manifestation*, he called it. But I've been believing so hard since we moved here, wishing so hard, I'm wrung out. He said it was that simple, but he couldn't even keep food on the table. He couldn't even save his marriage. What else that he taught me was a lie?

chapter ten

Cally

I'M GOING to Asher Logan's house. The thought makes me want to pinch myself and jump up and down all at once. I was planning to stay home, but Drew found out I was declining a party at Asher Logan's house (apparently his brand-new single "Unbreak Me" is "*amazeballs*"). She told me she would disown me if I didn't go and tell her all about it. So, twist my arm, I'm gonna party with a rock star.

And his girlfriend, who may or may not hate me.

Fuck it all. I could use a night out. Drew and Gabby had a good day at school, Dad's cough is getting better after a five-day course of antibiotics and some breathing treatments, and I used Dad's credit card to get some minimal supplies for my massage studio. All in all, I'm feeling *okay* about where my life is going.

When I turn onto Asher's street, I'm surprised to see there aren't many cars here. I don't know what I expected. Lines of Mercedes and Cadillac Escalades? There's a blue Mustang at the front of the drive and the Charger Lizzy said was hers, but other than that, only a pickup, a couple of sedans, and a yellow Ducati across the street.

I park along the road so I won't be blocked in if I decide I need to jet.

A hard tap on my window yanks me from my thoughts and makes me jump. Hanna pulls the door open, eyes bright, smile covering her whole face.

"You're really here!" she squeals, wrapping her arms around me before I can get out.

"I told you!" I hear Lizzy say.

"I had to see for myself!"

I push lightly against her embrace. "You're kind of squishing me, Han-Han."

She releases me and steps back to let me climb from the car.

"Dang, girl!" Hanna runs her gaze over me. "You left an average pretty girl and came back a freaking vixen!"

"Isn't she hot?" Lizzy says.

I feel myself blushing. I was pretty awkward during my early teen years, usually hiding in boxy T-shirts and behind my thick mop of hair. Brandon is the one who taught me how to dress for my curves and long legs. He even hired someone to teach me how to apply makeup with a modicum of skill. These, I suppose, are the souvenirs I get from a relationship I'd otherwise rather forget.

"Such a hottie!" Hanna agrees.

"She's a goddess."

I turn to the unexpected deep male voice and find myself facing William Bailey. Since we're going to be working in the same building, I guess I should get used to running into him, but I'm not sure I'll ever get used to the heat that fills me when he looks my way.

He takes in my tattered jeans and fitted black mesh top, making me extra grateful the boxes of clothes my friends shipped from my apartment arrived today. Even so, his careful perusal is worthy of a slinky formal gown, not some outfit thrown together to hang with old friends.

My cheeks are blazing by the time he returns those blue eyes to mine. Hot blue eyes that remind me of candlelit corners, sweet wine, and his calloused fingers on my thigh under the tablecloth.

"Hey, Cally," he says. "Good to see you again."

"Are you coming to the party, Will?" Hanna asks.

He shakes his head. "No, I just stopped by to get something from Maggie."

"You should stay," Hanna says softly. "It's going to be a good time." There's something tentative about the way she makes the offer, and I'm pretty sure I'm missing something.

"Thanks, but I have plans." His lips tilt into a half smile as he slides his gaze over me again before crossing the street. "See you around, Cally."

Just when I thought William Bailey couldn't get any sexier, he throws his leg over the Ducati and pulls on his helmet. The revving engine settles into a purr and, with a wave, he shoves off, and he's gone.

"Holy sexual tension, Batman," Hanna says.

"Yeah, after that we're going to need to cancel the party," Lizzy says. "There was so much tension between you two, it left *me* hot and bothered."

"What was that about?" Hanna asks.

I turn back to the girls to see them eyeing me expectantly. "What?" But I know the flush of my cheeks gives me away, and if they had any idea how hard my heart is pounding…

"Mmm-hmm," Lizzy says.

Then Hanna says, "You two were always so cute together. He needs someone like you, Cally."

Someone *like me*? They don't even know who I am anymore.

"He is such a good guy," Hanna adds, "and the last year has been shit for him."

"What happened last year?" I ask.

Lizzy nudges her. "Not now."

Hanna waves away my question. "Lizzy's right. That's for another time. Let's go inside and lust after Maggie's boyfriend."

"Are you going to tell me how she came to date Asher Logan?"

I ask, following the girls to the front door.

"She went skinny dipping in his pool after Will and Krystal's reception," Lizzy says.

"Lizzy," Hanna hisses.

Lizzy winces. "Shit."

I blink. "Wait. Will and Krystal? Like, your older sister?" Then the rest of her sentence sinks in, and I shake my head. "Reception?" Didn't he say he wasn't married?

Lizzy looks forlorn, and Hanna's biting her lip, but neither gets to answer before the door flies open.

"Cally?" Maggie's wan smile falls from her face but she quickly remembers herself and pastes it back in place. "Good to see you."

Lizzy nudges me toward the door. "Let's move! This tequila isn't going to drink itself!"

William

"NICE OF you to finally join us, Willy," Grandma says as I slide into a chair at her giant pine dining room table.

"I had to close up the gallery and run a few errands." I know it's useless trying to talk her out of the coming guilt trip, but old habits die hard.

She surprises me with a kiss on my cheek. "It's alright. You're a hard worker, and I'm proud of you."

I narrow my eyes at my grandmother. The woman doesn't pass up an opportunity to lay on a guilt trip unless she wants something.

"There's someone special joining us tonight."

So that's why I'm off the hook. There's nothing Grandma likes more than finding eligible young women for me, and I'm sure Cally's return to town will only make her redouble her efforts.

I look around the table but only see Grandma's friends.

"She's in the kitchen, making us a fresh pot of coffee. Why don't you see if she needs any help?"

"Easy on the matchmaking, okay?" I peck Grandma's leathery cheek and head to the kitchen, pretending I don't hear my grandmother's friends whispering, "At least she's not a Thompson," as I go.

About once a week, I meet Grandma and her friends for a couple of hours of Texas Hold 'Em. I'm under the impression that other people's grandmothers get together to do something respectable, like play Bridge and drink tea, but the old ladies in New Hope prefer poker for their nightly games and whiskey in their coffee. When I'm lucky, I get to enjoy the game with ladies whose skills at the table shouldn't be underestimated. When I'm unlucky, the little biddies use the opportunity to set me up with some unsuspecting great-niece/granddaughter/cousin's step-granddaughter once removed. It's only been worse since things didn't work out with Krystal.

In the kitchen, a tall, jean-clad blonde is filling the coffee carafe with water. Her eyes widen when she sees me and she puts the pot down and holds up her hands. "I'm so sorry. I had no idea you were going to be here."

I wave away Meredith's concern. "It's fine. Don't worry about it."

"I just don't want you to think I'm pushing myself on you. I heard your old girlfriend is back in town, and you probably don't want anything to do with me."

I cross my arms. "You *heard*, or she wanted to work for you and you turned her away?"

A rush of pink moves up her neck and blooms in her cheeks. "She told you?"

I shrug. "It came up."

She dries her hands on a towel and sighs. "I'm not a bitch, you know? But my business means everything to me, and I had to make a hard decision."

I'm not sure the decision was that difficult, but I can hardly be upset about it. Not when the result puts Cally so close to me. "It's going to work out after all. She's renting the apartment above the gallery, and she'll run her business out of there."

Her lips form a perfect circle of surprise. "Are you sure that's a good idea? People will think you approve of what she does."

My jaw tightens. "What do you mean by that?"

She lifts her chin. "I mean, her mom gave twenty-dollar hand jobs in her massage parlor. Maybe worse. Whether it's fair or not, people are going to assume like mother, like daughter."

I have to give Meredith credit for putting it out there like that. Most people tiptoe around the rumors. Regardless— "That's bullshit."

"Of course it is." She frowns. "Total bullshit. But people believe what they believe. It could really hurt the gallery. Just think about it."

I cross to Grandma's liquor stash beside the sink and pour myself two fingers of brandy. I shoot half of it back without tasting it. "I've thought about it. And my mind's made up."

"You're a good guy. She's lucky to have you."

I shake my head. "It's not like that," I say, then I toss back the rest of the brandy.

"I promise I had nothing to do with tonight," she says softly. "In fact, I'm a little embarrassed, but you know how Grandma and her friends go rogue in their matchmaking efforts. When I found out Cally was back, it was obvious why you started blowing me off. I don't want to be in the way."

And the Asshole of the Year award goes to *me*. I drag a hand through my hair. "I didn't mean to blow you off. I thought we were keeping things casual." Fuck. I even *sound* like an asshat.

Her cheeks bloom red again. "This is so embarrassing. I thought...I mean, when we seemed to get along so well."

Dammit. "I never meant to give you the wrong idea."

She holds up her hands. "It's totally my fault. I just hadn't wanted anything serious and then you...." She shakes her head. "See? Totally embarrassing. But no harm, no foul, right? I mean, we're on the same page now, and you can carry on with Cally without worrying about me."

"I'm sorry, Meredith."

"Don't be. Please. I owe *you* the apology." She drops her voice to a whisper. "I've been too much of a coward to tell my grandmother you're not interested, and I just want her off my back for a little bit, you know? I really hope you don't mind. I promise to tell her soon."

"So here we are." I take the carafe and finish preparing the coffee. "I don't suppose it would help if I told you that you can do better than me?"

Her cheeks flush. "I think we both know that's not true."

She's really pretty, but her red-tinged cheeks only have me comparing her to Cally, which isn't fair since all I've been able to think about for days is the way Cally responded to my touch in the back of that restaurant.

I press the brew button on the machine and pour myself a cup of coffee from the thermos on the counter.

"Grandma just wants great-grandbabies. And you know what? Things not working out between us was good for me."

"It was?"

"I realized I just need to do it."

I raise a brow. "Do what, exactly?"

"I've decided not to wait on babies," Meredith says in a rush. "So, even though I'd really like it if we could still be friends, it's probably good that you won't be around much. I don't want my store-bought sperm to get jealous."

I choke on my coffee. "I'm sorry?"

She pours her own cup of coffee and smiles. "It's the twenty-first century. I don't need a husband to start a family. My mom gets it, and when I have the heart to tell her, Grandma will too."

"Of course, but you're young." She's only a couple of years older than me, maybe twenty-seven. "Why the rush?"

Something like sadness draws down the corners of her eyes. "Sometimes you just know you're meant for something, and you go after it despite the logic."

"I can understand that."

The machine beeps, and we work together preparing a tray of mugs, coffee, cream, sugar, and whiskey. At my waist my phone buzzes a text alert.

"So what about you and Cally?" she asks. "Are you two working things out?"

"It's complicated." I pull my phone from my hip and smile when I see Cally's name on the screen. Maybe she's decided to stop avoiding me.

"I hope you can work it out," Meredith says. "She's a lucky girl."

I open the text and can only blink at the screen.

Just a week ago, we were at the restaurant and you were touching me under the table.

"Let me guess," Meredith says. "Mrs. Complicated?"

"You could say that, though I'm not sure our relationship has progressed to anything as official as *Mrs.* yet."

"You want more?"

I don't answer, but the truth must be in my eyes because she snags the phone from my hand and slides it into the pocket of her jeans. "What are you doing?"

"Helping you. If you want more from *Miss* Complicated, don't reply."

I fold my arms. "Isn't that a little childish?"

She shrugs, flashing me a grin over her shoulder as she strolls back in the dining room to join the card sharks. "Deal me in this hand?"

"Willy, what about you?" Norma calls.

"I'm in," I say and prepare myself to hand over my pride and my money to a bunch of old ladies.

chapter eleven

Cally

THIS MORNING is doing a fantastic job reminding me of the reason I stay away from tequila. No, make that *three* reasons.

1) Lack of moderation. My first shot gave me that fuzzy warmth in the pit of my stomach. The second had me feeling lighter and more carefree. By the third, I was definitely dancing, though I have no idea if anyone turned on any music. And then there were more shots. I just don't remember how many more.

2) Fuzzy memory. Pretty much everything after the third shot of tequila is fuzzy. A patchwork of unstitched memories—lots of pieces missing, no clear order.

I might have tried to get Asher Logan to sing to me.

3) Impulsiveness. I vaguely remember sending Will a text message...or two? (See reason two.) I'm scared to look and see exactly what I wrote, but I'm pretty sure I have to. Maybe I could lie and say Lizzy and Hanna got ahold of my phone?

I brace myself against the counter and take a tentative sip from my mug of coffee. Sliding my phone from my pocket, I open my text messages and click on Will's name.

Not just one sent message. Not two. *Four.* Four drunken, desperate, horny girl text messages. I lower my pounding head to the counter and whimper.

"Feeling good this morning?" I'm hung over, and Lizzy's voice is bright and perky enough to put the *justifiable* in *justifiable homicide.*

I crack open one eyelid and peer at her. "Don't talk to me."

"Don't be bitchy just because you drank too much." She pulls my phone from my fingers. "Did he ever write back?"

I lift my head. "You knew I was sending those? Jesus, Liz, you're supposed to have a girl's back when she's drunk."

She snorts. "I did have your back. God, after you told me about the restaurant, I did the only thing a real friend would do. I handed you your phone and tried to get you laid."

"I told you about the restaurant?"

Maggie and Hanna walk into the kitchen, heading for the coffee. "Sweetie, you told *everyone* about the restaurant," Maggie says.

My cheeks fill with heat. I wouldn't have thought embarrassment was possible with my head pounding this hard. "That is…mortifying."

"It wasn't too bad," Hanna says softly. "I mean, you didn't go into graphic detail about your orgasm or anything."

My face is on fire. "You're not helping, Hanna."

"You did tell us all about your panties, though," Lizzy says. "Now I want some like that. So fucking hot."

Asher walks into the kitchen and wraps his arms around Maggie, pulling her back to his front before whispering something in her ear.

I look at Lizzy and Hanna. "Are they always like that?"

Hanna leans on the breakfast bar and props her chin on her hands, sighing. "They're even worse when they think no one is looking. We're all jealous. Liz and I told him he has to find us our own rock stars, but so far, nothing."

Lizzy frowns at my phone. "I can't believe he never wrote back.

Most guys would have been knocking down the door to take you up on these offers. And this last one?" She whistles low and looks at me with a raised brow. "You are creative, I'll give you that." She shows the phone to Hanna, who takes it and cocks her head while reading.

"Wow. That's... You can actually...? And he never showed up? I wonder if he's in the hospital somewhere."

I snatch my phone back, then wince as pain ricochets through my head at the sudden movement.

"More than likely, he knew she was drunk," Maggie says softly, eyeing me. "Will's a good guy. He doesn't take advantage."

I rub my temples. Last night it became clear to me that Will has a history with both Maggie and her oldest sister, Krystal. Of course, no one wanted to talk about it, but I filed away the information. This is New Hope, after all. If I put my mind to it, I won't have to go far to find someone who knows the whole story and wants to gab.

"Maggie's right," Hanna's saying. "Call him today, sober, and I'm sure he'll be all yours."

"I don't want him to be mine."

Lizzy snorts. "*Bullshit*. The tequila-addled brain doesn't lie."

"It's a bad idea. I'm leaving in a few months—*max*."

Maggie is frowning at me, worry lines creasing her forehead.

Hanna puts her hand on my arm. "You were always the one telling us to keep an open mind and an open heart. You were the one convinced that if we just believed, good things would come into our lives. What happened to that girl?"

She sold out for a paycheck. "It's complicated. Being with Will would only hurt him in the long run."

"Then leave him alone." Maggie steps toward me. Asher touches her arm, but Maggie shakes her head and he backs off. "All Will wants in this world is to get married and make a family of his own. He might be attracted to Cally, but if she knows she won't give him that, she should stay away."

Hanna and Lizzy are looking at their hands, and Asher's eyes have gone sad. There's definitely more to this story than I've been told.

"I agree." My phone buzzes, and I take it back from Hanna to see a text from Drew.

Gabby had nightmares all night and I had to climb in bed with her, and dad made some sort of tofu-nugget sausage for breakfast that smells like roadkill. If you come home without an Asher Logan autograph on your boob, you are no longer my sister.

"I need to go."

"Don't rush away because of some silly texts," Lizzy says. "Asher's going to make us breakfast."

It isn't the texts that have me running. It's the reminder that some sexy texts sent to an old boyfriend are the least of my worries.

"But before I go...." I grab a Sharpie from the basket on the counter. "Maggie, is it all right if I have your boyfriend sign my chest?"

William

I DON'T want to wake up. I want to snuggle in closer to Cally and breathe in her scent while I sleep the day away. Then when I do wake up, I want to do it slowly, exploring her body with my hands and mouth before I bother opening my eyes.

Except she doesn't smell right.

I wrap my arm tighter around her waist and pull her closer. She must be using a different shampoo. She still smells good but more like perfume and less like...Cally.

But fuck sleeping, I'm hard just thinking about having her this close to me. I've been dreaming about her since she came back to town. About holding her. Touching her. Sliding inside her.

I fan my fingers under the waistband of her jeans, and she moans sweetly...

Only it's not Cally's moan.

My eyes fly open and I jerk upright in bed. Not my bed. My childhood bedroom at my grandmother's house. And it's not Cally next to me, it's… *Fuck.*

Meredith rolls over and smiles, peering at me from under half-closed lids. Then her eyes snap open and her face is masked with horror as her hands drop to investigate her clothing.

We're both fully dressed in the clothes we were wearing last night, and she appears to be as relieved by that as I am.

She tentatively lifts her hand to her head then grabs a pillow to press over her face.

"When did we start spiking our coffee like the old ladies?" I ask, rubbing my shoulder.

"When they were half drunk and kicking our asses," she mutters behind the pillow. "We decided it was giving them an edge."

"Rookie mistake," I mutter.

She lifts the pillow and peeks at me from under the corner. "We didn't? I mean…you don't think we…? Will Cally be upset?"

I shake my head. "We didn't do anything but sleep."

"I don't know if that's true," she mutters, sitting up.

"What do you mean by that?"

"I definitely woke up to someone groping me."

I drag my hand over my face. "I thought you were Cally."

The more I wake up, the more I remember about last night. It was Grandma's idea that we stay over, and we came to my room, laughing about how she was probably planning for us to conceive her great-grandchild.

We had fun. Meredith and me. I'm remembering how much I like her. She's funny and carefree and smart. Last night she stood up for herself when the old ladies were giving her a hard time about her series of love life foibles.

She didn't push herself on me. She even asked questions about Cally. About our history.

Cally.

She texted me last night, and Meredith didn't think I should reply. "You still have my phone?"

She pulls it from her pocket and tosses it toward me on the bed.

I pull up my text messages and see that I missed three more messages after the first. I blink at my screen.

"Is she mad you didn't text back?"

My stomach pitches and twists in a mix of worry, nerves, and boyish giddiness. "She must have been drinking," I say, more to myself than Meredith.

"Is she okay?"

"I think I'll go find out." I run a hand through my hair and attempt to smooth my clothes. "Can I get you anything? Coffee? Breakfast?"

"I'm good. Go get your girl."

"Thanks for being so cool about everything, Meredith."

She presses the pillow against her stomach and gives me a sad smile. "It's nothing."

I decide to drive over instead of call, but when I pull up to Arlen Fisher's house, I'm suddenly questioning my plan. What did I think I was going to do? Point at the last text and say, *This one, pretty please*?

Drew and Gabby are sitting in camping chairs out on the front deck, Drew's eyes on her phone and Gabby looking out toward the river.

I climb off my bike and head toward the house, but I haven't even hit the deck when I can hear Cally's voice—loud, angry.

"You had two thousand dollars in the savings account yesterday. Where did it go?"

I can't hear her father's words, just the deep murmur of him speaking.

"You're kidding me! A *guru*? You don't *need* a guru. The girls *need* textbooks. They *need* lunch. Stop giving your money away to some fraud promising things he can *never* deliver." *Pause.* "Kids are expensive. And this house is falling apart." *Pause.* "So, what?

You're just going to meditate your way to a better net worth? You *have* to get a job and you have to stop spending money on this bullshit."

"Dad dropped two grand on one-on-one counseling with his guru," Drew explains. "He wants to be enlightened or something stupid like that. And now Cally's mad because we can't afford the uniform for me to be on the cheerleading practice squad. Never mind that I don't want to be a stupid cheerleader. I only did it at home because my friends did. I don't have friends here."

More murmuring from inside. Then Cally, her voice less angry: "Well, you should have known better. Mom was never good with money."

"Translation," Drew drones, "Mom was a druggy."

I swallow, wondering what Cally would think if she knew I was here, hearing this.

"How many fucking autographed spiritual books do you have? Sell a few of those and beef up your checking account." *Pause.* "You're writing a book? Show me a big-ass contract from a real fucking publisher and I'll believe it. Call the college and get a *real job.*"

More murmuring.

"We should have stayed in Vegas," Drew sing-songs.

Cally: "If *politics* are the worst you have to face to put food on the table, you're one lucky bastard. Get over it." Then we hear the clack of footsteps, and she's pushing out onto the deck, the door slamming behind her.

She doesn't even see me. She's studying her shoes, her chest heaving. I can't tell if she's crying or just angry. I open my mouth to announce my presence, but Drew beats me to it.

"You have company."

Cally's head snaps up and her eyes widen as she spots me. "William."

"Cally."

"Did you hear all…. *Shit.*"

"Can we talk?" I ask.

She looks to Drew, then Gabby.

"We're *fine*," Drew says, shooing us away.

Gabby nods, giving me a half smile and a little wave of her fingers.

Cally draws her lower lip between her teeth, her brow wrinkling as she studies the girls.

Finally tearing her eyes from her phone, Drew says, "Go give your boyfriend a blow job and maybe he'll buy us a nice dinner."

Cally draws in a sharp breath, but before she can speak, Gabby says, "Behave!" It's one word, but it's clear and strong, and it wipes the rage off Cally's face. Drew's jaw drops.

Cally presses a kiss to Gabby's hair, then heads down the steps toward me.

"Wanna get out of here?" I nod to my bike, wanting to give her the break the strain around her eyes says she desperately needs. "We could go for a ride."

She shakes her head and tucks her hands into the pockets of her jean shorts. "Can we just walk?" She points to the gravel lane that meets up with the paved jogging path along the river.

"Sure."

It's a beautiful day, unseasonably cool for late August in Indiana and a nice break from last week's heat. Sunlight reflects off the water and makes her dark hair shine.

"I guess you're here about the texts I sent? I can only apologize. I had a little too much tequila."

I am, but that seems trivial in light of the argument I just overhead between her and her father.

"Do you need money? I can loan you—"

"Please don't. I already owe you for the groceries and the space for my massage studio." She looks out at the river. "We'll figure it out. We always do."

I let it drop—for now—and we walk in silence.

"You could do something for me," she finally says.

Anything. "What's that?" We wander onto a little dock and pause to look out at the water.

"See if there are any adjunct positions open at the college? Dad could use the work. Philosophy, religion. Anything like that. You know he's qualified."

"I'll make some calls, but don't get your hopes up. The fall semester starts on Monday, so they probably have all the classes covered."

She lets out a long, slow breath, her shoulders falling. "Right."

"I'll put in some calls. There are always temporary grant-funded positions he could consider for the short term. Research, maybe?"

"I appreciate it. I really do." She turns and wraps her arms around me and buries her face in my chest. "I'm lucky to have you."

I hug her back, pulling her close. God, I love the way she feels in my arms. Her hair is silky soft against my nose and I inhale deeply.

As if suddenly remembering herself, she stiffens and pulls away. "Sorry about that."

"Hmm...about those text messages...."

She grins and hits my stomach with the back of her hand. Her cheeks blaze red with her blush. "And here I thought you were going to let me off the hook."

"Maybe for the first three, but that last one isn't something a guy forgets."

She drops her gaze to the wooden planks of the dock. "I guess this is the part where I tell you that nothing can happen between us."

"I don't think we've been reading from the same script," I mutter.

"You haven't asked me why I didn't come to prom. You haven't asked why I ended things."

A crane spreads its wings and glides low over the water. "I figured you would have already told me if you wanted me to know." But my stomach folds over brutally at the reminder. Even seven years later, the memory still hurts.

"Can you promise not to ask me?" Her voice is so soft, and

she's studying me.

"If I asked, would I want to know the answer?"

She shakes her head and her eyes fill.

"You know my mind is going to answer the question anyway. I've had seven years to imagine what happened. The answers I've imagined have run the gamut. I've been pissed and worried and then pissed all over again. If you think *not knowing* is better, you're wrong." Stepping forward, I cup her face in my hands. Her eyes are moist but determined, and her cheeks are dry. I've thought about Maggie's words a lot in the last few days. "I think you'd be amazed what I've been able to forgive of people, Cally. And none of them have been you. If you slept with someone while we were still together...," I trail off as she closes her eyes.

"Don't," she whispers.

The light from the midday sun warms our shoulders, and the painful silence of regret wraps us in its barbed embrace.

Nothing can be done about the past, and I don't need to know what happened to forgive her.

"I promise," I say quietly.

chapter twelve

Cally
Seven Years Ago

A DRIVER picks me up after dark. I was told to wear something classy. *"A black dress will do. Don't be afraid to show a little ass."*

I tell myself I don't know what's going to happen. I tell myself not to jump to the worst possible conclusion.

I climb into the limo in a black skirt and matching button-up blouse, and I'm greeted by the man from the restaurant. Anthony.

"Hey, sweet thing." He runs his eyes over my body so slowly, my stomach churns.

When I broke down and called him for the money, I was only trying to keep my sisters off the streets and put some food in the fridge. He met me at the restaurant and gave me cash. For two weeks, everything was okay.

Then, yesterday, one of his guys showed up outside my apartment, looking for me to pay my debt with interest. I didn't have it. I still don't.

I swallow back my fear. "I'm sorry I don't have your money yet. I thought I could pick up extra shifts but then the girls both got sick and—"

He cuts me off with the wave of his hand.

"I've given you everything I can." Even as I say the words, I know they're ridiculous. There is no A-for-effort when it comes to owing money to men like this.

"I appreciate that you're trying to save your family from living on the streets, sweetheart. But your minimum-wage job isn't gonna cut it." He laughs, as if this is some big joke. "The longer you try to get by on pennies, the further behind you fall."

"We can go to a shelter," I whisper. "I'll get Mom to clean up first so they won't call CPS. Or…maybe I should just let them put my sisters in foster care." I don't mean the last. I won't let that happen. I can't.

He leans back in his seat, studying me. "That doesn't take care of the matter of money you already owe me."

I bite my lip and taste blood. "What do you want from me?"

His eyes leave my face and drop to my breasts, and I don't even care. He's been looking at me like that since the beginning. I hate him and his eyes on me make my stomach churn, but I'd let him look at me all day long if it would just make this all go away. "You work for me now. I have a client waiting."

"Please," I whisper. "I'm a virgin. I can't sell my body."

He claps his hands together. "Now, that's what I thought. Best news I've heard all day."

I can't allow my brain to process what that might mean.

Anthony narrows his eyes at me. "You don't have to have sex tonight, sweetheart. We'll give him a taste, but no intercourse, you hear me?" He tucks my hair behind my ear, and a shudder rocks through me. "We're going to save that for now. It's too valuable."

They drop me at one of those fancy high rises where the man at the front gets permission from the tenant before letting you up. The high security does nothing for my peace of mind, and as I am led to the elevator, I feel like everyone is staring at me, like everyone knows exactly why I'm here. My stomach knots.

When the elevator doors slide open, a servant greets me and

ushers me into the condo. It's beautiful with sleek contemporary furnishings and a marble floor. And the moment I step inside, I want to turn around and leave.

He takes me to a room at the back of the condo where the ceilings are vaulted and the walls are covered with bookshelves. The man sits behind a polished desk and motions for his servant to leave. He's attractive, probably in his mid-thirties with dark hair and striking hazel eyes, and he's obviously wealthy. The kind of man my mother throws herself at. What could he want with me?

"Close the door," he says softly.

I force myself to do as he asks. This isn't real. This can't be happening.

Moving from behind his desk, he settles into a winged back chair. "Come here." He crooks a finger at me.

My feet move slowly. One step. Two.

"Take off your shirt."

My hands shake as I obey, sliding the black plastic buttons free from their holes, telling myself it doesn't count if he doesn't touch me. This isn't real. No worse than a peeping tom looking in my window. I let the shirt slide from my shoulders and fall to the floor.

"Your bra."

Goosebumps break out on my arms, making my hair stand on end. I close my eyes as I reach behind my back. I think of my sisters.

"Now look at me," he says.

I force my eyes open and look at him. As I watch him run his greedy eyes over me, revulsion rises like bile in my throat. But not even my revulsion is as strong as my determination.

Shifting his hips forward in his chair, he pops the button on his slacks and pulls out his dick.

I back up a step. "He said no sex," I mumble stupidly.

My phone rings in my purse. William's ringtone.

"Not tonight," he says. "But soon. I can tell I'm going to like you. So you. What are you? Sixteen?"

"Yes."

"That's just perfect. You're going to do great."

The bright happiness of the ringtone is so sharp against the misery of this moment. My life with William feels so far away now. I was too much of a "good girl" to give myself to Will. And I'm supposed to suck a strange man's dick for money that's already gone. I ignore the call and drop my purse to the floor.

"It's okay, sweetheart." He stands up and crosses to me, his dick protruding between us.

I hate him for making me stoop to this. I hate myself for making the decisions that brought me here. I've spent so many years trying not to be my mom, and I've never felt so low as I do right now. Never so pathetic.

"You do a nice job and I'll bring you back." He tucks my hair behind my ear and smoothes it down. "You're beautiful, and I'll take care of you."

I'm trembling as I drop to my knees in front of him. My stomach heaves.

"That a'girl."

My phone rings again. William. As if he knows and wants to save me from this.

My chest shakes and my cheeks are damp with tears. I said I'd never stoop to my mom's level. I said I would never allow myself to be sold. I've spent years being proud about that. So fucking self-righteous.

I snatch my purse off the ground and grab my shirt and bra, running from the room. I thought I was better than Mom, but as I run to the elevator, I feel lower than ever because she did what she had to do. And I *can't*.

William
Present Day

"I JUST scheduled a massage for tonight," Max says, taking a sip of his beer. "I'm really looking forward to it."

I retrieve my cell from my pocket and pass it to him. "Would you like to call and cancel it or do you want me to do it for you?"

Cally's been working out of the apartment above my gallery for over three weeks now. She's been a consummate professional where I'm concerned, greeting me when we pass in the apartment kitchen, asking all the appropriate small talk questions while still managing to avoid having any meaningful contact with me.

Max eyes my phone, his lips twitching. "It's just a massage. Has she given you one?"

"Not since she was sixteen. Cancel it."

"Man, you've got it bad."

"Fuck yeah, I do." The smell of stale beer and onion rings is enough to turn my stomach off my lunch. Even so, I prefer this scene to the bars closer to the university, where I'm all too likely to run into my students.

"So, do something about it."

I set my jaw. "Hell, why didn't I think of that?"

"You're not on your A-game, man. She has you frazzled. You're not even seeing the obvious here."

I sit back in the booth and stare at my friend. Because he's right. Cally's been avoiding me and I've been waiting on her, rather than making my own move. "You know, I *could* use a massage."

"That's my boy," Max says. "You can take my spot. Tonight. Six p.m."

Cally

I HAVE a fifteen-minute break before my next client arrives, and I collapse onto the couch in the apartment's living-room-turned-waiting-room. We've started leaving the door between the gallery's loft reception area and the apartment open to encourage gallery visitors to check out my specials and encourage my clients to exit through the gallery.

Through the door, I can see Will sitting on the couch in the reception area, peering into his laptop. He does that a lot, I've noticed, choosing to work in the common space instead of his office, but he leaves me alone.

For three weeks, I've been taking clients in my little studio and avoiding him as best I can. But between giving massages and the horrible couch I'm crashing on at Dad's, I'm too exhausted to worry about limiting our exposure to each other tonight. The man might be a magic panty disintegrator, but the way I feel right now, he could make my panties dance the merengue against my girly bits and I still wouldn't be interested.

"Busy day," he says. He closes his laptop and heads toward me. He taught today and he's still wearing the button-up Oxford, the top unbuttoned, his sleeves rolled to his elbows.

"Lizzy and Hanna had their mom tell all the women at the country club about me and my introductory prices. And I'm doing this refer-three-get-one-free deal." I shrug. "It's working. People are finding me."

He rocks back on his heels. "I'm just impressed that you've had repeat business already. How many massages do people need in less than a month?"

I roll my head to the side so I can look at him while we talk.

I'm not about to waste the energy to lift it. "'I'm good at what I do."

He tucks his fingers into the pockets of his jeans, his shoulders looking impossibly wide. "I remember."

My cheeks flame to life. My mother had taught me massage when I was young, and I liked to practice on Will when we were dating. Of course, what started as my hands on his body usually ended as both of our hands and mouths *everywhere*. "Please don't use my techniques at sixteen to judge my talents now," I say. "I swear, I've grown remarkably more skilled over the last seven years."

He grins and runs those hot eyes all the way from the roots of my hair to the tips of my tennis shoes. "So have I."

Panties disintegrated.

I push off the couch, mentally preparing myself to find the energy for my last client of the day. "I'm going to have to ask you to leave," I say as sweetly as possible. "I have a client in a few minutes."

Will unbuttons his dress shirt and slings it over the side of the couch. Before I can ask what he's doing, he grabs the hem of his undershirt and tugs it over his head, leaving me staring at his gorgeous, solid chest.

What was I saying? "I have a client," I repeat, more for myself than for him.

"I know." He shuts the door between the apartment and the gallery. He turns back to me before unsnapping the button on his jeans and exposing another half inch of that soft, golden trail that travels down his belly. "You want me to take it all off, or should I leave on my boxers?"

William. Naked. Sexy stomach. My hands on William's stomach. My mouth. My tongue. I can't even…. "What?"

He pushes his jeans from his hips and steps out of them. "I'm your six o'clock."

"You're my—" He's wearing dark blue boxer briefs that hug his muscular thighs, and my panties might as well be dancing for as much as my girly bits are standing at attention.

"Cally, you keep looking at me like that and I'm going to find a new use for that massage table."

My eyes snap up to his. He's grinning that boyish grin, and I am swamped with the desire to shock him. To slide my hands down the flat of his stomach and lower until that smile falls away.

I roll my shoulders back. I am a professional. Pride myself on it and demand my clients treat me as such. That's not going to change tonight. I clear my throat. "I'm going to step out for a minute. You may undress to your comfort level and lie on the table under the sheets." Then I pretty much run from the apartment. *Right. A professional.*

Maggie is washing coffee mugs in the kitchenette, and she bites her lip when she sees me.

"You knew about this?" I hiss, crossing to her and scooping up my appointment book. "I thought my appointment was with…."

"Will's buddy Max?" she asks with a raised brow. "I don't think Will was going to let that happen. Guy code or something."

Dammit. "I've massaged many beautiful men. William's no different."

"Mmm-hmm."

"I've massaged *William* before," I say stubbornly.

She tries to stop her grin. "How'd that turn out for you?"

I spin on my heel and stomp back into the apartment and to my massage room, where I knock on the door twice before cracking it. "Are you ready?"

He's lying between the sheets face down. I usually start face up, but this will be easier. "I don't know. I thought I was getting a massage, but you look like you're ready to beat me."

"Sorry. You're not that lucky," I mutter. The sound of his chuckle brings a reluctant smile to my lips.

I prepare in my typical way, lowering the lights, adjusting the volume on the music, rubbing oil on my hands. When my hands touch his back, I expect instinct to take over. I have no problem separating my touch as a professional massage therapist from my sensual touch. There are people who struggle with that—that's why some don't enjoy massage and others think it implies something sexual. They believe that every touch between adults is sexual. Add in the naked or nearly naked factor and they totally squick out.

For me, it doesn't matter if my client is male or female, attractive or unattractive. The minute I begin a massage, my touch is therapeutic and all the other stuff falls away while I think about muscles and connective tissue and healing.

I know this isn't going to be the case with William the second I touch my hands to his lats. First of all, he's a moaner. Again, not something that normally affects me in the slightest. But with every touch, I am hyper aware of who I'm touching. This isn't just a massage. It's part of this long, drawn-out game of mental foreplay he's brought me into.

His body is amazing. I've seen a lot of bodies, and I appreciate them all as beautiful in their own right, but if I had to pick out a male body that was most beautiful to *me*, it would be William's. He works it hard. Not many adult men can say they're in better shape than they were in their high school football days, but Will definitely is.

"You're tight in your lower back." I apply pressure to the point and close my eyes against the sound of his moan. I wonder if he moans during sex? Did he moan when we made out as teens? How could I forget something like that? "You should come to my yoga class at the gym. It'll get this loosened up for you."

"Is that where you go when you leave here on Thursday nights in those tight little black pants and tank tops?"

"Yeah." I move up his back to the muscles over his shoulder blade. "This job is pretty hard on my body. I need yoga to keep my muscles from cramping up."

"And yoga involves a lot of watching you bend yourself in pretzels and stick your ass in the air?"

"Watching the *instructor* would probably be more appropriate."

"I can promise you, my eyes would be on you. Appropriate or not. And I don't think I should be in public while I witness that," he says, and I press a little too hard into the ridge under his shoulder blade. "Ouch!"

"Behave," I mutter. I soothe the area with gentle strokes and resume my massage.

chapter thirteen

Cally

I GROAN at the sound of my alarm and roll over to turn off my phone. Waking up is equal parts painful and welcome. The first night on the couch wasn't so bad. But after a few weeks on this Salvation-Army-find, I'm greeted every morning with an aching back and a sore neck, and now I hate it so much that sleep deprivation is less torturous than lying on the damn thing.

Dad has been helping herd the girls out the door in the mornings, but I've realized I enjoy spending a little time with them until they take off for the day. I'm at my massage studio until eight some nights, picking up the clients who like to come in after work, and sometimes I only get to see the girls for an hour or so before I make them go to bed.

My sleep was more restless than usual last night. I dreamed about William, him moaning in my ear, my oil-slicked hands running over his hard muscles. I made it through the whole massage without giving in to any of my...*baser urges*, and I got out of there as soon as I could. But after last night's dreams, I'm pretty sure I need to head into the gallery early and make good use of the fancy showerhead in the apartment's bathroom. Of course, sometimes Will showers there, and if I ran into him in the shower—

I push myself up and shake my head, trying to make my unwelcome fantasies scatter.

I'm hardly off the couch before Gabby is opening the door to the bedroom she shares with her sister. She flashes me that sweet smile before heading toward the bathroom. She's been talking more. Just a little here and there, but her teacher told me she'll answer questions sometimes in class, and the general sense of despair seems to be lifting off her shoulders.

The squeak of the old pipes and spray of the shower carry through the door. Satisfied that things are moving in the right direction, I decide to start a pot of coffee before waking Drew. My father has given up all "mind-altering substances," which apparently includes caffeine, so I had to buy my own coffee, but luckily I found his old pot in the attic and I don't have to settle for instant anymore.

After filling the pot and pouring the water into the reservoir, I add grounds to the filter and hit the switch to start it brewing before heading in to wake up Drew. There's no need to rush when the house only has one shower.

"Drew," I call, knocking softly on her bedroom door. "It's time to get up."

"No," she calls back. "Go away."

I crack the door and peek in to see her with the covers drawn up over her head. "You have thirty minutes to take a shower, dry your hair, and get dressed. If you don't want me sending you to school in your pajamas, get out of bed."

"I'm not going," she says, her voice muffled from behind the blankets. "You didn't finish high school. I don't see why I have to."

"Because I don't want you to have to do everything the hard way like I have." I sigh. To say that Drew "isn't a morning person" is a dramatic understatement. "Get up and I'll let you borrow my clothes."

She rips the covers down and glares at me, as if I just hurled insults as her instead of promising something she's been begging for.

"Come on, Drew. It'll—"

I don't get to say any more because my words are cut off by the sounds of Gabby's shrieks, and Drew and I both run into the bathroom to see what's happening.

"Oh, my God!" Drew screeches when I open the door. "That's so gross! I fucking *hate* this place."

I let her stomp away and try to hold back my own shudders of disgust. Gabby is standing on the edge of the tub, clinging to the shower curtain, eyes wide and focused on the floor.

I hear my dad's heavier steps behind me but I'm still too horrified to move.

"What's going on?" he asks, sleep slowing his words.

I swallow hard. I have to fight every instinct to climb on top of something—anything—and get my feet off the floor. "Dad," I say, impressed with how calm I'm able to keep my voice. "You have a rat."

William

"So," Meredith says. "What happened with Cally? Did you *uncomplicate* things?"

We're jogging along the river together this morning. Before Cally moved back to town, Meredith and I went running a few times a week. In retrospect, I can see why she may have thought our relationship would evolve into something more, so I've been finding excuses to cancel. When she texted me last night to see if I wanted to join her, I agreed. I'm a lot more comfortable about our friendship since we cleared the air during poker night with the grandmas.

"Things are still complicated," I answer. "Epically so. I had to endure a thirty-minute lecture from Grandma when she found out Cally was renting the space above the gallery for her massage studio."

"Ouch. You should have seen that coming, I guess."

She's right. I love my grandmother and like to tell myself she's only looking out for me, but sometimes she's so damn judgmental I can't understand how she's the same sweet woman who made me fresh chocolate chip cookies every Sunday afternoon while I was growing up.

"What's Grandma going to think when she finds out you and Cally are dating?"

I point to the turn and we follow it up the street to double back toward my house. I don't know what I expected to happen during the massage last night. Did I think she'd pick up where we left off seven years ago, where "massage" was code for heavy make-out session? The only thing that changed after an hour of her hands on my body was that I wanted her even more than before and she seemed more anxious than ever to get away from me. "I'll worry about that when she's finally willing to spend more than five minutes in the same room with me."

She slows to a walk, so I do too.

"I'm sorry," she says. "Do you mind?"

"Not at all. Are you okay?"

She nods and fans her hand in front of her face. "Yeah, I'm fine. Just a little under the weather."

"We don't have to run. Let's just walk."

She flashes me a grateful smile. "Thank you. I guess it's a good thing it's hot today since I have a cold shower waiting for me at home."

"Why's that?"

"Water heater broke. The guy's coming out to fix it tonight, but until then I'm roughing it."

I frown. "Why don't you just take a shower at my house?"

Her face brightens. "Hot water? Seriously? That would be awesome."

"It's no problem at all. I have plenty to go around."

We walk in silence for a bit, and my mind instantly wanders back to Cally, to her hands on me during my massage, to the way she's been avoiding me, to her eyes on my body when she thinks I'm not paying attention.

"Can I ask you a question?" Meredith asks.

"Of course."

"How long are you going to wait around for her?"

It's one of those questions I shouldn't honor with an answer, not with my complicated relationship with Meredith. But maybe she deserves the truth. "I'll wait until I have every reason to believe there's no chance for us."

Cally

I've only seen William's house the once, but it's bigger than I realized that first day in town, barely hinting at the *Mc* in McMansion. I knew he had a sizable trust fund, but judging by his house alone, his parents left him even more than I thought.

I press the doorbell before I can chicken out. I feel like I'm taking and taking from William and I hate asking for more.

I wait for a moment, listening for movement. I'm about to walk away when the door swings open.

"Holy shit." The words slip out of my mouth before I can stop them and my mouth goes dry at the sight of the man before me.

"Cally? What are you doing here?"

Fresh-from-the-shower William Bailey in nothing but a pair of gym shorts and all the muscles a girl's hands could ask for. His blond curls look darker wet, and he still has beads of water on his bare shoulders. Lord have mercy.

He blinks at me, and I realize I haven't said anything. "Hey," I say softly, "I need a favor."

"Come in." He pulls the door open wider.

I follow him into the house and try not to stare at the rivulet of water running down between his shoulder blades. "You caught me just out of the shower. Make yourself at home. I'm going to run upstairs and get dressed."

Please don't. "No problem."

"There's coffee in the kitchen. Want me to grab you a cup before I run up?"

"No need." I shove my hands into the pockets of my work scrubs. Too damn tempted to touch. "I'll just follow my nose."

The corner of his mouth pulls up in a lopsided grin. As his eyes scan the length of me, something flutters wildly in my stomach. "I'm glad you came by, Cally."

Then he's jogging up the stairs, and I'm alone in his expensive house, feeling like I'm sixteen years old again. The memories of waiting for him in his grandmother's living room are not my favorite. She would eye me disapprovingly and ask passive-aggressive questions about my parents. She knew them both and approved of neither. Such was my adolescence.

I follow the smell of coffee and have to bite my lip against the instinct to whistle when I step into his kitchen. Dark wood contrasts sharply with the shiny stainless steel appliances and cool stone counters. Sunlight pours from a bay window on the far wall and splashes against the polished wooden table in the breakfast nook.

I find the coffee pot tucked in a little alcove next to the refrigerator and a mug in the cabinet above. I fill it with shaking hands. There's no way I can drink this. Not with the riot of nerves making a mess of my gut.

Why am I so nervous? Because I'm going to ask him a favor, or because I'm alone with William in his house?

I'm not the girl I was when Will and I were together. Not

much makes me nervous anymore. But *he* does. Being so close to something I want so much and can't have does.

Settling into a chair at the breakfast nook, I take in his gorgeous backyard. Lush, green grass, flag stone patio, all bathed in delicious early-autumn sunlight that reminds me of my childhood and tempts me to indulge in *what-ifs* and *might-have-beens*. What if I had never taken money from Anthony? What if Mom had never made us move? What if I had taken that plane home for his senior prom?

It's hard to remember that I was once the one who believed so strongly in destiny. In us. I believed the Universe would find a way to bring us back together.

I squeeze my eyes shut and wrap my hands around my mug, willing the warmth to soothe my uncharacteristic nerves.

"You didn't have to sit in the dark." William's voice startles me, and the room fills with light.

"Your home is beautiful. I imagined you in a house like this."

"You imagined me, huh?" He pours himself a cup of coffee and settles into the seat across from me. "What else did you imagine?"

His hair is a mess of wet curls and his black tee stretches across his shoulders and over his sculpted pecs. He didn't have those muscles when we were teenagers. Not that he didn't have a nice body, but the good-looking boy has developed into a jaw-dropping man. And I want him.

It's nice to want things. Something I'm frequently telling Drew.

"I imagined you married with a couple of kids."

The pain that sweeps over his features at my remark reminds me to find out more about what happened with him and Krystal. Had Lizzy said something about a wedding reception? Was he divorced? And how did Maggie figure in to all of that? So many questions I have no business asking when I'm not willing to answer similar ones about myself.

"No wife or kids yet. But don't bring it up around my grandmother. She's doing her best to remedy the situation."

That makes me smile. Maybe his grandmother never was

much of a fan of mine, but I always respected her for the way she raised and loved her grandson. She would have done anything for him. We all deserve someone like that. "How's the old lady doing?"

"She's great. She's gonna outlive all of us."

I grin. "That's good to hear." Then, because I want to get it over with, I blurt, "I need a big favor."

"Sure. What is it?"

"I want your permission to move the girls into the apartment for a couple of days. There was a—" I take a breath and shudder, "—a *rat* in the bathroom at Dad's house this morning. I can't make them sleep there until we get an exterminator out."

He frowns. "How's that going to work? There are three of you, and the only bedroom has your massage studio set up in it."

"It'll have to work. We'll make it work somehow. Seriously, they flipped out. I just can't make them stay there until it's taken care of. I'll pay you more rent for use of the whole apartment, but…." God, I hate this. The IOUs I have out with Will are really adding up, and I hate owing people. "It might be awhile. I can't afford a hotel."

"Of course, Cally, but I think you're missing the obvious solution here."

I tense. "What's that?"

He waves his hand, gesturing to the space around us. "This house. I have more than enough room to take you all in for a few days. Longer if you need. Move in here with the girls and have the exterminator come out, but you can also use the time to get the carpets changed and do the painting you wanted to get done."

I'm speechless. I don't deserve anything from this man, and yet he keeps giving. "We couldn't impose on you like that."

"It's no imposition."

I tear my eyes away from his and look out into the yard, trying to remember my childhood here in New Hope, our rundown little house in town, never enough money and too many girls under one roof—just Mom, Dad, my two little sisters and me, wishing for a better life. They were good days. We just didn't have the perspective to understand it then. "I'm only agreeing because I think it's best for my sisters. If it was just me—"

"I know, I know. If it was just you, you'd stay far away from me and my hot body."

A giggle slips from my lips. "True story."

"I'm happy to help, and not just with this. Let me help you out at your dad's. I was really hands-on when I built mine, and I'm not without skills."

I stomach flips. "So you keep reminding me."

Tension, heat, and awareness pulse between us as our gazes tangle.

"Do you have a hairdryer?"

I jump at the sound of the unfamiliar female voice and turn to see Meredith standing in the kitchen in a terry cloth robe, her wet hair falling around her shoulders as she towels it dry.

"Sorry." She wrinkles her nose and draws her shoulders around her ears. "I hope I'm not interrupting."

Will pushes away from the table and stands. "Cally, you've met Meredith. She owns Venus Salon."

I force a shaky smile. What did Will tell me about their relationship? They're "friends"? Friends who shower together? I nod at her. "Meredith."

"Good to see you, Cally." Her smile lights up her whole face, and if I hadn't been there, I'd never believe this is the same woman who told me she'd rather have her company wither and die than let me work for her.

Will shoves his hands into his pockets but he looks perfectly at ease with both of us standing in his kitchen at the same time. Perfectly at ease about the fact that she's way too close to him for my peace of mind. "There's a hair dryer under the sink in the guest bathroom."

"Great! Thanks!"

I wait until she leaves before speaking. Even then, I'm sure to choose my words carefully. I don't want to sound jealous or spiteful. I might feel both, but I have no right to. "Maybe the girls and I should just stay in the apartment after all."

"What? Why?"

"You're kidding me, right? You really think your girlfriend is going to want your ex and her little sisters living with you? And Jesus, how long have you been seeing her anyway? Does she know only a month ago you were feeling me up in public?" The words spill out of me before I can stop them. So much for choosing them carefully.

Will's lips curl into a grin and he slowly closes the distance between us until I have to lift my chin to meet his eyes. "You're jealous?"

I shift and my breasts brush his shirt. "Of course not." *Liar, liar, pants on fire.*

"Meredith is a friend. We went running together this morning and I let her use my shower because her hot water heater broke."

"How convenient." I lift my chin. God, I can feel his heat. "She wants you. And I bet money she didn't need help finding the hair dryer. She just wanted me to know she was here. Naked. She *wanted* me to be jealous." I sound like a child throwing an irrational tantrum and I can't help myself.

"Hmm." His eyes drop to my lips. "Well, now you know."

"I'm not saying you can't date her. I mean, date who you want. It's none of my business. I just want to know what I'm walking into if I move in here for a few days."

"No, you're right." He toys with the ponytail at the base of my neck and tugs lightly, drawing me closer until I'm pressed against him and his eyes are on my mouth. Until *I. Want. More.* "She was totally trying to make you jealous. You should definitely get even by making out with me."

Just like that, all the tension knotting between my shoulder blades releases and laughter bursts from my lips. "You jerk." I put my hands to his chest and shove him back a step. "Don't make fun of me."

He shakes his head and runs his eyes over me. "I would never joke about something so serious."

chapter fourteen

William

"Oh. Em. Gee." Drew's eyes go big as she walks into my house. "*This* is what I'm talking about. Cally, you've been holding out on us. Making us live in that shithole while your boy here can give us the Ritz?"

She steps into the two-story entryway and spins a little circle, and I am so damn glad I convinced Cally to bring them here. I invited her father to stay as well, but he's not as sensitive to rodents as his daughters, and he said he wouldn't be comfortable taking advantage of my hospitality. Not the case for Cally's little sisters. Drew is looking around with the wide eyes of a child on Christmas, and Gabby's grin stretches from ear to ear.

"I'm glad you like it," Cally says to Drew, "but we're not staying long."

"*Like* it? You know, I think I was born to be rich. There's a pampered princess somewhere who really wishes she could live in that rat-infested cabin of Dad's and right now she's enduring her evening pedicure and facial. I was switched at birth."

"Hush," Cally says. "Your life is not that terrible. Will, do you want to show us where the girls will be sleeping? I'll bring in their suitcases."

Cally and the girls follow me upstairs, and I show Drew and Gabby the room they'll be sharing. The house has four bedrooms but one is set up with all my camera equipment and computers, so it's not fit for company.

"Your sister will in the room just down the hall if you need her."

"Not to be ungrateful or anything," Drew says, "but let's simplify things and put me in her room from the start. We all know Cally's going to end up in your bed anyway."

Cally's cheeks flame red. "Drew!"

"She's welcome there anytime," I say, "but we'll let her make that choice, okay?"

Drew just looks back and forth between us for a minute before shaking her head. "I don't get you two."

Cally avoids my gaze and studies the hardwood floor at her toes. "That makes two of us."

After we get the girls settled into their room, I show Cally to hers. "I apologize if the bed's not very comfortable. It's my old bed from Grandma's."

Something flashes in her eyes. Memories of what we used to do in that bed? Regrets about what we never did? "It has to be better than that couch I'm sleeping on." She rubs her forearm then digs her thumb into the palm of her hand.

"Are you hurt?"

She drops her hands to her sides as if she hadn't realized what she was doing. "I'm just sore from giving so many massages today. Sometimes my hands want to lock up at the end of the day." She shrugs. "It's normal when I'm putting in this many hours."

I take her hand and start working my thumbs into the muscles of her forearm, starting near her elbow and massaging my way down to the palm of her hand. As I apply pressure to the pad of her thumb, her eyes flutter closed. A low, barely audible moan slips from her lips.

Evening sun slants in the back window, spilling light across her face. She's so damn beautiful. The thick smear of her dark lashes across her cheek, the sweet curve of her lips. I could kiss her now. I could pull her close and put my lips on hers, slide my hands down her sides and curl my fingers into her hips as I seduce her with my mouth.

I could do all that. I want all that. But I want her near me more, and I know kissing her will scare her away.

"Cally."

Her lids flutter open and she blinks at me. We stand like that, staring at each other in the warmth of the evening sun, two people reorienting themselves after getting lost in a moment.

"Oh, God!" Drew's irritated tone snaps us both to attention. "Seriously, just give me this room and move her downstairs with you."

Cally

BRADY'S. BEER. *Pool. Girl time. Tonight.*

Grinning at Lizzy's text, I drop the paintbrush I was using on the front door and tap out a quick reply: *You have something against complete sentences, Miss Teacher?*

Bite me. <-- Complete sentence.

Minutes later, her cherry red Charger pulls into Dad's gravel drive, saving me from contemplating the painfully long list of repairs that need to be done to the house. Drew might not need the glam she says she wants, but even so, a couple of gallons of paint aren't going to cut it. While working here today, I realized the roof is leaking, causing God knows what kind of damage in the attic. Then when I was out on the back deck, I noticed a rotten board cracked under one of the girl's camping chairs. The place is a hazard and a money pit. At minimum, he needs a new stove, a new deck, and a new roof. None of those things come cheap.

Lizzy and Hanna climb out and survey the house.

"Ouch," Lizzy says, wincing. "Is that place…sanitary?"

"It's not *that* bad," Hanna attempts. "Maybe with some fresh paint?"

"It needs more than paint," I mutter.

"How's your dad's job search going?" Hanna asks. "Any luck?"

"He managed to find a part-time research position working for a faculty member at Sinclair."

"Oh, that's great!" Hanna says.

He needs something more, but I don't share any of that with my friends. They're worried enough about me without me piling it on.

Lizzy spins on me. "I can't believe you moved in with William and didn't tell us."

I shuffle back. "I didn't realize I needed to keep you updated."

"Save it for the margaritas," Hanna tells her sister. "Some conversations require tequila."

THE BAR is more crowded than I expected for a Wednesday night, but that makes the girls happy. I objected to the possibility of more tequila, so they've ordered us a pitcher of beer and staked out a booth by the pool tables, where they're scoping out the unsuspecting townies.

"Are you following me?" The question comes from right by my ear, and I have to resist the urge to lean into William.

"We got here first," I say. He brushes the hair off my neck, and I stand stock still and attempt to pretend I'm not affected by his touch. "I think that means *you're* following *me*."

The girls' eyes widen at the sight of Will.

"I see you brought your posse," Lizzy says, looking over Will's shoulder.

Will smirks. "I think you've already met my friends Sam and Max."

I was so focused on William, I didn't even realize he wasn't here alone. The guys slide out of a booth on the other side of the bar and join our little meet-and-greet. I recognize them from high school. Like Will, time has been good to them. They're both ridiculously handsome. The dark-haired one is in jeans and a fitted blue T-shirt that calls attention equally to impressive pecs and an amazing pair of baby blues. The other sports a dark polo and khakis. But neither of them is anywhere near the level of nuclear hotness that is my William is in a button-up white Oxford, sleeves rolled to his elbows, jeans hugging his narrow hips.

My William. Dangerous thinking.

"I don't know if you remember Sam," Will says, nodding to the one in the polo. He points his thumb toward the dark-haired one. "Or Max."

"It's been a while," I say.

"Good to see you again, Cally," Sam says, making me drag my eyes off Will. "How's your temporary roommate treating you? He doesn't drink out of the milk carton, does he?"

"He's a great host, and it's *very* temporary."

"Go finish your drinks." Lizzy shoos them toward their table. "We need some time for girl talk."

The girls slide into our booth, and Hanna sighs heavily.

"What's that about?" I ask.

She tucks a long, dark lock behind her ear and shakes her head.

"She's got a crush on Max," Lizzy explains. Hanna jabs her elbow into Lizzy's side, but Lizzy ignores her. "Can't say as I blame her. You could bounce quarters off the boy's ass."

"He has no idea I exist," Hanna mutters. "He's only had eyes for Lizzy since he came back to town and opened that gym."

Lizzy frowns. "I never would have gone on that date with him if I'd known Hanna liked him. I dropped him the minute I found out."

"Does he know how you feel?" I ask. Hanna looks nauseated just talking about it.

"God, no!" Lizzy snorts. "Are you kidding? Hanna doesn't tell guys when she's interested. She'd rather hide and tell herself she doesn't stand a chance. Which is stupid and a lie."

Hanna shakes her head. "What would he want to do with me anyway? He's an athletic trainer who runs his own health club, and I'm a fat girl."

"Hanna!" Lizzy and I say in unison. Hanna is bigger than her twin, plush and curvy with long dark hair, whereas Lizzy is tiny and lithe with blond curls. They look nothing like twins, but they're both equally beautiful.

Hanna shrugs off our protest. "It's *true.*"

"You're fucking gorgeous and any guy would be lucky to have you." Lizzy's face is drawn into a fierce scowl, daring Hanna to disagree.

"Time to change the subject, please," Hanna whispers into her beer.

Lizzy presses a kiss to her sister's forehead then turns to me. "Half the town is buzzing about you moving in with Will. I'm sure we had to find out from our *mom.* Why didn't you tell us?"

"Maybe there was nothing to tell?" The girls both stare at me like I'm trying to sell them land on the moon. I shrug. "What?"

"Sweetie," Hanna says, "there is so much heat in that boy's eyes when he looks at you, we can still smell the smoke. And now you're *living* with him?"

"You slept with him, didn't you?" Lizzy says, grinning. "We need details."

I cast a quick glance over my shoulder to make sure the guys can't hear. "I didn't sleep with him."

Lizzy's jaw drops. "Why not?"

"I screwed up with him once already," I whisper, holding up one finger. I add the second. "And I'm leaving after Christmas."

"You're really not going to sleep with him?" Lizzy's tone is more appropriate for talk of torturing kittens and killing puppies.

"I'm *really* not going to sleep with him," I growl.

"Will or no Will," Lizzy says, just as Will approaches our table, "I'm going to get you laid."

William

CALLY'S CHEEKS blaze and she shoots a lethal glare at her friend, then levels it at me, daring me to say something.

I bite back my smile. "A true friend, indeed."

Lizzy's gaze swings around to me and she bursts out laughing. "I had no idea he was there. I swear."

"What's going on over here?" Max strolls over to the table and runs his gaze over Lizzy. The guys want to hang with Cally and the twins tonight, and frankly, I'm game. I just want to be close to Cally.

We end up piling into a big booth together, me and Cally shoulder to shoulder on one side and Sam and Hanna on the other with Max and Lizzy pulling up chairs to the end, and before I know it the girls are all laughing and drinking and I'm sitting silently, nursing my beer and thinking how good it feels just to be *close* to her.

My phone buzzes in my pocket and I pull it out to see I have a text from Meredith.

Wanna get together for a drink tonight?

I key in a quick reply. *I'm hanging with the guys. Maybe another time?*

I look up from my phone and catch Cally watching me. "Sexting with your girlfriend?"

Max tips my phone down so he can see the screen. He groans. "Meredith? Girl can't take a hint, can she?"

Cally stiffens next to me, and Lizzy pipes up with, "*Meredith*?"

"She's a friend."

"Will's grandma set them up," Max says. "They went on a few dates and now she sends Will dirty texts day and night."

Shit. "We're just friends now."

"Dirty texts? How dirty?" Lizzy asks.

"*So* dirty," says Sam.

"Dirtier than the drunk texts Cally sent from Asher's party?" Lizzy asks.

Cally's eyes go wide. "Lizzy!"

"What drunk texts?" Sam asks. "Damn. Seriously, Will's phone gets more action in a day than mine has seen all year."

Lizzy winks at Sam and pulls out her phone. "What's your number, cutie?"

Cally's already gone stone cold next to me, and she's studying the table top like it explains the meaning of life.

I grab her hand and drag her out of the booth.

"What are you doing?" she asks.

I pull her over to the jukebox and drape her arms around my neck. "You're doing me a favor. I don't want to talk about Meredith right now, and when it comes to her, the guys are like a dog with a bone."

"Oh."

This isn't a slow song, but I don't care. I want her head against my chest, her body close to mine. She looks amazing in nothing more complicated than a little black tank top and jean shorts that show off her long legs. The second I walked into Brady's and saw her standing there, I started thinking about how much I want those legs wrapped around me, her nails digging into my back as I make her come.

"Do you exchange dirty texts with all of your *friends*?" she asks, her voice dropping low and lethal.

"We dated a little bit before you came back. It was supposed to be casual, but she ended up wanting more."

"I'm sure most girls around here would love a chance for more with you."

A Nine Inch Nails song kicks on, and I smile. "You remember this?"

Her eyes widen, her pupils dilating. We used to lie in my bedroom, listening to this album. We'd talk. Me about my controlling grandmother and her unreasonable expectations, Cally about her crazy father, her disappointing mother. We'd dream about going to college together and moving away, about a better life for her—she wouldn't have to worry about getting her sisters fed and to sleep at the end of the day—about an easier life for me—I wouldn't be expected to live up to every dream my grandmother ever had for the son she lost too soon. Then we'd explore each other, our bodies young and eager, our hands and mouths tentative as we learned together where and how to touch.

I lead her to the back corner of the bar and press my palms against the wall, pinning her in.

"What are you doing?" she asks in a whisper.

"This." I drop my mouth to hers before she can protest, and my hands move from the wall into her hair.

She doesn't hesitate and her mouth is greedy under mine as she kisses me back and wraps her hands around my biceps. I draw out the kiss, knowing damn well there are people watching, knowing damn well how fast news travels in this town. I want them to see. I'm ready to send the message that Cally is the only woman I'm interested in.

"I've spent the last month thinking about touching you at the restaurant," I whisper against her ear. "As long as I can remember the sound of you coming, you don't have to worry about any other woman laying claim to me."

"Speak of the devil," she mutters, looking over my shoulder.

"Who?"

"Meredith, and if looks could kill, you'd be holding a corpse."

I barely register her meaning, too busy burying my nose in her hair, trying to memorize her scent. It's something equal parts sweet and tempting.

Meredith is here. And if I'm not a dick, I'll release Cally and go talk to her. And yet, maybe Cally was right about Meredith laying claim to me.

Pressing my hand against Cally's back, I fan my fingers until two dip into the waistband of her jean shorts and under the silky smooth material of her panties. She draws in a breath and snuggles closer.

I'm tempted to brush my fingers over her and tease that sensitive skin of her lower back, tempted to whisper something wicked in her ear. But I don't. I just move my hips to the music, savoring the moment until the song ends.

Her dark eyes hold arousal and sadness and so much I don't understand. "I'm going to go back to the table," she whispers.

I nod but I don't follow her. I need to catch my breath, to get my head right.

I head to the bar and order a beer. Within seconds, Meredith has joined me. She leans against the bar and frowns. "I thought you were out with the guys."

She's smiling, as if she's trying to make it a joke, but the hurt is in her eyes. Meredith is sweet and pretty and sexy, and if I had any sense at all I'd be chasing her instead of a girl who once shattered my heart.

But Meredith isn't the one I want.

"Cally and her friends were already here."

"You should have told me she was here with you. Now I feel like an idiot for showing up."

"What did you think would happen if she wasn't here?"

She drops her gaze to her hands. "We were good together. I just…I just want you to remember that."

"This isn't fair to you, Meredith. You should find someone who deserves you."

She frowns, her carefully painted lips drawing into a pout. "You said you didn't want anything serious, and I didn't believe you because everyone knows that you want to get married. You want to make a family. It's part of who you are. Only, you were telling me the truth. You didn't want anything serious. At least, not with me. Those rules don't apply to Cally."

"Meredith—"

"No." She holds up a hand, cutting off my explanation. "Don't. We're just friends. That was the deal." She shakes her head and tucks her purse under her arm. "I'm not a bad catch, you know? Your grandma loves me, and things were going great between us. But suddenly you're pushing me away because Cally's back, and Cally... Cally's not even staying. She's heading back to Vegas in a few months. Add to that the fact that your grandma can't stand her. Never could. Never mind that she dropped you without a thought back in high school."

"That was a long time ago," I growl.

She shrugs. "People don't really change, Will. Not much. I hope you know what you're doing. I don't want to see you hurt."

chapter fifteen

Cally
Seven Years Ago

I'm headed to work when the dark SUV slows alongside me and the window rolls down. A man pokes his head out and smiles at me, a sick, calculating smile. I don't recognize him, but I know without asking that Anthony sent him. His nose is crooked, as if it's been broken a few too many times, and his dark hair is slicked back with too much gel. He looks so much like a stereotypical movie bad guy, I almost want to laugh. Only there's nothing funny about the way he's looking at me or the fear tearing through my stomach.

"Your little sisters sure are cute," he says.

I freeze in my tracks, my feet glued to the sidewalk.

"That little one, she sure does like the swing at Tyson Park. And the older one, she's got potential. A couple years and think of the things she could do." The man grins. "Boss said you can either work off the loan or your sisters can do it for you."

A chill whips through me, sharp and angry. "No."

"Anthony doesn't do second chances, sweetheart. It's your

lucky day. The client you ran out on took a special liking to you. He wants to see you again, requested you personally. You couldn't have played it better, actually. That one likes a little bit of the chase, and now he won't take any of the boss's other girls. Only has eyes for the sweet dark-haired virgin." His laugh is more like a cackle. "We'll pick you up tonight. No fucking around this time." He doesn't wait for an answer before his window slides back into position and the car pulls away.

I don't bother going to work. What's the point? I head home and stare at my phone, trying to figure out what will happen if I call the police. They'll help me. I won't have to go to that man again tonight. I won't have to do the unspeakable things I'm sure to have to do. But what will happen to my sisters? And how long can the police protect me from Anthony and his men?

So I shower and change and wait for Anthony's car to pick me up.

When my phone rings, William's name looks at me from the screen of the phone he bought and paid for to keep us together. I send the call to voicemail and steal two pills from Mom's secret stash.

Cally
Present Day

"You little lying, hooky-playing twerp!" I growl as I tap out the text to Drew: *Where are you?*

I burst into William's house looking for her. After I walked Gabby to school, Drew's truancy officer called to let me know that Drew wasn't in her first class. Was she sick today?

I caught her playing hooky once before, and if she's doing it again, I'm going to ground her for a month. If she thinks she's going to get away with skipping school just because I'm working all the time, she's got another thing coming.

I storm up the stairs, my anger growing as I burst into the room she and Gabby share. The room is unoccupied. Empty.

"Drew! Where are you?" I head back downstairs, not bothering to quiet my tear through the house. William was already gone when I left with the girls this morning—heading to the gym to squeeze in a workout before opening the gallery. I avoided him after getting home from Brady's last night. I shouldn't have let myself dance with him. It felt too good to have his body close, his breath on my ear. By the time he kissed me, I was already too far gone to make a sensible decision.

After hitting the family room and the kitchen, I still haven't found Drew. I'm starting to worry when my phone buzzes with a text from her.

I'm at school.

"No," I grumble. "You're a liar."

Then the shower kicks on down the hall, and I'm darting toward the Master before I think about it. His shower is one of those with showerheads on three walls and Drew has been chomping at the bit to try it out.

The door to his bedroom is open and I'm more incensed with every step. William has done so much for us, and this is how she thanks him? Skipping school and using his freaking shower?

I open the door to his bathroom and blink when Will's running clothes greet me in a neat pile by the door. I freeze, staring at the rumpled pile of cotton, remembering the look of his sweat-slicked skin when he comes off a run.

Move, Cally.

But I can't.

Then I hear a long and low groan come from the direction of the shower and what I see when I lift my head has my heart racing and my breath going shallow.

Drew isn't anywhere to be seen. Only William.

Behind the steamy shower door, he stands under the spray,

one hand braced against the tile and the other…*oh, hell*…the other wrapped around his shaft as he moves over it in long, even strokes.

His body is gorgeous—broad shoulders tapering to narrow hips. Hard, sculpted muscles that I want to touch with my hands, taste with my tongue, and test with my teeth.

From the angle he's standing, with only five steps and the steamy glass between us, I see more than I should and so much less than I want. I need to take these feet—the ones that are glued to the bathroom tile—and put them in reverse. I need to back myself right out of this bathroom and figure out where Drew really is. Or hell, maybe I need a shower of my own. A really cold one.

But what I really want is a better view. I want to see the expression on his face as he works himself over. I want to see the ripple of his muscles as he strains against the need to come. I want to open the shower door and—without a word—drop to my knees and replace his hand with my mouth.

Just the thought of it has my legs unsteady. Who knew the thought of giving a blow job could turn me on so much? With anyone else it probably wouldn't, but this is William, and my heart slams in my chest as I imagine filling my mouth with him, his hands in my hair as I take him deep, his ass flexing under my hands.

The thought is more than enough to turn me on. It's almost enough to get me off.

He groans again, longer, lower, deeper this time, and I know this is the moment I have to make my decision. Either get the hell out of dodge or muster up enough courage to join him.

As much as I hate to leave, I'm too much of a coward to stay. I stumble back. My heel hits the trash can and I jump. My hands fly out to the sides to catch my balance and my arm whacks the sink as I go down.

The next thing I know, Will is out of the shower, dropping to his haunches in front of me. Worried. Naked. Dripping wet. "Are you okay?"

"Yeah. Fine. I was…." *Wishing I was brave enough to join you?*

Fantasizing about sucking you off? "Looking for Drew." My eyes drop involuntarily to the erection still standing strong between us. I have never wanted to taste something so badly in my life.

"Cally." He clears his throat, and I lift my eyes to his face. He's smirking. "She's not in here."

Tonight, maybe tomorrow, I'll probably think up a genius smart-ass retort, but right now the capacity for speech seems to be escaping me.

He offers his hand, and I take it, trying very hard to keep distance between our bodies as he helps me up. I should go, but I'm caught under the spell of those hot blue eyes.

He traces my jaw with his fingertip, moving from behind my ear down to the tip of my chin before touching his thumb to my lips. "Join me in the shower?"

I swallow. Hard. Whisper, "Tempting."

He groans, low and long and so much like the sounds he was making when I caught him stroking himself in the shower that it takes everything in my power not to strip down, follow him under the spray, and act out every second of my fantasy. Then he dips his head so his lips brush my ear. "Having you watch me while I stroked myself in the shower was one of the hottest experiences of my life."

A tiny thrill dances down my spine and blossoms, wild and nervous, in my belly. Lower. "You knew I was here?"

Again with the low groan, but he presses closer this time, the hard length of his erection pressing against my belly. "I was already thinking about you. Thinking about how badly I wanted to take you in the shower. Thinking about touching every inch of your body with my soapy hands. Thinking about making you come like I did at the restaurant, but this time you could cry out as loud as you want. You have no idea how much I want that."

It's my turn to moan. My body is alive with pulsing sexual energy as if we were hours into foreplay. The wild nerves dancing in my gut play on the unwelcome arousal churning beneath. His breath against my ear sends shivers down my spine. Need and desire spiral low, and I know that if he slid his hand into my panties now I'd be slick, ready.

I lift my hand to his face. I can't resist. He didn't shave this morning, and his cheek is rough against my palm. I slide my hand into his wet curls.

"I don't know what you're scared of, Cally." He brushes my hair out of my face and behind my ear. "But I won't push you beyond anything you're ready for. Just tell me what you want. Tell me what you need."

I press my lips to his. He tastes of toothpaste and fresh water, and when our mouths first touch, he stays perfectly still. I brush my lips over his once, twice, three times.

My fingers trace the edge of his jaw, then the top of his shoulders. I explore the firm muscles of his chest. He doesn't move. Doesn't touch me. When I finally reach his abdomen, my fingers find the V of his hipbones, and he draws in a sharp breath.

"Cally," he whispers.

I let my lips find his. He kisses me back softly, tentatively, as if he's afraid I might run away. Maybe that's fair, and maybe I should, but right now I'm his. I'm not going anywhere.

He tucks a lock of hair behind my ear and runs his thumb down my cheek, and I decide I don't care about before or after. I decide I'm going to do something stupid and wonderful right *now*.

William

CALLY'S IN my bathroom, touching me. I am all too aware that I'm naked and aroused. All too aware of what I was doing before she attempted her clumsy escape.

Her eyes flick back south again before she catches herself and pulls them back to my face, tongue darting out to moisten her lips.

I could press her against the wall. I could talk her into what we both want. But before I can make a move, she glides the palm of her hand against the flat of my stomach and fans her fingers until they're brushing the base of my cock.

"Jesus," I hiss. I lift my hands to touch her, then clench my fists and drop them to my sides.

"Let me touch you," she whispers. Her fingertips dance along the underside of my erection. "No strings. No expectations. Just let me do this for you. Please."

"Cally." Her name is a whisper and a prayer, but she's already dropping to her knees.

She runs her hands down my body and wraps one around my cock in a movement so sudden and so unexpected, I have to steady myself on the vanity. My heart pounds wildly in my chest and I want to close my eyes and sink into the fucking amazing sensation of her hand sliding over my dick, but I won't. I can't bring myself to miss a second of Cally on her knees before me, her lips parted as she looks up at me through those thick lashes and strokes.

"I've wanted to do this for so long," she whispers. Then she touches her barely-parted lips to the head of my cock and sweeps her tongue along the underside. When she opens her mouth over me and takes me deep, I can't resist touching her anymore and my hands find their way into her hair.

Her soft moans fill my head as she slides her mouth over me, sucking me deep before pulling back and repeating the motion. When her hand slides up the inside of my thigh to cup my balls, my fingers tighten in her hair and I have to fight the instinct to rock into her, to press myself deeper into the heat of her mouth.

She squeezes lightly on my sac and then, when I don't think it's possible for her to take any more of me, she slides her lips down my shaft, taking me in nearly to the root. Then I can't take it anymore. My dick so deep in her mouth, her hot tongue curling around me, and that sexy ass moan makes her lips vibrate just barely against me.

I tug gently at her hair. "Baby." She doesn't pull back but

somehow takes me another fraction of an inch deeper. "Sweetheart, I'm gonna come."

My words only seem to steel her determination and she adds just enough suction that I can't hold back. I knot my hands in her hair as I release into her throat. Hard and fast and so intense I'm almost worried about her.

Pulling her to her feet, I lean against the wall to catch my breath. I hug her against me. "You're so fucking amazing," I whisper.

Her lips, pink and swollen and apparently my true Kryptonite, curl into a smile before she can bite it back. "Thanks."

I reach for the hem of her shirt and she stiffens. "What is it?"

"Fuck. *Drew.*" She squeezes her eyes shut and presses her palms against my bare chest until I step back.

Only then do I hear the music down the hall. Before I can ask what's going on, Cally's headed in that direction.

I reluctantly pull on some jeans and try to come to terms with the fact that I'm not going to be getting her naked any time soon. By the time I join her in the living room, she and Drew are already facing off, arms crossed and bodies tense in nearly identical stances, faces drawn into nearly identical scowls. I would laugh if I didn't think it would get me hit.

"I don't see why high school is so important." Drew is saying, "You didn't finish and you're doing fine."

"*Fine?*" Cally says. "What about my financial situation seems *fine* to you?"

"You would be fine if you stayed with Brandon. He used to buy you stuff and take care of you. What's so wrong with that?"

Cally's hands are balled into fist at her sides, and tension has made her posture stiff. "That's your great plan? Find some guy to take care of you?"

"It's better than what Mom did for her clients. It's better than what the people at school say you're doing."

I can see the moment the words register with Cally. Her shoulders sag and she sinks into the couch and leans forward, elbows on knees, head in her hands.

Drew's face falls, regret wiping her expression clear of its former bitterness. "I don't believe what they say. I know that you don't... I'm just...." Her gaze shoots up to meet mine, as if I might be able to take her words back for her.

Cally lifts her head. "Drew, go to your room, please." There's something unsaid between them. Old promises drudged up by a strained relationship.

"I'm sorry," Drew whispers, then she runs past me and up the stairs.

I cross to the couch and sit next to Cally.

She takes my hand before I even offer it. "I shouldn't have moved them. I should have had Dad sign custody over to me. I could have talked him into it. We would have figured out... something."

"She's at a tough age. She'll be fine. She just needs more time."

She nods, tugging her bottom lip between her teeth. "She's pissed at me because she wanted to sleep over with this new friend this weekend. I told her she had to work on Dad's house with me instead."

"You're working on your dad's house this weekend?"

"The exterminator is done, so...yeah. We can't stay here forever."

They could. I wouldn't mind.

She shrugs. "Anyway, I think Dad misses them."

"What all are you doing at the house?"

"Not as much as I want. Everything is so expensive. But we can paint and deep clean. Don't worry. We'll be out of your hair in no time." She shakes her head and pushes herself off the couch. "I have to get that pipsqueak back to school before my first client."

"Cally," I call, stopping her when she hits the first stair. "You're not in my hair at all." *Please stay.*

"Just in your bathroom." She bites back a smile. "Sorry about that."

A groan I hardly recognize rumbles up from my chest. "I'm not."

chapter sixteen

Cally

WHEN I climb out of the shower, the house is still. The last of the homework is finished, dinner put away, the television turned off. The giggles from the girls' room have quieted.

I pull on my robe and wrap my hair in a towel before heading to my room, stalling at the staircase halfway there. He's down there. Maybe tinkering with his photos on his laptop, maybe sitting in the living room with his feet up, grading student papers. Maybe taking a shower of his own. My eyes float closed as I conjure up the image of him under the spray, muscles taut as he strokes himself.

Maybe he's in bed. Maybe he's thinking of me, of my mouth on him this morning. Maybe he knows I'm thinking of him.

I pad to my room, closing the door quietly behind me—for privacy or to put another obstacle between us?

Over the last few nights, I've found myself heading back downstairs after the girls go to sleep at night, just hoping I might run into William in the kitchen. I love the way his eyes roam over me every time we're in the same room, as if he's trying to memorize me, and I find myself craving those moments, looking for them.

I could throw on some clothes and go down to find him, but I won't. Not tonight. Not when the girls are in the house and I'm so close to giving in to temptation. Every day I'm realizing it's not a question of *if* I'll acquiesce the attraction between us. It's a question of *when*.

My phone buzzes, vibrating against the nightstand, and when I pick it up, I see William's number on the screen.

"Hey there," I whisper.

"How was your shower?"

"Wonderful. Hot. Long. Water pressure to die for. Much needed."

His hum of approval carries over the line and rumbles through my body, vibrating through my core and settling between my legs. "You could have taken it down here. You'd like my shower."

"And have it ruin me for all other showers?" I grin and plop onto the bed. "Hardly."

"I had a good time hanging out with you and the girls tonight." His voice drops low, seducing me with treble alone. "I like having you around, Cally."

I like being around. "I owe you so much for all of this. I really can't thank you enough."

"You're welcome. It's been my pleasure."

The silence rises up between us. It's not an empty silence, eating up space in our conversation. Instead, it's this loaded silence, charged with attraction and unfulfilled desires. Fantasies. Memories. Unspoken secrets.

"Remember our phone calls after you first moved away?"

"I remember."

"Lock the door, Cally."

"Are you trying to keep me in or keep yourself out?" Even as I ask, I turn the lock on the handle.

"You don't have to worry about me coming up there."

"I don't?" Why am I disappointed?

"No, sweetheart. Your sisters are up there, and when I'm finally inside you, I want to hear you scream."

My knees turn to jelly, and I sink onto the bed.

"The lock is so you won't be interrupted while I'm listening to you touch yourself."

"William." His name comes off my lips like a plea.

"I left you something on the dresser."

"Wine," I whisper, standing to pour myself a glass.

"Strawberry wine," he corrects. "I sprung for the kind with the screw-off cap."

"Classy." I giggle and take a sip. The taste and the smell work together to snare my senses and carry me back in time. The dock behind the old warehouse on Main. The moonlight reflecting off the water. William's tongue circling my navel....

"Are you nude?"

His words pair with my anticipation and send a thrill up my spine. "I have a robe on. I believe it's the one your 'friend' Meredith was wearing the other day."

"Jealous much?"

"Maybe a little." I smile. "Maybe I should send you more dirty texts. I can't have your phone thinking she's better at that than me."

"Maybe you should."

I could. I like the idea of sending him a dirty message while he's teaching.

"What are we doing?"

I'm talking about *this*, about *us*, but he says, "I'm not sure, but let's start with that robe and see what happens." His voice has gone deep, gravelly. "Untie it for me, Cally."

My hands shake slightly as I obey. I let the ties fall to the side and slide my hand down the flat of my belly. "What about you? What do you have on?"

"Boxers."

I lick my lips. I'd tell him to take them off, but I like the image of him in nothing but boxers. "Since I started staying here, I've been wondering how you sleep," I confess.

"Honestly, I haven't done much sleeping at all. I think about you sliding between those sheets, your body laid out on the same bed I used to touch you on."

My breath hitches. "How am I supposed to resist you when you talk to me like this?"

"You're not."

"There are so many reasons we shouldn't do this." But I already know we will. I surrendered the moment I locked the door. "I'm afraid I'll hurt you again."

He hesitates a beat. "That's a chance I'm willing to take, Cal. Let me make that choice, okay?" Then, before I can reply: "Are you nude under the robe?"

"Yes."

He groans. "You've got the upper hand here."

"How so?"

"You saw me naked in the shower. It's been too damn long since I've seen your bare body. I want to see those curves I felt at the restaurant."

I shift back on the bed and fan my fingers over my belly.

"Touch your breasts for me. Touch them like I would. Let me hear you as you play with your nipples."

Desire ripples through me as I lift one hand to my breasts, cupping them, teasing my nipples with my fingers.

"God," he groans. "I love hearing you breathe when you're aroused. You're so damn responsive. It is such a turn-on."

"It's not...." I hesitate, embarrassed to say it but needing him to know, to understand. "I'm not always like this. It's you. No one else does this to me. No one else could ever turn me on this fast."

"How aroused are you? Slide your hand between your legs and tell me."

My breath comes faster as I trace my hand down my body to the needy spot between my thighs. My body is humming with arousal. Greedy with desire. When my fingers find the slickness between my legs, I whimper because my hand is a sorry substitute for his, the quiet of this empty room a poor consolation prize when I crave the weight of his body on me, his breath in my ear. "I can't," I whisper. "I want *you*."

He moans softly. "It's good to hear you say it."

I shake my head and remove my hand. This is too much. And I've reached my breaking point. "Will, I have to go."

Then I hang up the phone.

William

WHAT THE hell just happened?

I blink at my phone, try to make sense of the words telling me the call ended. *Fuck.*

I squeeze my eyes shut and throw my head back on my pillow.

Not that I'll be sleeping much tonight. Not with Cally in my head. Not with the image of her just upstairs, parting her legs at my command. Not while I'm remembering the soft, barely audible almost-purr that she makes when she's close to coming. I keep thinking of how soft her lips look before I kiss them. How swollen they are after.

At the first knock on my bedroom door, I think I'm imagining things. But it sounds again, and then someone whispers my name quietly. "William?"

After I pull open the door, I have to blink a few times to be sure my eyes aren't playing tricks on me. Cally's standing there in nothing but a white terry cloth robe.

"Cally."

She just looks at me with those big brown doe eyes. Then her hands are in my hair and her mouth is on mine. And holy hell, her lips are so damn soft, her taste so damn sweet that I'm lost.

Cupping her face in my hands, I kiss her back without hesitation. I pull her bottom lip between my teeth, and she lets out this little kitten mewl that makes me crazy. My thumb skips down her jaw until she opens under my mouth, because I have to get inside. I need to taste her, to explore her.

Mine.

"Are you sure?" I ask.

"I promise to be quiet." She rubs a thumb over my lips, and I have to resist the instinct to pull it between my teeth and suck, to watch those expressive eyes of hers flare with desire. "Please," she says softly. "Please, William. I need this. I need someone good to touch me. Please."

I drop my hands to her waist and tug her close. The slide of my hand in her robe and I'm skating my thumb across her navel. "I'm not good, Cally. I've screwed up so many times."

"You are," she breathes. "So good you can't even see it."

I yank her robe open and crush my mouth down on hers. I mean it to be a warning—because I'm not letting her go without a fight this time. But she doesn't withdraw. She moans and rocks her hips. She meets my brutal desire with her own, tugging at my hair, biting my lip.

I kick the door closed and back her against it, as if a solid surface might contain this wild and dangerous hunger pumping through me. When I move to her neck and suck that tender skin, she gasps and presses harder into me.

Another wave of lust slams through me, and suddenly I need to see her eyes, to see the pleasure on her face as I touch her.

When I pull back, she's watching me. Her lips are red and swollen, her lids heavy with desire.

I move my hand up her torso. As I brush the underside of her breasts, her eyes float closed and she arches into my hand.

"God, you're beautiful." My words are thick with arousal, gritty with the desperation I've felt since she watched me stroke myself in the shower. Fuck. I'm lost.

I dip my head to her breast, wetting it with my tongue. Cupping her in my hand, I draw her nipple into my mouth. She cries out against my neck and digs her nails into my shoulder blades as I suck and bite, rough and soft by turns. Maybe too rough, but I can't help it because she's moaning and I am desperate to claim her, to brand her.

She rocks into my thigh. I run my hands down her legs and draw her knees up, lifting her between me and the door until my cock is nestled right between her legs, only the thin fabric of my boxers between us. She wraps her legs around me and squeezes me tight.

"Goddammit, Cally." My eyes close, and I have to grit my teeth. "You're so wet I can feel it, and I haven't even taken off my shorts yet."

"What are you waiting for?" She slides her fingers into my hair and tugs my mouth down to hers.

I growl against her and curl my fingers into her hips. "Do you have any idea how much I've thought about this sweet body of yours? Do you have any idea how crazy it made me to have you sleeping upstairs, so fucking close but off limits?"

I peel the robe from her shoulders and let it drop to the floor. "You are so insanely beautiful." I drop my head to open my mouth against her breasts. One at a time, I draw the taut peaks into my mouth, between my teeth, until she cries out and arches closer.

"William," she whimpers. "Please."

I lift my head, my fingers picking up where my mouth left off and rolling a perfect pink nipple between my fingers. "What, baby? Please what?"

She shudders and presses her breast further into my hand. "Please, can you?"

I need to hear her say it, to hear the words from her lips, but I can't resist another taste and have to lower my head to her breasts again and roll a nipple against my tongue.

"God, you taste good."

Her hands thread through my hair and tug, and when I close my mouth over her and suck, the cry that rips through her is almost enough to make me go off in my shorts.

"William," she whimpers, and I love the way she says my full name. "Inside me. Please."

My breath leaves me in a rush. There they are. The words I've been waiting for. But I'm not ready.

Sliding my hands under her ass to support her, I swing around and take four long strides to the bed. I slowly slide her down my body until she's sitting on the bed. Grabbing her hips, I tug her forward until she's leaning back on her elbows and her hips are at the edge of the bed. Then I kiss my way down her body—across her collarbone, between her breasts, down her belly.

I scrape my teeth over one hip then trail my mouth across her stomach. Stopping at her navel, I circle the little jeweled piercing with my tongue before opening my mouth against the soft flesh and sucking.

She bucks her hips, and I cup her, hot and wet, between her legs.

"God, you're amazing," I murmur. She gasps at the touch of my hand.

I position her feet back on the bed so her knees are bent and she's open to me. Then I sink to my haunches and look at her.

She reaches for me. "What are you doing?"

A smile curls my lips, and I press lightly against her inner thighs until her legs fall open and she's completely exposed to my gaze.

"William," she whimpers as I trace my finger down her swollen, sensitive sex.

Her legs come together, and I press them open again and lower my head and taste her. She arches against me, crying out again until the sound of her moans, the feel of her fingers tangling in my hair, and the taste of her against my tongue has my cock aching impatiently in my shorts.

But I won't be rushed. I circle her clit with my tongue, and she trembles under me.

Lifting my head, I lock my eyes with hers. "Don't hold back, Cally. Let me make you come."

I sink two fingers inside her. She pulses around me. So damn close. Taking her clit between my lips, I suck the same moment I cover her mouth with my free hand. She trembles under my mouth, until she's pulsing around my fingers and her cry is muffled against my hand.

chapter seventeen

Cally

"God, you're beautiful when you come." His eyes are hot on mine as he works his way back up my body, one hand still cupping me between my legs. My limbs are limp, my body relaxed, but just the heat in his eyes reignites something in me.

Just like that, I need more.

William climbs on top of me, and I wrap my legs around his hips. I'm greeted with the long, thick shaft of his cock pressing against my clit through his cotton shorts. Just that contact and I'm whimpering—with that dangerous cocktail of pleasure, need, and nostalgia.

"I made so many damn mistakes when you were out of my life. When I you left, I lost more than my girlfriend. I lost myself." He traces my lips with his thumb, and the tenderness in his eyes nearly undoes me. "Be with me, Cally. You're my compass. My north star."

My throat is thick, and his words have tears pushing at the back of my eyes.

"I love you," he murmurs. He kisses the corner of my mouth, my ear, then my cheeks, where his lips press the wet heat of my tears into my skin. "I've always loved you."

I shake my head, needing him to understand. "You don't love me. You love the girl I used to be."

"Do you have any idea how amazing you are *now*?" His eyes lock with mine as he whispers the words. "Everything you've done for the girls and your father...the way you just picked up and left your old life? Not many people your age would do that. You work nonstop, and you're always doing for them. I don't need my memories to be head over heels in love with you, Cally. All I have to do is know you."

My heart is full and broken all at once, and I can't allow myself to return his words. I've said *I love you* so many times since leaving William, and every time it was a lie. I won't let the words be tainted by my lips. "Make love to me, William."

Something flashes over his face. My choice of words doesn't escape his notice. But that's what this is. That's what it will be between Will and me. Some people have sex or intercourse. Some people fuck. But with Will, no matter how fast or slow, tender or rough, after all these years of waiting, I know it will be making love. And that's what I need now. More than anything.

In seconds, he's off me, standing beside the bed and shucking his shorts. He slides on a condom from his end table, and I swallow hard at the sight of him—long and thick, and a little intimidating.

He lies back on the bed, his head propped against a pillow, and crooks his finger at me.

Placing a knee on either side of his hips, I straddle him. He guides me until he's pressing against my entrance.

My eyes close in anticipation of the pain-laced pleasure I know his size will bring.

"Look at me," he commands, fingers digging into my hips.

I open my eyes and lock them on his as he slowly slides inside me. My body has to stretch to accommodate his size, but he's patient and lets me adjust to him. Just having him inside me brings me close again. He stretches me and presses deep, and his eyes don't leave my face until I start moving over him, creating a rhythm for our bodies as he slides deep again and again. Pressure building, my body tightening.

He pulls me forward and cradles my ass in his hands. When his mouth latches onto one of my nipples and draws it tight, I come apart again, and he tightens his hold on my hips and rocks into me with three hard strokes before coming with me.

"WHY DID you keep resisting this?" We're lying in bed nude, our sweaty skin drying under the soft breeze of the ceiling fan. He took care of the condom in the bathroom and then came back to bed and drew my body against his.

"Maybe I wanted you to beg," I tease.

He grunts. "If I thought that would do it, I would have."

The humor leaves me suddenly. He deserves a real answer. "Because I'm not staying. Leaving you once almost killed me. I don't know if I can survive leaving you a second time."

He hooks his foot behind my knee and rolls us over so he's above me, his hands framing my face. "So don't leave. You have a job here. A place to live. What are you so anxious to get back to?"

My heart squeezes in my chest. Because I want what he's offering. I want to be the girl who believes in happily-ever-after again. I want to trust that everything happens for a reason.

But I'm not that girl I used to be, and Will deserves more than for me to pretend I am.

"It's not that simple."

"It can be." He presses a kiss to my collarbone. "Are you really so desperate to get back to something there, or are you running away from something here?"

My throat grows thick. I can hardly speak because I can't swallow my own lies when he's looking at me with so much love.

"Stay." He presses a kiss to the corner of my mouth. "There's nothing you need to run from. I've got you. No matter what." He kisses me again, this time right between my breasts. Right over my heart.

He settles next to me and pulls my body against his to sleep. "Hello, Cally," he whispers, and seconds later, I feel his breathing change against my neck as he relaxes in his sleep.

I lie there, wide awake, wishing it were all as simple as he believes it to be.

William

SLEEPING BEAUTY is in my bed.

The morning sun slants in my bedroom window and across Cally's face, and I can't bring myself to leave her, though I have to open the gallery in fifteen minutes. There's something about being with this woman that washes away all the ugliness of the past two years. My mistake of an engagement to Maggie, my bigger mistake of an engagement to Krystal. I hate to think of myself as some easily analyzed psyche. A cliché case of a guy who lost his family when he was young and has spent his life since trying to build a new one.

But with Maggie and Krystal, I was always caught up in what *would* be. Securing that future—the family, the children—it was all this elusive high I couldn't stop chasing.

It was never like that with Cally. Not when I was eighteen. And not now. Cally grounds me in the moment, roots me in the here and now. She makes simply *existing* so damn perfect I forget all my anxieties about tomorrow.

Her dark lashes flutter against her cheek and she moans softly, rolling to her side and curling into me. After I made love to her the second time last night, she fell asleep in my arms. I watched her for awhile, reminding myself she was real, and here, that it wasn't a dream. I was almost back to sleep myself when she started talking in her sleep. *"I'm sorry."* That was all I could make out her long stream of murmurs. *"I'm sorry. I'm so sorry."*

She was dreaming, but I felt like the words were for me, and it shook me to think she's carrying around so much guilt. But sorry for what? For standing me up that weekend? For dropping me with a text message and just as quickly making herself unreachable? For falling into another guy's arms before a month was out? Or maybe she's sorry for all that and more. Maybe she's sorry for something I don't even know about. Something I wouldn't want to know.

Whatever it is, it doesn't change how I feel. Here, in my bed, the morning sun warming our skin, I'm surer than ever that only Cally matters.

"Mmm," she murmurs against my chest. "I need to get out of bed and get the girls to school."

I stroke her hair back from her face, tucking it behind her ear. "Already taken care of."

She jerks upright and looks at the clock. "Shit. I'm so sorry."

"Don't be. They wanted to let you sleep." I tug her hips until she slips down in bed next to me again. "And I wanted to keep you in bed as long as possible."

She rolls over and curls into my chest. "I haven't slept that well in ages."

"Sounds like you should sleep in my bed more often."

"So you're going to use my insomnia as an excuse to have your way with me?"

"When it comes to getting your naked body next to me as often as possible, I have no shame."

"You smell good." She presses her lips against my chest and licks up my sternum. "Taste good too."

I grab her hands and roll us so she's under me, her hands over her head, trapped at the wrists by mine. Her eyes flash hot as they meet mine.

I nuzzle her neck, relishing the knowledge that I'm branding her with my unshaven face.

"When are you moving back to Vegas?" I have to ask. I need to remind myself that she isn't going to be in my life forever. That she doesn't want to be.

"I don't know." She lifts her eyes to mine, her insecurities written all over her face. "I'm not a fan of long-distance relationships."

"Me either. But I think they can be done. If it's really necessary."

She sinks her teeth into her bottom lip. "Maybe it's not necessary."

"What do you mean by that?" I'm afraid to hope.

"I mean I was going back to Vegas because it was the default, the obvious next move, and—" She watches me. Hesitant. Careful. "—I'm saying I'm going to consider other options."

Something floods my chest, threating to overwhelm me. I bury my face in her neck and squeeze her tight.

Kissing a path up her neck, I draw her earlobe between my teeth, sucking until she cries out. She's like a dream in my arms. There's no way I can go into the gallery today. I need the whole day with Cally in my bed.

"I have to make a phone call," I whisper. Releasing one of her hands, I snatch my phone from the bedside table and lift my head enough to dial Maggie.

It rings four times before she picks up. "Hello?" She sounds like I woke her up. Too fucking bad.

"I need you to open the gallery for me today."

Cally's moved her free hand to my back, and she's smiling at me as she traces her fingers down my spine.

"I have plans with Asher," Maggie says.

Cally slips her hand between our bodies and skims the head of my dick with her fingertips. I growl. "Cancel them." I hang up the phone and toss it across the room.

Cally giggles beneath me. "Bossy."

I recapture her straying hand and replace it above her head. "I *am* the boss."

"You're good at it," she murmurs.

"You like being told what to do?"

"Not particularly, but when you do it, it's pretty hot." Her lips quirk and she rubs her bare, slick heat against my cock. She doesn't even need use of her hands to make me lose my fucking mind.

"Dammit, Cally. You're going to kill me."

She repeats the motion, tucking her hips. I'm all but inside her. "Don't make me wait."

"I need to get a condom." I grit my teeth as I shift so my cock isn't so irresistibly close to her wet heat. I've never wanted to be inside a woman without a condom as much as I want to be inside her. I'm already thinking about what it would be like to slide inside of her, skin to skin.

"I have a clean bill of health," she whispers. "Before you, I hadn't had sex for four years. And as for the rest, that's what birth control pills are for."

I still and study her. I'm not worried about pregnancy. Unfortunately, that's not something I ever need to worry about. "Are you sure?"

She sinks her teeth into her lip and nods.

Just as I move to slide into her, she stops me with her hands on my shoulders.

"What is it?" I ask. The idea of being inside her without that barrier is so damn appealing, but I'll stop if she's changed her mind.

"I wanted you to be my first. I wish you had been."

Aw, hell. "That doesn't matter anymore."

She runs her fingertips down my cheek and nods. "What's done is done. I know. But this? I've never had sex with a man without a condom before. I've been diligent. So, this is…a first."

I cup her face in my hands and crush my mouth to hers, hoping she feels every painful and beautiful ounce of my love for her in this moment. "That's amazing," I whisper. Then I slowly sink into her, our eyes locked as our bodies join so intimately. Skin to skin.

Cally

"STAY. THERE's nothing you need to run from. I've got you. No matter what." William's words haven't left my head since he whispered them in my ear yesterday morning. I'm considering. Maybe I could stay. Maybe this could be my life. My days working across the hall from this man who makes my heart race, my nights in his bed, his hands on my body. Could I really be that lucky? Will he want all that with me once he finds out the truth?

Sickness eats at my stomach at the thought. I should have told him the truth before sleeping with him. I owed him that. But I'm terrified that he won't look at me the same once he knows, and I'm not ready for the end.

"Lots of water," I tell my client. I force myself out of my reverie and offer her a bottle of water. "And no more workouts today. Let your muscles rest."

The woman takes the bottle and slips me a twenty—that tip in addition to the seventy she paid for her massage makes this a great start to the day.

"I'll be back," she promises. "Don't you leave town yet, or I'll have to come to Vegas for my massages."

"I'm considering staying in New Hope permanently," I admit. "I just need to work out some details."

"That would be amazing. You totally should. I'll send a ton of business your way."

"That would be wonderful."

I see her out the back doors and decide to head down to the gallery for a little break between clients.

Maggie is chatting with a young woman in the back, and

William isn't around anywhere. I try to squelch my disappointment but I can't help it. I'm becoming accustomed to his face, his laughter, his eyes on me as I walk through the room. But I make myself resist. I'll see him tonight. Surely I can make it a few hours before setting eyes on him again.

"Cally?"

I turn to find the familiar voice. The smile falls from my face.

"I found you." Hazel eyes, broad shoulders, enough silver peeking through his dark mop to make him look distinguished. Brandon McHugh is as handsome as the day he set out to make me his.

My stomach flips and my heart pounds so fast and hard I need to sit down. "Hello, Brandon."

He runs his eyes over me, my ponytail, my mint green medical scrubs, my tennis shoes. "You're working." He's smiling but the disapproval is in his eyes.

"I am." Brandon doesn't care to have his women work. If they work, how can they do his bidding? If they work, they may not rely on him. Not that I ever dared speak these thoughts to him. Four years out from under his control, and I'm only now daring to *think* them.

"God, I've missed you."

"I—" I try to force the lie he wants to hear from my lips. *I missed you too.* That's what he wants to hear—that I love him, that he broke my heart when he started screwing around with Quinn, that I miss him desperately and I need him. But love and heartbreak have nothing to do with the mess happening inside me. It's fear.

I'm not ready for this. I wasn't prepared for my worlds to collide—my world in Vegas creeping in to infect my New Hope world. I don't want it here.

He frowns as he takes my hand. "Why are you shaking?"

To my horror, I realize I'm trembling. *How did you find me?* Not that I covered my tracks. I didn't think I needed to. He'd only been back in Vegas a month or so before Mom died. I thought he'd get used to the idea that I've moved on. I thought *he* had already moved on. Had I really been so foolish? "What are you doing here?"

His eyes crinkle in the corner as he gives his bashful smile. "I came for you."

chapter eighteen

William

CALLY IS on the showroom floor talking to a man who reeks of money. I watch from the loft, jealousy tearing through me, which is absurd because she's not doing anything inappropriate. Hell, she's still dressed in her massage scrubs. He could be a client for all I know. But there's something almost proprietary about the way he positions his body by hers, the way he's touching her hand.

After what happened this morning, I told myself I was going to give her some space today. I'm too damn tempted to touch her when we're together, too damn tempted to beg her to stay in my house after the girls leave, to stay in New Hope indefinitely. To stay with me. She needs time to come to those decisions on her own. She doesn't need me pressuring her.

Even before I realize what I'm doing, I'm headed down the stairs toward Cally, determined to put some space between her and this stranger.

"Good afternoon." I offer my hand. "I'm William Bailey, the gallery owner and manager. Can I help you?"

The moment the man turns to face me fully, the force of

recognition slams into me so hard, I stumble back a step. He carefully releases Cally's hand and takes mine, his grip confident and strong. "Brandon McHugh."

"It's nice to meet you, Brandon," I manage, but I can feel my jaw hardening. I know that face, those eyes. Could it really be? It may have been seven years ago, but I'll never forget seeing those hands on my girl. It's him. And now he's here. "Is there anything I can help you with today? I'm sure Cally needs to get back to get clients upstairs."

"Is it going well?" Brandon asks, that proprietary hand returning to her shoulder.

"Yes," Cally says quickly. "Very well." Then, to me, "Brandon is visiting from Las Vegas. He was just—"

"Just looking for some new artwork for my New York apartment," he finishes for her.

They exchange a look, and I wonder what their relationship was. I never let Cally know I came to Vegas that summer. When I saw her with Brandon, his hand on her thigh under the table, I assumed they were together, despite how inappropriate—not to mention illegal—such an age match would have been. Was I right? Were they a couple? Her sixteen to his thirty-something? And what are they to each other now?

"Let me show you some of my favorite pieces," I offer.

"I do need to go," Cally tells Brandon. Her voice is softer, almost hesitant. She doesn't sound like herself. "We'll talk later."

"I'd like that." He runs his eyes over her until my fists are almost ready to fly at his face of their own volition. "I'd like that a lot."

Cally scurries upstairs, and I do my best to hide my jealousy and a long-held resentment he wouldn't understand. I won't give in to my caveman need to drive my fist through his face. Not until I have a reason. Instead, I usher the man toward the most expensive pieces in the gallery.

Because I'm a spiteful dick, I suggest that he probably can't afford the gorgeous glass mosaic bowl that Maggie priced at fourteen hundred dollars as a joke. And because this is obviously some sort of pissing contest to him, he buys it *and* an overpriced watercolor of the moonlight reflecting off the New Hope River. I ring him up with a smile and don't bat a lash when he pays with cash.

Only when he's gone do I feel like I can breathe again. But I'm plagued by questions about his visit and his relationship with Cally. This morning Cally suggested she may stay in town. Will his appearance here change that?

Cally

"You came." He opens the door to his hotel room and runs his eyes over me as I step in.

The black dress and tall heels I purchased for this meeting cost me everything I made this week and more, but I didn't dare show up in an outfit that would displease him. Brandon believes my appearance is for his pleasure alone, and he expects me to dress accordingly. When he finishes his visual tour and returns his eyes to mine, I know he approves. First hurdle, crossed.

I don't bother asking how he can afford the swanky downtown Indy hotel. I'm sure he had cash reserves hidden somewhere. Besides, the question would insult him. Brandon will tolerate only the best; therefore, he's in the top floor Presidential suite. He used to take me to hotels like this all over the country when he was traveling on business. He claimed to be an international jeweler. Though his business was certainly international in scope, it wasn't the jewels the Feds were worried about when they caught up with him four years ago.

"Champagne?" he asks, but his servant hands me a glass before I can answer.

I haven't stopped shaking all day. I never imagined he'd bother to come after me. I'm twenty-three now, after all, which might as well be fifty for all Brandon's concerned. Even before he was caught and thrown in prison, he was starting to get bored with me, starting to find younger girls to fulfill his desires.

I used his incarceration as an opportunity to get away from him. The feds froze all his assets, so it wasn't like I could have kept living the high life if I'd wanted to. So I found the apartment with my stoner roommates and hawked most of the jewelry and designer clothes Brandon had given me over the years. When I found out another girl had been visiting him at the prison, I had the perfect excuse to pull away. Not that I was jealous, but being a little too clingy and pretending I was hurt worked. Brandon likes the chase too much to tolerate a clingy woman. I had to work him like that. One doesn't just *leave* Brandon McHugh.

When he was released from prison and I told him I'd moved on, he took it so well. I thought he'd let me go. But he never would have showed up in New Hope if he had any intention of letting me live my life without him.

I should have known better.

I settle into the couch across from him, trying to calm my shaking hands. I need to convince him to go back to Vegas and let me finish my business in New Hope, but I have to be careful I don't piss him off.

Thinking to take a sip for courage, I put my lips to the glass then think better of it. Brandon isn't above slipping drugs in my drink to get his way. I settle my champagne on the glass-topped coffee table that sits between us.

"You're working too hard," he says, narrowing his eyes as he looks at my face. "You need more sleep. Those bags under your eyes don't do you justice."

"Maybe I'm just not as young as I used to be." I stick out my lip in a pout, as if I'm desperate for his reassurance.

"You're still beautiful, but you're tired. You can't hide that from me, sweetheart."

I shrug. *Hard work* was always a dirty word to him—especially when it came to me. He wouldn't even let me finish high school. I change the subject. "What made you decide to come?"

"You know I don't like to wait for what's mine."

A chill steals through me at that old, determined tone of a man who gets what he wants. "You took me by surprise." I force a smile and lean forward. "A nice surprise."

"Our flight leaves tomorrow," he says. "That should give you enough time to pack your things."

I'm not going with you. It's not lack of courage but presence of mind that keeps me from speaking the words. Instead, I say, "You're really going to tease me with that when I already promised the girls I'd stay until after Christmas?"

"So break your promise. I'll fly you back here with so many presents for the little rugrats that they'll be glad to send you back to me and wait for more." He comes to sit next to me and takes my face in his hands. "I need you more than they do."

When his lips touch mine, I don't try to move away. I put my hand on his sculpted shoulder and let him kiss me. When his tongue brushes my lips, I open to him, knowing the invasion will cost me far less than the consequences of denying him.

When he pulls away his eyes are smoky and he's breathing heavily. "I'd missed those lips. Four years is too long."

"It didn't seem to bother you when you were with Quinn," I pout. I hate playing this game, but I don't have a choice.

He cups my face in his big hand. "Forget her. I'm here for you now."

"Give me more time," I whisper, stroking my thumb down the side of his face. "Please, Brandon?" Before he was arrested and sentenced, I'd gotten so good at manipulating him. His obsession with me was his weakness. But I got cocky. I never should have believed he would let me be.

"Stay with me tonight," he growls. "It's been too long since I fucked that hot little body."

I lean forward and touch my lips to his, then, carefully, I reposition myself so I'm straddling him, and he's leaning back. My body wants to recoil from his kiss, but I push forward. Only when he's pulled the skirt of my dress to my waist and his hands are reaching for his belt do I pull away.

"Could I ask you for something?" I whisper.

"Of course."

"Would you book a room at that hotel where we were together for the first time? You remember? With the view of the mountains? I want our first time being together again to be special."

His hands still. "It will be."

Sinking my teeth into my bottom lip, I cut my eyes away from his. "Yes, but I'm on my...my monthly," I lie.

He growls and pushes me off his lap. "Why'd you go and get me all worked up then?"

Righting myself on the cushion next to him, I bow my head and look at him through my lashes. "I guess I was too anxious to touch you again. Not so long ago, I thought we were over."

His fingers grab my wrist and wrap tight. "We will never be *over*. You can't get rid of me."

"You left me for four years," I say, trying for a pout. "And then there was Quinn. I thought you wanted *her* now."

He yanks me forward and the skin under his fingers burns. "How can I prove myself to you? She was a passing fancy. You are the only one I ever wanted as a permanent fixture in my life."

Fixture. What an appropriate word choice. "Give me two months with the girls. Then I'll be home and everything can go back to the way it was before." I place my hand over the one he has wrapped painfully around my wrist. "You can stay with me." The offer is a gamble, but one that I must take.

"I can't stay," he growls, and there's something like anger in his eyes. "Damn parole officer doesn't want me leaving Nevada at all. I have to get back before he realizes I've gone."

"We'll make up for lost time when I get home," I promise.

"Stay my good girl. I'd hate to have to replace you."

I couldn't be so lucky.

He insists I let his driver take me back to New Hope, and I

have him drop me off at Dad's because I can't risk Brandon finding out I'm staying with William.

I have two months of borrowed time. But I won't be heading back to Vegas when it's over. I *won't* go back to Brandon. But I can't be here when he comes back for me either. If I don't want to be forced back into a life with him, I'll have to hide.

chapter nineteen

William

IT'S NEARLY midnight when Cally walks in my door. The girls knew she'd be late and had dinner with their dad. Drew took care of all the necessary bedtime rituals with Gabby. But I didn't get the memo, and I sat in my dark living room, watching the front door, willing her to come through it. I'm foolishly hoping she spent the evening with Lizzy and Hanna, but I know better.

She's in a high heels and short black dress that shows off her long legs. Oblivious to my presence, she goes straight to the kitchen.

I catch her at the sink, splashing water on her face, and I spin her around and slide my hands into her hair, pressing my mouth to hers. She lets out a little squeak and lifts her hands to my chest as she opens her mouth under mine.

Her kiss is so sweet, so full of something that feels like love.

My hands go to her ass, and I pull her hard and fast against my body, needing to feel her close to me. When that's not good enough for this raging need inside me, I draw her skirt up around her waist and lift her onto the counter. She spreads her legs and tugs me forward by my shirt. I break the kiss to trail my mouth to her neck. A sexy moan of protest slips from her lips as her hands slide into my hair.

Closer, something primal demands. I nearly forget everything but our bodies. Everything except this roaring need to own. To claim. To *keep*. Because that's what's there at the root of this desire—my fear that she's going to leave me again.

I try to catch my breath and slow this down. Tracing her lips with my thumb, I skim my hand down the side of her neck before tangling it in her hair.

She tilts her head to the side to give me better access to her neck. I kiss and nip there as I find her zipper and peel the dress from her shoulders. I go to work on her bra, releasing it at the back and throwing it across the kitchen.

Her breasts are full, her nipples already hard. I take one into my hand and tease her nipple. With my other hand, I trace down the column of her spine and dip into the waistband of her panties.

She's panting in my ear and tugging on my hair to pull me closer. Moaning, she wraps her legs around me. The stiletto points of her heels dig into my back.

"Be mine, Cally. You belong to me."

She cools in my arms and presses me away. "What did you say?"

"I need to know you're mine. The asshole in the gallery. He's here for you. I can tell."

Her whole body stiffens. "How did you know?"

"Aside from the fact that he was two seconds away from whipping it out and pissing on you to mark his territory?" I take her thumb between my teeth and bite gently before releasing it. Then I place my mouth to her earlobe and treat it to a similar torture until she's pressing into me again. "You were with him tonight, weren't you?"

"Let's not do this, William," she whispers. "Not now."

She doesn't deny it and that tears me apart, but I need her too much. "Forget about the past. Forget about the future. You're here now, and what's happening between us is inevitable. You're *mine*." I roll her nipple between my fingers and pinch until she cries softly, rocking her hips into me. "Say you're mine."

"No," she says in a harsh whisper. She shoves away my hands. "I'm not."

I stagger back. "I'm supposed to believe you belong to him? After last night?"

The sadness in her eyes makes a vice around my heart. "I'm not anyone's. I'm a human being, not a possession." She tugs off her heels and hops off the counter. Pulling her dress back up, she grabs her bra off the floor and is headed to the stairs when I stop her.

"Cally?"

She hangs her head but keeps her back to me. "I'm sorry I can't tell you what you want to hear."

William
Seven Years Ago

THE INDIANAPOLIS Airport is buzzing with late Saturday morning traffic, and I wait for Cally at baggage claim, pacing, too nervous to sit.

Her plane from Las Vegas arrived twenty minutes ago, and I haven't seen her yet, but I refuse to assume the worst.

I rented a little cabin for after prom, and I already have it set up with rose petals, candles, and strawberry wine. We're going to be together tonight. For the first time.

But it's not the sex I'm looking forward to the most. It's having her in my arms again, smelling her hair, reassuring myself that I haven't lost her.

The people around me reunite with their loved ones and I try to shake this sense of impending disappointment. A mom drops her bag as she sinks to her knees and gathers a little girl in her arms. A young woman with bright eyes wraps her arms around her pierced and tatted boyfriend. I scoot back to get out of the way, scanning the crowd for her face.

The traffic around the baggage carousel clears, person by person. My heart turns stony in my chest and sinks to my gut as I watch the shiny conveyor belt turn.

All the bags are gone. Cally is nowhere to be seen.

My hands are unsteady as I pull my cell phone from my pocket and punch in her number. It rings once and goes to voicemail.

I try again. This time it goes straight to voicemail.

I'm ready to dial again when her text comes through: *Something came up. I'm sorry I can't come.*

I sink onto a bench and cradle my head in my hands. It's over. I ignored the signs because I didn't want to believe it, but I can't deny it anymore. I've lost her.

How am I supposed to let her go when she still has ahold of my heart?

✧

Cally
Present Day

"JUST IMAGINE we're on one of those renovation shows Mom used to like watching so much."

"Does that mean the sexy hosts are going to show up?" Drew asks, stumbling forward on the riverside trail. She still hasn't completely opened her eyes, but I woke up early after a night of anxiety and little sleep, and I didn't have the patience to let her sleep in this morning. "I'm going to need some decent scenery if I'm going to be working this early on a Saturday."

"No sexy hosts, but the exterminator also promised no rats, so it's a trade-off."

It's a gorgeous morning, and I'm determined not to let last night's falling out with William ruin my day. It had to happen eventually. Better sooner than later.

As I tossed and turned last night, I realized how much I need to do before I leave New Hope. First, I need to prepare the girls for life without me. I've been taking everything on myself for too long. They're old enough to scrub walls and push a vacuum, and it's time I made them pull their weight. After all, the cabin is going to be their house, and I won't be here to take care of it. I probably won't even be able to risk coming back to check in.

I can't think about that too much.

"I better get to pick the paint color for our bedroom," Drew grumbles.

"I want to knock down a wall," Gabby says.

"No knocking down walls. I'm afraid the house would fall down."

We turn off the trail and into the woods toward Dad's.

"Who's here?" Drew asks.

I follow the direction of her gaze and my steps stutter. Dad's driveway is filled with cars, and from here I can see William and two guys I only vaguely recognize. As we get closer, I see Hanna and Lizzy leaning against Lizzy's Charger, and behind them—

Drew squeezes my arm and stops cold. "Oh. My. God."

I see him the same moment she does. Asher Logan is climbing into the back of a big black pickup, handing supplies to the guys.

Drew looks like she might vomit.

I bite my lip to keep from laughing at her. "What were you saying about needing decent scenery?"

"He's beautiful," Gabby whispers.

I roll my eyes. "Seriously? You too?" But then I realize she's not looking at Asher. She's looking at one of Will's friends, the tall, dark-haired guy with broad shoulders and wicked smile. The one Hanna likes. Max. "Come on, girls," I say, heading into the fray. "First rule is to never let them see you drool."

"Surprise!" Lizzy calls when she sees us approaching.

I prop my hands on my hips. "Are we having a party here that no one told me about?"

"A renovation party!" Lizzy says, hopping up and down so her curls bounce.

Drew grimaces next to me. "No one should be that perky before nine a.m."

My eyes connect with William's. I know without asking that he's responsible for this. He just winks at me as if last night in the kitchen never happened. *Too. Damn. Good.*

"You didn't have to come."

The guys shrug, and Max says, "We owe Will. Anyway, we're happy to help."

"Okay, everyone," Will announces. "The Dumpster will be here any minute. Let's start with the carpet and the linoleum in the kitchen. Once we get all that out, we'll tackle the walls and be ready for the new flooring by this afternoon."

"New flooring?" I whisper. Everyone's already headed toward the house and I'm standing here, blinking at Will like an idiot.

"New flooring," he says carefully, his eyes on me. "A couple of appliances."

I don't even have words. I know I should feel…something. Anything other than this crazy out-of-body confusion, like I've been dropped into someone else's life. "But…how?"

"Hey, Bailey!" Max calls from the front porch. "Where do you want the furniture?"

"Coming!" He winks at me and then disappears into the house.

A couple of hours later, the old carpet and linoleum are gone, Sam and Asher are patching the bad spots on the roof, and Max and William have started working on the rotted planks on the deck, pulling off the bad ones and replacing them with new. The sun is high in the sky and cutting through the trees, turning the autumn day hot. William peels off his shirt and tosses it aside, giving me a hell of a view as I try to tape the windows for painting.

Next to me, Drew clears her throat and nudges me in the side with her elbow. "The first rule is to never let them see you drool."

By lunch, I don't know whether to tell William off or kiss his feet. First, the truck arrived with the flooring, then another truck brought a new stove and refrigerator, and a third brought new living room furniture and loft beds for the girls and desks that go under each.

It's too much, and if it were all for me, I wouldn't accept it. If it were all for me, I'd be angry. But Gabby and Drew are practically bouncing with excitement, and instead of being angry I'm just... grateful. I'm grateful William could do this for them. I'm grateful that, for once, it's not all on my shoulders. But even so, there's something unsettling about the grand gesture. Something that doesn't sit right.

"How much do you hate me right now?" William asks behind me.

I turn slowly. He's a sweaty mess from tearing up the carpet, and he looks a little unsure as he studies me, but I've never been so attracted to someone in my life.

I grab his hand and pull him around the side of the house, where we can talk without curious eyes watching us. "Thank you for arranging this."

He shifts his hand under mine and entwines our fingers. "You're welcome."

I force myself to ask the question that's been needling me more and more with every gift he's given. "You know this doesn't change things between us, right?"

The smile falls from his face. "What do you mean?"

"You can't buy me, William. I appreciate everything you've done for us, but I'm not for sale."

"I didn't think you were." His hard jaw starts to tick. He runs a hand through his curls and looks up at the trees as it trying for patience, but his eyes burn with anger when they turn back to me. "Is that why you think I did this? Is that why you think I'm giving you a deal for your studio, why you think I let you and your sisters stay with me? You think I'm trying to *buy* you? What the fuck kind of asshole do you think I am?"

467

"No! Of course I—" But I can't deny it when that's exactly what I just accused him of. That's exactly what I'm afraid of.

"Last night you accused me of treating you like possession, but I have *never* thought of you that way. A possession is something you own, something you control." He tugs me close until my body is pressed against his and his mouth is brushing my ear. "I don't want to control you. I want you to be mine. Don't you see the difference?"

My heart pounds in my chest, stumbling painfully as if it's trying to race away from this conversation. "There is no difference for a lot of guys." *There was no difference for Brandon.*

"I want your heart. I have no interest in buying it or controlling it. I want you to give it to me freely. Because you already own mine. You always have. You always will."

"And my body?" I can't help myself. I have to ask. "For some men, being *his* means wearing the clothes he picks out, expressing the opinions he wants me to hold, and letting him fuck me the way he wants to fuck me."

One hand drops to my waist, lower, and he draws my body close to his, fingers squeezing my hip. "I don't want to dress you. If you're in a sexy skirt or in those scrubs your wear for work, all I want is to *un*dress you. And I don't want to own your mind, I want to explore it." His mouth brushes my ear as he speaks. Arousal shoots like an electric pulse down my spine. "But I *do* want you to let me fuck you the way I want to fuck you. But only because I'm yours as much as you are mine, and every time I touch you, I feel like I've been put on this Earth to make you come."

His mouth opens over mine. I'm clinging to him, my nails biting into his shoulders, my legs unsteady beneath me. He backs me up until has me against the side of the house, and I suddenly wish everyone else was gone, so I could take him up on the promise in his eyes.

"You're mine, Cally," he whispers. "I don't give two fucks if that sounds too caveman or possessive for you, because when it comes to you, I am."

chapter twenty

William

TODAY HAS been shit. Because I want Cally so much it hurts. Because despite our little conversation outside her dad's house yesterday, she avoided me after the girls were in bed last night. Because even angry with her, I'm happier than I've been in years.

But mostly my day has been shit because I know Cally and her sisters are moving back home tonight, and even though I'm going to see her at the gallery most days, letting Cally go in any form goes against every instinct I have.

When I get home from work and walk in my door, my nose is assaulted by garlic and basil. I don't make it more than a few steps before Drew appears in a white dress shirt and black pants, a linen napkin draped over her arm. "Your table is this way, sir," she says, motioning toward the dining room.

"What's going on, Drew?" I walk into the dining room, and Gabby, dressed just like her sister, pulls out a chair for me to sit.

The table is set for two with taper candles burning in the center and flickering shadows on the walls. Bowls of spaghetti, salad, and garlic bread wait, and a wine bottle sits on ice in a stainless steel bucket. I pick it up to see they've chosen strawberry wine.

"Did Cally do this?"

Drew grins and shakes her head. "Nope. She's not home yet." She slides her phone from her pocket and looks at the time. "She'll be here any minute."

"Does she know?"

"It's a surprise." Gabby grins. "To thank you for letting us stay."

Tenderness toward both of these girls tugs in my chest. "The strawberry wine?" Out of all the wines in the rack, I'm curious how they knew to choose this one for me and Cally.

"It's Cally's favorite," Drew says with a shrug. "She doesn't drink often, but when she does, this is what she likes."

Damn. I swallow. "Thanks."

The front door opens. "Drew?" Cally calls. "Gabby?"

Drew scurries to greet her, and Gabby just grins at me.

"This way," Drew says, ushering Cally into the dining room. "Your dinner awaits."

Cally's jaw drops and her eyes go wide as she looks at the table and then me. "Did you do this?"

I shake my head. "Your sisters were the masterminds behind this evening."

Gabby pulls out the chair opposite mine. "Please, have a seat."

Cally obeys and watches in mute fascination as the girls fill our plates with food and our glasses with wine.

"Enjoy," Drew says, placing a silver bell on the table. "And please ring this if you need anything. We'll be in the family room with our movie."

"Unless you call us, you'll have *plenty* of privacy," Gabby says with a nod.

With that, both girls leave the room.

Cally runs her finger over the condensation on her wine glass. "Strawberry wine," she says with a baffled shake of her head.

"Drew said it's your favorite."

She smiles at me and takes a sip. "She's right."

"Not much changes."

She stiffens. "Everything changes."

I don't want to argue. Not tonight. So I change the subject. "Are the girls looking forward to sleeping in their new beds?"

"They are, and Dad's ready to have them back. He misses them. I think they miss him too. He's planned this big trip to the Indianapolis Children's Museum, and Drew isn't even complaining about it." She smiles. "Did I tell you Dad got another job?"

"Really? That's great."

"Apparently his obsession with everything spiritual is finally paying off. He got a guest-lecturing gig up at The Center. It doesn't pay a ton, but it will help a lot until he can get adjunct work at the college next semester. That plus the part-time research gig and I'm finally feeling semi-confident in his ability to support the girls."

Her phone rings and she slips it from her pocket and looks at the screen. Something flashes across her face. Worry? Anxiety? "Do you mind if I take this?"

"Go ahead."

She steps into the hall to take the call, but I can still hear her side of the conversation.

"Hello?… I'm glad…. I miss you too…. I know…. No, I can't talk about this right now. I'm in a meeting…. I promise…. You too."

She avoids my eyes when she slips back into her seat.

"Brandon?" I ask.

She stops her fork halfway to her mouth and lowers it before speaking. "Yes."

I won't bother pretending I wasn't eavesdropping. "You miss him."

"It's…complicated." She shakes her head. "How do you know about us anyway? What did he tell you when he was at the gallery?"

I take a long drink of my wine before answering. She has no idea I came to Vegas looking for her after she dumped me. "He's the one you left me for," I say carefully.

Her brow furrows. "I didn't leave you for another man. I— Wait. Why would you even think that? What did he tell you?"

"I came to Vegas seven years ago. That summer? I came and I tracked you down and your neighbor told me you were at some fancy restaurant, so I took a cab and sure enough…there you were. You were in this fancy dress drinking wine and sitting with this rich older guy. It was Brandon."

"You came to Vegas?"

"My girlfriend fell off the face of the earth," I say softly. "I wasn't okay at letting that text message be the last words between us."

"I had no idea you came."

"Brandon was the one you were talking about yesterday. The one who told you how to dress, what to think—" I lower my voice. "—how to fuck."

She pushes her food around her plate and avoids my eyes.

"Everything changed after he showed up."

"Brandon's visit was just a reminder that my life isn't as simple at it was when I lived here as a teenager."

"You don't have to be with someone like that. You deserve better."

"Please. Let's not do this?"

I take a breath and make myself ask the question I've been pushing from my mind. "Do you still love him?"

She lifts her head and her eyes connect with mine. "If I did, would you still insist I be *yours*?"

"No." My chest aches and I can't understand her question in the context of the desperation that's written all over her face. "If you loved him, if he was the one you wanted…." I swallow. "I want you to be mine. I'm won't lie about that. But you can't belong to someone you don't give yourself to."

Her jaw goes slack and her eyes soften. "It says a lot that you believe that, William Bailey."

We take our meal in silence for the next few minutes, though in truth neither of us is eating much. When I can't stand it anymore, I reach across the table and take her fingers in my hand, squeezing. We finish our meal and take the dishes to the kitchen before finding the girls in the family room.

"So are you madly in love and going to have babies yet?" Drew asks from the couch, her tone bored.

Cally picks up a pillow and knocks Drew softly on the head with it. "Twerp. Get your things. We need to get going."

Someone honks out front and Drew and Gabby jump to their feet and grab their bags. "That's Dad!" Drew calls, running toward the front door. "You two behave."

Then the slam of the front door echoes through the house, and we're alone.

"I shouldn't stay," she whispers, looking at her shoes.

"Just for a drink," I promise. There's too much we've left unsaid tonight. "I hate to see a fine bottle of screw-top wine go to waste."

"I guess you know my weaknesses. Meet me on the patio?"

I grab the wine and head out to find Cally looking at the stars.

"I should have known you'd be looking at your stars."

She gives me a sad smile. "It's really beautiful. I guess I'd missed it more than I realized."

"You still wishing on stars?" I settle into the chair beside her and hand her a glass of wine.

"Thanks." She takes the glass but doesn't drink. "Not in a long time."

"Why not?"

"Kid stuff, I guess."

"That doesn't sound like the Cally I used to know."

She eyes me wearily. "I'm *not* the Cally you used to know."

My jaw tightens. "You're not the only one who's changed. You're not the only one who's had to make shit decisions."

"Says the man who just up and bought us a house of new furniture." She crosses her arms then shakes her head, looking away.

I'm instantly pissed. "Money doesn't make everything easy. I know you always thought it did, but you have no idea what it was like to grow up without my parents, no idea how much I would trade to have known what it was like to have them there."

"But it helps," she says softly. "Having money means you didn't have to make as many 'shit decisions' as I did. And my parents? They might have been alive, but—" She shoots up out of her chair. "Dammit, I don't want to do this."

I catch up to her at the French doors and press my hand against the glass before she can open them. Frustration ticks in my jaw. Fear of losing her churns my stomach. I'm sick of everything being left unsaid between us and too scared of the answers to demand the truth. "You don't want to do *what*?"

She turns to face me, leaving her body between me and the door, my hands blocking her in on either side. "I don't want to play the *who-had-the-worst-childhood* game."

"That's not what I was doing. You just shut me down every time the past comes up, like I'm incapable of understanding what your life was like after you left."

She scoffs. "Like you're an open book about yours?"

"Try me."

"You and Maggie were together." It's not a question.

"Briefly." I don't want to go there. Not with Cally. But if this is the conversation she needs to have in order to open up to me, so be it.

"She still cares about you. She's worried I'm going to hurt you. Again."

"I'm a big boy. I don't need Maggie looking out for me."

"But she does." Her hand slowly rises to touch my face, and I stay perfectly still, resisting the urge to turn a kiss into her palm. Resisting the urge to kiss her until we have both forgotten this conversation and are thinking only of each other's bodies. "And then you married her sister Krystal."

She caught up fast. But what do I expect? This is New Hope. There are no secrets here. If anything, I should be surprised she had to come all the way back to New Hope for the grapevine to deliver the news. "Krystal and I were never officially married." Not that we didn't get way too fucking close for comfort. Stupid on my part. "It seemed like the right decision at the time, but it didn't work out, and that was for the best."

"But they're all so protective of you. You're not the bad guy to them."

"I screwed up. They've forgiven me."

Her eyes dip to my mouth before lifting to connect with mine. "Which part was the screw up?"

I ball my hands into fists, resisting the urge to touch her. "All of it. Both of them."

"Yeah, you're an open book, alright."

"Jesus? Is that what you want? You want to know where I fucked up? You'll show me yours if I show you mine? Is that it? What are you so desperate to hide from me?"

"We *all* have parts of ourselves we don't want anyone to see."

I drag a hand through my hair and turn away from her. Because she's right. And I can't look her in the eyes while I confess my life's biggest failure. "After I went to college, Maggie...she needed me."

"The poor little rich girl needed you? I'm sure she did."

"It's not mine to tell, Cally, but *I* can tell you I fucked up. She came to me, she needed help, and I put her back on a bus and sent her home."

"You weren't responsible for her. A college student, you were barely more than a kid yourself."

And I was hung up on a girl who dumped me for a rich asshole at least fifteen years older than me. I hang my head. "It doesn't matter. She was terrified, and I sent her right back into the fray."

"What fray?" She shakes her head. "I don't understand what could have been so bad. The maid didn't clean her room well enough? Not enough boys falling at her feet?"

She's trying to pick a fight, but I won't take the bait. "Exactly. You don't understand. You aren't the only one who's had to make shit decisions, and neither am I. When I realized what I'd inadvertently done, I couldn't forgive myself. I was obsessed with protecting her, and when I came back home from grad school, that obsession turned into something else."

"You fell in love with her."

I shrug. "I loved her. That doesn't mean it was a healthy love."

"Then Krystal?"

"Krystal picked up the pieces when Maggie left me. She loved me and she wanted all the same things I wanted. She made me forget that I'd lost Maggie."

"And Krystal? Did you love her?"

"Of course I did. I wouldn't have put a ring on her finger if I didn't."

"But Maggie had just left you. You poor thing, so broken-hearted you only needed two-point-five seconds to fall for her sister. Was it that easy for you to get over me too?" I turn, and she's thrown her hand over her mouth. Regret pulling at her features. "I shouldn't have said that."

"Because you already know the answer."

"I'm not so different than Maggie," she whispers. "You always wanted to save me. To fix me and my broken family. Hell, look at us now. You're just coming to the rescue again."

"I can help and I want to. What's *wrong* with that?"

"I want more."

She can have more. She can have anything. Everything. "Then it's yours."

She tilts her chin, looking up at her stars again. "I don't want to be rescued. Been there. Done that. Lived with the self-loathing."

"Tell me what you want."

"I want a man who's just as saved by my love as I am by his." She lifts her shoulders. "Someday. But I don't *need* it. All I need now is to help my sisters and get by."

"I'm sick of you dancing around your past."

I don't really expect her to reveal anything, so I'm surprised when she speaks. "Mom's love affair with Vicodin became an obsession. She was too stoned to even give twenty-dollar hand jobs anymore."

I flinch. "Cally…."

"We got food stamps, but she'd sell them for drugs. A hundred dollars that was supposed to buy my sisters and me dinner became a handful of precious pills for her." Her eyes fill and she looks away from me. "Within a month of moving to Vegas, I got a job, two jobs, but it was never enough. And then I'd talk to you, and you were planning for college and picking out the car your grandmother was going to buy you for a graduation gift. You lived in a completely different universe than me, and I couldn't handle it."

I take her shoulders and turn her to look at me. "I wish you would have told me. I could have helped. I could have—"

"What?" She laughs. A cold, hollow sound that doesn't hold an ounce of humor. She pushes at my chest, and I back up and drop my arms. "What would you have been able to do? Send money? And then keep sending money? An eighteen-year-old boy responsible for supporting a family of four? Mom would have had your trust fund cleaned out before you even finished college."

"I don't care about the fucking money. I would have given it all up for you."

"I loved you," she whispers. "I loved you enough to let you go. That's the truth. Someday soon I'll have to do it again, and it will still be the truth, even if you can't accept it."

I wrap my arms around her and crush her against me, holding on too tight because I'm terrified of what will happen if I let go. "Don't. I need you to believe again. I need you to be brave. You hold on to me, and I'll hold on to you."

She clings to me, her hands wrapped around my biceps as she lifts to her toes and presses her mouth to mine. I hold her tight, pouring everything I feel into the kiss until all the tension has drained out of her body. "I can't stay," she murmurs. "This is only for now. It can't be forever. Please don't ask me for something I can't give."

I don't answer, don't let myself think about what she's leaving me for—or whom. I scoop her off her feet and carry her to my bed. I undress her slowly, exploring her body with hands and mouth. When I slide into her, she clings to me, cries her pleasure into my neck. I make her come again and again, taking everything she offers from her body since she won't give me her heart.

chapter twenty-one

Cally

IN THE last month, the leaves have turned, days have cooled, and I feel like we're racing toward the end of my time in New Hope. Every day I stay is another day I'm risking Brandon returning. He promised me two months, but the promise of a selfish man means nothing, and I would be smart to leave now.

Life has been deceptively good since the girls and I moved back into Dad's. William and I go to football games and cheer on his alma mater, and then he takes me back to his house and makes love to me. I insist our affair is temporary, but I can tell he thinks he can change my mind.

Dad has settled into his role as primary care provider for the girls, and though money hasn't been easy, there's been enough that I've been able to put some back for my new life. Thanksgiving is just around the corner, and this morning William told me he wants us to host a dinner for our friends and families at his house. I need to disappear before Thanksgiving, so his plans only fill me with despair. He misunderstood my reaction and teased me about my lack of cooking skills until we were both laughing away my fears. Then he spent the rest of the morning making love to me.

Each day, I find myself counting down the minutes of my workday, anxious to get home to William, to savor these last days together. Today is no different.

But first I have to finish with this client. This is the third time in as many weeks that Carl York has been in for a massage. Normally that wouldn't bother me. The fact that he's mentioned his wife leaving him and how lonely he is *at least ten times* leaves me a little uneasy. But I shrug off the feeling.

"That's our hour." I reposition the sheets to cover his chest. "Take your time, and I'll meet you in the waiting area."

He moans. "When's your next client? I'd like to add thirty minutes."

"Okay." This is something I usually don't allow unless the client makes arrangements before we start, but I'm available, and as much as I need the money, it's foolish to say no. "I could do another thirty. Is there an area you want me to focus on?"

Before I realize he's grabbed my hand, he's pressing it onto his hard-on over the sheet. "Right there, baby."

I slam my fist down on his dick, then twist around to bend his to the back of his hand. "*Bitch!*" he cries.

I release him and step back, queasiness churning my belly. "We're done, Mr. York. But if you ever try anything like that again, I'll be doing some deep tissue work on your balls. Understood?"

He rolls to his side and draws his knees up to his stomach, moaning. Fucking asshole deserves it. I'll go back to living on peanut butter sandwiches and invite rats to be my roomies before I work with a guy who treats me like that.

I turn to leave but when I reach the door, his words stop me. "Don't act so fucking righteous. I know who you are. I checked up on you. You want to act like you're better than your mama, but I know the truth."

When I leave the room, I'm shaking. I don't want to be here when Carl leaves, so I exit the apartment and go out into the gallery's loft reception area. Maggie shoots me a worried look from the couch where she's tapping away at her laptop. "Are you okay?"

I force a smile. "Yeah. Everything is fine. I just—"

I run to the sink and vomit, heaving and heaving until my stomach is wrung dry and my mouth tastes like bile.

"Yeah, you're downright peachy," Maggie mutters. I hear her getting up, but I don't look. I need to compose myself. I've been practicing massage professionally for almost four years, and I've never had anyone try anything like that. But none of my clients knew about my past. None of them knew I once sold myself to keep my sisters off the street.

I rinse out my mouth and clean out the sink, but even then I leave the water running. The sound gives me the illusion of privacy I need right now.

When I finally turn it off and turn around, Maggie's leaning against the wall, her arms crossed. "Carl York? Seriously, you let that piece of shit on your massage table?"

I plaster on a smile. "Made a good impression on you too, did he? Is he still here?"

"He's gone and not very happy with you. What happened?"

"He wanted me to jack him off. Pushed my fucking hand onto his hard-on."

Maggie's breath leaves her in a rush. "That's assault, Cally. You need to call the cops, file charges."

I shake my head. "That's the last thing my business needs. I can't take that sort of hit." Not now. Not when I'm stockpiling as much cash as I can so I can start a new life.

"It's exactly what your business needs. File charges when some asshole pulls that shit. That sends a message loud and clear about what kind of business you run. You have to make sure people know that's not what you're about."

"And why is that?" I lift my chin and feel all the anger that's been simmering inside me for the last fifteen minutes rise up. "Does the spa by campus have to make sure their clients know they aren't there to give 'happy endings'? Why am I any different?"

"Don't be like that."

"I want to know. Why is it different for me? Because I'm poor, so my massage practice is really just a front for my real specialty of giving hand jobs? Is that what people think? Or maybe they think that because my mom felt like it was what *she* had to do, I'll feel the same way?"

Her eyes go sad. "Just because what people think about you isn't fair doesn't mean they won't think it. Trust me. I know."

"What do you know?" I laugh, and it sounds so empty, so miserable. "You're a *Thompson*. You have money and influence. Everyone in this town loves you guys."

Her face changes and the sympathy in her eyes is replaced with something else. Something harder. "Nobody cared that I was a Thompson when they found out the sheriff was fucking me. I was fifteen, and he was cheating on his wife. With me. The fact that I said *no* was just a technicality to people around here. He left town, and some people saw what he did for what it was—a man with power over me, a much older man, using that power to fulfill his own sick desires. Some people got that. They got that I was a victim. They got that even when you have a crush on your dad's best friend and wear tight shirts around him, *no* still means *no*." She shrugs. "But others? Others *never* got that. You weren't here to see a good portion of this town turn against me because of the sins of a grown man, but it happened, and don't you dare tell me that I don't *get it* just because my family has money."

My throat is thick with shame and embarrassment. Not only am I being as judgmental as everyone else, I should have known better. This was what William was talking about when he said he failed Maggie. This is the part he wasn't telling me. "Jesus, Maggie. I had no idea."

Her shoulders rise on a long inhale and her expression softens. "It's better now, but I had to stop allowing them define who I am. You're going to have to do the same thing. Don't let what they think about your mother influence the way you see yourself. Your mom did stuff for money, but you're better than that."

I blink at her, stepping back until my shoulder hits the wall. "My mom did what she had to do." I just didn't understand that until I was pushed into the same corner. At least she called the shots when she sold out.

"I don't know one way or the other," Maggie says. "But it doesn't matter what she did or didn't do. The truth is irrelevant to some people. They believe what they want. Especially assholes like Carl who are just looking for an excuse."

"Don't tell William about what happened today."

She chews on her lower lip for a moment, studying me. "I think that would be a mistake."

"I won't take another appointment from Carl. It'll be fine. Please?"

She crosses her arms, disapproval clear in her eyes. "It's not mine to tell, but think about what I said, okay?"

I don't know what Will would do if he found out about what happened tonight, but I'm sure that, like Maggie, he'd want me to file charges. But I can't tell anyone what Carl did because I'm too terrified he'll share what he knows about me.

"Maggie, what does Carl do for a living?"

"He's some sort of PI, I think. Pics of husbands cheating on their wives, that kind of thing."

I swallow and make myself ask, "Do you have any idea who might have hired him to find something out about me?"

Maggie frowns. "Who would do that?"

But I already know the answer.

"You want to act like you're better than your mama, but I know the truth."

If someone hired a private investigator to look into my past, it won't be long before William finds out what I haven't had to courage to tell him. I got caught and sent to juvie when I met with the second man Anthony sent me to. I have no doubt that's how Carl York found out the truth. I assumed my juvenile record would be sealed, but I wasn't so lucky. When I was arrested for breaking and entering at nineteen, the court decided not to seal it. I had a box of jewelry in one of Brandon's homes that I was trying to get to after he was sentenced. Only it wasn't his house anymore, and I got caught.

Was I ever going to tell William the truth about my first years in Vegas? Or was I hoping my past would just disappear if I wished hard enough?

I know what I need to do, and when I leave my massage studio I go straight to my car. There's no question in my mind who hired Carl, and I need to make sure she lets me tell William the truth before she can.

Venus Salon is a swanky place by campus where all the sorority girls get their hair foiled and nails painted. The place is bustling on this Friday night, with every chair in the salon occupied and several people in the waiting area.

I'm two steps inside the doors when I spot Meredith.

She crosses her arms around her middle at the sight of me, hugging herself as she approaches. "Can I help you?"

All eyes are on us. "Can we go somewhere private to talk?"

Her jaw is hard, her disgust with me all over her face, as if my presence repulses her. "Fine. Follow me."

We cut through the salon. The stylists stop working and stare as us as I follow her back to the office. I could swear I hear one of them mutter *"Home wrecker"* as I step into the office.

Meredith closes the door behind me. "What can I do for you?"

I frown as she lowers herself into a chair. Her face is pale. "Are you okay?"

She waves a hand. "I'm fine."

"I…." I should have thought this through. What am I going to say? How am I going to convince her to stay quiet? And if she agrees to wait, do I really have the courage to tell William myself?

Before I can figure out what to say, she motions to the chair across from her. "Will you sit? I wanted to talk to you anyway, so I'm actually glad you're here."

I swallow. Shit. Am I too late?

"I have a proposition for you."

"A what?"

"Twenty thousand."

I cross my arms. "Twenty thousand what?"

"Dollars."

I blink at her, then my breath rushes from my chest. "You're blackmailing me?" My heart pounds.

"What? How could I blackmail you?"

"I don't have that kind of money."

"Exactly. That's why I'm offering it to you. Twenty thousand dollars. A little gift from me to you. I know about your dad's house."

I feel like I've been dropped into the wrong conversation. Nothing she's saying makes sense. No matter what she tells William, she hates me. Why would she want to give me money? "What about Dad's house?"

She raises a brow. "The foreclosure? The auction? What, are you so busy screwing my man that you aren't even reading the mail that comes to your house? I have friends at the bank. Your dad is eighteen months behind on his mortgage. They've given him every opportunity, but time's up. The bank is auctioning it off? I suppose you don't mind. You'll just move your crew in with Will, continue to suck him dry, huh? Real classy."

My stomach flips, turns sour, and tightens on itself all in one painful moment. "Dad's house is being foreclosed on?"

She leans forward and narrows her eyes at me. "Are you seriously that clueless?"

"I had no idea." And she's not far off the mark. I've been too caught up in my own temporary fairytale.

Is she telling the truth about the house? Does Dad know? Has he been keeping this from me? Then the rest of her words sink in. "You're offering me twenty thousand dollars to save my house?"

She laughs. "There you go. Finally catching on. Good girl."

"What's the catch?"

She drops her gaze to the desk where she drums her perfectly manicured nails. Her voice isn't as cocky when she speaks again.

"I think you know."

"William," I say softly.

"You came back into town like you'd never left. Swept in and stepped right back into his life, with no mind to the fact that you were pushing me out. I'll give you twenty thousand. You can save your little sisters' home and then leave town." She crosses her arms and leans back in her chair. "Or maybe you'll just take the money and run, screwing over your family like you screwed over Will by coming back. I don't care. I just want you gone."

My world spins wildly as she explains what she's already arranged—an account in my name that she'll wire the money to as soon as she's satisfied I've made a clean break with William and left town.

When she's done explaining, I ask, "And if I don't take it?"

Sighing, she shakes her head. "Don't be stupid, Cally. Eventually William is going to come to his senses and see that you're not the girl he wants to spend his life with."

"Is this why you hired Carl York? So I wouldn't have a choice? So I'd have to take your money?"

"Carl York? The PI? Why would I hire him? The foreclosure is public record."

I feel like I've been sucker punched in the solar plexus. If she didn't hire Carl, who did?

"Think about it," she says. "It's a lot of money."

"Bribing me to leave isn't going to buy you William. He's not for sale." I put the words out there. Intentionally baiting her to see if she knows more than she's saying, to see if she'll say, *"But you are."*

"That's a chance I'm willing to take. Will and I were good together. He'll come around. But do you want to know that truth?"

No. I don't want to know the truth. I want to hide from it in fantastical beliefs about wishes and destiny. The truth has done me no favors.

"Even if he doesn't want me back—which, let's face it, he will—it would be worth every penny just so I didn't have to see him with you."

ELECTRIC BILL, gas bill, water bill. My hands shake as I tear through the stack of mail on Dad's kitchen counter.

I freeze when I see it. The New Hope Bank logo on the front left corner. The letter is addressed to my father and explains how the auction will work and the amount he must pay by next Friday if he wants to keep his house.

My stomach goes into a free fall, my heart following shortly behind.

I don't realize he's watching me until I hear him clear his throat. "I've been sending them as much as I can." Worry wrinkles my father's brow and draws his features downward. Suddenly, he looks much older than he is.

"If you've been sending money, why are you going into foreclosure?"

He takes the letter from my hands and taps it nervously on the counter. "I was already so far behind, and I wasn't able to catch up fast enough."

I close my eyes. "If you would have told me, we could have cut our losses on this place and moved you and the girls somewhere else. Instead, you've been throwing good money after bad, and now you're going to lose it all."

"I thought it would work out." His eyes are so sad, and my heart breaks for him. One of the smartest men I've ever met caught up in a delusion.

"*This* is how things 'work out' when you don't take care of them, Dad. *This* is what happens. Everything falls apart and all the work you've done, all the sacrifices you've made amount to nothing."

"Then maybe *nothing* is exactly what the Universe knows we need," he says softly.

"No!" I point my finger in his face and my body trembles with sudden rage. "The *Universe* wants you to take care of your shit. This isn't something that's going to get better by wishing on stars. *Destiny* can't swoop in and save the day."

"Everything happens for a reason, Cally. You have to believe that."

"Believe it? I believe it's an excuse for people who don't want to take responsibility for their own decisions. It's a dream world for men who can't deal with the fact that they've let their families down." I want to rail at him, to tell him the rest. I want to scream that while he was in India telling himself that 'everything happens for a reason,' I was in Vegas, spreading my legs for the highest bidder.

But I bite my tongue. I keep the truth locked inside because I may have sold my body but I didn't sell my heart. And my heart won't let me destroy my father with what I've done.

"You *set me up* for disappointment. You taught me all that magic bullshit and we lost everything." I might spare him from the whole truth but he needs to understand the consequences of his beliefs. "When we first moved to Vegas, I thought the shit life we were living was *my fault*. I hadn't wanted to leave and I had a terrible attitude about it. When Gabby cried at bedtime because her piece of bread wasn't enough to fill her belly, I thought I wasn't *believing* hard enough. Don't assign all your spiritual nonsense to us losing this house. Because that's on *you*."

Dad's eyes fill with tears, and I regret even that much of my confession. Then, out of the corner of my eye, I see Drew as she runs from the room.

"Shit," I mutter.

"I had no idea," Dad says, and the horror on his face is so terrible I wish more than anything I could take it all back. I wish I could package up the terrifying reality of those early days in Vegas and lock it away where it can't hurt anyone else.

"Of course you didn't," I whisper. My anger leaves as quickly as it came, and now I just feel empty.

"I wish you would have…If I'd known…Your mother said…"

"Yeah. I wish you would have known too." I shrug awkwardly. "What's done is done. And we made it out alive."

"You're mother never told me how bad it was."

She was too stoned. But I don't say it. "I need to talk to Drew."

I leave my dad to deal with his shock and find her alone in her room, sitting in a corner, her knees drawn to her chest.

"You made me love this piece-of-shit house," she mutters. "You made me love it, and now I'm losing it too."

"I'm sorry, Drew," I whisper. "I'm going to find a way to fix it. I promise."

"Call Brandon," she says. "Call him and tell him we need money for the house. He'll give it to you."

I squeeze my eyes shut. I've limited Drew's understanding of my relationship with Brandon on purpose. I wouldn't want her to know the truth about her big sister. But as a result, she sees him the way he sees himself, as a knight in shining armor who swept in and saved my family from a life on the streets. "We can't ask Brandon," I say carefully. "I'm not with him anymore."

"Well, it was stupid. Really fucking stupid moving us here. Gabby's finally acting like a normal kid and now she's going to be homeless."

I swallow, but I can't choke down the guilt and regret clogging my throat.

She shrugs, picks at the carpet with her big toe. "Does this mean we have to leave New Hope?"

"No, of course not," I say in a rush. "You're staying. I have to figure out what to do about the house, but you're absolutely staying."

She flicks her eyes up to meet mine. "What about you?"

"I can't," I whisper. And the words tear my heart in two.

chapter twenty-two

Cally

I AM head over heels in love with William Bailey, and it hurts like a bitch.

When I was a little girl, I believed I would grow up and fall in love. I believed that loving would be as natural as breathing. I believed love was inevitable and that it would feel like being wrapped in a warm fleece blanket on an autumn day.

I was right about everything but the last. I had no idea how much love could hurt, and it feels like it's done nothing but hurt me for seven years.

For the last four hours, I covered the floor for Will at the gallery while he set up the new exhibition for opening night this weekend. His muscles bunched and stretched under his T-shirt, and when he caught me watching, I pretended not to be hot and bothered.

Every stolen glance, every time he passes me and stops for just a second to kiss my lips, every squeeze of my hand or pinch of my ass, fills me with hope and breaks my heart all at once.

I haven't told him the sordid truth about my past. Though if someone hired Carl to find out, Will's going to find out soon, whether I tell him or not. I haven't told him about Dad's house either, and time's running short on that too.

William positions another painting and turns to me with a grin, his baby blues sending my girly bits into a whining fit of, *Please!* and *I want that.* "You okay?"

"I'm fine. Good. Great." *I'm a babbling idiot incapable of constructing an intelligent sentence in your presence.* I've been like this since I found out about the foreclosure yesterday. Because the only choice I have is to take Meredith's money. It's pretty ironic that she's offering, since I was planning to leave anyway, but it still kills me to take it. Because if Will doesn't hate me when he finds out what I did seven years ago, he'll hate me for taking her bribe.

He steps closer and takes my face in his hand, tilting my chin up as he studies me. My heart slams in my chest, and my whole core is filled with the push-pull, pain-comfort that comes with loving someone you have to let go. "I think you're working too much."

"I'm fine," I promise.

The bell over the front door jingles, and Hanna and Lizzy Thompson stroll into the gallery.

"We're here to kidnap Cally," Lizzy announces.

Hanna nods. "She works too much, and we're dragging her along for martini night with the girls."

"You guys—"

"We won't take no for an answer," Lizzy says, cutting me off.

"I have to close up for Will so he can finish putting up the fall exhibition."

"Stop being such a workaholic and *live* a little," Lizzy says.

"Back us up, Will," Hanna says. "She works constantly. It's not healthy."

Will's studying me, and I duck my head under his assessing gaze. "They're right," he says. "You need a break. And it's slow today. I've got this. No problem."

"I told you I'd stay and—"

He waves away my objection. "It's not a big deal. The twins are right. It's not healthy to work all the time. You'll burn out." He tugs me against him and lowers his mouth to my ear. "Or you could take me up on my offer to run away with me for a weekend. Cancel your appointments? Spend next weekend in bed in our hotel suite?"

My stomach flips—because, if I take Meredith's money, by next weekend, I'll be gone. I turn to the twins. "Fine. I'll go for one drink."

Lizzy grabs my arm and pulls me toward the door. "Let's get her out of here before she changes her mind."

"Bye," I call lamely over my shoulder as I leave.

"Hello," William calls back.

"Hello," I whisper.

Lizzy pushes me through the doors and rolls her eyes. "I think I just threw up in my mouth a little."

Her Charger is parked out front and she doesn't release me until she's opened the passenger door and shoved me half inside.

I rub my wrist. "Man, you weren't kidding when you said *kidnap*."

"Are you okay?" Hanna asks from the back. "Lizzy doesn't know how strong she is sometimes."

"She's fine!" Lizzy slams my door and comes around to climb in her side. "Brady's for margaritas, or The Wire for martinis?" she asks as she slides her key into the ignition.

"Martinis," Hanna says.

Lizzy turns the car in the direction of The Wire, and I'm almost relieved that they came for me. This might be the only chance I have to say goodbye.

"Would you stop thinking so much?" Lizzy asks. "All you're doing is sitting there, but those wheels in your brain are so busy cranking away, it's making my brain feel like a slacker."

Hanna taps my shoulder. "Thank you for coming with us. We've missed you."

Something squeezes in my chest. "I've missed you guys too."

Lizzy flashes me a sad smile before returning her gaze to the road, and I know there's something they're not saying.

AT THE Wire, it appears every table is taken, but I follow the girls back to a booth and am surprised to see Maggie waiting there.

"I didn't know you were joining us!" I slide in next to her and grab the martini menu.

Maggie exchanges a meaningful look with her sisters, who have taken their positions in the booth across from us.

I set down the menu. "What is it?"

Again with the secret sisterhood of exchanged glances, then, Lizzy: "We need to talk."

"Drinks first!" Hanna protests.

Maggie nods. "Hanna's right. This calls for vodka."

So I sit there with anxiety tearing up my stomach as we wait for our drinks to arrive—Grey Goose with olives for Maggie, chocolate for the twins, and a vodka tonic for me.

"Enough with the suspense," I say after we get rid of the waitress. "What's up?"

"There are some rumors," Hanna hedges.

"And we think you should know about them," Lizzy finishes.

I smile but I don't need a mirror to know it's shaky and doesn't reach my eyes. The PI. Whoever he was working for has told everyone the truth about me. I was hoping it wouldn't get around until after I left. I wince, thinking of my sisters. No. I was hoping it would *never* get around. "What is it?"

Again, the girls exchange looks. Lizzy clears her throat. "Meredith is pregnant."

"Everyone is saying it's Will's," Hanna continues, "and…the timing is right."

I take a swig of my drink. "Pregnant," I murmur. *Holy shit.* No wonder she wants me to leave town.

"She's not coming out and *saying* that it's his." Lizzy puts her hand on mine.

"But she's not denying it either," Hanna adds.

"People are starting to whisper about you," Lizzy admits. "They're calling you a home wrecker."

"Because apparently men in this town aren't responsible for their own dicks," Maggie mutters.

"We're telling them what's what," Hanna assures me. "Despite how she likes to spin it, Will and Meredith were *not* an item when you got to town."

"We don't think Will knows," Lizzy says softly. "But we think you should tell him before she does."

Maggie clears her throat. "Ladies, would you let me and Cally speak privately for a minute?"

The twins scoot out of the booth, leaving me and Maggie alone.

"Listen," Maggie begins, "I like you, and I like how happy Will is when he's with you, so I'll tell you something I wouldn't tell anyone else. There's no way that baby is Will's."

My mouth is dry, and I down half of what's left in one gulp. "I'm pretty sure they slept together," I say. "Even assuming they used protection, nothing is one-hundred-percent effective." What was it Maggie said after I first moved back? That all Will wanted was to get married and have a family? If I hadn't shown up, would he and Meredith be happily pursuing that dream by now?

She gives me a sad smile and drops her eyes to her drink. "Would you just trust me on this one? Meredith may be pregnant, but it is not his baby."

Slowly, I nod. I'm sure she's trying to reassure me because she sees the panic on my face. But she doesn't understand that I can't give William what Meredith can. And I love him enough to let him have with her what he can't have with me.

"Would you excuse me for a minute?" I push out of the booth before she can answer. Suddenly it's too hot in here and I need some fresh air. I don't make it to the door before someone grabs my arm.

When I look up, Meredith's eyes are boring into mine. "Look who's here."

I step back. Shit. I don't want to face her tonight. "Hey, Meredith."

I try to side step her, but she holds on tight. "I had an interesting chat with Carl York today." She actually smiles, as if what Carl told her about me is the best possible news. "I wonder how much William knows about your escapades as a *call girl* back in Vegas."

I stumble backward and my feet tangle under me as my back hits a tray. The next thing I know, glass is shattering and I'm soaked with beer. The smell is more that my stomach can handle but I force myself to take slow, steady breaths.

"I'm so sorry," I say to the waitress, who is also soaked, eyes wide in horror.

"It's okay," she mumbles, dropping to her haunches to pick up shards of glass.

Meredith shakes her head slowly. "Some people cause you nothing but trouble."

I'm stuck in place and before I can unfreeze myself, Lizzy rushes over and grabs towels off the bar. "Let me help you with that." She flashes me a worried look before dropping to her haunches.

"My offer still stands," Meredith says, and then she turns and leaves.

As I busy myself with helping the girls clean up the mess, my stomach surges into my throat at the thought of that bitch living the life I want. A life with William. His babies in her belly. I'll get out of the way and let Will make his choice, but now I know I can't take her money. Because I'm not for sale anymore.

I make excuses to leave early, but Maggie follows me outside. She takes me by the shoulders, determination gleaming in her eyes. "It's not whether or not you make the mistake. It's how you handle it."

"I—"

She squeezes my shoulders. "Do you understand?"

I blink at her and realize she heard Meredith. Maggie knows. "I can't *fix* that," I whisper, and to my horror, tears are spilling down my cheeks. "I can't change what I did."

"You explain what happened. You tell him the truth. You'd be amazed what William Bailey can forgive."

chapter twenty-three

William

"Hey there, Bailey, Carl York here. You're one difficult man to get ahold of!"

I frown into my cell phone. I've been sending his calls to voicemail, trying to forget I hired him. Carl doesn't seem to want me to forget. "What's up, Carl?"

"I got that information you wanted. About that Brandon McHugh guy." He whistles, long and low. "It's a good 'un too."

"I don't need it anymore." Anything I need to know about Cally's ex, she can tell me.

"Oh boy, you want to know this. Trust me."

I close my eyes and rub my temple. The gallery is closed for the night, and I'm alone in my office preparing the last minute details for this weekend's exhibition opening. I don't want to deal with Carl. I want to go find Cally and take her home to my bed.

"Listen," Carl says, "it's up to you, but you already paid me. Might as well get what you paid for, right? You don't have to decide now. I'll put it in the mail so you'll have it all. I gave you an extra piece in there too—did a little digging on Cally Fisher. I was curious, so it's on the house. In the meantime? I wouldn't touch her with a ten foot pole...." He chuckles. "If you know what I'm saying. I know I won't be getting any 'massages' from her again, that's for sure."

I can practically hear his air quotes around the word *massages*. Fucker. I hang up before he can say more.

Cally

MY DAD is going to have to face losing the house. My little run-in with Meredith tonight made that clear to me. The reality of the situation sucks, but I don't see an alternative. The truth is, I won't be around to bail Dad out, and he needs to learn to make better decisions.

When I pull up to the cabin, my heart drops like a thousand shards of glass into my already aching stomach.

Brandon McHugh is leaning against a black SUV. His long legs are crossed at the ankle as he flashes that charming smile in Drew's direction.

The way he's looking at her makes me want to cut off his balls with a rusty razorblade.

I hurry out of my car. "Drew, go inside and set the table for dinner."

Drew scowls. "I'm not hurting anything."

"Go!" I order.

He watches her run into the house. My fifteen-year-old sister. And all at once, I both wish I had a gun and am glad I don't. He turns his attention back to me and shakes his head slowly at my jeans and T-shirt. "Cally baby, I hate seeing you dressed like that."

"You're early," I say softly. "We said two months."

"I have business in Indianapolis and Chicago, so it appears

your time's up. Your sisters are settled, and I'm done waiting."

There's no use arguing. I knew this could happen. "Okay." I look over my shoulder to make sure the girls aren't around to hear. "When do we go?"

His jaw tightens. "I have business to attend to. I'll come for you tomorrow night. But buy some new fucking clothes before then." He sneers. "I can't look at you in that shit. You look *old*."

I force a smile. "Of course."

"You should bring your sisters with you. They're cute. I'll take good care of them."

My stomach pitches. "Not an option," I say steadily. "Dad has legal custody."

He grins. "Drew likes me."

"I have to get their dinner ready." And buy a gun. I really have to buy a gun.

Cally
Seven Years Ago

THE MOONLIGHT calls my name through the bedroom window, and the stars wink at me from the dark midnight sky. Stardust kisses my fingertips. My wishes float in the air like dandelion fluff, waiting for me to catch them. I try to concentrate, to focus so I can stretch to take one into the palm of my hand.

He stops me before I can grab the wish. His hand on my arm, his erection at my back.

His mouth is hot on my ear, and I think of William in a tuxedo. Good, beautiful William, waiting for me to get off the plane so he can take me to prom.

I lost my virginity tonight, just like William and I planned. I wore a beautiful dress that clung to my curves. Sipped wine through the dinner at a fancy restaurant. Danced. An evening orchestrated for perfection. So much just as we planned, and nothing as we planned.

Goosebumps race across my bare skin as his fingers skate up the back of my spine.

"I wanted you from the first moment I saw you. I would have paid anything to have you." Fantasy mingles with reality. His words are hot against my neck, and I close my eyes and imagine William is holding me, speaking to me. The way it was supposed to be. The drugs make that easier than it should be, but I hide inside the fantasy of me and William as this man slides his hand between my legs. I imagine William is holding me after prom, seducing me with his fingers until neither of us can resist, imagine it's William preparing to slide into me again.

"*William*," I murmur.

The man flips me to my back—suddenly, painfully, violently. He pins my hands on either side of my head, squeezing. "What did you call me?"

I blink up at him, and my fantasy skitters away into the night.

"What's my name, sweetheart?" The man over me demands. "Tell me my name."

I try to catch my breath, reorient myself. I lock my gaze to the piercing hazel eyes of the man who bought and paid for the right to my body. The man who owns me now.

"Say it."

"Brandon," I whisper. "Brandon."

William
Present Day

BRANDON MCHUGH is outside Arlen Fisher's cabin, leaning against a gleaming black Cadillac Escalade, smoking a cigarette. He gives me a disinterested once-over as I swing my leg off my bike.

I went to The Wire to track down Cally after Carl York's call, but the girls told me she went home. Idiot that I am, I assumed that meant my house, but she wasn't there.

"Can I help you?" Brandon asks.

"I'm here for Cally."

"She's not available right now. Want me to tell her you stopped by?"

Her car is parked right in front of me, but I'm not going to argue. I shove my hands into my pockets and glare at him. "What are you doing here?"

"I could ask you the same question."

"Me? I'm her boyfriend."

He inclines his chin. "Hmm. That's funny, because when Cally and I made plans for her to move back to Vegas with me, she didn't say anything about a *boyfriend*."

His words are a punch in the gut, and I have to hold strong against my instinct to stagger back. "I'm sure there's a lot she hasn't told you."

"Oh, hell." He chuckles. "I'm such a fan of irony."

I want to knock that grin right off his face. "Where is she?"

He grunts, then cocks his head. "You're not fucking my girl, are you?"

"If you have to ask, is she really your girl? Why don't you get out of here? If she wanted to be with you, she'd be living in Vegas."

He laughs again. "My *wife* and I were just figuring out the details of her return."

Wife. The word slams into me, and I spin on him, nails biting into the flesh of my palms. "Excuse me?"

"Cally's little sisters showed me everything you fixed up for their daddy inside, not to mention the outside. Well done. Can't say I blame you. But she's good. You have to give her that. Not even a couple of weeks away from having me to take care of her, she found you. I guess she knows what men will do for a taste of that pussy."

I don't even make the decision before my arm is swinging. And soon I'm nothing but my anger and my fists and the sharp pain radiating from where his fist connects with my jaw. His fists land twice—a wrecking ball into my cheek and nose—before I manage a solid swing at his jaw. Then I lose track of where I've been hit and the number of punches we've thrown. All I care about is bringing this asshole down, and we're wrapped up in each other, still going hard, when someone pulls me off him.

I'm breathing hard and my vision's blurry. My face feels wet, and I wipe my nose and find my hand covered with blood.

I can faintly make out Cally's dad standing over me, and she's standing a few feet beyond him, hands on her hips. Between us is the asshole. Her *husband*. He hops to his feet and grins like it's nothing.

"There will be no violence on my property," Arlen Fisher growls. He's a quiet man, and that's probably the most I've heard him speak at one time. I wonder if he'll say more or threaten to call the cops, but he just nods, as if he has complete faith that his order will make it so, and then he turns and walks into his house.

"What do you think you're doing?" Cally asks, and I don't know if she's talking to me or him or both of us. I don't fucking care. I just want away from this. From her.

I push myself off the ground, and pain starts settling in places I don't remember getting hit. My side, my left bicep. My knuckles are screaming and the whole right side of my face is on fire.

He slaps her ass, and even though I just promised myself I was getting out of here, I'm ready to go again.

"Will, please," she whispers before I can swing. "Don't." For a quietly whispered word, it's wrapped in enough sadness that I know I've already lost her. He's here for her, and she's going with him. He's the reason she told me she can't stay. Can't or won't?

Her father reappears and hands me a wet towel. I nod gratefully and press it against my bloody nose while Cally takes Brandon's arm and walks him to his car.

"I can't believe she'd be with someone like that."

Her father is staring at me, and I realize I said the words out loud.

"Don't make the mistake of thinking that people don't continue living their lives just because you're not around," he says softly. "Cally isn't the same girl you were with seven years ago, and if you keep trying to pretend she is, you're both going to get hurt."

I draw in a breath. Cally's been trying to give me the same warning and I've ignored her, but suddenly it's painfully obvious that she was right.

I walk back to my bike and every step sends pain radiating through my ribs. Cally is standing at the SUV, using a washcloth to wipe blood from Brandon's face. When she sees me watching, she steps back and drops her hands to her sides. Her eyes go sad as she looks me over.

"Are you okay?" she asks.

I swing my leg over my bike and pain ricochets through my core. "Fucking fabulous." Then I start the engine and pull away. Because I can't handle the idea of her seeing me like this. And because, for the first time, I finally understand what she was telling me. She's not the same woman she once was, and we can't have the relationship we once had.

Cally

"Baby," I whisper. "You're hurting me." William's gone, Brandon's pissed, and my world is shattered.

Fury burns in Brandon's eyes. "You little slut. You've been fucking that asshole."

I shake my head. "No," I whisper. "It's not what you think." My purity, the idea that I had only ever been with *him*, was everything to Brandon. I don't want him going after Will. I can't have him hurting Will more than he already has.

"You fucked him and now you expect me to take you back, to take care of you?" His hands slide from my shoulders to around my neck, resting there, waiting for an excuse. My dad is just inside the house and I say a silent prayer that he's watching, that he'll be able to protect me if Brandon snaps.

"I didn't sleep with him," I say, slowly lifting my hands to his face. "I don't want to be with anyone but you." I have to calm him down before his hands tighten any more at my neck.

"Don't lie to me, Cally. Not about this."

"I wouldn't." The lie is a dangerous one. All he would have to do is ask around town and he'll learn the truth. I've been careless, too determined to soak up every ounce of a life I knew I'd have to leave behind.

"I *saved* you," he whispers, his face going sad and his hands dropping from my neck to take mine. "You were days from being on the street and I saved you."

That's his favorite story to tell. He'd hold me at night and repaint our ugly beginnings in the broad strokes of his twisted perception. As if he didn't pay Anthony tens of thousands of dollars for the privilege of taking my virginity. As if he didn't force me to marry him so he could control me even more than before. "I helped your family. How do you repay me? You don't even visit me while I'm in prison."

"I—I didn't think you wanted to see me," I lie. "You were with her." But I can tell he sees through my excuse now. He always has.

"I told myself I would get you back as soon as I got out, but you tried to push me out of your life like I didn't *save* you." He has tears in his eyes. Actual, glistening *tears*. "You. Hurt. Me," he growls, hands returning to my neck. "I thought you would need me again after your mom's drug overdose. I was so sure that would bring you back to me."

"Brandon," I gasp when his hands tighten. "You're hurting me."

He stumbles back, his hands curling into fists. "I can't look at you right now." Then he climbs into his car and tears out of the drive, kicking up dust.

I don't know how long I'm standing there before I feel Gabby at my side. "I don't like him," she says. "He came to the apartment the morning Mom died. I never liked him."

I turn and blink at her. "Brandon was at the apartment the morning mom died?" Then Brandon's words sink in. *"I thought you would need me again after your mom's drug overdose. I was so sure that would bring you back to me."*

I never told Brandon mom died of a drug overdose. I told him she had a heart attack. Just like I told everyone else.

"I was so sure that would bring you back to me."

Suddenly, everything is too clear. After years, Mom was doing better, even holding a steady job. Then suddenly a drug overdose? And how did Brandon know?

I thought I could run away. I thought I could hide from Brandon. I thought leaving New Hope would be enough to protect the people I love. But the only way I can protect them is if I give Brandon what he wants. They won't be safe until he has me or he's in prison again.

WILL'S HOUSE is dark, but I'm sure he's here. Where else is he going to go with his face torn up like that?

The door's locked, but he gave me a key last month when I was staying here with the girls. When I tried to give it back, he insisted I keep it. Now I'm glad.

Evening sunlight slants through the windows and spills across the hardwood floors at the back of the house. I know I haven't seen the last of Brandon. He'll be back for me soon. He was pissed. Ugly, nasty angry, and I don't have long. Not unless I want him to come after William. Brandon bought me years ago, and in his mind he still owns me.

But my heart belongs to William.

William's kitchen and living room are empty. He's not resting on the couch in the family room like I thought he might be. I follow the dark hall to the master bedroom and find his curtains drawn, making it darker in here than the rest of the house. In the dim light trickling in from the hallway, I spot him, sprawled on top of the comforter in nothing but his boxer briefs.

I step into the room quietly. The soft and steady rise and fall of his chest gives me the courage to go closer so I can look at his face. His cheek is twice the size of the one opposite it, and the bruise there extends up to his eye, which is puffy and possibly swollen shut. His lip is cracked.

I continue my study of his injuries and drop my gaze to his bandaged knuckles and the angry red bruise at his ribs.

"What are you doing here?"

I jump at his words. He's awake but not moving. "I just came to check on you," I say softly, lowering myself on the edge of the bed by his side. "I've been worried."

He reaches to the bedside table and clicks on the light. "You seemed real damn worried about me when you were tending to your *husband's* injuries."

I swallow the hurt his words bring and don't bother defending myself. "I didn't want him to hit you again."

"I can handle myself."

Of course he can against most guys, but Brandon eats and breathes fighting. God knows what new skills he learned while he was locked up. Just remembering coming outside to see Brandon swinging at Will is enough to make me lose my breath all over again.

I have to touch him. In the near-darkness, I find his lip and trace the split with my fingertip. Then I touch his swollen cheek, his puffy eye. "I thought he was going to kill you." He doesn't reply, nor does he complain as my fingers take inventory of the rest of his face—the injured and healthy spots equally.

After my hands have finished their tour and slide to his hair, my lips follow the path of my fingers in reverse. I kiss his swollen eye, his cheek, his jaw. He doesn't move.

When I come to his mouth and finally press my lips to his injured ones, he grabs my wrists and holds me still. Suddenly, my tentative exploration of his wounds becomes his exploration of my mouth. His hands are in my hair, and he's pulling me down on the bed, rolling until I'm under him.

And today sucked so badly I let myself have this moment like a reward for enduring. Here, in the dark of his bedroom, his nearly naked body over my fully clothed one, everything between us falling to pieces, this kiss is the least we deserve. It feels like a secret gift we're both entitled to. So I open under him, kissing him back and rubbing my tongue against his, and when his hand snakes up my shirt, hot and greedy, I arch into his touch like Brandon isn't coming for me, like kissing William when I need to be telling him goodbye isn't the worst idea I've ever had.

I have to touch him. I need it more than I need air. But when I explore his body, his breath leaves him in a hiss and his lips abandon mine.

"I'm leaving tomorrow night," I whisper.

"He's making you. Before he ever showed up in town, you were thinking of staying. He's making you leave, isn't he?"

"I want to go." The words are heavy with lies and I fight to heave them off my tongue. "I'm sorry."

"You can tell me if you're scared. I'll protect you from him."

But who will protect you from Brandon? I swallow. I don't know what's going to happen tomorrow, and I need William to let me go. "Why would I be scared of my own husband?"

"You can tell me the truth, Cally."

I roll back my shoulders. "The truth is that I'm leaving, just like I planned from the beginning."

The pain in his eyes isn't just the physical kind. I've hurt this man. Just like I knew I would.

chapter twenty-four

William

"You CAN leave then." I roll off her and sit on the edge of the bed, cradling my head in my hands. When she doesn't move, I growl, "Go back to your husband, Cally."

She sits up and positions herself next to me. So damn close it hurts. She rests her elbows on her knees, her head in her hands, and I realize for the first time what a wreck she is. She looks like she hasn't slept for days, like she's been ravaged by grief and worry and...more.

She lets out a long, slow breath. "Meredith's pregnant. Did you know that?"

"What does Meredith have to do with anything?"

"Everyone is saying it's yours."

I have to laugh at that. Same old joke coming back to me. "I can guarantee you it's not mine."

"But you slept with her before I came back. It could be."

"Just—" I shake my head and push off the bed. Why are we even talking about this? "Believe what you want, okay? It doesn't fucking matter anymore."

"It does matter," she whispers. "It matters because she can give you the life you want. The marriage, the children. I can't."

"Right. Because you're already married."

"I'm sorry I didn't have the courage to tell you the truth about…my past. But I was up front with you about what I could and couldn't offer."

I can't stomach this conversation. I love Cally enough to need more from her. "You weren't *up front* with me about the fact that you were married." She draws in a shaky breath, and I'm so damn hurt, her pain only pisses me off. "Whatever. I'm done with this conversation."

"I was selfish and I'm sorry for that." She turns to me and puts her hand to my face. A tear rolls down her cheek. "I hope you have an amazing life. You *deserve* an amazing life."

"*Leave*," I growl. "Put your key on the front table on your way out."

She walks to the door and hesitates.

"Goodbye, Cally."

Cally

SATURDAY NIGHT, I'm waiting for Brandon with a packed suitcase and an illegally purchased gun.

If I tell Brandon I won't go with him, I risk him hurting me, or worse, hurting William, Dad, or one of the girls. But I can't go back to being his doll and living under his rule. Three years of that was three too many. The worst kind of prison is the kind that disguises itself as home.

My grand plan is to wait until I know Brandon has drugs in his possession and tip off the police. It shouldn't take long since I know that's the "business" he's in town for. The gun is Plan B. A pretty shitty Plan B, but better than none at all.

My phone rings. I don't recognize the number, but I accept the call because I expected Brandon to be here by now and I'm starting to get nervous. If he killed mom, what else will he do?

"Hello?"

"Cally?"

"Drew? Where are you?"

"I'm in Indianapolis." She's whispering and her voice is thick with tears. "I'm at the big hotel by the stadium. Can you come get me? Please?"

The whole world goes still around me. She told me she was staying with a friend tonight. "What are you doing there?"

"I'm scared. Please come get me." She takes in a shaky, hicuppy breath. Hell, she's crying. "Please."

"Are you with Brandon?" Even as I hope she'll say no, I already know she is.

"Don't be mad. He said that if I came with him, he'd give me the money for Dad's house, but he's scaring me. He gave me these clothes. A dress and this skimpy underwear and he made me put them on." Another shaky sob. "He said he'd kill me if I called the police. He has some people here in the other room now. He doesn't know I'm on the phone. He keeps calling me *Cally* and he won't let me leave. I'm scared. Please come get me."

"I'm on my way." Fear skates through my stomach on a razor edge, leaving shreds behind. I close my eyes and grab my purse. My gun is inside, and I say a prayer I won't have to use it. "I'll be there as fast as I can."

William

THE LAST thing I am in the mood for tonight is the opening for the fall exhibition. The doors to the event opened an hour ago, and I've spent most of it in my office, hiding my face and my mood from unsuspecting patrons.

There's a knock on my door, and I ignore it, leaning back in my chair and closing my eyes. My solitude is destroyed at the scrape of a key in the lock. Which can mean only one thing: Maggie. No one else has the key to my office.

She sweeps through the door, wearing a long, strapless black dress, her hair in some sort of twist at the back of her head. The minute she sees me, her jaw drops and her eyes widen.

"Holy shit!"

"I know. I really make this suit, don't I?"

She grins and tilts her head to inspect the bruises on my face. "Of course you do, and once I get past the ground burger someone made of your face, maybe I can appreciate that. What happened?"

"I cut myself shaving."

She props her hands on her hips and narrows those sharp green eyes. "Does this have something to do with Cally?"

"She's not responsible for my stupidity."

"Who did this?"

"Give the credit to the asshole she's married to."

Her face falls and she lowers herself into a chair. "She's married?"

"She's not only married, she's leaving. Or she already left. Fuck if I know." I lean back. My body aches in places I didn't know I had, and my heart hurts so fucking bad I wish I could cut it out of my chest. "I knew she had secrets, but I never imagined this."

"Did she tell you the rest of her secrets?"

"The rest of what secrets? She's fucking married. If there's something worse than that, I don't want to know it."

"The truth is always more complicated than it appears," Maggie says softly. "Maybe the same is true of her marriage."

I shake my head. "She was talking about staying until the first time he showed up, then everything changed. I thought maybe she was afraid of him."

"How do you know she's not?"

I set my jaw against the pain, remembering the conversation. "I asked. I told her I'd protect her." And fuck if my pride isn't in worse shape than my face. She chose him over me. I should be used to this shit by now.

"You big idiot. How hard did he hit your head? A woman who's afraid of her husband is going to lie about it nine times out of ten. But when looking at the mess said husband made of her lover's face, she's going to lie about it one-hundred percent of the time. She's trying to protect you."

I hear a sharp gasp and I look up to see Meredith standing in the doorway.

"Who did this to you?" she demands. Her heels click against the floor as she rushes over to me and gently touches my face. "You don't have to tell me. I already know that girl has something to do with this. I wish you'd stay away from her."

"You should see the other guy," I grumble.

She turns to Maggie. "What happened to him?"

"I'm sitting right here," I growl.

"He got in a bar fight."

Meredith narrows her eyes. "A *bar* fight?"

Maggie nods sagely. "I told him he needs to stop hanging out at the titty bar, but does he listen to me? *No*, he doesn't."

I scowl at her. "Seriously?"

"I don't believe for a second this happened at a titty bar," Meredith says.

She shrugs. "Tell your sweet little girl here the truth, Will. Tell her you can't get enough of the titty bar."

"Would you both stop saying *titty bar*?" I blow out a hard breath, hoping to send some of my frustration with it. "Maggie, will you excuse us? Meredith and I need to talk."

"Fine," Maggie says, standing begrudgingly. "I'll be downstairs doing *your job* if you need me. But think about what I said."

I wait until Maggie closes the door behind her before I speak. "I hear congratulations are in order."

Meredith's cheeks flush and she drops her gaze to her hands. "Thank you."

"I also hear everyone thinks it's mine."

"I didn't say that. Not to anyone."

"But you didn't correct them."

"I thought it would be better this way. You know, in case we reconcile."

"Do you hear yourself? You're batshit crazy, woman."

She lifts her eyes to mine and they're glistening with unshed tears. "I'm not crazy. I'm in love. Your grandmother told me you can't have children. She told me about the football accident. I knew how much you wanted a family and I thought....Well, I thought if I could give it to you, maybe you'd choose me."

She's biting her lip and worry lines crease her forehead. She's really beautiful, and I know she can give me all the things I've spent the last three years craving madly—a life, a family, love. But I don't just want those things. I want them with Cally.

"I'm sorry," I say. "You and I will never work."

"Because you love Cally."

"Yeah." And it's true. I still love her. Still want her. I'd forgive her for all of it to have her in my arms just one more time.

"Well, at least you know she loves you too."

"How do you figure?"

She looks at her hands for a minute before bringing her eyes back up to meet mine. "I offered her twenty-thousand dollars to leave town and stay away from you."

"You did what?"

"I thought she was going to take it. I really did. But she didn't." She shakes her head. "I love you, and I knew she needed the money."

"Jesus, Meredith! That's not love! That's manipulation. You've got to be kidding me."

She throws her hand over her chest. "I don't *want* her dad to lose the house. I thought it was a nice compromise. But apparently she's going to let you pay for *that* too."

"Why would her dad lose the house? What are you talking about?"

"She didn't tell you? Arlen Fisher's house is in foreclosure. The bank is going to auction it off."

"Shit." I drag a hand through my hair. Of course she didn't tell me. She doesn't want my money.

"Can I ask you something without you getting angry with me?"

"You just told me that you offered the woman I love twenty-thousand dollars to leave town."

She nods. "Okay. Point taken. So, nothing to lose, right?"

"I don't want to talk to you about Cally." I push back my chair and stand.

"This isn't about her. Not exactly." She stands too and skirts around me until I'm looking at her. "You say you want family and stability, but have you ever noticed that you tie yourself to women who you know can't or won't give you that?"

I step back. "I don't know what you're talking about."

She lifts a finger. "First, Maggie, who never loved you, not the way you deserve at least." She holds up a second finger. "Then Krystal, who would have been the perfect choice—except she's Maggie's sister, so that was doomed from the start." She holds up three fingers. "And now Cally? Even if you can get over her juvenile record, she's married, and to a man who spent the last four years in prison no less. You say you want something real and I'm standing right here, but you're choosing her instead."

My jaw hardens and it aches from where Brandon's knuckles connected with it yesterday. "What do you want from me, Meredith?"

She shrugs. "I just want you to be honest with yourself. It's okay if you want to be alone. It's really all you've ever known— being alone and wishing for more. That's safe for you. But at least do me the courtesy of admitting it."

"I don't want to be alone. But that doesn't mean I want to be with you." I exhale slowly. "I never meant to hurt you." Then her words sink in. "Cally's husband spent the last four years in prison?"

Jesus. How young was she when she married him?

"Didn't you read the file Carl York put together for you? It's all in there. The dirt on her husband, their marriage certificate, the juvie record from her escapades as a call girl."

Her words hit me hard and unprepared. "Her escapades as what?"

"You didn't even look at it, did you? You're rejecting me for a former *prostitute*. Don't you get that?"

I ignore her and dig through the stack of paperwork on my desk until I find the unopened manila envelope Carl York mailed to me. I tear it open and flip through the papers, past the background check on Brandon McHugh, past Cally's juvenile record, until I reach the copy of their marriage certificate. The date stares up at me in bold, black print. "She was sixteen."

"Her mom would have had to give written consent. You'd think she would have looked into him before permitting it." She leans over me and flips through more papers until she pulls the one she's been looking for. "Two years before he married Cally, he got picked up with an underage prostitute. Apparently he has a thing for the young ones. Heck, maybe prostitution is how they met. Like in *Pretty Woman*."

I'm already grabbing my keys. I need to find her. I need to stop her from leaving. Her words echo in my head. *"I loved you enough to let you go. That's the truth. Someday soon I'll have to do it again, and it will still be the truth, even if you can't accept it."* She isn't leaving with Brandon because she loves him. She's leaving because she loves me.

"You really don't care about her past?" Meredith asks behind me as I rush toward the door.

"It's called unconditional love, Meredith. I recommend you try it."

Maggie bursts into the office. "I just got a call from the Marion County jail. They're holding Cally for shooting her husband."

chapter twenty-five

Cally

LAST NIGHT, I did something I've wanted to do for seven years. I told my story to the police. The whole thing. From my mom's drug addiction to the loan I took from Anthony to how I came to meet and marry Brandon McHugh to why I shot him.

Okay, I did two things I've wanted to do for seven years. I told the police my story and I shot the bastard who thought I was something that could be bought.

Honestly, once I'd told my whole story, I think the detectives were surprised I didn't aim for center mass when I found Drew in his hotel room.

Brandon will be going back to prison. There was already a warrant for his arrest in Nevada, and he had all sorts of drugs in his hotel room. I don't know too many details. I don't care about anything but the fact that Drew is safe, and I managed to get away from Brandon without killing him.

When the police cruiser drops me off at Dad's, the sun is starting to rise. The first thing I do is look for Drew. She's sitting on the couch, arms wrapped around her middle, and I sink down next to her and pull her tight against me.

The silence is sweet, and I'm scared to break it. When the police came, they separated us for questioning, so I didn't get to ask any questions.

Right here, in this quiet moment, I am blissfully ignorant of what happened to her before I got to the hotel room. I almost don't want her to speak, as if me not hearing the truth could save her from it. But that only works one way, and tonight it's Drew that needs saving.

"I'm going to ask you questions, and I need you to tell me the truth."

"You're going to be so mad at me," she whispers. It's dark in the living room, the morning sun just now starting to show her head outside our windows. I can barely make out the tear streaks that glow against her perfectly smooth skin.

"What's done is done, Drew. I need to know some things."

"Okay."

I take a breath. It feels like the first I've taken in days. My chest is still tight with panic. Even with Drew next to me—safe—it's still hard to breathe. "Are you hurt?"

"He slapped me. Shoved me a little. But I'm okay."

My squeeze my eyes shut. Questions are screaming through my brain at a hundred miles an hour. *Why did you go to a hotel room with him? Why did you lie to me?* What were you thinking? I have to push them all aside. *Triage.* "Did he rape you?"

She spins to me. Her eyes are big and her red-painted mouth is slack, her cheeks smeared with mascara. She looks so young. Like a child caught playing in her mother's makeup.

"I need to know, Drew." But more, she needs to tell it. I can't have a dark secret eating my sister from the inside, not when I know the kind of damage that can do.

Her teeth sink into her bottom lip and she tugs at her too-short skirt. I recognize the outfit as the one Brandon had me wear the first night he had sex with me. God help me, he was trying to recreate that night with Drew. "No. He didn't touch me. He kissed me. Groped me over my clothes a little. But I cried and that pissed him off. He didn't have a chance to do anything else."

Thank you, dear God. Something loosens in my chest and I can breathe a little deeper. "That's good. That's so good."

"I was so scared, Cally. I know that's what he planned." Her words are muffled by her sobs. "I thought that maybe I should do it, you know. He said he wanted to help us. To save me, to save our house. I just had to be—" She hiccups out a sob. "I just had to be his good girl. But I couldn't…."

"Never!" I force myself to relax, force my voice to quiet. I could scream at her. Scold her. Tell her how stupid that was. And maybe I'll do all of that. Another day. When my heart isn't so completely pulverized. "You don't ever sacrifice yourself like that. You are worth more than a pretty dress. More than a meal on the table. More than a house. You hear me? Never forget what you're worth." It hurts so much to have this conversation that I almost want to ask her to stop. Instead, I reach over, and grab her hand from where she's fidgeting with her skirt. I lace our fingers together, and I squeeze. "There are some parts of yourself that, once you sell, you can never get back."

"Are you in trouble? For shooting him?"

"Not much." I'll have to go before a judge, but my lawyer didn't think I'd have to do much beyond some community service hours for the illegal handgun.

"I should have listened to you. You told me to stay away from him."

"Shh." I pull her against my chest and stroke her hair. "It's over now. You're safe."

William

CALLY'S LEAVING. I keep repeating the words to myself, as if maybe that will make them finally sink in.

She's here now. I can hear her in the apartment upstairs. But she's leaving.

I turn off the gallery lights and lock the door. When I went to Indianapolis last night, they were questioning her and wouldn't let me see her. Then this morning when I went to her dad's place, the trunk of her car was open and suitcases were piled inside. I tried not to panic, but Maggie heard her on the phone canceling her appointments for next week, and I can't deny the truth anymore. *She's leaving.*

I need to see her before she goes. Feel her. Taste her. I need to make sure I never forget her.

I catch her in the massage room.

"Are you okay?" My voice is rough, as battered as my heart and body.

"I'm fine." She gives me a soft smile but it falls away when I push her against the wall. "Well, hello to you too."

Pushing close, I spread her legs with my knee until she's positioned against my thigh.

"I'm so sorry," she whispers, sliding her hands into my hair. "For everything."

I open my mouth against her neck and suck, not caring that it will leave a mark. I'm desperate to chase away the gnawing pain I've felt since Brandon called her his wife, to wash away the horror I felt at reading the file Carl put together. When I think about her selling her body to someone, when I think how bad things must have been to make her resort to that, I want to punch something. I want another shot at Brandon.

I grip the bottom of her shirt in both hands and pull it off over her head before shoving her pants from her hips.

"Yes," she whispers. "Please. I need you." But then I drop to my knees and press my open mouth against the cotton polka dots of her underwear, and she stops talking altogether.

I slide my tongue against her panties, saturating them with my tongue as my hands find their way up the back of her thighs and take an ass cheek in each hand.

"Oh my God."

Repositioning my mouth right over her clit, I suck at her through the cotton. Her hands are in my hair, pulling as her hips rock instinctively toward my mouth.

I grab her wrists and position them at her sides, holding them there as I kiss my way up her body.

Her eyes are on me, dark and smoky with need, and I draw her hands from her sides to above her head, where I shackle them with one of mine.

She's so fucking gorgeous in a lacy pink bra and polka dot panties, her chest rising and falling as she tries to catch her breath from my assault.

I can't resist those perfect lips, so I press my mouth to hers, slide our tongues together until she's rocking into my thigh again.

"I'm going to release your hands, but I want you to leave them above your head."

Her dark eyes go smoky with approval as I pop open the front release on her bra. Her breasts fill my hands and I lower my head, drawing her nipple into my mouth, toying with it with my tongue, then teeth. She cries out and her fingers tug on my hair, forcing me to stop too soon.

"Hands above your head," I order. Heat flashes in her eyes as she obeys, and I return to her neck, trailing my mouth over the sensitive bit of flesh under her ear and down to her collarbone. I flatten my palm against her stomach and fan my fingers over her hipbones, my thumb over the ring in her navel.

"Turn to face the wall," I command.

She obeys without question and leaves her hands above her head as I explore the bare skin of her back with my hands and then my mouth. She obeys me completely with her stillness as I explore her. As I trail kisses down her spine, I slide off her panties. With one hand around her hip, I slide the other between her legs.

"Slide your legs apart for me."

She leans into the wall and does as I ask, arching enough to expose her sweet sex to me.

"*Jesus.* You're so damn beautiful." I cup her with my hand, using my fingers to tease her as I scrape my teeth over one ass cheek then the other.

She whimpers, and I drive two fingers inside of her, curling them until her legs are unsteady and her muscles are flexing. When she's close, I open my mouth to that sensitive spot just at the base of her spine and suck until she's coming apart on my hand.

Cally

I'M CLINGING to the wall for dear life as I recover, but I've hardly caught my breath when William's mouth is back at my ear. "Face me, sweetheart."

I turn on wobbly legs and reach for the button on his jeans, desperate to get him nude, to feel his skin against mine. I unzip him and release him from his boxers. Before I can push them off his hips, he's hoisting me up between his body and the wall, sliding into me fast, hard, and hungry.

I cry out in pleasure as he pushes deep.

"That's right, baby," he murmurs. "Let me hear you."

He uses the strength in his arms to hold me up, and his muscles bunch under his shirt. He's manic, driven by something he isn't sharing with me. He presses his face into the crook of my neck, and all I can do is hold on and pray he's finding what he needs in me.

He's swelling inside me, so close to the edge, and he groans into my neck and presses my weight into the wall so he can slip his hand between our bodies. He's holding back, putting off on his own release.

"Come for me again, sweetheart. Let me feel you." His fingers are relentless against me, his whispered demands hot in my ear. It doesn't take long before I shatter. Only then does he let go, his hips jerking and his head falling back as he finally releases inside me.

After, he takes me to the shower in the apartment and washes me slowly and thoroughly, pressing gentle kisses to where his mouth was rough minutes before.

We don't bother going back to his place or getting dressed. We lock the doors to the apartment and curl up on the couch, clinging to each other.

I keep thinking the words I need to say but they refuse to find their way to my tongue. But I don't want to ruin the perfection of this moment by explaining my ugly past.

"Why'd you do it?" His question is so soft, I almost don't realize he's speaking.

"What?"

He swallows so hard I can hear it. "Is it true? You were a prostitute?"

My heart pounds, but I concentrate on the feel of his skin under my cheek, his arms wrapped tightly around my waist. "It's true."

"That's why you broke up with me, isn't it? Your mom was stoned out of her mind and you sold yourself for money for your sisters." His voice is so calm, so rational—a complete contrast to the chaos of pain and hope warring in my chest. How can he know this and not hate me?

"I messed up," I confess. "I took a loan from a man I knew I shouldn't trust, and when I couldn't pay it off, he threatened Gabby and Drew."

"You became a call girl to pay off a loan?"

I shake my head against his chest, then push myself up so I can look at his face. His eyes are full of hurt, and I wish I could take that away for him. "This is what the man does. He finds women who are in trouble and he gives them loans to keep them afloat. Then he requires them to 'work off' their debt."

"Jesus," he breathes. He squeezes me tight and pulls my head down to his chest again.

"I can hardly think about it. I hate thinking that anyone else touched you, but to think men paid for it." A shudder moves through him, and he sits me up and climbs off the couch to pace. "Dammit, Cally, you were a fucking virgin. Didn't he know?"

I close my eyes. His agitation makes me feel both better and worse. Better because I'm not alone. Worse because now he's suffering with me. "I was more valuable to him once he found out." I swallow hard, not wanting to share this ugliness with him, but knowing I need to tell him more. "I gave blow jobs to a few of his special clients, and then he played them off each other and gave the highest bidder my virginity." I want to spare him the pain I see on his face, but I make myself keep going. "Brandon won that honor."

He stops pacing and runs a hand over his face.

I make myself keep going. "Knowing I'd been a virgin only fueled Brandon's obsession with me." An obsession that began the moment I ran out of his condo, too terrified to do what I'd been sent to do.

"But what you told me was true? You've been tested? You're healthy?"

"Of course! I wouldn't have risked giving you something."

"I'm not worried about me, Cally!" He pulls me off the couch and crushes me to his chest. "You're all I care about. Don't you get that?"

"I was telling you the truth when I told you I haven't been with anyone for four years. It's true. Brandon bought my virginity, but the man who'd given me the loan expected me to keep working. He threatened my life, my sisters. Brandon said he'd pay the guy off, get him to leave me alone, if I'd marry him. He promised to take care of me and give me money for my family, so I told mom I was in love with him and made her consent."

"Did the girls know any of this?"

I shake my head. "Not about the loan or the prostitution or even the marriage. Mom and I thought it would give them the wrong idea about when they should get married and agreed not to tell them. Brandon gave me just enough to keep them off the streets but never enough that I felt like I could run away. He controlled every aspect of my life from the moment he bought me until he was put in prison four years ago."

He pulls me into his arms. "I wish you would have told me."

"I hated the idea of you knowing what I'd done."

He presses his lips to my hair. "I think I knew. I told you I would imagine the worst, and when I saw the look in your eyes when I brought up the past, I knew it was much worse than anything I'd imagined before."

"I'm sorry I couldn't tell you. I thought you'd hate me."

"How could I hate you for something like this?"

I shrug. "I made a choice."

He takes my shoulders and steps back until I'm looking him in the eyes. "A choice made out of fear is no choice at all."

I snuggle back into his heat. Through the sliding glass doors that look out over the river, I can see the stars cradled in the dark night sky. I take my time, selecting a favorite for the first time in seven years, and then I muster the courage to dare one more wish. "I love you," I confess. "I never stopped."

"I love you too. Always." He tangles his hand in my hair and holds me close. "Don't leave me, Cally. You fill my hollow places. You make me whole. Please stay."

I lean back and frown up at him. "Where do you think I'm going?"

"I saw you packing your car this morning. There were suitcases in your trunk, and you were canceling all your appointments."

"Just five days. Asher Logan's letting me use his beach house on Lake Michigan for a week with the girls. Drew needs some time before going back to school."

He squeezes me tighter. "And after that? You're staying?"

"There's nowhere else I'd want to be."

chapter twenty-six

William

SEEING CALLY for the first time in a week is like a punch in the gut and an instant high all at once. Midweek, I caved and asked Maggie to tell me the address, but she refused, promising me the best thing I could give Cally right now is time.

So I made it five days and now she's standing in front of me in long sleeve T-shirt, her hands tucked into the pockets of her jeans. The wind whips her dark hair around her face, and she looks so damn beautiful I can't resist reaching out to tuck some of those wild wisps behind her ear.

"What are you doing here?" she asks softly.

"The bank is auctioning the house today," I explain, as if she wasn't already painfully aware of this fact.

Her shoulders tense. "I know you mean well, but sometimes people need to face the consequences of their decisions. For my dad, that will be losing this house."

"You won't let me buy it for you then?"

"I won't," she whispers.

"What about us?" Lizzy asks from behind me. She and Hanna

were in the back of my car and apparently decided now was as good a time as any to make their presence known.

"What?" Cally asks. "You guys don't have enough money to buy this house."

"Not alone," Lizzy says, "but maybe if we went in with some friends."

"They say when you're young is the best time to invest," Hanna says sagely.

I nod, just as an oversized black pickup pulls in the drive.

"What's Asher Logan doing here?"

"I guess maybe he's looking at investment properties too," I say. "And this is a prime piece of real estate, right by the river, not to mention the sentimental value it holds. He and I bonded over that roof, you know. Can't put a price tag on male bonding."

Max and Sam appear next, cutting through the grass up the trail from the paved path along the river. "Count us in, too," Max calls. "That dock back there has the best fishing all along the river."

Cally's eyes brim with tears. "You guys."

"I'm in, too," Gabby says behind her. Cally turns and Gabby places a bright pink Minnie Mouse bank in her hands. "You got this for me when you took us to Disney Land. You told me to save for something magical. I think this place will do just fine."

Drew steps forward next, her jaw hard and her eyes moist. "I'm in, too," she says, handing Cally a wad of cash. "That's what I was saving for a new iPhone, but I don't need it. My best friends are all here in New Hope."

Cally looks at the Minnie Mouse bank and cash in her hands. "So you're all going to go in together and buy my dad's house?"

I lift my hands. "Not me."

Her brow wrinkles. "Not you?"

I shake my head. "I can't have you accusing me of trying to buy you when I ask you to be my girl. But the rest of them, yes."

"As long as you're in this town," Hanna says, "you don't have to face anything alone."

"I—I don't even know what to say."

"You can tell them that won't be necessary," Arlen calls, the porch screen squeaking behind him as he comes down into the lawn to join everyone else. "I visited the bank this morning and got it taken care of."

Cally's jaw goes slack, but I'm sure mine does too.

Arlen shifts uncomfortably as everyone stares. "While you girls were gone last week, I auctioned off my books."

"The autographed ones?" Cally's eyes are wide. "You've been collecting those my whole life."

He lifts a shoulder in an awkward shrug. "My daughters are more important than some autographed papers."

"Daddy," Cally whispers. Then in three long strides she's wrapping her arms around him and leaning her head into his chest.

"Does this mean Asher Logan isn't going to be part owner of a house with me?" Drew asks. "Because that is a total bummer."

Asher grabs something out of his truck and walks it over to Drew. "Here you go, kiddo. How's that for a consolation prize?"

Her eyes go wide as she takes the CD from his hands. "Oh. My. God. Is this the new album? It doesn't even release for months!"

He grins. "Thanks for being such an awesome fan."

"Huh," Lizzy says. "My mom said she wanted to see me do something responsible with my money. I guess I'm going to have to find something else now."

"We could go shoe shopping?" Hanna suggests.

"That's a plan," Lizzy says. "Maggie, can you and your stud give us a ride back to Mom's?"

Everyone clears out and the girls head back into the house with their dad, and finally I'm alone with Cally.

I clear my throat. "I have a bone to pick with you."

Cally

I spin around at the sound of Will's voice.

His eyes blaze, nearly predatory, as he takes three slow steps and closes the space between us. "You tried to get rid of me by pushing me off on some other woman."

I hang my head and study my shoes. "I just want you to have the best life possible."

"Yeah, but I would have thought you'd do better. Meredith? She's scheming and manipulative and kind of a bitch."

I snap my head up and bite back my smile.

"I mean, sure, she's beautiful, and you're right about me wanting kids. It's true, I do. And I guess it's nice that Grandma likes her, though—between you and me—I think me falling in love with troubled girls keeps Grandma's mind young. You wouldn't want my grandmother to get senile, would you?"

"No," I say, keeping my face somber. "I wouldn't want that."

"And, anyway, Meredith is a blond, and I know that's a thing for a lot of guys, but I really prefer brunettes."

"It's important to know what you want."

He's so close I can feel his heat and have to fight the urge to wrap myself up in his warmth. "If you wanted to choose the woman for me to spend my life with, you totally missed the boat. I thought you knew me better than that."

"My apologies. Maybe I could try again if you gave me a bulleted list."

"Hmm…well, I'm not really into girls who will let me own their mind. I'd like a girl who can think for herself."

"That's important."

He settles his hands on my hips and lowers his mouth next to my ear. "And I don't mean to be picky, but she needs to be amazing.

You know the type, loves with all of her heart and thinks I'm a sex god."

A wicked tendril of electricity zips up my spine. "Hmm, and how would you confirm that?"

He nips at my earlobe. "Maybe by the way she screams my name when I make her come."

I swallow. Hard. "I'm not sure I want to know how other women sound when you make them come."

He pulls back and his eyes drop to my mouth. He's a breath away. I could push up on my toes and taste those lips. "But you asked what I want."

"The baby's really not yours?"

"I can't have kids, Cally. The baby's not mine." He cups my face in his hand. "So I guess you need to add to that list a woman who could handle life with a man who can't have children. She'd need to be okay with fertility interventions or adoption."

My eyes fill. "I could handle that."

"I could also use a decent massage." He grins and rolls his shoulders back.

"We might be able to arrange that."

"I want you, Cally." Then his mouth is on mine and his hands are in my hair. This isn't the gentle, loving kiss of my high school sweetheart. And I don't kiss him back like an innocent girl with her first love. This is the hard, punishing, demanding kiss of a man who's finally taking what he wants and the woman who's giving it to him.

I open under him and moan into his mouth, clinging to his shirt as I surrender to the kiss—the brush of our tongues, the wicked nipping of his teeth.

When we finally break the kiss, he leans his forehead against mine and we both struggle to catch our breath. "Now it's time for you to head back in the house and break the news to your father."

"What news?"

"That his girls won't all be living with him. That you're moving in with me. I'm also going to need you to divorce that asshole you're married to. Call me a caveman if you must, but I don't share."

epilogue

Cally
Six Months Later

WHEN I get home from the massage studio, the house is dark and empty.

My phone buzzes in my hand, and I open the text message: *Go to the bedroom.*

Biting back a smile, I follow my boyfriend's command and make my way down the hall. But when I get there, I don't see William like I expect to. Instead, there's a formal black gown draped across the bed, a floor-length number with ribbons tied in little bows at the shoulders. It looks vaguely familiar, but I can't place it.

I'm not surprised when my phone buzzes again.

Get dressed. I'll pick you up in thirty minutes.

What's he up to?

I'm pulling off my clothes when another text message comes through.

Wear the black silk panties, the ones with the ties at the sides.

I text back, *Care to tell me where you're taking me?*

And ruin the surprise?

I shower quickly with the floral body wash that makes him crazy, then I dress carefully. I take special care as I tie the panties at each hip, imaging him untying them later. For my bra, I choose black lace that makes his blue eyes go smoky when he looks at me.

The dress is a soft flowing material that glides against my skin and makes me feel beautiful.

I don't put on much makeup, just a little lip-gloss and some eyeliner and mascara, and I leave my hair down so he can tangle his hands in it when he kisses me.

I'm just stepping into my shoes when he texts me again. *I'm out front when you're ready.*

A ridiculous case of the nerves has my stomach somersaulting as I walk out the front door.

William is leaning against a black stretch limo dressed in a tuxedo, legs crossed at the ankle as he waits for me. He holds a single red rose.

"I thought you said you didn't want to dress me?"

His lips turn up in a grin. "I didn't. Drew pulled that dress out of storage for me."

I blink down at the familiar gown and have to shake my head. How had I forgotten my own prom dress? "Where are we going?" I ask again.

He winks at me and opens the door, taking my hand to help me into the limo. "You'll know soon enough."

When he's seated next to me, he pours me a glass of champagne, and I have to shake my head in awe. "Am I forgetting some sort of special occasion?"

He dips his head and presses his lips to mine. "Every day you're in my life is a special occasion."

I take a single sip from my glass before he takes it from my hand and the limo comes to a stop. "Short ride," I mutter, only a little disappointed that I didn't have enough time to enjoy it.

"Don't pout. The limo's ours all night." He winks at me as he helps me out onto the sidewalk. "Later, we'll let him drive us around while we make out."

I frown at the building before me. I'm missing something. "You brought me to New Hope High School?"

He offers me his arm, and I slide my hand through it and allow him to escort me inside the heavy gymnasium doors. The doors swing closed behind me and I can hardly believe what I'm seeing. The room is dark save for the twinkling white lights draped across the ceiling and a dim light illuminating the dance floor. My best friends are already dancing—Lizzy, Hanna, and Maggie wearing prom dresses, arms draped around their dates.

I spin around and William pulls me close. "Happy prom night," he whispers in my ear.

Wrapping our arms around each other, we start to dance from where we stand. "I thought about taking you to the actual prom," he says, his hands cupping my butt. "But then I couldn't touch you like this. I didn't want to finally get prom night with my girl and be expected to behave."

I grin. "We couldn't have that."

His fingers tie something cool around my wrist.

"Diamonds?" I shift my hand back and forth, watching them twinkle in the light.

"Stardust," he corrects. "I want you to always believe you deserve whatever you can wish for, Cally. As long as you'll let me, I'll make your wishes come true."

"They already have," I whisper. "I love you so much, William Bailey. You're my dream come true, and I'm so grateful I found you again."

"Hmm...then do you mind if I borrow them to make a wish of my own?"

I grin. "What's that?"

"I know you've already given me more than I should ask for, but I'm one of those spoiled rich kids who thinks he should have everything he wants."

"You're not spoiled. What is it? What do you want?"

He releases me and draws a box from his pocket. "I wish you

would marry me, Cally Fisher."

My throat is thick with tears and happiness, but I nod and press my lips to his. "You don't have to wish for me, William. I'm already yours."

The End

author's note

There is a common argument that prostitution is a victimless crime—a transaction between two consenting adults that harms no one. However, in the United States, we're beginning to take another look at what is truly happening in these so-called "consensual" transactions and, in some cases, reclassify them as human sex trafficking. Authorities have found that very often the prostitutes are coerced into a life they don't want to be living, manipulated through addiction, poverty, and fear. It is all too easy to dismiss a prostitute's troubles, to tell ourselves "she made the choice," but as William tells Cally, a choice made out of fear is no choice at all.

acknowledgements

I must thank my husband first. Without him, my books just wouldn't be possible. Brian, thank you for the time, encouragement, and patience you gave me through this book and all the others. For sending me to the "satellite office" to work when the kids won't leave me alone, for listening to my endless out-of-context plot concerns, and for proving day after day that happily-ever-after exists outside of my head. I love you and those rotten kids something fierce.

My friends and family, who celebrate my successes as their own, cheer me on every step of the way, and pimp my books out to every literate adult they meet. I am humbled by your enthusiasm and grateful to have built a life surrounded by such amazing people.

To everyone who provided me feedback on and cheers for William and Cally's story along the way—especially Adrienne Hogan, Marilyn Brant, Violet Duke, Megan Mulry, Annie Swanberg, and Lauren Blakely—you're all awesome and I'm lucky to call you my friends.

Thank you to the team that helped me package this book and promote it. Sarah Hansen at Okay Creations designed my beautiful cover, and if I have my way she will do many, many more for me. Rhonda Helms, thank you for the insightful line edits, and Sara Biren at Stubby Pencil Editing for proof reading. A massive shout-out to Jessica Estep of Ink Slinger PR for your amazing and tireless work to promote me and my books, and to all of the bloggers and reviewers who help her do it. Amazing. Every one of you.

To my agent, Dan Mandel for getting my books into the hands of readers all over the world—you're making my dreams come true.

To all my writer friends on Twitter, Facebook, and my various writer loops, thank you for your support and inspiration. I must say, ours is the coolest water cooler in all of the workforce.

And last but certainly not least, thank you to my fans. To those who read *Unbreak Me* and sent me notes begging for William to get his happily-ever-after, knowing you wanted to read his story as much as I wanted to write it was a thrill. I appreciate each and every one of my readers. I couldn't do this without you and wouldn't want to. Thank you for buying my books and telling your friends about them. Thank you for asking me to write more. You're the best!

~Lexi

playlist

Gotye, Kimbra—*Somebody That I Used to Know*
Kings of Leon—*Sex on Fire*
Passenger—*Let Her Go*
Ani DiFranco—*Sorry I Am*
Miley Cyrus—*Wrecking Ball*
Sara Bareilles—*Gravity*
The National—*Slipped*
Ani DiFranco—*Letter to a John*
Kodaline—*All I Want*
William Fitzsimmons featuring Rosi Golan—*You Still Hurt Me*
Katy Perry—*Roar*
One Republic—*Counting Stars*

about the author

A *New York Times* and *USA Today* bestselling romance author, Lexi Ryan considers herself the luckiest chick she knows. Her books have been described as intense, emotional, and wickedly sexy. Lexi herself has only been described using two of those adjectives (feel free to guess but she's not telling). When not writing, she enjoys watching football, perfecting her chocolate martini, and reading her way to the title of Biggest Romance Fangirl Evah. A former college professor, her biggest fears include faculty meetings and large stacks of ungraded freshman composition papers. She now writes full-time from her home in Indiana, where she lives with her husband and two children and their neurotic dog. You can visit Lexi at her website www.lexiryan.com or find her on Twitter @writerlexiryan or Facebook at facebook.com/lexiryanauthor.

This paperback interior was designed and formatted by

www.emtippettsbookdesigns.com

Artisan interiors for discerning authors and publishers.

www.ingramcontent.com/pod-product-compliance
Lightning Source LLC
Chambersburg PA
CBHW031334070726
47496CB00017B/888